DAVID NOBBS

Second
from Last
in the Sack Race

MANDARIN

A Mandarin Paperback

SECOND FROM LAST
IN THE SACK RACE

First published in Great Britain 1983
by Methuen London Ltd
This edition published 1989
Reprinted 1990 (four times), 1991 (three times), 1992 (twice)
by Mandarin Paperbacks
an imprint of Reed Consumer Books Limited
Michelin House, 81 Fulham Road, London SW3 6RB
and Auckland, Melbourne, Singapore and Toronto

Reissued 1992

Copyright © David Nobbs 1983

ISBN 0 7493 3606 4

A CIP catalogue record for this title
is available from the British Library

Printed and bound in Great Britain by
BPCC Hazells Ltd
Member of BPCC Ltd

For Dave, Chris and Kim

Contents

Contents

1 Death of a Parrot

Upstairs, in the tiny back bedroom, Ada's pains began. Ezra heard her first sharp cry at twenty-five to seven in the evening.

He shuddered and tried to bury himself in that morning's *Sheffield Telegraph*. 'Do women want careers or husbands?' he read without interest. 'County valuation officer dead,' he noted without pleasure or regret.

The parrot listened and watched, unaware of its impending doom.

Silence reigned briefly in Number 23 Paradise Lane, Thurmarsh, on that night of Wednesday March 13th, 1935.

Ezra sat in front of the lead-polished range, in the rocking chair. On the floor, in front of the range, was a rag rug. It had black edges, and a red diamond in the middle. Ada had made it, out of old coats and frocks.

A burst of molten light came from the open-hearth furnaces of the great steelworks of Crapp, Hawser and Kettlewell, which lay on the other side of the main road, dwarfing the dingy, back-to-back terraces, and a dun-coloured Thurmarsh Corporation tram clanked noisily down the main road.

'Bugger off,' said the parrot.

Ezra examined the bird sadly. It had been a bad buy. Henderson had assured Ada that it was a master of Yorkshire dialect, and would amaze her visitors with comments like 'Where there's muck, there's brass,' 'Ee, he's a right laddie-lass. He's neither nowt nor summat,' and 'Don't thee *tha* me; *tha* thee them that *tha's* thee.' Ada had spent long hours rehearsing it. All it ever said was 'Bugger off.' Admitted, it said it in a south Yorkshire accent, but that was scant consolation to its disappointed owner.

Ezra lit a Gold Flake. It had never occurred to him to ask to be present at the birth. Such a thing would have been unnatural. He had carried his obligations quite far enough by announcing his unavailability for the dominoes match at the Navigation Inn. Sid Lowson was substituting. (Don't bother to remember the name

Sid Lowson. Substituting for Ezra at the dominoes is the nearest he will come to the centre of our stage. He will acquit himself with credit, incidentally, sixing it up with aplomb at a vital moment.)

Cousin Hilda popped her head round the door.

'She's started,' she said.

'Aye, I've heard,' said Ezra.

'Bugger off,' said the parrot.

Cousin Hilda sniffed. Her nose looked as if it disapproved of her mouth, and her mouth looked as if it disapproved of her nose, and probably they both did, since Cousin Hilda was known to disapprove of orifices of every kind.

'I don't blame t' parrot,' she said. 'It doesn't know owt different. I blame Henderson. That sort of thing comes from t' top. Look at Germany. Pet shop? Sodom and Gomorrah more like. Every animal from that shop's the same. Foul-mouthed.'

'They can't all talk,' protested Ezra. 'Fair dos, our Hilda. Tha's not suggesting Archie Halliday's goldfish swears, is tha?'

'It would if it could,' said Cousin Hilda, with another sniff. 'Have you seen the look in its eye? Foul-mouthed. I don't know why you didn't complain. Your Ada spends good money on a parrot guaranteed to be an expert in the Yorkshire dialect, and what does she get?'

'Bugger off,' said the parrot.

'Exactly,' said Cousin Hilda. 'That's modern shops for you. Craftsmanship? They don't know the meaning of the word. Any road, she's doing just fine, so don't worry yoursen.'

Cousin Hilda returned upstairs. Ada cried out. Sid Lowson played a crafty domino (the double five). A tram screeched furiously round the corner by Saxton's the newsagent. The parrot, perhaps mistaking it for a mating call, shrieked back. And Ezra worried.

He tried to concentrate on the paper. 'Air service opened – Doncaster to Croydon in 95 minutes', 'Razor Affray on Ship'.

'In your garden,' read Ezra, who had no garden, not even a back yard. 'When overhauling mowing machines it should be noted. . .'

Ada gave another, louder, sharper cry.

'Begonias must not be over-watered,' read Ezra desperately.

'Venizelos flees to Italian island. Greek rebel fleet surrenders.'

'Come on. Come on, Ada,' he implored. 'Get it over with.'

He went to the sink in the corner of the room, filled the kettle, and put it on the hob.

Big Ben began to strike nine on the wireless at number 21. They only had the wireless on once a day, for the news, so as not to wear it out, but they made up for it by having it on very loud, so that all the neighbours could hear.

The ninth stroke died away, and then came a tenth, a shriek of shocking physical agony that tore into Ezra's heart. He sank into his chair, stunned. His hands shook.

The parrot cocked its head to one side, listening intently.

There was another shriek from Ada. Ezra looked up at the ceiling, and shook his head slowly, as if reproving his maker for not coming up with a better way of bringing people into the world.

There was silence. He made the tea. Another tram clanked past.

'There's nowt so queer as folk,' said the parrot.

Ezra stared at the bright green bird in amazement. It twinkled maliciously in its cage above the sideboard.

He longed for Ada's agony to be over, so that he could bring her the glad tidings about her pet, so that she would know that the long hours of tuition had not been entirely in vain.

'Fifty-four years ago a postcard addressed to a Norwich firm was posted in London,' he read. 'It was delivered this week.'

'Please God,' he prayed. 'Let our child be delivered quicker than that.'

Ezra Pratt was twenty-nine years old, a thin man, a frail man, a shy man.

Her Mother came downstairs next, a big woman, a strong woman, not a shy woman.

'It's a right difficult one,' she said encouragingly. 'Our firsts allus are on our side. I had t' devil's own job wi' our Arnold.'

He closed his eyes. Arnold had been killed at Mons. He couldn't be doing with it just then.

'Was it worth it,' she said, 'in view of what happened?'

She went outside, to the lavatory, which was two doors away, in the yard.

He turned to the *Thurmarsh Evening Argus*. 'Youths Daub House with Treacle', 'Speed Limit of Thirty Miles an Hour in Built-up Areas from Monday', 'Headless Corpse could be Missing Thurmarsh Draper'.

Her Mother returned, shaking her sad, carved head.

'She hasn't scoured it out or owt,' she said.

They shared the lavatory with number 25, and they were supposed to take turns at cleaning it. It was a constant bone of contention.

He longed for her to go upstairs. He wanted to be alone with his tension.

Ada cried out again.

'Tha wouldn't think it'd be such a to-do,' said Her Mother. 'She's big enough.'

She managed to make it sound like a criticism of his smallness.

'We haven't heard owt from our Doris, then,' she said.

Ada's sister Doris was a social climber. She had married another social climber. Roped together, they were taking on the North Face of Life. They had, as yet, no children. Her Mother probed, hinted, joked that pregnancy was catching. 'Tha wants to be careful, Doris,' she'd said. 'It's smittling, tha knows.' It seemed that Doris had been careful.

She gave Ezra an assessing look. Was it just his imagination, or was it one of surprise that he had managed to sire the infant who was so reluctant to enter this world?

'It wouldn't surprise me if it's not born while Friday,' she said, and with this encouraging shot she was gone, and he was alone again with the parrot and his thoughts.

The Navigation Inn closed its doors. The peripheral Sid Lowson went home and out of this tale. The trams grew fewer, and Ada's screams more frequent. They were the shamed, reluctant screams of a dour woman who had been brought up never to make a fuss. The parrot listened intently. A thick film spread over Ezra's forgotten third cup of strong sweet tea.

On Wednesday, March 13th, 1935 Hitler had announced air parity with Britain, Golden Miller had won the Cheltenham Gold Cup for the fourth time and the Duke of Norfolk had shot a rhino. Now, at last, at three and a half minutes before midnight, Ezra heard the healthy protest of outraged young lungs, asking; 'What *is* this? Am I to be constantly ejected from warm, dark places into cold, light ones? Is this what life is?'

He leapt from his chair.

'Hey up, our parrot,' he said. 'I'm a father.'

'Bugger off,' said the parrot.

Ezra Pratt stared down at the pink, podgy, wrinkled infant. Everything seemed normal, blue eyes, wet mouth, snotty little nose, bald pate, chubby arms, wet podgy hands, fingers and thumbs like tiny sausages, little red stomach distended as a wind-sock in a gale, then a portion discreetly veiled from the world in a nappy. Below the nappy, there were two plump little legs with puffy knees. The legs ended in hideous but apparently normal feet, and ten absurd, angular toes.

'It's a boy,' said the midwife.

Ezra was aware that speech was expected of him, but no speech came.

He clutched Ada's arm.

'Ee, Ada,' he said at last.

She smiled wearily, proudly.

'Ee, Ada,' he repeated.

He glanced at Cousin Hilda, his eyes asking her to come downstairs.

She came downstairs, and stood by the door while he sought reassurance from the rhythmic movement of the rocking chair.

'Under t' nappy,' he began, and stopped.

'Well?' said Cousin Hilda, who had never helped a man in her life, and was too old to start now.

'I didn't like to ask in front of Her Mother and t' midwife,' said Ezra.

'Get on with it, man,' said Cousin Hilda, investing the last word with a goodly measure of disgust.

'Well. . .I could see t' nipper were all right as regards what I could see. Features, like. Extremities, like. What I could see,' said Ezra.

'So?' said Cousin Hilda.

'Under t' nappy,' said Ezra awkwardly. 'There's nowt wrong wi'

13

'im under t' nappy, like, is there?'

Cousin Hilda sniffed.

'It's all there,' she said, as if blaming the father for the presence of genitalia in the offspring.

'Aye,' said Ezra, clenching his fingers round his long-forgotten mug of cold tea. 'Aye. . .but. . .I mean. . .is it all normal?'

'I didn't examine it in close detail,' said Cousin Hilda. 'Such things don't interest me.'

'Aye,' said Ezra, 'but I mean. . .'

'I wouldn't have owt to compare it with, would I?' said Cousin Hilda.

'Aye. . .but. . .' persisted Ezra, 'is that safety pin all right?'

Cousin Hilda stared at him blankly.

'T' safety pin. On t' nappy. Is it correctly positioned?'

'Ask the midwife. She did it,' said Cousin Hilda, hand on the sneck of the door, eager for escape.

'Aye,' said Ezra, 'that's all very well, but I wouldn't like his little willie to get scratched.'

Cousin Hilda uttered a hoarse cry and then, with one last sniff, she was gone.

At eight minutes past five, on the morning of Thursday March 14th, shortly after the first tram had rolled down the deserted road towards Thurmarsh, there came a shriek of shocking physical agony which made Ezra sit bolt upright in bed, and sent the sweat streaming from his every pore. Poor Ada was having another baby.

Such a thing couldn't be. So why had she cried out? He reached over and gently patted the amplitude of her buttocks. She was asleep.

He swung out of the bed, fumbled for his shoes with his feet, tightened the cord of his thick, striped pyjamas, faintly clammy with sweat, and lit the candle at his bedside.

Another cry of agony rent the air, longer and rising to a crescendo. It was Ada, yet it could not be, for she still slept. She stirred, moaned tensely, but did not wake. The baby in his simple cot gave a cry that was half-gurgle, half-alarm, half-human, half-animal.

A hob-nailed boot rang out on the main road.

He peeped into the tiny front room, where Her Mother slept, snoring loudly, but certainly not shrieking in agony.

Another cry shattered the night. It came from downstairs, and the truth dawned on Ezra.

He hurried to the top of the stairs, the candle protesting at his speed. He crept down the bare, narrow staircase. A startled rat scampered off. The seventh stair creaked. The ninth groaned. The house smelt of soot and damp.

He entered the little room which served as kitchen, dining room, living room, bathroom and parrot house. It was warm from the heat of the range. The walls sweated gently with condensation.

He lit the gas mantle. The parrot's eyes shone wickedly. His cup of cold tea still lay on the dresser.

The parrot's eyes challenged the world. It screamed. It was Ada to a tee, and Ezra realised that the bird intended to reproduce faithfully the whole of her agony, scream by scream.

He grabbed the bird by the throat. It gave a dreadful scream which began as Ada's agony, became a brief squawk of outrage, then a choking almost-human gurgle, and finally a parrot's death rattle. Then silence.

He continued to strangle the parrot long after it was dead.

Grey, unshaven dawn found a still tableau in a terrace house in south Yorkshire. A polished range. A thin man with a grey face, rocking slowly in a chair. In his hands, a dead parrot.

Her Mother found him there. At first she thought that they were both dead.

Later, when he had dressed, Ezra wrapped the dead bird in the women's page of the *Thurmarsh Evening Argus* – headline: 'Cami-Knickers – Are They Here to Stay?' He took it along the road and up the alley into the yard, and tossed it into the midden.

Later still, he tried to talk to Ada about it.

He tried to say: 'I love thee, Ada. No creature has the right to mock thy suffering and live. I killed the parrot for love of thee, my darling.'

What he actually said was: 'It were a dead loss, Ada. All it ever said were "Bugger off".'

He hadn't the heart to tell her that it had also said: 'There's nowt so queer as folk.'

2 Brawn and Brain

Three days after Henry was born, Hitler introduced conscription.
Twenty-five days after Henry was born, his Auntie Doris bought a
genuine crocodile handbag for a pound at Cockayne's Hand Bag
Event in Sheffield. Eighty-six days after Henry was born, Baldwin
became Prime Minister. Slowly the shadows of war grew darker.
Slowly Britain rearmed. Henry remembered none of this.

Away to the south-west lay Sheffield and cutlery country. To
the east was pit country. The road north led to textiles country.
Thurmarsh and its immediate environs were steel country.

Many of the men in Paradise Lane were steelworkers at the
giant works of Crapp, Hawser and Kettlewell, across the road.
Some of them worked on the Thurmarsh trams. Others were in
the army of the unemployed. Ezra Pratt made penknives. He
wasn't strong enough for the steelworks. Penknives were more his
mark. Her Mother infuriated him by referring to them as pocket
knives. 'I don't make pocket-knives, Norah,' he'd say. 'I make
penknives. I'm a two-ended man. I wouldn't lower mesen to
pocket-knives.' In the end he decided that she called them
pocket-knives deliberately, and so he denied her the pleasure of
seeing that it annoyed him. 'I won't give her t' satisfaction,
mother,' he told Ada. He called his wife 'mother' and he called
Her Mother 'Norah'.

Ezra Pratt was paid fifty bob a week, and after Christmas he was
usually laid off for two or three days a week until trade picked up
again in March. Ada became a dab hand at making things go a
long way. She baked her own bread, and her brawn was legendary.
Once a month they had roast beef for Sunday dinner, preceded by
Yorkshire pudding served separately with gravy so that you weren't
too hungry when you came to the joint. Ada Pratt added herbs to
her Yorkshire pudding, and it was grand. Her Mother made the
gravy. Nobody could touch Norah Higginbottom when it came to
gravy, and so it came to gravy fairly often.

Every Sunday, after dinner, Her Mother took little Henry out.

Sometimes they went over to Thurmarsh Lane Bottom, to see her son Leonard. She'd had three sons. The eldest, Arnold, had been killed at Mons. Leonard was unemployed. Walter lived in Durban, and had never invited her over 'because of Jenny's nerves'. Dead, unemployed, and living in Durban with a nervous wife. She did not feel that she had been lucky in the matter of sons. Of daughters she had but two. Ada and Doris. One Sunday she took Henry to Sheffield to see Doris, but by the time they got there it was time to come back again, and Henry cried.

She was never sure whether these Sunday outings achieved their object. Certainly, no little brother or sister for Henry came along. Babies abounded in Paradise Lane and adjoining cul-de-sacs, but Ezra and Ada Pratt only ever had the one. 'And what's tha been up to?' she'd say on her return, but Ezra could make a clam seem talkative when he'd a mind to it.

'That parrot hasn't come between you, has it?' she enquired once, to no avail.

'Oh, well, it's none of my business, any road,' she said when she received no reply. 'Tha knows what tha's doing.'

'Or not doing,' she noisily refrained from adding.

Henry remembered none of this.

Many years later, when Henry was thirteen, and living with Uncle Teddy and Auntie Doris, Uncle Teddy showed him some photographs of his childhood. There weren't many, because Uncle Teddy and Auntie Doris were the only relations with a camera, and they rarely came to Paradise Lane. 'What's to do, Teddy?' Her Mother had said, noting Teddy's unease on one of these brief visits. 'Does tha think poverty's smittling or summat?' Uncle Teddy had flushed, because she had touched a nerve, and Ezra had flushed too, at the thought that he represented poverty.

In 1936, George V and Rudyard Kipling died. Edward VIII came, saw and abdicated. Her Mother, who considered herself a student of politics, announced: 'There's one good thing about t' abdication. It's shown up that Churchill for what he is. We've seen the last of 'im. Hitler invaded the Rhineland, Italy over-ran Abyssinia, the people of Jarrow marched to London, and the Spanish Civil War broke out. Henry's life during that momentous year was recalled only by two photos, taken in Uncle Teddy's garden. He'd just begun to walk. In one snapshot he stood between his highly self-conscious, stiffly-posed parents. On his left Ezra, small, ill-at-ease in his serge suit, dwarfed by his flat cap. On his right, Ada, large, shapeless, defiant, challenging the camera not to explode. The other shot, taken by Ezra, showed him with Uncle Teddy and Auntie Doris. Auntie Doris was wearing a well-cut suit and a Tyrolean-style hat with feathers. She looked very sunburnt. Probably Uncle Teddy looked very sunburnt too, but it was impossible to tell as his head was missing. They had just returned from a cruise on the *City of Nagpur*, calling at Oporto, Tunis, Palermo, Kotor, Dubrovnik, Venice, Split, Corfu and Malaga. It had cost them twenty-five guineas each. Uncle Teddy had gone on about it, and Auntie Doris, who always made things worse by protesting about them, had said: 'Give over, Teddy. Don't rub it in to them that hasn't got.'

1937 was a year of slow continuation. The world continued to advance slowly towards war. The factories continued to turn slowly to munitions. The dole queues continued to grow slowly shorter as the nation slowly discovered that it had a use for its manpower. Baldwin shrewdly retired, Ezra bought a wireless set, and there were two more photos of Henry in Uncle Teddy's scrapbook. They were taken on the beach at Bridlington. In one of them he was howling at being made to paddle. In the other he was with Auntie Doris, who was wearing one of the new two-piece bathing costumes. Henry had a bucket and spade, but didn't seem to know what to do with them. He'd been sick all over Uncle Teddy, just beyond Driffield. Uncle Teddy had been upset, but Auntie Doris had been very understanding, and had said that it had been Uncle Teddy's fault for driving too fast. On the way home Uncle Teddy had driven with exaggerated care, and Henry had been sick all over Auntie Doris, just beyond Goole.

That day, in his fourteenth summer, as Henry sat on Uncle Teddy's settee, facing the open French windows, looking at his unremembered youth, Uncle Teddy said: 'Now then, Henry. Doesn't my Doris look a picture in that two-piece bathing suit?'

'She certainly does, Uncle Teddy,' said Henry, who could

never think of anything interesting to say in Uncle Teddy's presence.

'Interested in girls yet, Henry?' said Uncle Teddy.

'Give over, Teddy,' said Auntie Doris.

'I'll tell you one thing,' said Uncle Teddy, stabbing at the old snapshot with a nicotined finger. 'Look at that bust. You don't get many of those to the pound.'

'Teddy!' said Auntie Doris.

Henry blushed, partly out of embarrassment and partly out of confusion at being seen to be blushing.

'It's part of his education, looking at a fine pair of Bristols,' persisted Uncle Teddy.

Henry felt the blood rushing to his face. He felt humiliatingly crimson. He wished he was two again, at Bridlington.

'Teddy!' hissed Auntie Doris, who always made things worse by protesting about them. 'Bristol was where it happened.'

'Oh Lord,' said Uncle Teddy, reddening in his turn. 'Oh Lordy Lord.'

Henry rushed through the French windows, hurtled across the lawn, tripped over the tortoiseshell cat, and fell into the goldfish pond. It wasn't the last pond that he would fall into, but it was infinitely the most humiliating

1938 was represented by a picture of Henry with Cousin Hilda, by the river at Bakewell. He was clinging to her hand, and she was looking down at him, her face radiant with affection, all sniffing forgotten.

Later still, when he was sixteen, and living with Cousin Hilda, he showed her this photo. She gave a stifled sob and rushed from the room. It was years later still before he realised why.

She was looking at herself as she might have been, if she had been born into a different time.

But I anticipate.

All the pictures of young Henry Pratt showed a distinctly podgy child. Since he was of a lively and nervy disposition, everyone knew that he would soon grow out of his podginess. But everyone was wrong. He never did.

When he looked at these pictures, Henry tried to fill in the gaps. He could summon up the old living room without too much trouble. The flagstone floor was covered with a brown carpet square, and lino edges. The rag rug stood in front of the leaded range, with oven, coal fire and hob. In one corner, behind a faded curtain, there was a sink with a square Ascot geyser. The window was over the oak dresser, and the street door led straight into the room. An army blanket hung over this door, to keep out the draught. Another door led down into the cellar. A tin bath with a handle at each end hung on this door. There was a battered mahogany sideboard, and an anonymous table. Over the mantelpiece there fitted an over-mantel. It was decorated with oak leaves and acorns. There were cracks in the walls and loose plaster hung threateningly from the ceiling. Condensation and rats were frequent visitors.

He could summon up Paradise Lane, the uneven cobbles, the two rows of brick terraces, wine-red, grimy. The cul-de-sac ended in a brick wall, beyond which was the canal. Between numbers 25 and 27, a narrow alley led to the yard, which was surrounded by blackened brick walls. At each side of the yard there were two lavatories, with a midden between them. Two houses shared each lavatory. You poured your rubbish in the midden, and when the midden men came they stood in the midden and scooped the rubbish out. The yard smelt of refuse, and the rats liked it.

He could summon it all up, but he couldn't be sure that these were genuine memories of his early childhood. After all, he had known that same world many years later, after the war, for Paradise Lane survived the Thurmarsh Blitz, and the Baedeker raids didn't touch it.

1938 brought his first genuine memory, dim and confused though it was. It involved the aforementioned wireless set, an argument, a sporting record and a dismembered insect. The date, had he known it, was Wednesday, August 24th.

Binks and Madeley Ltd were on holiday. Ezra had a whole week without making penknives. He didn't go for a cruise on the *City of Nagpur*. He didn't even go to Bridlington. He couldn't afford it, because he'd bought the wireless. His parents had come over for the day. His father had been a miner, and he coughed a lot, and spat into his handkerchief. His mother was small and steely. They had another son in Sheffield, but they lived with their daughter, who had married one of Penistone's foremost coal merchants.

Ada, Her Mother and Ezra's mother were out shopping. They would soon return with the ingredients for the making of brawn, and a fish and chip dinner from the Paradise Chippy. Ezra and his father had been ordered to keep an eye on Henry and lay the table. They had done neither, being too engrossed in the wireless.

Len Hutton was approaching Don Bradman's record of 334, the highest score ever made in a Test Match. Don Bradman himself was captaining the Australians. The tension in south Yorkshire was palpable.

Henry sat in the road, unwatched. A large, black beetle crawled over the warm, uneven cobbles towards him. He grabbed it, and began to pull its legs off. Quite soon it was dead.

He rushed excitedly into the house. His father and grandfather were crowded round the wireless, staring at it as if worshipping it, because they were afraid that they wouldn't be able to hear it if they didn't sit close to it and stare at it.

His grandfather smelt of moustache, blue cheese, tobacco and old age.

Fleetwood-Smith was beginning a new over, at the exact moment when Henry announced, proudly, 'I killed a inseck.'

'That's right. Now 'ush,' said Ezra.

'I deaded 'im a lot,' said Henry, producing a handful of limbs and organs to prove that this was no idle boast.

'Grand. Shut up now,' said Ezra.

'Dad, Dad. Look, Dad, dead,' said Henry, thrusting the evidence in front of his father's face.

'Bugger off, will yer?' shouted his father, as a great roar came from the wireless. 'Bloody hell. I missed it.'

'He cut Fleetwood-Smith for four,' said his grandfather, choking and getting out his handkerchief. 'He's got record.'

Henry wailed, hurled bits of beetle onto the floor, and began stamping them into the carpet, screaming.

The three women returned with their purchases, chatting happily, ignorant of the mayhem inside the house.

'There's nowt Cousin Hilda doesn't disapprove of,' said Her

Mother. 'I don't like that.'

'Betty Crabtree's another one,' said Ada.

'Tha what?' said Ezra's mother.

'Betty Crabtree,' said Ada, 'She never has owt good to say about folk. She's a right misery, is Betty Crabtree.'

'She gets it from her mother,' said Her Mother.

'That's Henry screaming,' said Ezra's mother.

They hurried into the house. Henry was still screaming. On the wireless the crowd was cheering and singing 'For He's a Jolly Good Fellow'.

'Shut that thing off,' shouted Ada. 'I can't hear mesen talk.'

'Tha what?' shouted Ezra.

Ada switched the wireless off.

'Ada!' said Ezra.

'That was cricket on there,' said Ezra's father.

Henry's cries grew quieter now that they had no competition.

'What's t' mess on t' floor?' said Ada.

'Henry's been stamping on an insect,' said Ezra.

Ada slapped Henry, and he began to scream again.

'Nay, mother, give over,' said Ezra. 'It weren't his fault.'

'Weren't his fault?' said Ada. 'Weren't his fault? Well whose fault was it? Neville Chamberlain's, was it? Or was it Lord Halifax? Did Lord Halifax pop in and show our Henry how to trample insects into t' floor?'

'I told him to bugger off,' said Ezra in a small voice.

'Lord Halifax?' said Ezra's father, and immediately wished he hadn't.

Her Mother began to clean the carpet with a great show of virtue.

'I'm keeping out of this,' she said, sweeping the beetle remains into the dustpan.

Henry howled.

'Tha told thy son to bugger off?' said Ada.

'Aye, but there were extenuating circumstances, Mother,' said Ezra.

'Extenuating circumstances?' said Ada. 'There'd better be and all. He's not content to strangle parrots now. He's got to swear at his own son. Animal.'

Ada put her arms round Henry, and made sure that her huge frame was between Henry and his father. Henry's sobs subsided slowly.

'Can I put t' wireless back on?' said Ezra's father, and immediately wished he hadn't.

Ezra's mother glared at her husband.

'Well, they were having drinks,' said Ezra's father.

'I thought it was cricket,' said Ezra's mother.

'It was cricket,' said Ezra's father. 'Then it was drinks.'

'He wants to listen to people having drinks now,' said Ezra's mother.

'Don't look at me,' said Her Mother.

'It weren't drinks as drinks,' said Ezra's father. 'It were drinks as a celebration of a Pudsey lad getting highest ever score in test cricket.'

Ada glared resolutely at Ezra. She seemed to swell, and he to shrink.

'Let's get this right,' said Ada. 'Tha told our Henry to bugger off because of cricket?'

'Aye. . .well. . .' said Ezra. 'It were the exact moment, does tha see? Fleetwood-Smith dropped one short.'

'Hutton, coolest man on t' ground, cut it to t' fence,' said Ezra's father, and immediately wished he hadn't.

'I'll drop thee both one short before I'm through,' said Ada. 'I'll give thee both Fleetwood-Smith.'

'I'm saying nowt,' said Her Mother.

'Shut up, Mother,' said Ada. 'Tha's getting on me nerves.'

'I haven't said owt,' said Her Mother.

Henry's sobs were merely exhausted remnants now.

'This is what happens when men are left to look after things,' said Ezra's mother.

'It's sport,' said Ada. 'They're sport mad, men. I'd abolish sport, if it was me.'

'Aye, but be fair, mother,' said Ezra. 'It was the greatest moment in English cricket history, ruined.'

'Good,' said Ada.

The fish and chips were getting cold, so they ate them straight from the newspapers. It was a subdued meal.

As he reached the end of his fish and chips, Ezra's father began to read the newspaper in which his had been wrapped.

'United have signed a new winger,' he said, and immediately wished he hadn't.

Ezra promised treats. But it takes a lot of atonement to make up to a child for one hurtful moment. The hurting is spontaneous, the atonement calculated. Henry sensed the difference, and never felt quite the same about his father again.

The first of Ezra's treats was not a success. It consisted of a visit to Blonk Lane to watch Thurmarsh United versus New Brighton in the Third Division North.

Henry enjoyed the tram ride, past the long, black corrugated-iron sheds of the great steelworks, up out of the Rundle Valley, and down the long hill into Thurmarsh Town Centre. A second, noisier, smokier tram, a football special, took them past the soot-black Gothic town hall, ringed by sandbags. The fear of war was everywhere. Men were digging a slit trench beside the old men's shelter in the Alderman Chandler Memorial Park.

There was a lingering smell of sweet baking and golden roasting around the biscuit factory. Then they were in the low, bleak eastern suburbs. They walked up Blonk Lane towards the stadium, in a tide of cheery, beery, flat-capped men. Newspaper vendors and hard-faced men with spare season tickets shouted, and Henry was frightened. When he had to leave his father to go through the turnstile of the juveniles' entrance, he screamed, and his father took him away. A great roar announced a Thurmarsh goal as they waited for the tram back. When they got home, the clothes horse was in front of the range, and the house was filled with the nourishing smell of steaming pants and singlets. There was brawn for tea, and Ada rebuked her husband, saying, 'He's nobbut three. Tha should have had more sense, tha great lummock.'

'I'm saying nowt,' said Her Mother.

Sunday dawned bright, if breezy.

'There'll be a hundred thousand gassed in t' streets on first day of hostilities,' said Her Mother cheerfully.

Ezra took Henry into Derbyshire, for a treat, to help him

recover from his treat. Ada did not accompany them, on account of her legs being a liability, and Her Mother was not invited.

A Sheffield Corporation tram, with dark blue and cream livery, took them to Sheffield. Even on Sunday, the industrial mist hung, dimming the sun.

'A mucky picture, set in a golden frame,' said Ezra proudly.

A gleaming cream bus took them out of the mucky picture and up into the golden frame. Hikers and cyclists abounded. The atmosphere was cautiously frenzied. They didn't know how many more summers there would be, and this one was almost over.

Henry sat rapt with wonder, wrapped in excitement, as the womb-bus rose warmly through the leafy, stone suburbs and out into the high country. There were stone walls and fields and then miles of lifeless swaying grass. Groups of hikers descended outside square stone pubs, and briefly a cold wind blew into the bus.

Soon came the moment that Henry had begun to dread. Out of the womb into a wide and empty world.

They walked for a few minutes, and then came to a place where the land fell away abruptly, and the view over the valleys and hills of the Peak District was splendid, but too large for a child's eye.

'Right, then,' said Ezra. 'We've got us brawn to contend with.'

Far below, a toy train came out of a tunnel, and its white smoke filled Henry with longings – to be on that train, to be that smoke, to be other than he was.

They sat in a hollow with their backs against a rock, and ate their brawn butties.

'I hate brawn,' said Ezra. 'I hate gravy, too. I like me food dry. It's more than me life's worth to tell her that. In life, Henry, tha has to eat a lot of gravy that tha doesn't want. There's going to be a war. That's what Reg Hammond reckons, any road. The world is changing. Think on, though, our Henry, before tha blames us for bringing thee into t' world. Remember this. Tha's English. Tha's Yorkshire. Tha could have been born Nepalese or Belgian or owt. Thank me for that, at least.'

Henry was puzzled. His father had never talked to him like that before. And he was a sensitive child, aware of the fear and unease around him, although he knew nothing about Hitler, and cared even less about the Sudetenland than all the hikers and cyclists.

'It's not going to be easy, lad,' said his father. 'But tha'll frame. Thy little mind's never still. Tha's got brains.'

Ezra handed Henry a last corner of brawn sandwich.

'Brains and brawn,' he said. 'Tha'll do. Tha'll do.'

They walked on, away from that hollow, which could have become a womb, given half a chance.

They walked along a track, across a featureless expanse of sheep-cropped, wind-stunted coarse grass. And Henry, sensitive, brainy young Henry, believed that he understood. His father was abandoning him, to fend for himself in the world. His father had encouraged him, told him that he could do it. His father, who had so recently told him to bugger off, was going home without him.

He clung to his father. He screamed. He yelled. His father had to pick him up and carry him, frail father struggling with podgy prodigy.

'Nay, lad. Nay,' said his father, disappointed that this day too was going to end in tears, totally unaware of what was going on in the little boy's brain. 'Ee, Henry, tha's not nesh, is tha? Does tha know what "nesh" means? "Nesh" means feeling t' cold, like cissy. We don't want t' lads at school calling us nesh, do we?'

He put Henry down, and they walked towards the road, hand in hand. Henry clutched his father's hand and whimpered. He was still whimpering when the bus arrived, and Ezra had to sit him on his knee throughout the journey home.

He didn't take Henry on any more treats.

The following Friday the headline in the *Daily Express* read 'Peace'. In smaller print were the words: 'The *Daily Express* declares that Britain will not be involved in a European war this year, or next year either.' Neville Chamberlain flew back from Munich and said: 'You may sleep quietly – it is peace for our time.' Her Mother said: 'I knew there'd be no war. All that worriting about nowt. It just goes to show. Tha can't believe all tha reads in t' papers. It were just a scare to take folks' minds off unemployment. Hitler? All it needed were a strong man to stand up to him. He's shot his bolt, he has.'

Henry's world began to expand. It was a world of parallel, cobbled, back-to-back cul-de-sacs called Paradise Yard, Back Paradise

Yard, Paradise Lane, Back Paradise Lane, Paradise Hill, Back Paradise Hill, Paradise Court, Back Paradise Court, Paradise Green and Back Paradise Green. All these cul-de-sacs rose gently from the main road to end in a brick wall, beyond which lay the stagnant, smelly waters of the Rundle and Gadd Navigation.

A narrow footpath, with posts to prevent cycling, ran between the cul-de-sacs and the brick wall. A gate in the brick wall led onto the towpath, which crossed to the other side of the canal on a bridge behind Paradise Court. Beyond the canal, and below it, were the less stagnant but equally smelly waters of the River Rundle, even in those days a Mecca for lovers of the polluted. Beyond the river was the railway, and beyond that, marching in rows all over the hills, were the semi-detached houses that had been built between the wars.

The canal and the river were out-of-bounds to Henry, for safety reasons, and he went there whenever he could.

It was a lively world, Henry's little womb-world to the south of the Thurmarsh-to-Rawlaston road. The cul-de-sacs were full of children. Barges and narrow boats chugged frequently along the canal. Trains roared regularly along the railway line. Dogs from the semis cavorted on the waste ground between the river and the canal. Thirty years later, when Henry came back, the trams were gone, the main road was clogged, the canal barely used, the railway derelict, whole streets razed to the ground and empty. But in his youth, before the planners got to work, it was all busy and bustling.

One Sunday morning, in 1939 – it was September 3rd, as it chanced – Henry slipped off along the cul-de-sac, through the gate onto the towpath, across the Rundle and Gadd Navigation, over the waste ground, and onto the wide footbridge over the Rundle.

Four boys were standing on the bridge, four boys near to his own age, four boys from Paradise Lane, four boys who often played together, four boys with whom Henry had often longed to play, four boys by whom Henry had never been accepted. Tommy Marsden, Martin Hammond, Billy Erpingham and Chalky White, who was the only West Indian for miles around in those days.

Henry approached them diffidently, trying to pluck up his

courage, a timid, brainy little boy. His podgy white knees stood out like headlights between his long, thick socks and his drooping, baggy shorts, proclaiming their owner's lack of physical strength and presence.

'Can I play?' he asked pathetically, although pathos had no power to touch the hearts of the four-year-old gang of four. Only Tommy Marsden could answer his question, because Tommy Marsden, black-haired, gaps in his teeth, dirt on his cheeks, rips in his shorts, paint on his jersey, scabs on his knees, was their leader. Tommy Marsden watched him like a hungry crow. Whim, not compassion, would decide his answer.

If Tommy Marsden was a crow, Martin Hammond was an owl. A solemn, intense, little old man with yellowing shorts. Chalky White smiled his gleaming, beaming, more-the-merrier smile. I forget what Billy Erpingham did.

'Can I play?' repeated Henry.

'All right,' said Tommy Marsden, generous only in order to prove that generosity was his to give.

Many years later, Martin Hammond wrote: 'I don't think there was a single one of us, however small, however deplorably apolitical the home environment that helped to shape us, who was not aware that an event of cataclysmic importance was casting its shadow over our little world and over the great world beyond our little world. I remember we played some kind of game on that fateful morning. I forget the rules. They don't matter. What matters is that we felt a compulsion to play a game, a clean game, a game with rules, because we knew, with the untainted instincts of youth, that the world was embarking on an adventure which was definitely not a game, and that for many years to come there would be no rules,' which was pitching it a bit strong, because Martin had been four at the time, and the clean game of his recollection consisted of racing dried-up dog turds along the sulphurous river.

If those scruffy youths had ever heard of Christopher Robin and Poohsticks, they might have called their game Pooh-Dried-Up-Dog-Jobs. But they hadn't. So they didn't.

Why did they use dog turds? Because it was exciting: some sink, others disintegrate, the element of chance is high. Because human beings are disgusting until lucky enough, in some cases, to be taught not to be. Because there were no trees in their environment, and therefore no sticks. Because, ultimately, as always, they were there.

The line up on the footbridge was Martin Hammond (Labrador), Tommy Marsden (Alsatian), Billy Erpingham (I forget), Chalky White (Cocker Spaniel) and Henry Pratt (Whippet).

Tommy Marsden lowered his left arm. Five tiny turds fell through the air. Henry's dropped into a dark corner under the bridge. He leant over to watch its early progress. Maybe he leant too far in his excitement. Maybe Tommy Marsden pushed him. He followed the dog turds into the filthy water.

He went into the Rundle head first. It was not the last river into which he would fall, but it was definitely the least prepossessing.

The foul waters met over his head. He took a great gulp of untreated sewage and chemical waste. He was choking, bursting, dying. Tommy Marsden's frail craft brushed his cheek. He struggled upwards, broke surface for a second, then sank again.

Then hands were underneath him, he was being lifted out of the water.

He was on the bank, upside down, gasping, heaving, retching, too concerned with survival yet to wail.

Slowly he recovered. The other four children had disappeared, as children will, given the slightest opportunity.

His two rescuers took him home. They were Fred Shilton, the lock-keeper, and Sid Lowson, that adequate domino substitute, suddenly proving less peripheral than expected.

His mouth tasted foul, his left knee was bleeding, his clothes were dripping, he was filthy and soaking and cold, he was crying from delayed shock, but he was alive.

The two men led him across the waste ground, over the canal, along the towpath, through the gate, and down the footpath until they came to Paradise Lane.

Neville Chamberlain's voice could be heard from the proliferating wirelesses: '. . . no such undertaking has been received. . .cannot believe there is anything more or anything different I could have. . .no chance of expecting that this man will ever give up. . .know that you will all play your part with calmness and courage.'

Fred Shilton knocked on the door of number 23.

'Now, may God bless you all. May He defend the right. It is the evil things that we shall be fighting against. . . .'

The door opened. Her Mother stood before them.

'There's been a bit of a to-do,' said Fred Shilton.

'Aye. I know,' said Her Mother. 'Hitler has not responded to our ultimatum. We're at war with Nazi Germany.'

'No,' said Sid Lowson. 'Your Henry's fallen in the Rundle.'

3 War

'I've decided to volunteer,' said Ezra.

'Volunteer?' said Ada.

'Volunteer,' said Ezra.

'Don't look at me,' said Her Mother.

Henry sat on the floor and looked from one face to another, forgetting his game, in which an empty tin of Parkinson's Old-Fashioned Humbugs, brought by Uncle Teddy and Auntie Doris on a rare visit, had represented a Thurmarsh Corporation tram. He sensed that this was important.

'Volunteer?' repeated Ada incredulously.

'Aye. . .well. . .' said Ezra. 'Let's face it, mother. It isn't a reserved occupation, isn't penknives.'

The month was May, the year 1940. Hitler had not invaded Thurmarsh. The Paradise cul-de-sacs had suffered only two casualties during the Phoney War. They were Archie Halliday and his goldfish. Archie Halliday had been knocked down by a car which hadn't seen him in the blackout. His goldfish had frozen to death during the long, hard winter.

'I've got to serve my country,' said Ezra. 'We all have. Think on, mother. What would tha reckon to me if I let t' others do all t' fighting?'

'There's ways to serve thy country baht volunteering,' said Ada.

'I know. I've tried 'em,' said Ezra

'I'm saying nowt,' said Her Mother.

Henry's life had hardly been affected by the war. He had his Mickey Mouse gas-mask, which he liked. A white circle had been painted on the wall of number 1 Paradise Lane. Ezra had explained that the letters inside the circle were an S and a P. They indicated that number 1 Paradise Lane, had the stirrup pump for the street.

'Look at him,' said Ada, pursing her lips. 'Is he fighting material? If Hitler's crack Panzer divisions see a scranny feller like him coming towards them, will they panic?'

'All right,' said Ezra. 'They may fail me, but I can try.'

31

'Pigs may fly,' said Ada.

The Phoney War was coming to an end. Hitler had invaded the Low Countries. Holland had fallen. Belgium was fighting for her life.

'I thought tha liked being an air raid warden,' said Ada. 'Tha looks just grand wi' t' helmet and navy blue pullover wi' yellow stripe.'

'Navy blue suits him,' said Her Mother. 'I've allus said that.'

Ezra stood up, drew himself up to his full five foot three, and glared down at the two large women in his life. Henry clutched his empty tin of Parkinson's Old-Fashioned Humbugs tightly. A railway engine whistled furiously, and a dog barked.

'I'm talking about resisting t' evil territorial demands of t' fascist dictator, not helmets,' said Ezra. 'I'm talking about survival of human freedom, not navy blue pullovers wi' yellow stripes. They don't want us part-timers any more any road, now they've got their paid officials. They complain we can't work eight-hour shifts because of us jobs. They say it upsets their rostering. Thus is the common man's idealistic spirit constantly thwarted by petty officialdom. That's what Reg Hammond says, any road.'

'Reg Hammond!' said Ada, as if that explained everything. 'Reg Hammond! He's allus got plenty to say for hisself. Is he volunteering?'

'He can't,' said Ezra. 'He's in a reserved occupation.'

'Nobody can make thy mind up for thee,' said Her Mother. 'That's what my Herbert used to say, any road.'

Henry couldn't sleep. Sleep was funny. There wasn't any way of making yourself fall asleep, so when you couldn't sleep you couldn't understand how you ever could.

It was a hot night in August. The Battle of Britain was in full cry. Germany had occupied the Channel Isles. The invasion of mainland Britain was expected at any moment. Her Mother said parachutists had landed at Rotherham. In the morning, Ezra would join the war. They hadn't failed him. They had failed Sid Lowson, who looked twice as fit as Ezra, but they hadn't failed Ezra. This surprised Ada, but not Henry. It was common knowledge that his father had strangled a parrot. Henry was still rather vague about the war, but he knew that the object of it was to kill Germans, and supposed that his father must be going to take a pretty exalted role in the strangling section of the British army.

Henry was frightened of his father, but he didn't want him to go off to the war. For one thing, his mother didn't want him to, and Henry loved his mother. For another thing, all change frightened him.

For many weeks the atmosphere in the terrace house had been tense. Production of brawn, that local barometer of stress, had increased dramatically. Now the moment had come. The night was stifling. Her Mother had gone to bed early, making a point of leaving Ezra and Ada alone together on their last night, displaying her tact so coyly that it became tactlessness. Henry could hear her snores from the front bedroom. He slept in his parents' room. There was barely room for the two beds. Normally he slept soundly, and didn't hear them come to bed.

That night it seemed to him that they would never come to bed. He couldn't bear it alone any longer. He would go downstairs, and tell them that he couldn't sleep.

As he got to the top of the stairs, he could hear their low voices, the hum of grown-up night-talk, from which he was always excluded. He knew straight away that they were talking about him, and he decided that he must hear what they were saying.

He crept carefully down the bare, narrow staircase. His legs were still too little to miss out a step. He trod softly on the seventh stair, which creaked, and on the ninth, which groaned.

Their voices continued. They hadn't heard him.

He pressed himself against the wall and listened.

'Take him to Kate's,' his father was saying. 'Get him away from here.'

'Become evacuees, does tha mean?'

'Not evacuees, mother. It's not evacuees, isn't staying wi' relations. I want to know he's safe, mother. In front line, fighting Jerry, I want to know our kid's safe.'

Conflicting emotions gripped Henry. It was nice to know that you were talked about when you weren't there. It provided reassuring evidence that you existed. It provided reassuring evidence that you were important to folk. But it was disturbing to hear your destination being discussed as if you were a parcel. It brought home to you how powerless you were. And it was worrying to learn of the prospect of massive change.

'We won't be any safer up there if there's an invasion,' she said.

'Course you would,' said Ezra. 'And there won't be one, any road.'

'Mother reckons it's imminent.'

'That's what I say. There won't be one. There'll be bombing, though.'

'They won't bomb civilians.'

'We won't. We've said we won't. They will. They're ruthless killers. Look at London.'

'London's London. They won't bomb us.'

'They'll bomb steelworks, mother. They'll bomb t' canal and railway. They'll try and cripple t' munitions industry and t' lines of communication. That's what Reg Hammond reckons, any road. There'll be stray bombs, Ada. There's forced to be. It isn't pin-point accuracy, isn't aerial bombardment.'

'Reg Hammond!' she said. 'Tha doesn't want to believe all he says. Him at chippy reckons he's a fifth columnist.'

'Him at chippy! Portions he serves, I reckon he's the fifth columnist. Go, Ada. It's best.'

'Will she want us?'

'Course she will. She likes having folk around her.'

'What about him?'

'He's all right.'

'What about t' house?'

'Evacuees can live here.'

'Evacuees?'

'Evacuees.'

'Why should evacuees want to live here?'

'Because it's safer.'

'So why are we going?'

'Evacuees come from London and Liverpool and Channel Isles and that, because it's safer here. We go to Kate's because it's safer still there. That's t' principle of evacuation, mother. That's how it works.'

34

Henry was in a quandary. He wasn't interested in the finer points of evacuation. His mind was whirling with the terrible possibility that he was going into the unknown, to Kates, wherever that was. He wanted to rush in and ask them about it, to beg them not to go. But that would reveal that he had been spying. He had done that once, and punishment had resulted.

'Ada?'

His father's tone of voice was different, softer.

'I've gorra headache.'

'Headache? It's me last night. I may never come back.'

'Ezra! Don't say that.'

'It's a possibility, mother. It's got to be faced.'

'I'm not making excuses, father. I have gorra headache.'

Henry decided to go back to bed. This business about headaches was boring.

'Is it a bad headache?'

'It's not that bad.'

'It's me last night, mother.'

'Go on up. I'll just make t' door.'

Up? His father was coming upstairs? Henry had begun to creep carefully up the stairs. Now he increased his pace. The stair which groaned groaned. The stair which creaked creaked. He prayed that the bedroom door wouldn't squeak. It didn't.

He snuggled down into the dark, warm womb of his bed. He pulled the bed-clothes over his head. The bed smelt pleasantly of himself. It was dark, warm and wonderful down there. If only he could stay there for ever.

He heard his father come upstairs. He heard the groan and the creak of the two errant steps. He pretended to be asleep. It was hard work pretending to be asleep, especially when your head was whirring with thoughts and worries. Perhaps if he pretended to be asleep hard enough he would find that he was asleep, except that you couldn't find that you were asleep, because when you were asleep you were always asleep, so you never knew you were asleep.

He heard his mother's heavier tread. The errant steps protested loudly. The house shook. He breathed deeply, rhythmically. He heard them getting into bed. He essayed a light snore. Their bed-springs were creaking. His father was grunting. His mother

35

was groaning. What on earth was going on?

His father was strangling his mother!

He leapt bravely from his womb and rushed over to the writhing, twisting couple. His mother was putting up brave resistance, but his father's strength belied his size, and she was definitely going under.

He grabbed his father with his frantic, podgy arms.

'Stop it! Stop it, dad! Give over!' he screamed. 'Don't do that to mam.'

'Hell's bells,' said his father. 'Hell's bells, Henry.'

They saw his father off at Thurmarsh (Midland Road) Station. The platform was crowded. Henry was frightened when the train roared in. It was packed. There were many soldiers. Ezra couldn't find a seat.

Henry wasn't so frightened as the train chugged out. All along the train, men with fixed smiles leant out of the windows and waved. On the platform, little groups of relations clutched each other helplessly. His dad waved until he was just a speck among many specks waving, and then the last carriage disappeared round the corner of the carriage sheds, and they walked away through the cruel August sunlight. Ada walked in the middle, with Her Mother on her left and Henry on her right. It was the first time that Henry had ever been exposed on one of life's flanks, the first time he had been required to give support, not receive it. He was tiny, and solemn, and frightened, as they waited for the tram home.

When they got home, Ada cried very briefly, and then busied herself mightily about her tasks. She gave him an extra portion of brawn as a treat. He asked the question that he could not contain within himself.

'Where's Kates?' he said.

'Kate's?'

'Aye. Where's Kates?'

'I've never heard of it,' she said.

'There's no such place,' said Her Mother.

'Only Kate's I know is your Great Aunt Kate's,' said Ada. Her mouth dropped open. 'Was tha listening last night?'

36

'No,' he said. Too late he added, 'What to?'

'Kate's our Ezra's father's sister,' said Ada. 'She married a farmer. They live on a lovely farm with cows and sheep and green hills all around. It's a grand life there. Come on, get thesen agate of that brawn. Was tha standing there, on t' stairs?'

Henry nodded miserably.

Ada raised her cup of tea to her lips, then lowered it without drinking.

'Happen it's best out,' she said. 'Ezra made me promise.'

'Promise what?' said Her Mother. 'Promise what, Ada?'

Ada's eyes avoided Her Mother's.

'To take Henry to Kate's.'

'To take Henry to Kate's? For how long?'

'Just for t' duration.'

'Just for t' duration?'

'I reckon I've got me parrot back again.'

'I don't want to go to Kate's,' said Henry. 'I 'ate Kate.'

'What about me?' said Her Mother. 'Did tha forget about me, or what?'

'Tha'll come wi' us,' said Ada. 'Tha lives wi' us, doesn't tha?'

'I'm not going there,' said Her Mother. 'I've lived all me life in Thurmarsh. I can't be doing wi' countryside, me.'

'It's a right nice place, mother. There's lovely hills and that.'

'Hills? They're nobbut lumps of muck. I'll go to our Leonard's. Now he's working.'

'Mother!'

'I'm not upset,' said Her Mother. 'I'm not hurt. T' lad comes first, and that's as it should be. I've had my life.' She sighed, thinking about it. 'It wouldn't matter if a bomb fell on my napper tomorrow. Nobody'd care. I wouldn't blame them. It's natural when tha's getting old.'

'Mother!'

'If Hitler doesn't oblige, I'll go and live wi' Leonard. It's all settled.'

'I feel awful now,' said Ada.

'Nay, luv, don't take on,' said Her Mother. 'I don't want to upset thee, not when tha's so upset. Countryside's safest for youngsters. I don't like t' countryside. Our Leonard's my son, and

37

it's about time I lived wi' 'im. Let's leave it at that.'

'Well what about our Doris? She's got more room than Leonard.'

'I wouldn't impose on her.'

'If anyone has thee, it should be Doris.'

'I'd never axe our Doris for owt. I wouldn't demean mesen.' Ada took a sip of tea.

'I don't like to see Doris getting away wi' it,' she said.

'Not doing her stint at putting up wi' me, does tha mean?' said Her Mother. 'Tha makes me sound like an air raid, not her mother.'

'I didn't mean that,' said Ada. 'I just meant Doris allus wriggles out of doing her bit.'

'I'm her bit now, am I? I'm summat unpleasant has to be undergone in line of duty, for t' war effort.'

'I don't want to go to Kate's,' said Henry. 'I 'ate Kate.'

'Mother!' said Ada, almost sobbing. 'I just know what Doris'll do. She'll wait till tha's settled wi' Leonard, then say, "You should have asked to come to us. We'd have been happy to have you, wouldn't we, Teddy?" '

Henry wondered if he had become invisible and inaudible at the same time. He made another plea for attention.

'I won't go,' he said. 'I won't go.'

'It's all settled. I'm not going to Doris,' said Her Mother. She took a piece of bread, and spread an ostentatiously thin scraping of margarine on it. She managed to make the gesture into a criticism of Teddy and Doris's whole lifestyle. This is my final word on the subject, said her eloquent knife.

Henry tried to be good, and reconcile himself to going to Kate's. He tried to support his mother, helping her scour the steps with the donkey stone, trying to carry the aspidistra out when it rained and everybody took their aspidistras out to stand on the causer edge. He went with her to the corner shop, holding her hand to reassure her. Her at the corner shop refused to take a slurpy halfpenny, because she couldn't see Britannia. Ada said, 'Some folk don't know there's a war on,' and almost cried, and Henry squeezed her hand.

38

They grew used to life without Ezra. For a week, Ada couldn't bring herself to mention him to Henry, for fear that she'd break down. Then she broached the subject that could not be avoided.

'Come here, Henry,' she said gently.

It was afternoon. Four pairs of stockings were drying on the clothes-horse in front of the range. Three of the stockings were laddered. Her Mother was over at Leonard's, discussing her room.

'That night, our Ezra's last night, upstairs,' she said. 'He wasn't trying to strangle me.'

She had to tell him that much, in fairness to Ezra.

'What *were* he doing, mam?'

She sighed. She'd known he'd ask it, of course. Why not describe the act in detail? He'd be as bored as he was bemused. He'd think it ridiculous. He'd have a point. But no, she couldn't tell him.

'Summat men do to women when they're grown up. Summat that happen tha'll do thysen one day.'

'What?'

'That's enough now. I just wanted tha to know that thy dad's a good man. He's gone to fight t' war so we can be safe.'

'What'll I do one day, mam?'

'We'll see.'

When Her Mother returned, she was well pleased with the room she had been allotted. 'It faces north, but it's got a nice outlook,' she said. 'I said to our Leonard, "It'll do, but tha can get shut of yon alablaster bust." He said, "That's Lord Hawke." I said, "I don't care if it's Lord Muck. It's going." He said, "Aye, but Lord Hawke were doyen of Yorkshire cricket." I said, "Aye, and he'll be doyen of bloody dustbin an' all in a minute. Get shut of him or I will."'

German bombers blitzed London and the Midlands. Allied bombers carried out night raids on German towns. There were fierce dog-fights in the skies over south-east England. The railings in front of the Georgian town houses behind the Alderman Chandler Memorial Park were ripped down and sent to join the war. Her Mother went to live with Leonard. 'It's a bit of a squeeze,' she said, 'but they can cope. She's quite nice when tha gets to know her. Me room faces north, but how much sun do we have any road? It'll be nice to have an inside toilet for a change, even if it has got an alablaster bust of Lord Hawke in it. So don't feel badly about it, Ada. It's my choice. I don't feel unwanted. I don't feel neglected.'

Their belongings were all packed and standing by the door of the little house. Uncle Teddy and Auntie Doris had insisted that everything be ready by the time they arrived.

'They said they'd be here early doors,' said Ada. 'Some folk have a funny idea of early doors.'

Soon there would be evacuees in the house. Moving had proved no problem. Him at corner shop didn't mind where his rent came from, provided it came.

Henry wanted to cry, but he was determined not to.

Uncle Teddy and Auntie Doris arrived at last.

'Cup of tea?' enquired Ada.

'No, no,' said Uncle Teddy hastily, and then he tried to soften the refusal with explanation. 'We've a long way to go, and there's the blackout.'

'I wish mother'd asked to come to us,' said Auntie Doris. 'We'd have been happy to have her, wouldn't we, Teddy?'

'Is this all there is?' said Uncle Teddy, surveying their meagre baggage.

'Teddy!' said Auntie Doris.

'Well there's not much, to say they're going for the duration,' said Uncle Teddy.

'Tact,' mouthed Auntie Doris.

'Tact?' said Uncle Teddy.

'Don't rub it in that some folk haven't got as much as others,' hissed Auntie Doris, who always made things worse by protesting about them.

'Oh. Right,' said Uncle Teddy. 'Travelling light, eh? That's the ticket. The rest'll be quite safe here.'

There was ample room for their luggage in the boot of the Armstrong-Siddeley 'Twelve Plus' Four-Light Saloon De Luxe.

And then Henry knew that he couldn't go.

'Don't want to go,' he whimpered.

Uncle Teddy gave Ada a sharp glance.

'It's nice there, Henry,' said Ada.

'I 'ate Kate,' said Henry.

'Don't be silly. Tha's never met her,' said Ada.

Henry began to scream.

'We'll be in the car,' said Uncle Teddy grimly. 'Come on, Doris.'

Henry screamed and screamed and screamed. At first he screamed because he was terrified of leaving this cobbled, terraced, canal-side womb. Then he screamed because he was upset with himself for giving way to his fear. Then he screamed because he was angry with life because he was a helpless thing about which other people made decisions, and he had no choice about being put into positions where he had to scream. Then he was empty of fear and anger and shame, and he screamed because he couldn't think of a way of stopping screaming without looking ridiculous.

In the end he stopped out of sheer exhaustion.

Ada closed the door for the last time, and led Henry to the waiting car. The top half of the headlights had been blacked out.

'I thought it best if we were out of the road,' said Uncle Teddy. 'I thought it might get it over with quicker if the performance was mainly for our benefit.'

'It wasn't a performance,' said Ada.

'Now you've not forgotten anything, have you?' said Uncle Teddy. 'We're late. We've been delayed. I'm not turning back.'

'He never turns back,' said Auntie Doris, whose perfume filled the car.

'I've not forgotten owt,' said Ada.

Uncle Teddy handed Ada a paper bag.

'In case he's car-sick,' he explained.

'You didn't have to say what it's for. It's obvious. You could just have handed it to her. You've made things worse,' said Auntie Doris, who always made things worse by protesting about them. 'You've put the idea of being car-sick into his head.'

'You won't be car-sick, will you, Henry?' said Uncle Teddy.

'No, Uncle Teddy,' said Henry in little more than a whisper.

'Let's gerron wi' it,' said Ada.

'He has to have his little argument,' said Auntie Doris.

'I do not have to have my little argument,' said Uncle Teddy. 'I do not have to have my little argument, Doris.'

'Don't clench your teeth at me,' said Auntie Doris.

'Tha can go now,' said Ada. 'T' whole street's seen her fur wrap.'

'I'll put that down to tension and ignore it,' said Uncle Teddy, crashing angrily into first gear and setting off with a jerk.

Henry Pratt had lived at number 23 Paradise Lane for five years and almost six months. Never, in the rest of his life, would he remain in one home for so long.

The nearest that he would come to it would be at Low Farm, near the village of Rowth Bridge, in the spectacular landscape of Upper Mitherdale.

But I anticipate. They weren't there yet. There were problems on the long journey from womb-cobble to world-hill.

The first problem was petrol. Or rather, the lack of it. 'He always leaves it too late,' said Auntie Doris, as Uncle Teddy trudged back into the distance with his can, towards the garage at which he had declined to stop because he 'didn't like the cut of its jib'.

The second problem was the signposts. Or rather, the lack of them. Most of them had been taken down, and the others had been pointed in the wrong direction, to confuse the Germans. It confused Uncle Teddy.

'It's lucky I know my county,' he said. 'I might get lost otherwise.'

The third problem was Uncle Teddy's war effort. Or rather, the lack of it. It came to the surface just after they had found themselves lost for the third time.

'Who are we supposed to be fighting, the Germans or ourselves?' said Uncle Teddy.

'Nobody, in your case,' said Ada.

Uncle Teddy slammed the brakes on. The car slewed to a halt across the road, almost catapulting Auntie Doris through the windscreen.

. 'I have flat feet,' said Uncle Teddy. 'I have very flat feet. I have fallen arches. I have very fallen arches. My worst enemy couldn't say that I am a man not to face the music when the chips are down. I want to do my bit. With my feet, I've no chance. No chance.'

'I'm sorry,' said Ada.

'We'll forget it,' said Uncle Teddy. 'We'll attribute it to tension, and wipe it from the minutes.'

They had left the big towns and the factories behind long ago. The hills were growing higher, the dale narrower. The little towns and villages were all of stone, plain, square, unadorned, and handsome. They crossed the river twice, catching glimpses of it slipping placidly over the rocks.

They came to another small town. There was no place-name to greet the Teutonic invader.

'If it's Troutwick, we turn right,' said Uncle Teddy.

He pulled up in a pleasant, jumbled square, and asked two elderly men, 'Is this Troutwick?'

The elderly men stared at him in amazement.

'Well of course it is,' said one. They had lived there all their lives, and they couldn't see how there could possibly be any doubt on the matter.

'How do I get to Rowth Bridge?' said Uncle Teddy, speaking more loudly and slowly than usual, as if to foreigners.

'Tha turns right,' said the second elderly man.

'Yes, but where?' said Uncle Teddy.

'Does tha see t' lane along o' t' Trustee Savings Bank?' said the first elderly man.

'Yes,' said Uncle Teddy.

'Not there,' said the first elderly man.

'Carry on along t' road,' said the second elderly man, 'till tha comes to an old inn, t' Three Magpies, that were demolished ten years ago.'

'More like twelve,' said the first elderly man. 'Our Annie were carrying our Albert.'

'Mebbe,' said the second elderly man. 'Tha turns right there, any road.'

Somehow they managed to find the turning. Soon they were in a narrower, steeper dale, with a smaller, livelier river. The road was slow and winding, the houses further apart, the villages

43

hamlets. Dry-stone walls criss-crossed the fields and hills, and at regular intervals in the walls there were stone field barns, like wayside chapels.

Some of the land was under the plough. Some was pasture for cattle. Most of it was a huge sheep run.

They crossed the old stone hump-bridge that gave Rowth Bridge its name. The river Mither was little more than a rocky beck up here.

They twisted through the village, a tight-packed cluster of low stone buildings, huddled together for warmth, for protection, and out of kinship.

Beyond the village the road ran on to the head of the dale, which was bounded by high fells to the north, with the impressive bulk of Mickleborough dominating the scene. The infant Mither tumbled joyously down from these hills, chuckling delightedly over its miniature gorge.

All this was unfamiliar and terrifying to Henry. He could see nothing good in this spectacular place. It was impossible to believe that life here could have anything in common with life in Paradise Lane.

There, tucked under the hills on their left, was Low Farm. It was a very long, low, seventeenth-century stone building, a typical long house of the Yorkshire Dales, with the cow barn built into the end of the house, as if it were part of it. Anywhere else it would have been a row of cottages.

A bumpy track led up to the farmhouse. Uncle Teddy negotiated it slowly, in pained silence, veering from side to side to avoid the worst potholes and cowpats. Sheep watched him, and protested.

'We'd have suggested you came and lived with us,' said Auntie Doris. 'But we're almost as likely to get bombed as you were.'

The track took them round the side of the house. There, at the back of the house, at the kitchen door, stood Ezra's Auntie Kate and her husband Frank.

Frank, five foot nine of solid rock, gazed at them with his expression of amiable gentleness which verged on a smile without ever quite breaking into it. Kate, five foot one of bouncing energy, beamed from ear to ear.

44

Their expressions did not say, 'We are prepared to have you here.' Their expressions said, 'We are grateful to you for coming.' Suddenly, Henry knew that it was going to be all right.

4 Peace and War

Ada and Kate stood at the landing window, watching little Henry marching sturdily up the hill in his Wellington boots. They were putting up paper-chains for Christmas. The paper-chains were sober and tasteful, in pastel colours.

It was Tuesday, December 17th. The Battle of Britain had been won. Churchill had said that never in the field of human conflict was so much owed by so many to so few. Dowding, whose planes had won the battle, had been relieved of his command. The war cabinet had agreed that the civilian population around the German target areas must be made to feel the weight of the war.

On Sunday night, Sheffield had been blitzed. Henry Hall and his band had been forced to leave the city without their instruments, and there were more than five hundred homeless. Uncle Teddy and Auntie Doris were not among them. On Monday night it had been Thurmarsh's turn. 173 houses had been struck, and there had been a direct hit on the biscuit factory, with an attendant loss of custard creams on a large scale. Paradise Lane had not been affected. Nor had Her Mother, Leonard and his family, or the alabaster bust of Lord Hawke. Cousin Hilda survived unscathed as well, although a bomb demolished the house three doors away.

Henry's right hand was firmly clasped in the left hand of the farm hand Billy, who wasn't quite all there. Beside them trotted Sam, the sheepdog.

Ada sighed.

'Is summat wrong, Ada?' said Kate.

'I don't like Henry being so friendly wi' animals,' said Ada.

'What does tha think he'll catch, Ada?' said Kate. 'Milk fever? Mastitis? Hard pad?'

Ada flushed, and Kate felt sorry that she had been so tart. She had been a town person herself once. She had been the only person not to be surprised that they had arrived without Wellington boots.

'I'm not o'er pleased that he's such friends wi' Billy,' said Ada.

'Billy's safe enough,' said Kate. 'Manpower's short. There's a war on.'

Kate flushed now, and her hand went to her throat in distress. Ada knew more about the war than she did. She was on her own, in a strange place, without the support of her husband.

'I'm sorry,' said Kate. 'I'm sorry, Ada.'

'It doesn't matter,' said Ada. She felt tears coming into her eyes. A hot flush drenched her body in the illusion of sweat. Her legs, which she knew to be huge and horrible, were on fire. She stumbled towards the bedroom she shared with Henry.

The bedroom was the only thing she shared with Henry. She had lost him. Her husband had been taken by the army. Henry had been taken by Kate, by Frank, by Billy the half-wit, by Jackie the land-girl, by Sam the sheepdog, by the River Mither and the age-old hills.

By the time Henry got home, she had recovered.

'Well, what's tha been up to?' she asked him.

'Picking earth,' he said smugly.

'Picking earth?'

'Aye.'

He led his mother downstairs to the kitchen, and pointed to the flagged floor. Lumps of dark, wet, thick, winter earth lay on the beautiful bluish Horton flags.

Ada struck him violently, a big blow across the right ear.

'Clear it up,' she ordered, and rushed from the room.

Henry fell to the ground, his ear ringing with pain which exploded inside his head.

Tears filled his eyes, but he wouldn't cry. Wouldn't wouldn't wouldn't. Nearly did. Didn't.

His Great-Aunt Kate came in with a handful of turnips, and found him sitting there, lips puckering, a lone tear drying on his cheek, on the flagged floor, beneath the hanging hams, in front of the huge, leaded range, among the earth that he had dumped on the floor.

'What's to do?' she said.

'Mam hit me.'

'Why?'

'I picked lots of earth.'

'Why did tha pick lots of earth, Henry?'

'I'm nobbut a lad. I have to be naughty sometimes.'

He hurried from the room, before he could be hit again.

Frank came in before Kate could clear the earth from her beautiful floor.

'Problem,' said Kate.

'Aye,' said Frank. 'I can see. Henry.'

'No,' said Kate. 'Ada.'

'Ada?'

'Ada.'

Frank sat in the big, wide-backed wooden chair which looked huge until he sat in it. He stretched his weary legs.

'Ada spilt earth on t' floor?'

'No. Henry,' said Kate.

'I don't know what she's on about half the time,' said Frank.

'Ada?' said Kate.

'No. Thee,' said Frank. 'I were just confiding in t' Lord.'

It had been a great sorrow to Uncle Frank – he refused to be known as Great-Uncle Frank: it made him sound so old, and he was only just the wrong side of sixty – that he had had no sons. The three Turnbull daughters had been famous throughout the district for their vitality and beauty. Their ephemeral charm and grace had contrasted exquisitely with the stark timelessness of the gritstone landscape of Upper Mitherdale. They could have had anybody, and for two worrying years it had seemed that Fiona had. Now they were gone, married (and who were Uncle Frank and Auntie Kate to say that their husbands were unworthy of them, just because everyone else said so?). Uncle Frank had been proud and amazed that he could have helped to produce three such lovely creatures, but he was a farmer, and he wanted sons.

Now Auntie Kate – she refused to be known as Great-Aunt Kate: it made her sound so old, and she was still the right side of sixty, if only just – saw Ada worrying about Ezra, and gave thanks to God that she had no sons. In war-time sons get killed.

She began to keep Ada busy. She tried to encourage her to talk about her worries, while they made bread and havercake and Christmas cake and Christmas pudding and stuffing for the goose and all the other things which Auntie Kate could have made in half the time if she hadn't been trying to get Ada to talk about her worries without appearing to do so.

The kitchen was large, but warm and cosy. A huge dresser occupied the wall opposite the range. The scrubbed deal table was covered in the preparations for a feast. Ada relaxed enough to explain the reasons why she found it impossible to relax.

These were 1 Ezra. (a) Was he sleeping well? He needed his sleep. He always had. (b) Was he getting enough food? He was a right gannet, despite his size. He'd be missing his brawn. She'd heard that the Red Cross sent parcels, but would they include brawn, or would it all be soft, southern stuff? (c) Would his food, even if adequate, be too dry? Ezra needed gravy to help him digest. (d) Would he be killed? 2 Self. (a) Was she a sour old hag, although only thirty-four years of age? (b) Were her legs getting bigger still? (c) She was still. . .tha knows. . .so why was she getting hot flushes? 3 Henry. (a) Why was he getting naughty? (b) Why was she jealous of him? (See 2 (a).) (c) Would he get mastoids because she'd struck his ear?

Auntie Kate felt that her responses were inadequate. They were 1 (a) Like a log, undoubtedly. (b) Definitely. An army marches on its stomach. Temporary brawn starvation might be a good thing. Absence makes the. . .etcetera. (c) Armies are great places for gravy. They're known for it. Hence the expression, the gravy train. (d) I don't know. 2 (a) No. (b) No. (c) God moves in a mysterious way. 3 (a) Because he feels more secure. (b) Because you're a mother. (c) Unlikely.

'That were t' best Christmas I've ever 'ad.'

Auntie Kate looked at Henry sadly, gladly. She was torn in two. A casual observer might have thought her possessive. She needed people. She needed to be useful to people. But she did not want to impinge upon their close family attachments. She had no wish to cross the demarcation lines of emotion. She was not vying with a mother's love. There had been hopes that Ezra might get leave before he went abroad, but he had not. Auntie Kate had been disappointed that Henry hadn't seemed disappointed. How could she make his life here secure and rich without leading him to compare it unfavourably with what Ada and Ezra had been able to offer him?

'It were t' best Christmas I've ever 'ad ever,' he repeated.

Jackie, the land-girl, had gone home for the holiday. Fiona, their youngest, had come over from Skipton with her husband, who was an assistant bank manager and had an artificial leg. They had married in October last year. The bride had looked charming in Burgundy marocain, with hat and shoes to tone. She had worn a spray of pink and white carnations, and carried her gas-mask. She had dark, deep eyes which were full of fun. Henry had liked her, but not her husband, who was right dull, in his opinion. Laura, their eldest, had come over from Nelson on Boxing Day with her husband and their three aggressive children. Laura was putting on weight. What her husband gained by being not quite as dull as Fiona's, he lost by being a Lancastrian. Norma's husband, who was duller than Laura's, but less dull than Fiona's, suffered from a far graver character defect than being a Lancastrian. He was German. They lived near Nuremberg. It had added insult to injury that Norma's husband was fit enough to fight for Germany, but neither Fiona's husband nor Laura's husband were fit enough to fight for Britain. People were right when they said that the lovely Turnbull girls could all have done better for themselves.

On Christmas morning they had gone to church. Henry had stared at the people from the big house, in their family pew, as at creatures from another planet. Except for Belinda Boyce-Uppingham, aged six. He had stared at her as at perfection. She had looked right through him. Ada had hoped that nobody would notice that she didn't know when to stand and when to kneel and when to sit. All the Boyce-Uppinghams had noticed. After church, people had lingered in the little churchyard and outside in the lane beside the aptly-named Mither. They had wished each other a happy Christmas. Humble villagers had touched vocal forelocks to the Turnbulls. The Turnbulls had touched vocal forelocks to the Boyce-Uppinghams. Old Percy Boyce-Uppingham had tapped Henry with his walking stick, as if he were a barometer, but instead of saying, 'Looks like rain,' he had said, 'So you're our new little town boy, then. Well done,' and had given him sixpence, and Auntie Kate had nudged Henry, and

Henry had said, 'Thank you very much, sir. Happy Christmas,' and then they had gone home and had roast goose with all the trimmings, and on Boxing Day they had had home-cured ham. And there had been a Christmas tree, and Henry had had a stocking, in which there was an orange, a Mars bar, an apple, a comb, a box of coloured pencils and a little woollen camel which squeaked. Round the Christmas tree there were other presents, which included a Dinky toy (a London bus), a book with stories and pictures, another book with pictures that you coloured and a humming top.

Now it was over, and Henry sat at the scrubbed deal table in the spacious kitchen, and managed to read a few words from his book out loud in a solemn, slow, artificial voice. It had been Auntie Kate's idea that Ada should teach him to read before he went to school in January.

'This is my best home ever,' he said.

Auntie Kate turned grave eyes upon him.

'This isn't your real home, Henry,' she said. 'Always remember that. You like it because it's new, and there are animals. It can be right lonely and cruel sometimes, specially in winter, and there's not many folk thy own age here, and that's why it can never be your real home.'

She hoped that this had made an impression on him, but what he said next was, 'I were right put out at first about eating t' goose, cos I knew him. He were my friend. Bur I et 'im. He were right tasty too.'

The words came slowly, solemnly, articulated with exaggerated care. Auntie Kate wanted to laugh at the grown-up sound of 'I were right put out' coming from the five-year-old boy, whose podgy legs were swinging above the flagstones as he sat in his kitchen chair.

'There were two things I didn't reckon much to,' said Henry.

Auntie Kate waited.

'Doesn't tha want to know what they were?' said Henry.

'Aye. Oh aye. I do. What didn't tha reckon much to, Henry?' said Auntie Kate.

'Children's party and Auntie Laura's bairns. I hate kids.'

Perhaps it was a mistake, holding him back from school till he'd

51

settled down, thought Auntie Kate. Certainly Henry had not distinguished himself at the children's Christmas party in the Parish Hall. Local ladies had given entertainments comprising charades, sketches and musical items. A Mr Elland from Troutwick had made interesting shapes out of newspapers – all of which, he emphasised, would later be sent for salvage. Patrick Eckington and one or two other children had given turns. Father Christmas had put in an appearance, and there had been a gift of savings stamps for each child. They had played games including musical chairs. The evacuee children had been rowdy. So had the Luggs. Lorna Arrow had been sick. Henry had been paralysed with shyness and had just stared at everybody and reverted to sucking his thumb.

He didn't tell Auntie Kate the thing that he had hated most, which was being tapped by old Percy Boyce-Uppingham as if he were a barometer. He didn't tell her because he had fallen in love with Belinda Boyce-Uppingham, and everything to do with the Boyce-Uppinghams was therefore too private to be talked about. Old Percy Boyce-Uppingham's stick had made a deep impression on him. Its effect was seminal, he later decided, wondering at his youthful ability to feel to the full the horrors of being patronised many years before he even knew of the existence of the word 'patronising'.

'Auntie Kate?'

His solemnity was comical. He spoke with the air of someone who has thought long and hard about a subject of deep importance, as indeed he had. But she had herself under control. She wouldn't laugh at him now.

'Aye. What is it?'

'I saw me dad on top of me mam doing summat that weren't strangling, and I don't know what it were, and when I asked me mam she were right cagey about it. Does tha know what they were doing, Auntie Kate?'

Auntie Kate didn't reply. She was leaning on the window-sill and shaking.

'Only I thought tha might know what it were cos I thought happen Uncle Frank might have tried it with thee,' said Henry.

Auntie Kate threw back her head and roared with laughter. She

52

went bright red with mirth.

Henry went red too. The shame of being laughed at and by Auntie Kate of all people was too much. The terrible hot shame of it.

Auntie Kate stopped laughing.

'I'm sorry,' she said.

And then, the unexpected happened. Henry Pratt, frightened of being laughed at, frightened of his own father, frightened of falling into water, frightened of railway engines, frightened of children, and frightened of being ejected from wombs, discovered that he had a fighting spirit.

'It's not fair to laugh at me because I don't know things,' he said. 'I can't know everything. I'm only little.'

'Oh dear. We've made a puddle, haven't we?'

It was Henry's first day at school. The exciting world of education was about to open up before him. He'd made a puddle.

His mother had walked with him down the lane to the village. The school was through the village, over the hump-bridge, on the right, beyond the Parish Hall. It was a square, stone building with high, Gothic windows and solid triangular gables. There was a large bell over the porch. He had his sandwiches in Fiona's old, stained satchel. He'd begun to want to go before he'd even crossed the playground.

Miss Forrest, the headmistress, tall and efficient, had pointed him in the direction of the junior classroom, and there he had met Miss Candy for the first time.

Miss Candy was fifty-three years old, and rode to school from Troutwick on a motor bike. She had three chins, and skin like leather. Her nose was large, her eyes were too close together. Her body had no definable shape. Her grey hair was pinned up into elaborate curls and rolls. A tuft of darker hair sprouted from the middle of her middle chin. Those who said that her moustache resembled the Fuehrer's were exaggerating.

There were children's paintings all round the walls of the classroom. Some of the paintings were just about recognisable as crude impressions of various local scenes. Others were less good. Pale winter sun streamed in through the high Gothic windows. The little desks were arranged in five groups for pupils of different ages. There were three small portable blackboards on easels. In front of the large, fixed blackboard there hung a blind covered with a picturesque representation of a farmyard. Yet it remained a classroom, filled with twenty-five strange children and presided over by a teacher of fearsome aspect. The pressure on his bladder grew rapidly, and he was far too shy to be able to ask to be permitted to relieve it.

Miss Candy sat him in a group with five of the youngest children, and asked him his name.

'Henry,' he mumbled.

'Oh dear. That's a little unfortunate, Henry, because we already have a Henry, don't we, Henry?'

'Aye, miss,' said a fair-haired boy in Henry's group.

'We can't have two Henrys in the same group, can we, Henry?' said Miss Candy.

'No, miss,' said the fair-haired boy, whose name was Henry Dinsdale.

'Have you got another name, Henry?' said Miss Candy.

'Aye,' said Henry.

'Well what is it?' said Miss Candy.

'Pratt,' said Henry, and a boy in the group giggled.

'Hush, Jane, there's nothing funny about names,' said Miss Candy to this boy, who was actually a girl. This was Jane Lugg, who came from a regrettably long line of Luggs.

'Haven't you got another Christian name?' said Miss Candy.

Henry nodded miserably.

'Well what is it?'

'Ezra,' he mumbled, hot with shame, wild with fury.

'Ezra,' said Miss Candy. 'Well, I'm glad to say we don't have any other Ezras here, so we'll be able to call you Ezra, won't we, Ezra?'

'Aye,' mumbled Henry, glaring at Henry Dinsdale, who had forced him to become an Ezra and inherit the curse of being a parrot-strangler.

It was lucky that Henry didn't know that Henry Dinsdale's real name was Cyril, but he'd had to be called Henry because there was already a Cyril. He had only just got over the problems associated with this change, and Miss Candy judged that to call him by a third name might provoke a severe identity crisis. So, Cyril remained Henry and Henry became Ezra.

The remaining members of Henry's group were Simon Eckington, the younger of the two Eckington boys from the Post Office, Cyril Orris, whose father was a farmer, and Pam Yardley, an evacuee.

There was no sign of Belinda Boyce-Uppingham. Henry was glad of that as he made his puddle.

'You'll have to go to the utility room, Ezra,' said Miss Candy. 'Take your trousers and pants off, wash them in the sink, and hang them on the pipes to dry. Show him the way, Henry, and bring me the bucket, the mop and the disinfectant.'

Cyril/Henry led Henry/Ezra to the utility room/locker room/boiler room, and there he spent his first morning at school.

In one corner there was a large sink. In another corner was the boiler. Hot pipes ran round the dark-green walls. There were many pegs on which hung satchels and coats, and all round the floor there were lockers. There was a window of frosted glass. There was nowhere to sit.

Henry took off his trousers and pants and washed them with a bar of green carbolic. He had never washed clothes before. The soap didn't produce lather, just a greeny-white slime. The world of rinsing was also an unexplored continent to him, and despite his best efforts, much of the soap proved impossible to remove. He gave up, and put the long, baggy shorts and thick yellowing pants on the pipes to dry. Time passes slowly when you're five years old and have nothing to do except stand and watch your clothes drying. That morning was an eternity of misery to Henry, standing with his fat legs bare, and his shirt not even covering his cowering little willie, in the hot little room with the noisy boiler and the frosted-glass window. His legs ached. There was a sudden eruption of children's voices and screams. It must be dinner-time, but nobody came into the utility room, and eventually the noise died down again. There was a distant slamming of doors, and silence reigned, save for the roaring and gurgling of the boiler.

Please, God, he said, as he stood beside his steaming clothes, I'm sorry I never came to see thee in Thurmarsh, but I didn't really know about thee, but now I do, so I will come in future. Please, God, kill Henry Dinsdale so I don't have to be an Ezra. Amen, and

55

lots of love. Henry.

He began to wonder if everybody had gone home and left him. Perhaps he was locked in. Several times he felt that he would cry, but he fought against it.

Suddenly children were pouring into the utility room and looking at him and giggling as they collected their coats if they were going home to dinner or their sandwiches if they weren't. One older boy said, 'Look at his little willie,' and Patrick Eckington said, 'I can't. I forgot me magnifying glass,' and there was laughter, and then Miss Candy was there, saying, 'Your clothes are dry. Why haven't you put them on?' and he mumbled, 'Didn't tell me to,' and Miss Candy, who had a bottomless supply of minatory saws of her own invention, said, 'Mr Mumble shouted "fire" and nobody heard,' and he put his pants and shorts on with difficulty because the soap had caked hard, and the afternoon was a blur, and that was his first day at school, and it was to be the first of many, and they would all be like that, and life was awful.

There was still no sign of Belinda Boyce-Uppingham.

The snows came. Huge drifts swept up to the dry-stone walls. The ash woods were a magical tracery of white. Henry rushed into the kitchen with a snowball, and hurled it wildly in his excitement. It knocked a plate of best Worcester porcelain off the dresser. The plate smashed. Uncle Frank, who was never angry, strode abruptly from the room.

'Snow isn't funny here, Henry,' explained Auntie Kate. 'Uncle Frank's been out for hours, making sure his sheep are all right.'

Henry felt that awful hot shaming feeling all over.

Uncle Frank was out for hours again, with Billy and Jackie, taking fodder to any sheep they could find, but there were many more cut off in the huge drifts.

'Won't they die?' Henry asked Uncle Frank that evening.

'Grown up sheep are very tough,' explained Uncle Frank. 'We don't mind early snows so much. It's when we get snows in t' lambing season that we're in trouble.'

Henry was very thoughtful. If the sheep could survive out there, he thought, he wouldn't make any more fuss about going to school.

56

That Saturday afternoon, after the snows had stopped, and the sun was shining crisply, there was tobogganing down the lower slopes of Mickle Fell. Uncle Frank asked him if he'd like to use the girls' old toboggan. He tried to get out of it, on the grounds that it was unfair to sheep to enjoy the snow, but really because he was frightened. But Uncle Frank insisted, and suddenly it was important not to seem a coward in front of Uncle Frank.

The children of Rowth Bridge hurtled down the white slopes with apparent fearlessness on that ice-blue Saturday afternoon in war-time. Some had toboggans, some wooden boards, some tea-trays. The older children set off from quite high up. Some of them were fighter pilots, dive-bombing the vicious Hun.

Henry trudged up the slope somewhat fearfully. Patrick Eckington hurtled past. Surely this was high enough? And then he saw her. Belinda Boyce-Uppingham. Ravishing. High above him.

He couldn't start from below her, so he trudged on. Between him and Belinda a sturdy young man was carrying a tea-tray.

At last Belinda stopped and turned. The sturdy young man stopped beside her. They stood and waited for him.

He approached them, wheezing breathlessly. The sturdy young man turned out to be Jane Lugg. He wanted to speak to Belinda, but no words would come.

They began their descent. As his wooden toboggan gathered speed, Henry grew terrified. Faster and faster he went. Jane Lugg on her tea-tray was outclassed. Belinda Boyce-Uppingham, streamlined on her superb metal bobsleigh, was narrowly ahead of him.

Their speed increased. The field below was full of tiny figures.

Belinda Boyce-Uppingham was heading for the side of the field, where a slight incline slowed the toboggans and enabled you to stop quite gracefully. But Henry's toboggan was heading down to the bottom of the field, and there was nothing he could do to stop it.

Belinda dismounted from her bobsleigh gracefully. Jane Lugg landed underneath her tray in a clumsy, laughing heap. Henry's toboggan breasted the snows piled against the wall. It soared over the top, hurtled towards the thinner snow of the lower field, and landed with a bruising crunch. It gathered speed again. Wide-eyed and petrified he saw the trees at the edge of the ash wood rushing towards him.

He missed the trees by inches, and shot straight into the icy waters of the infant Mither. It was not the last river that Henry Pratt would fall into, but it was easily the smallest.

After that, things were better at school, and he began to settle in. Not quickly. Not easily. But steadily.

Within a week he had received two overtures of friendship. One he accepted, one he rejected.

The overture that he accepted was from Simon Eckington. Like him, Simon was shy. And Simon's father was also away at the war. His mother had her hands full running the Post Office and General Store, and his elder brother Patrick bullied him unmercifully. He was glad to find a good friend.

The overture that he didn't accept was from Pam Yardley. She was an evacuee, from Leeds. She had been taken in by the Wallingtons. Jim Wallington was the bus driver. Pam Yardley made the mistake of appealing for friendship on the grounds that they were both evacuees. Henry denied this angrily. He didn't add the clincher which prevented any possibility of friendship. Pam Yardley was a girl. Girls were useless, with one glorious exception. That exception was Belinda Boyce-Uppingham. Pam Yardley was not Belinda Boyce-Uppingham. Therefore she was useless.

The great strength of Belinda Boyce-Uppingham was that she was a beautiful and wonderful human being, despite her family.

The great weakness of Belinda Boyce-Uppingham was that she didn't go to the village school. Henry plucked up courage and, blushing, asked Auntie Kate why this was.

'The Boyce-Uppinghams send their children to private schools when they are young and then to public schools,' explained Auntie Kate.

It sounded to Henry as if the Boyce-Uppinghams were somewhat confused people, who had no cause to go around smugly tapping people as if they were barometers.

The school day started with a hymn and a prayer. Then they did painting and drawing. Henry's paintings were beautiful in his mind, but ghastly messes by the time they reached the paper. The younger children moulded plasticine and the older ones carved wood. Sometimes they would dance and even sing, quietly, so as not to disturb Miss Forrest's class. Sometimes they would dress up and perform little plays. Most of the class liked this part of the day, but Henry was doubtful.

There followed a bad time. This was the break. The playground was divided sexually by a tall wire fence. Miss Candy had argued against this. 'Put them in cages and they'll behave like animals,' she had said. 'Put them together and they'll behave like animals,' her superior had retorted. Henry didn't like the break because it exposed him to the bullying of *his* superiors. His tobogganing had not transformed him into a hero overnight. It had to be weighed against the puddle. It wasn't certain yet whether he was to be counted as an evacuee or not. More evidence was needed before judgement was passed on him.

After the break there came the best part of Henry's day – the lessons. They learnt reading and writing, and the basics of arithmetic, and he proved good at these things.

Dinner came next. The risk of bullying was less great than in the break, because many of the children went home. On the wall of the playground, however, a goal had been marked in chalk, and here football was often played. Henry had nothing against football, except that he couldn't play and always got hurt. There were also three stumps chalked against the wall, and when the summer came Henry would learn that his lack of talent extended to cricket also. These perils, when added to the lingering threat of brawn, made dinner a dangerous time.

In the afternoon, they applied their arithmetic, and their reading and writing, to various practical ends, like running a shop, or planning the farming year, or holding auctions, or even, as they got older, writing a local children's newspaper.

We have seen Miss Candy from the outside, a shapeless, greying motor-cyclist with an excess of chins, hair in unfortunate places, and a distant hint of the porcine in her features. Come with me now on a journey into the interior.

Miss Candy had always known that she would be a teacher. She had believed that she would be a good, perhaps even a great teacher. She was steeped in educational theory. She identified with those two alliterative lady educationalists, Maria Montessori and Margaret McMillan.

It was because of the influence of Maria Montessori that there was no rivalry in Miss Candy's class. Each child went at his or her own pace. There were no rewards. Punishment was reserved for naughtiness and breaches of communal discipline, and was never used as a weapon against the slow-witted. The communal discipline included tidying up the classroom before going home. Miss Candy believed that Maria Montessori, the great Italian, would approve, if only she could ever see Miss Candy's class of five- to ten-year-olds at Rowth Bridge Village School.

Being herself from Bradford, it was natural that Miss Candy associated herself even more closely with Margaret McMillan, who did much of her best work in that city between 1893 and 1902. Margaret McMillan believed that many schoolchildren went through school life using only a minimum of their powers and expressing only a fraction of their personalities. She believed in the importance of nursery schooling, where children could be given adventure, movement, dancing, music, talking, food and rest within the school environment. Extracts from her writings hung on the wall of Miss Candy's bedroom. 'You may ask why we give all this to the children? Because this is nurture, and without it they can never really have education. For education must grow out of nurture and the flower from its root, since nurture is organic. . . . Much of the money we spend on education is wasted, because we have not laid any real foundation for our educational system. . . .'

Nobody would ever read the educational theories of Miss Florence Candy. Her wise saws would hang on no one's bedroom wall. No international seminars of educationalists would ever hang breathless on her words. She looked ridiculous. She lived in a world which judges men partially and women almost entirely by appearance. The junior classroom at Rowth Bridge Village School was therefore her pinnacle. Her satisfaction was that she was achieving as much as could possibly be achieved by a woman of her appearance, in a classroom split up into five different groups of children who had not been to nursery schools, in a tiny village school with holes in the ground for lavatories, under a head teacher who disapproved of her, insisted that the children marched into school in lines, and would try to get rid of her as soon as the war was over.

It is time to reveal another of Miss Candy's secrets. She had always believed that one day one of the human seeds that she had helped to nurture would grow into a plant that would make her life worthwhile. One day she would have a pupil through whose reflected glory her work would live on.

She had a hope, just a faint hope, that she had found that pupil at last.

On Sunday mornings, as Henry got ready for church, cleaning shoes, brushing hair, he listened to the repeat of Tommy Handley in 'It's That Man Again' on the kitchen wireless. He didn't understand it very well but the grown-ups laughed a lot, and he was determined not to be left out.

This Sunday he didn't laugh. Henry Dinsdale, né Cyril Dinsdale, had not been to school for three days. Ezra Pratt, né Henry Pratt, remembered a prayer made in a utility room. Please, God, kill Henry Dinsdale, so I don't have to be an Ezra.

He was terrified that God had answered his prayer.

When they all knelt, in the little, squat-towered church beside the Mither, he prayed fervently.

Please, God, he prayed, it's me again. Tha knows I axed thee to kill Henry Dinsdale. I didn't really mean it. Bring him back to life, will tha, like tha did thy kid?

He had the utmost difficulty in eating his dinner that day.

After dinner, they listened to the gardening advice given by Roy Hay. Uncle Frank kept up a running commentary. 'I disagree!. . .Not up here, tha won't!. . .Never wi' our soil!'

The day dragged endlessly. Henry didn't sleep that night.

In the morning, Henry Dinsdale still wasn't at school. God had failed him.

He toyed listlessly with his plasticine.

'What's up, Ezra?' Miss Candy asked.

'Nowt, miss.'

In the break he longed to ask Miss Candy about Henry Dinsdale but he didn't dare. Patrick Eckington punched him in the tummy for no reason, and he didn't care.

His turn came to read out loud. Usually he liked that. Not

today. The words danced in front of his eyes. 'The young blind is not only hedgehog born, but deaf.'

He didn't even bother to scratch Pam Yardley's hand when she put it on his knee under his desk.

When dinner-time came, Miss Candy asked him to stay behind.

'What's wrong, Ezra?' she said.

'Nowt, miss.'

'You must tell me, Ezra.'

'I prayed to God to kill Henry Dinsdale, cos I didn't like being called Ezra, and now he's dead, miss.'

'Henry Dinsdale has measles, Ezra,' said Miss Candy.

Henry Pratt's measles came on the Wednesday. He lay, feverish and aching, in a darkened room, listening to the snow dripping off the roof. Outside, the country sounds were unusually sharp. Sam barking. A cow mooing. Billy the half-wit laughing. Jackie the land-girl sneezing. Henry pretended that Belinda Boyce-Uppingham was in the bed, having measles with him.

As a treat, while he recuperated, they bought him the *Beano* and the *Dandy*. He couldn't read them very well yet, especially the stories, but he managed to make sense of most of the cartoons. He liked Big Eggo, the ostrich, and Korky the Cat, and Freddy the Fearless Fly, but Keyhole Kate was horrid. He read out the words to himself with difficulty. Pansy Potter, the strong man's something.

Fiona came to visit, with her dull husband, and she came upstairs to see him. 'It's daughter,' she explained. ' "Pansy Potter, the strong man's daughter. Pansy's teeth are cracked and bent, eating a cake made from cement." '

'That's Jane Lugg,' said Henry. 'And Pam Yardley's Keyhole Kate.'

'My husband's Hungry Horace,' said Fiona.

Henry couldn't imagine her dull husband eating a lot, but he made no comment.

'Read me a story,' he said.

Fiona read a story about Derek, the wild boy of the woods, an outlaw branded as a traitor by Bagshot, Head of the Secret Service. Derek alone knew that Bagshot was a Nazi spy, and he foiled Bagshot with the aid of Kuru, his eagle pal. At the end of the story, the real British officer congratulated him. ' "If it hadn't been for you," he grinned,' read Fiona, ' "this 'U' boat would have got away with the secret plans of our new battleships. We owe everything to you and the wonderful eagle you have trained so well." '

Henry sighed ecstatically. He would be the wild boy of the woods when he was better.

'How did he grin all that?' he asked.

' "Grinned" means "said with a grin",' explained Fiona. 'In comics you never say "said". You say "suggested", "grunted", "snorted", "breathed", but not "said".'

'Why?' queried Henry.

'I don't know,' chuckled Fiona. 'I suppose that's their style, to make it more exciting.'

'Read me another one,' demanded Henry, the Boy with the Magic Measle, whose Every Wish was Granted.

That afternoon made a great impression on Henry, with dark-haired, brown-eyed, flashing Fiona, who smelt so nice, reading stories in her sparkling voice, glad to be free of her evil, greedy husband, whose Artificial Leg Contained Secret Plans of British Battleships.

When she had gone, Henry decided to learn to read better, to get better quickly, and to rescue Belinda Boyce-Uppingham from her Wicked Family, who were Nazi Spies.

Pssst!!!! Someone was coming. Who would it be? The foul Bagshot? Pansy Potter, the strong man's daughter? Or Keyhole Kate, eavesdropping again?

It was another Kate. Auntie Kate.

'Who's a lucky boy, then?' said Auntie Kate. 'Who's got pilchards for tea?'

They gave Henry the option of not going to church on Sunday, as he'd been ill. To their surprise, he chose to attend.

How he loved her! Who was the man sitting beside her in army uniform?

'That's Major Boyce-Uppingham, Belinda's father,' said Auntie Kate after the service.

'And a Nazi Spy!' breathed Henry to himself.

People stood around and discussed the weather, the losses in the Atlantic, the rationing, and their arthritis, but not God. They'd done that part.

Kit Orris, father of Cyril, approached.

'Now then, Frank,' he said.

'Now then, Kit,' said Uncle Frank. 'It's right thin and parky, i'n't it?'

'How's young Ezra, then?' said Kit Orris.

'I'm Henry,' said Henry. He wasn't going to start being called Ezra out of school. He began to suspect that Kit Orris was Another Nazi Spy.

'How's t' blackout, then, Kit?' said Uncle Frank.

'Well, I didn't know,' said Kit Orris, sheep-farmer, sheepishly.

The story had swept the village. Jim Wallington, who was air-raid warden as well as bus driver, had called out, 'Put out them lights.' 'Lights?' Kit Orris had said. 'All t' lights at back of t' house.' 'Oh. Does tha have to black out t' back and all?'

Very suspicious, thought our hero. It sounded to him like a Beacon for Messerschmitts.

The Nazi Spy Boyce-Uppingham was approaching with his beautiful daughter. The Nazi Spy Kit Orris raised his eyes to heaven and hurried off as if he didn't want to meet him. That ruse did not fool Henry!

Major Andrew Boyce-Uppingham, to do him justice, did not tap Henry as if he were a barometer. He prodded him as if he were a potato. But instead of saying, 'Nearly done. Just needs another minute,' he said, 'A little bird tells me that somebody we know isn't exactly short of grey matter. Well done!'

Henry smiled at Belinda Boyce-Uppingham.

She looked straight through him.

'Play it that way if tha wants to. Keep us love secret,' thought the Wild Boy of the Woods.

Spring came late and fragile to Upper Mitherdale, and ripened uncertainly into summer. 'It's That Man Again' came from the seaside now, and was known briefly as 'It's That Sand Again'. Germany invaded Russia. In the Middle East, Wavell failed to dislodge Rommel. The losses in the Atlantic continued. The war was becoming long and grim, not exciting and heroic. The nation seemed to have survived so far through a chaotic mixture of luck and genius. Now luck had run out, and genius wouldn't do on its own any longer. The war was being rationalised. The planners were coming into their own, thus ensuring, did Henry but know it, that the nation would win the war and lose the peace that followed.

There was a heavily censored letter from Ezra, who was somewhere doing something, and was well. Clothes, jam and tinned food joined the list of rationed goods, and Henry enjoyed his first summer in the country.

He enjoyed collecting the hens' eggs with Billy, from the huts in the hen coop, which smelt of sweet, hot, healthy decay. He liked to go over to the new shippon, across the thick-mudded, glistening, treacly yard, to watch Jackie milking the red, white and roan cattle with her gnarled, agile fingers. The old shippon, built onto the house, was used for hay and crops now.

On her evenings off, Jackie looked an awesome sight, striding off to the Three Horseshoes in her baggy corduroy riding breeches, in search of men. Now, at work, she was jolly and friendly. She explained that the cattle were shorthorns, dual-purpose cattle, bred for milk and beef. The future belonged with the specialists even among cows. Uncle Frank was a bit old-fashioned. He hankered after the olden days.

Uncle Frank took him round in the cart, which was pulled by a Dales pony. A few of the better-off farmers had tractors, but most still used horses.

The sheep were Swaledales, with black heads and small, curved horns. The little lambs looked as if they had black socks. They all talked in individual voices. Some sounded like human babies, some like gruff old men.

War regulations had compelled Uncle Frank to put twenty-five per cent of his land under the plough. The land wasn't suited, and his two small fields of oats were indifferent in quality and quantity.

Henry's reading and writing were improving apace. Miss Candy attributed it to her nurturing, but it was because he wanted to be able to read his comics.

When he went out for walks with Simon Eckington, they were

two shy lads who sat and chatted, threw stones into the Mither and discovered the quiet pleasures of friendship. They were also naturalists. Simon taught Henry to recognise dippers, and pied wagtails, and how to tell yellow and grey wagtails apart. Once, a kingfisher flashed turquoise along the river. They watched common and palmated newts in the farm pond. They kept tadpoles in jars, which got knocked over. Simon kept budgerigars, but Henry rarely went to Simon's home, because Patrick was a rotter, who was not above tearing up a chap's cigarette cards.

They were also in part explorers, known as Sir Simon Eckington of that Ilkley, and Lord Pratt of Thurmarsh, surveying the millstone grit moorland around Mickleborough. High above the valley the two little boys trudged through the cotton-grass and heather in their Wellington boots and baggy shorts. Curlews were albatrosses. Buzzards were vultures. Redshank were Eckington's Cranes, named after Sir Simon Eckington of that Ilkley, who first discovered them.

They were also in part adventurers, the Wild Boy of the Woods and the Kid with the Magic Wellies. It couldn't have been mere coincidence that only one Hun was seen in Upper Mitherdale throughout the whole of 1941.

Some of the evacuees were fish out of water, tadpoles in knocked-over jars. Henry discovered that he was a country lad at heart. It was as if Paradise Lane, Thurmarsh, had never existed.

On the Sunday before the hay harvest began, Henry was determined to speak to Belinda Boyce-Uppingham.

They stood by the churchyard, after the service. Uncle Frank was talking to Kit Orris.

'Now then, Frank.'

'Now then, Kit. It's a right dowly day.'

There she was, with her mother and grandmother and older brother. Please look this way, Belinda.

'How's t' oats?'

'Rubbish. Regulations! Land's not suited. Those Whitehall willies wouldn't recognise a field of oats if they fell over it.'

She was coming this way!

'I'd like to see them come up here.'

'So would I. I'd set t' bull on 'em.'

He walked up to her.

'Belinda?' he said.

'I don't talk to evacuees,' she said, and walked on, her exquisite little nose pointing straight up to heaven.

This time he couldn't pretend that it was part of a game.

The hay harvest was below average, but store lambs fetched good prices.

One day, Jane Lugg followed Henry and Simon as they set off on one of their walks.

'There's a funny smell around here,' said Simon. 'Is it a dead hedgehog?'

'No. It's Jane Lugg,' said Henry.

But she persisted. 'Can I come too?' she kept saying.

The two six-year-old boys went into a huddle.

'She's a girl,' pointed out Simon.

'Aye, but be fair, she doesn't look like a girl,' said Henry.

They decided to admit Jane Lugg to their friendship as an honorary boy. She proved all right, for a Lugg. Where other people grew marrow and cabbage, the Luggs put their garden down to prams and rusty bikes. In 1909, in a brawl after a dance at the Troutwick Jubilee Hall, five Luggs had fought six Pitheys from Troutwick, and a Pithey had died. The Luggs bred like rabbits, and kept rabbits, which bred like Luggs. But Jane Lugg proved a keen naturalist, a resourceful explorer, and a doughty fighter against the only Hun seen in Upper Mitherdale that year. The fiendish Hun had a Magic Body, and could Disguise Himself as Anybody. That day he was disguised as Pam Yardley. He ran away, but Jane Lugg, alias Pansy Potter, the strong man's daughter, caught him and settled him. It was a long while before Pam Yardley dared go out on her own again.

Both boys would have got a lathering if they dared go to the Lugg abode, and the Post Office and General Store was dangerous also on account of Patrick, so the three often congregated at Low Farm. Henry wasn't banned from seeing Jane Lugg, but he was discouraged. Sometimes she would be sent home. Simon was sent home as well, to make it fair, but when Simon was there without

Jane he was never sent home. Henry defended Jane stoutly, and vowed to marry her when he grew up. He wouldn't have been heart-broken if news of his intention had reached the shapely little ears of Belinda Boyce-Uppingham.

The brief Dales summer slipped all too quickly into autumn. It began to look as if the Russians might hold out against the Germans till the winter. In Upper Mitherdale, the sickly oats were stooked. School began again. Maria Montessori did not visit Miss Candy's classroom, but the nit lady did. It was widely known that the evacuees were not clean, and it would be no surprise to find that they had nits.

None of the evacuee children had nits. Jane Lugg did. Henry's ardour cooled, and autumn slipped imperceptibly into winter. The oats were threshed communally, since there was only one machine.

Belinda Boyce-Uppingham rode past Henry on her pony, and he decided that he must ride. One Satuday, in late October, his riding career began. Fifty-three seconds later, his riding career ended.

It was the age of the wireless. It was on almost all day, in the dark, cosy kitchen of Low Farm. News bulletins were eagerly awaited, and a tense silence fell during them. Then the music began again. Charles Ernesco and his Sextet. Falkman and his Apache Band. Troise and his Banjoliers. And always, wafting faintly over the darkening, misty dale, one Reginald or another at the theatre organ. There was 'Music While You Work' twice a day, and Ensa concerts with Richard Tauber. And comedy. Slowly Henry was beginning to grasp the concept of humour. Apart from ITMA, there was 'Breakfast with the Murgatroyds', 'The Happidrome', with stars like Izzy Bonn and Suzette Tarri, who sang 'Red sails in the Sunset', 'Varie-tea' at tea-time, 'Workers' Playtime' and 'Works' Wonders', and it was all a wonder that it worked, that the bright, far-away world came flooding into the quiet, gas-lit farm kitchen beneath the stark, silent hills. For the children there was 'Children's Hour'. Henry liked the animal programmes, with David Seth-Smith, the Zoo Man, and 'Out with Romany', but 'Children's Hour' was of an improving nature, on the whole, and Henry didn't want to be improved, on the whole, and so, on the whole, he preferred the alternative programme, which was called 'Ack-ack, beer-beer' and came from the canteens of balloon barrage centres and anti-aircraft units.

The Japanese attacked Pearl Harbour, and the United States entered the war. In the school nativity play, Henry played a passer-by. He had one line, 'Look at them three funny men.' He forgot it, but he did remember to pass by. Jane Lugg, shorn and humiliated, was given the part of an angel by Miss Candy, for psychological reasons, and much against the wishes of Miss Forrest. As Henry passed by, an angel belted him round the ear-hole.

Christmas was quiet, but enjoyable. Henry's presents included an apple, an orange, a Mars bar, two Dinky toys (a Packard and a Lagonda) and a kaleidoscope. 'I'm right set up wi' me prezzies,' he said with satisfaction.

There was a letter from Ezra. He was in. . .they were hoping to advance to. . .before. . .and he loved them both very much.

Summer sunshine streamed into the kitchen. Reginald Foort at the theatre organ streamed out into the fields. Auntie Kate was bottling soft fruit. Ada was humming cheerfully. Henry was buried in his *Beano*. After the sad business with Jane Lugg, he was less sure about Pansy Potter, the strong man's daughter – 'Pansy laughs, the cheeky elf – she makes a 'U' Boat shoot itself' – and he could never quite forgive the Boy with the Whistling Scythe for replacing the Wild Boy of the Woods. His favourite was Lord Snooty and his Pals, who were Rosie, Hairpin Huggins, Skinny Lizzie, Scrapper Smith, Happy Hutton, Snitchy and Snatchy, and Gertie the Goat. They had some hard battles with the dreadful Gasworks Gang. He quite liked Cocky Dick – he's smart and slick – and Musso the Wop – he's a big-a-da flop. He liked it best when people bopped Huns. The Huns went 'Der Wow!' and 'Der Ouch!' and serve them right. Henry hated them. That was why, on this, his first day of the summer holidays, Simon and he were going to open up a second front. They owed it to the nation.

His dinner was in his satchel. A ham sandwich, an egg sandwich, a cake made by Auntie Kate out of cornflakes coated with chocolate, and an apple. A dinner fit for a man going to battle. Especially when supplemented by a Mars bar out of your own pocket-money. His pocket-money was threepence a week. This bought him the *Beano* and the *Dandy* on alternate weeks. If he had enough coupons he would spend the rest on sweets. In those days of rationing, sweets were luxuries to be savoured. At his peak, he could make a Mars bar last an hour.

The first seven months of 1942 had passed quite smoothly. One of Simon's budgerigars had won second prize in the cobalt or mauve cock or hen class at the Barnoldswick Fur and Feather Society. Henry's progress at school had been steady. The nation fought germs almost as keenly as Germans in this era of food shortages and rationing. The newspaper adverts aimed at the authority of military commands. 'Fortify those kidneys!' 'Yes, sir.' 'Stop that terrible itching.' 'Sorry, sir.' 'Wake up your liver bile.' 'Righto, sir.' Even in Upper Mitherdale, where ways of circumventing rationing were not difficult to find when you kept your own pigs, Henry was made to consume cod liver oil and Californian syrup of figs with the utmost regularity. There had been a big nationwide competition to see which area could collect the most waste-paper. Henry's *Beano* was full of poems exhorting him to save paper:

Waste littler, paste Hitler.

and:

Come on girls! Come on chaps!
Dot Hitler on the napper.
Save up all your little scraps,
And be a 'paper scrapper'.

and again:

Bop the Wop, Slap the Jap,
Stun the Hun, with paper scrap.

Dutifully Henry had added his old *Beanos* and *Dandies* to the Rowth Bridge pile much as he longed to keep them. Uncle Frank and Auntie Kate had rewarded his patriotic efforts by taking him and Ada to Skipton to see the opening of the Skipton and District Warship Week. The week was opened by Viscountess Snowden, and there were loud cheers as she moved the indicator to show that £109,557 had already been collected. The indicator had been made by members of the Skipton College of Art. There was a march past by the Skipton Home Guard, the Skipton A.T.C., the St John's Ambulance Brigade, the Civil Nursing Reserve, the Civil Defence workers, the Women's Land Army, which included Jackie, who looked very solemn, the Boy Scouts, the Wolf Cubs and the Girl Guides. Many of the stores featured attractive window displays with a naval theme. Henry wished that he was taking part in the march, although he knew that if he had been he would have wished that he wasn't.

In the war there had been losses on all sides and victories for nobody. The British had bombed Lübeck and Rostock. The old wooden houses had burnt well. The Germans had responded with the 'so-called' Baedeker raids, on historic British cities. Once or twice, Henry had heard Ada crying in the night. This morning, a letter had come from Ezra. He was safe. The battle of. . .had been a right. . .they were now dug in at. . .and likely to be there for some time. The food was very. . .but he was well, and he loved them both very much.

So Ada was smiling, the sun was shining, Reginald Foort was playing, Auntie Kate, was bottling soft fruit and it was good to be alive.

Henry and Simon climbed the hill on the east side of the dale, past the remains of the old smelt mill. It was a clear morning, with just a few puffy clouds forming above Mickleborough. They disturbed an oystercatcher, and above them lapwings tossed themselves around joyfully.

They lay in the cotton-grass, commanding a view of the dale from Mickle Head to Troutwick, and kept their eyes skinned for Huns while they ate their Mars bars slowly.

Their conversation was an attempt at the style of the comics.

'Gasp!' said Henry. 'Is that a Hun over there, Eckers?'

'A Hun? Ho ho, you silly twerp! It's a horse.'

Henry pointed excitedly.

'I think *that*'s a Hun,' he said.

'Let's go and bag the blighter,' said Simon.

They crawled along the ground towards the unsuspecting enemy, which was actually Pam Yardley again. It was the first time the Leeds girl had dared brave the fells since she had last been taken for a Hun. She was collecting sphagnum moss to hand over

71

to the Red Cross for use as padding in splints.

They got to within twenty yards of the Hun without his suspecting them. Then they charged. He ran off. They chased him. Henry brought the fiend crashing to the ground. It was the only successful rugby tackle he would ever make in his life, wasted on a lonely evacuee girl who didn't even know that she was supposed to be a Hun.

'Give over,' said the Hun, picking himself up and trying not to cry.

'Tha's a Hun. We've just captured thee,' explained Henry.

'Oh. Right,' said Pam Yardley, a little more resourceful than on her last capture. 'Hang on a sec.' She worked herself up into being a captured German. 'Der wow!' she cried. 'Der ouch! Der Gott in Himmel! Der lemme go, Britisher swine!'

The Deadly Duo discovered that capturing German prisoners was a mixed blessing. You had to share your dinner with them. They did think of starving her, but had to admit that she had been a pretty sporting blighter, for a rotter.

They saw no more Germans, and fairly soon grew bored. As they returned to Low Farm, they could hear the music of Reginald New at the theatre organ.

Henry volunteered to escort the prisoner home, but as soon as Simon had gone home, he abandoned the pretence that she was a Hun, and told her that he liked her. She kissed him quickly, and skipped off into the Wallington home, clutching her puny collection of sphagnum moss in her hot little hand.

Stay-at-home holiday activities were laid on in the towns that summer, and Skipton was no exception. Ada was to take Henry in the bus. He was so excited that he got up at half-past six. If he hadn't, he wouldn't have seen the Real Live Hun!

Uncle Frank had gone out early, to examine some sick sheep, whose complaint he was unable to diagnose.

Henry wandered up the field towards his great-uncle. The dew was heavy, and cloud hung over the top of Mickleborough.

Suddenly there was a great roar, and an aeroplane with a swastika on its side came rushing up the dale towards Mickle Head. A long trail of dark smoke was pouring from its tail. The pilot had a faulty compass, and was trying to get home after being the only man ever to make a Baedeker raid on Burnley.

Henry and Uncle Frank stared open-mouthed. The plane tried vainly to gather height. The pilot ejected, tumbled headlong for a hundred feet, then his parachute opened. The plane crashed into the side of Mickleborough and a great flame spurted into the air. Silence fell, save for the bleating of the surprised Swaledale sheep in the next field, as the Hun fiend landed gently among them.

Henry's flesh came out in goose-pimples as they approached the Terrible Teuton.

The pilot gathered up his parachute and walked towards them nervously. To Henry's surprise, he looked young, bewildered and frightened and really quite nice, not like a fiendish killer with bared teeth and a snarl.

The German youth looked at Uncle Frank nervously, but Uncle Frank seemed quite calm.

'Now then, lad,' said Uncle Frank. 'Does't tha know owt about sheep?'

It was a long day for Ada. There was the bus ride, on two buses, changing at Troutwick, down winding roads bordered by stone walls and grass verges flecked with meadow cranesbill. An advert on the village bus showed a drawing of a conductress. The caption was 'Give her a big hand – with (if possible) the correct fare in it!' On the village bus the conductor was the driver, Jim Wallington. He gave out brightly coloured tickets from his clip board. On the outskirts of Skipton, in the second bus, they passed a static water tank. They watched a display of blitz cookery by a team of Girl Guide camp advisors in the Friendly Society's yard. The girls demonstrated the use of the sawdust cooker, the haybox cooker, the camp cooker and the W.V.S. blackout cooker. They lunched in style on Australian minced-meat loaf at the café in the bus station. They joined a large crowd on the rugby field. The crowd were amazed at the speed with which the Home Guard put up barbed wire entanglements. She took him to the cinema for the very first time. They saw 'The Wizard of Oz' at the Plaza. It was his best film ever, so far. It was quite a day, and by the end of it Ada's ankles, large at the best of times, were swollen horribly. You couldn't have said that Henry hadn't enjoyed his day, but Ada felt that much of her thunder had been stolen by the real-life German prisoner.

Back at Rowth Bridge, Germans and outings over, the summer continued placidly, and Henry wrestled with his secrets.

His secrets were that he liked girls and evacuees! He liked the two in one! He liked Pam Yardley! He couldn't think why boys thought girls were soppy. Pam had a nice, square, honest face, and chubby, smooth legs, covered in bites and scratches. It gave him a warm feeling in his body to be near her. He went to the Wallingtons' house and listened to 'Children's Hour' with her. They sat with pencil and paper and tried to do puzzles, questions and catches set by P. Caton Baddeley. They listened to 'Mr Noah's Holiday', a Toytown story by S. G. Hulme-Beaman. They laughed together at an evacuee boy from the south who didn't know that 'laiking at taws on t' causer edge' meant playing marbles on the pavement. Pam Yardley showed Henry her marbles. They exceeded expectations. She came to Low Farm and they watched the harvest and listened to the faint strains of Reginald Dixon at the theatre organ wafting over the fields. Always there was music at Low Farm, exotic names from a magic world outside. Nat Gonella and his Georgians. Don Felipe and the Cuban Caballeros. The Winter Garden Orchestra under the direction of Tom Jenkins. They laughed together at Stainless Stephen, Jeanne de Casalis as 'Mrs Feather', Revnell and West, and Gillie Potter speaking to them in English from Hogsnorton, although they barely understood a quarter of it all.

Henry invited her to church one Sunday, and outside afterwards he held her hand and waited for Belinda Boyce-Uppingham to notice them and realise what she had missed.

Uncle Frank was chatting to Kit Orris.

'How's t' lambs, Frank?'

'Nobbut middling, Kit.'

There she was. If only she'd turn and see them.

'Tha's only got feed for six months. Tha feeds 'em up. They come on grand. Then they deteriorate. It's a bad do.'

Belinda Boyce-Uppingham turned and looked straight at them. Henry squeezed Pam's hand. Belinda Boyce-Uppingham turned away, her sang-froid apparently undisturbed, but Henry fancied that the thrust had gone home.

Pam came for Sunday dinner. Afterwards, they listened to the gardening advice of C. H. Middleton. 'Not at this latitude,' commented Uncle Frank. 'April! Tha'll be lucky. . .Six inches apart! Give over!' The young love-birds slipped out and wandered down by the river.

Simon Eckington was approaching. When he saw them he veered away.

'Simon!' shouted Henry.

He watched his best friend walk away without looking back.

'Forget him,' said Pam Yardley. 'Good riddance to bad rubbish.'

She put her arm round Henry. He blushed. He hoped nobody would see them, especially Simon.

'Give over,' he said, shaking himself free. 'Gerroff.' Then, so as not to seem unfriendly, he said, 'Race thee to t' top.' They ran up the slope, away from the river. The sheep, just about over the shock of the German airman, retreated before them in panic.

Pam Yardley beat him by about forty-five yards.

She flopped on her back and waited for him to arrive.

'What a weed,' she said. 'I couldn't marry a weed.'

'Marry,' he gasped.

Pam Yardley put her hand on his private parts.

'What's tha doing?' he said.

'Don't know,' she admitted, 'but I saw Debbie Carrington do it to Stanley Lugg, and he liked it.'

'Aye, well, he's a Lugg,' said Henry.

Pam Yardley squeezed.

'Give over. Tha's not doing it right, wherever it is,' he yelped.

Luckily, Pam Yardley gave over.

'Are we to get married when we're grown up then?' she said.

He considered the question seriously.

'I think we're a bit young to decide,' he said.

A cool evening breeze sprang up, and they ran helter-skelter down the hill, and tumbled breathlessly back into the farm fields.

They could hear the music of Reginald Porter-Brown at the theatre organ.

In the morning, Henry asked Auntie Kate if there was anything he could get at the Post Office and General Store. He needed an excuse to see Simon.

He stood in the cool interior of the shop, gazing longingly at the almost empty bottles of sweets. He'd used up his ration. He wanted two stamps, a packet of snap vacuum jar closers, some Eiffel Tower lemonade crystals, Gibbs Dentifrice (No Black Out for Teeth with Gibbs Dentifrice) and he could try for Reckitt's Blue.

Mrs Eckington served him and he asked for Simon. Simon came into the shop and hissed, 'Come outside.'

They went outside.

'What's up?' said Henry.

'I don't go around wi' evacuees,' said Simon.

'I'm not an evacuee,' shouted Henry.

'It's Patrick,' whispered Simon, and disappeared back into the shop.

School began again. The nit lady came. Pam Yardley had nits. Her brown hair was shorn and she was sent to Coventry and Henry didn't dare speak to her and Simon came up to him in the playground, and Henry knew that Simon was only pretending not to be his friend because he was frightened of Patrick, so he thought everything might be all right now he wasn't seeing Pam Yardley any more, but suddenly Simon's face was twisted into hatred, and he shouted, 'Pam Yardley's got nits. Pam Yardley's got nits.'

On account of his divided loyalties, Henry had ended up without a friend in the school. His little group of six had changed slightly. They had left Cyril Orris behind, and caught up with Lorna Arrow. Jane Lugg, Pam Yardley and Simon refused to speak to him at all. Henry Dinsdale was distant. Lorna Arrow, fair, tall, thin and toothy, tried to be friendly once on the way home, but he spurned her offer. 'It's nowt personal,' he said kindly, 'but girls are more bother than they're worth.'

Montgomery defeated Rommel at El Alamein. There was no news of Ezra. His son, Henry, buried himself in his studies and his reading. He listened to his good friend, the wireless. He heard an all-star concert with Naughton and Gold, and Rawicz and Landauer, Music Hall with Elsie and Doris Waters, Randolph Sutton and Magda Kun. On 'Children's Hour' there was 'Stuff and Nonsense', fun fare on the air concocted by Muriel Levy, with

Doris Gambell, Violet Carson, Wilfred Pickles, Muriel Levy and Nan. But, without friends, there was no fun in his heart any more.

Christmas drew near. One day, as he reached the end of the village on his way home, he found his path blocked by Simon and Patrick Eckington, Freddie Carter and Colin Lugg. They took him to Freddie Carter's.

Colin Lugg and Patrick Eckington grabbed him, and twisted his arms. Colin Lugg's breath smelt of sick and Patrick Eckington's breath smelt of freckles. They forced him to the lavatory, and thrust his head deep into the bowl, which was the creation of Cobbold and Sons, of Etruria. But Cobbold and Sons could not help him now.

The bowl was dark and smelt vaguely fetid. They held his head there until each boy had flushed the cistern, which took a long time to fill.

They let him go then, without a word. Simon Eckington couldn't look him in the eye.

At the Christmas carol service, Belinda Boyce-Uppingham sang a solo of 'Gloria in Excelsis Deo' quite exquisitely. Henry fancied that she was inspired by the desire to humiliate him.

He refused to go to the children's party in the Parish Hall. By all accounts he missed a treat. Coon songs were given by Mr Ballard, who also proved his ability with the banjo.

In April, news came that Ezra had been injured. He was on a troop ship, which would dock at Plymouth.

Ada set off to meet him. Henry wanted to accompany her, but was told that this was a crisis, not a treat. Nobody could be sure how badly Ezra had been injured.

On Troutwick Station, windswept among the high hills, Ada said, 'Now tha'll be a good, brave lad, won't tha?'

'Oh aye,' he said. 'How many wheels does tha think t' engine will have?'

The engine roared in and shuddered gasping to an exhausted halt.

'It's got ten wheels,' he told her. 'Two little 'uns and three big 'uns on each side.'

'Oh aye?' said Ada. 'Now think on. Be a good lad.'

77

The train started with such a display of skidding and coughing from the engine that Henry felt sorry for the iron monster.

Some chickens which had arrived from Carlisle in a wicker basket protested volubly.

Ada waved until she was just a speck.

'It had ten wheels,' said Henry on the way home. 'Two little 'uns and three big 'uns on each side.'

'Oh aye?' said Auntie Kate, who was determined not to give him too good a time, so that he would miss his mother. 'Now remember what our Ada said. Be a good boy.'

The summer term began. Miss Candy asked them about their experiences in the holidays.

'My dad's been injured in t' war,' he said proudly.

'My grandad was hurt in t' Dardanelles,' announced Henry Dinsdale.

'Does anybody know where the Dardanelles are?' said Miss Candy, ever the improviser.

'Just above the knackers,' said Jane Lugg. Everybody giggled.

'That's a bit silly, Jane,' said Miss Candy. 'And it's not the sort of thing we laugh at.'

Miss Forrest entered the classroom without knocking, which irritated Miss Candy, because if she had ever entered Miss Forrest's classroom without knocking there would have been ructions.

'Your great-uncle's here to see you, Ezra,' said Miss Forrest.

Uncle Frank stood in the corridor, in his battered green tweed jacket with leather elbow patches. He was twisting his hat in his hands. His face was as old as the hills and as dry as a stone wall. He put his hand on Henry's shoulder and led him out into the playground. It surprised Henry that the sun was shining.

So his father had died! He couldn't really feel much. He had almost forgotten his father.

Uncle Frank led him towards his car. Pleasure motoring was forbidden now, but this journey had not been for pleasure.

His father got out of the car with difficulty, and hobbled to meet him. His left leg was in plaster. He looked gaunt and old.

'She stepped straight in front of a bus,' he said. 'She never knew what hit her.'

·

His father's injuries had healed. He was going back to the war. Henry was glad, although he knew that he must never say so.

They sat beside the infant Mither. It worried away at its stones. Three months of its ceaseless efforts had passed since Henry had learnt of his mother's death.

They had so little to say to each other, father and son. It was nearly harvest time, and the sky promised rain again. There was to be bad weather for the harvest of 1943, although the hay crop had been good, and prices for sheep and calving cows had been good all year.

Henry dived off the top board of the pool of silence that separated them.

'Why does God kill people?' he asked.

Ezra had longed for, yet dreaded, some question such as this.

He would never tell Henry about the funeral. She'd gone to Bristol, on her way to Plymouth, to visit his sister, who had married a bus driver, and to arrange for them to break their journey there on the way back. She'd gone shopping. Perhaps she'd been dreaming of his return. The driver hadn't stood a chance.

His sister and her husband had gone to Plymouth to meet him. Her husband had said, 'I'm only glad it wasn't my bus.' They hadn't been church-goers, and there had only been three mourners at the funeral. Ezra, his sister and her husband. The harassed vicar had referred to Ada as 'our dear departed brother'. They hadn't told anybody at Rowth Bridge, because they might have felt obliged to come, and there was no point, and it was best that Henry should be told by his father.

'He doesn't kill people,' said Ezra at last. 'He lets them get on wi' things, and if they happen to get theirselves killed, well, that's it. He looks at them, and if they've been good, he takes them to a better place.'

'Was my mam good?'

'Aye. Very good.'

'Has she gone to a better place?'

'Oh aye. Happen.'

'Where is it?'

'Up there. In heaven.'

Henry looked up at the scudding clouds. Sometimes the sky was blue and you could see that it was empty. He found it difficult to believe that his mother could be up there.

He felt a spot of rain.

'Is rain t' people up there crying?' he said.

'I don't reckon so,' said Ezra. 'They're happy up there.'

'Doesn't she miss us?'

'Oh aye. She misses us. But she hopes she'll see us one day. That's why it's so important for thee to be good.'

Ezra was quite proud of that, and also a little ashamed.

'Tha's a lucky lad to be wi' Uncle Frank and Auntie Kate,' said Ezra. 'I doubt this war'll go on while next Christmas or more. Owt can happen to me, tha knows. Look at it this road. Uncle Frank and Auntie Kate, they're thy parents now.'

'I don't reckon there is a God,' said Henry. 'If there was, he wouldn't have killed me mam.'

Henry exchanged a big mother and a small father for a small mother and a big father, and life went on. At first, the nights were the worst times. His bed, which had been a womb, had become a prison. Perhaps, when your mother had died, you could no longer go back to wombs.

One day, not long after it had happened, he saw Simon and Patrick Eckington waiting for him, on his road home from school, and his blood ran cold.

Patrick Eckington's freckled face was blazing. He thrust a brown paper parcel into Henry's hands.

'Peace offering,' he mumbled.

Henry took it as if he had been handed a bomb. He opened it cautiously. It was a book about birds and animals. On the fly-leaf, there was written, 'To Henry, from his friends Simon and Patrick.'

'Thanks,' said Henry.

'Are we friends again, then?' said Simon.

'Happen,' said Henry.

One day, Henry and Simon climbed Mickleborough. On the way up, they saw a peregrine falcon. At the top they knighted each other. First Henry knighted Sir Simon Eckington of that Ilk (they knew now it wasn't Ilkley). Then Sir Simon knighted Lord

Pratt of Mitherdale (Thurmarsh was forgotten) and explained that he had never wanted to be beastly to his chum, but had been forced to, owing to the threats of his elder brother, Sir Freckle de Fish-face, who had regarded Lord Pratt of Mitherdale as a filthy swot, and a silly twerp to boot. Sir Simon apologised. Lord Pratt accepted. They became friends again, a little awkwardly at first perhaps, never quite the same again perhaps, but friends.

Miss Candy gave Henry special attention without the other children realising it. Even Jane Lugg and Pam Yardley declared an unspoken, uneasy truce. Lorna Arrow made passes at him. (Can it be that our podgy hero is going to turn out to be attractive to women? Women are strange in these matters. We have seen on what dross the lovely Turnbull sisters threw themselves away.) Uncle Frank and Auntie Kate no longer felt that they had to hold back to avoid stealing a mother's love. Not that they spoilt him. Food wasn't too short up here. You had your own pig, and you used every bit bar t' squeak. But thrift was still the order of the day. Auntie Kate put a bottle of borax by the wash-basin to add to the water in order to use less soap (even if at the cost of using more borax, a perfectionist might complain). She washed plum and prune stones, cracked them and retrieved the kernels. She made buttons out of small circles of calico. She encouraged still greater effort in the saving of scrap metal and waste paper. (Luckily she never knew that Jackie kept all her love letters *and* bound them with elastic bands.) Nevertheless, they treated Henry now as if he was the son they had never had. Love and attention were not spared. And the welcoming wireless thundered on. Gwen Catley singing. Sandy Macpherson at the theatre organ. Felix Mendelssohn and his Hawaiian Serenaders. 'Hi, Gang' with Bebe Daniels, Vic Oliver and Ben Lyon. 'The Happidrome' returned with Ramsbottom, Enoch and Mr Lovejoy, and guests with magical names like Flotsam and Jetsam and Two Ton Tessie O' Shea. He loved them all, utterly without discrimination. He had loved his mother, but he was eight years old, and gradually it became like trying to commemorate a drowned woman by preserving a hollow in the ocean where she had plunged. Life closed slowly over Ada's head.

The United States were leading the allies' effort now. In the *Dandy* and the *Beano*, more stories had American settings. Big Eggo was as likely to catch a Jap as a Hun, and Musso the Wop had long since been put on-a-da scrapheap, his propaganda value exhausted. The allies' shipping losses were plummeting as the battle against the 'U' boats took a 'U' turn. It was permissible to talk about eventual victory. Men's minds turned to thoughts of the kind of world that victory would bring. Sir William Beveridge was planning for universal social security. Poverty and mass unemployment were to be things of the past. R. A. Butler was preparing his plans for equal opportunity of education for all. Was it too much to hope that this time men would get it right after the war?

' "I feel a bit of a frost, Mr Barrett – always catching colds and letting the office down," ' read Henry. He had developed the habit of reading aloud from the newspapers, to prove how proficient he had become. Today it was the turn of the adverts. 'What's "a bit of a frost", Auntie Kate?'

'Somebody who lets the side down,' said Auntie Kate. 'Like tha'll be if tha doesn't go to Leeds with Miss Candy.'

Miss Candy wanted to take Henry to Leeds on Saturday. He didn't want to go. It wasn't what schoolteachers did. There was bound to be a catch in it.

'Why does she want to take me to Leeds?' he asked.

'Happen she reckons thee,' said Auntie Kate.

He agreed to go. He could hardly refuse after they'd said he could go to Troutwick on Jim Wallington's bus *on his own*.

He loved every minute of the bus ride, on that morning of Saturday, November 14th 1943. Mist clung to the hillsides. A black-market pig squealed under the back seat.

Miss Candy met him off the bus. She was wearing a brand-new utility skirt and jacket. Her grey hair was piled up on top of her head in a fearsome Victory Roll.

The train was late. On the platform opposite, the adverts stated 'Dr Carrot, your winter protector', and 'The navigator swears. By Kolynos, of course.' Henry read them out loud. He read everything out loud.

He'd never been on a train before. He'd only watched them disappearing into the distance, while he waved at vanishing parents.

The smoke from the engine poured past the window. Sheep ran away across the sodden fields, as if this was the first train they had ever seen. People got on at every station, many of them in uniform. By the time they reached Leeds, the train was jam-packed. Miss Candy chatted easily about the things they saw, and he completely forgot that he hadn't wanted to come.

They went to the British Restaurant and had Woolton Pie. Then they caught a bus to Elland Road, to see Leeds play Bradford, in the Wartime League North. There was only a small crowd in the large, windswept stadium.

Henry enjoyed the game, which was the first football match he had ever seen. Miss Candy was rooting for her native Bradford. 'Other way!' she shouted angrily at the ref, and flat-capped men turned to look. There weren't many women present, and certainly none with booming, posh voices, three chins and a moustache. Henry wished Miss Candy wouldn't draw attention to herself.

Leeds took a well-deserved lead through HENRY and HINDLE. Miss Candy was a picture of dejection, and Henry, who had begun by wanting Leeds to win, because they had a player called Henry, who, to Henry's delight, scored, found himself switching his allegiance after Leeds had gone 2–0 up.

'Where's your white stick, ref?' shouted Miss Candy.

In the last twenty minutes, Bradford equalised through STABB and FARRELL, who netted from the penalty spot. In fact Bradford might have snatched victory, had Butterworth not kicked off the line with the goalkeeper beaten.

They went back into the City in a state of physical well-being. Henry was particularly thrilled, because although it had been a two-all draw, the team he had been supporting at the time had scored all four goals.

The train to Skipton was crowded, and slow, and there was nothing to look at. The blinds were drawn. A dim bulb gave a light too faint for reading.

At Skipton they caught a local train. The only other person in their compartment was an airman, who was fast asleep.

Henry had felt sure that there would be a catch. There was. It came now, on the rattling, blacked-out little local train.

'Henry?' said Miss Candy. 'I want you to tell me what people say about me."

'Tha what?' said Henry.

'The children say things about me. I must know what they say,' said Miss Candy.

Miss Candy had given him a nice day. She didn't tell him that she had delivered her part of an unspoken bargain, and now it was his turn. She didn't need to.

'I won't be upset,' she said. 'And I won't be angry. But I must know.'

'They say tha used to ride in a circus,' said Henry. 'They say tha loved a Yank, and he went home and left thee broken-hearted. They say. . .'

He hesitated.

'Go on,' breathed Miss Candy.

If only the airman would wake up. But he snored deeply, as if to reassure them that it was safe to continue.

'They say tha drinks a bottle of a gin a day,' said Henry. 'They say tha has a pet wolf. They say. . .' He hesitated.

'Go on,' breathed Miss Candy.

'They say tha's got a special tube so tha never has to go to t' lav.'

'Go on,' breathed Miss Candy.

'They say tha used to be a stripper in a club in Wakefield,' said Henry.

'Really?' said Miss Candy, amazed. 'It must have been the masochists' club.'

'Tha what?'

'Never mind. Go on.'

'They say. . .'

'Go on. I won't be cross.'

'They say tha has great tufts of hair hanging down from thy nipples.'

There was silence. The train rattled on. The airman groaned and his head lolled.

'What an amazing woman I must be,' said Miss Candy.

Christmas came and went. Strikes were frequent. The British and Americans landed at Anzio. In the Far East the war was fierce.

The Rowth Bridge knitting circle knitted its two thousandth woollen garment. Every Sunday evening, Henry listened to 'Variety Band Box'. Then Albert Sandler and the Palm Court Orchestra played 'a programme of the kind of music heard in the Palm Court of your favourite hotel in the days before the war' and Henry, who had never been in the Palm Court of any hotel before the war, listened, because it was there.

One day, towards the end of May, 1944, he received a letter from his father, who was now in. . .and hoping that by Christmas he would be in. . .he was well, and he loved Henry very much. And Henry realised, with a shock, that the letter had come as a shock. He was happy here. Uncle Frank and Auntie Kate were his parents now. There wasn't any room for his father. And then he felt guilty about that, because he knew that you were supposed to love your father. That afternoon, after school, he saw one of the five-year-old boys crying. His name was Sidney Mold. He came from Five Houses, which was a tiny hamlet of six houses on the Troutwick road. He had to walk three miles on his own, and the previous day Simon Eckington had offered to escort him, but half-way home, Simon Eckington had dug his nails into him viciously. Henry sympathised. In fact he was shocked that his friend Simon could have done that. He offered to escort Sidney Mold home in good faith, but half-way to Five Houses he dug his nails into him viciously and made him cry.

In school the next day, Henry wondered if Miss Candy could see what he had done, and he felt guilty. He looked at Simon and felt shocked by Simon's cruelty more than by his own, and he wondered if Simon was thinking the same. He wandered home slowly. The weather was humid. He felt tired and nasty.

It is easier to cope with the shame of yesterday than with the shame of years past. Henry suddenly recalled the last time he had ever seen his mother. The last words he had ever said to her were, 'It's got ten wheels. Two little 'uns and three big 'uns on each side.' He could cope with the guilt of knowing that he had dug his nails into Sidney Mold and probably would again, much as he didn't want to. He couldn't cope with the guilt of his neglect of his mother.

He trudged towards the head of the valley, nine years and two months old, his chubby white legs still in short trousers, his shoes scuffed, his shirt grubby and hanging outside his trousers, a tiny, leaden figure in the great, natural bowl of Upper Mitherdale, and he vowed that from now on his heart would be a shrine for his mother, and he would be a loving son to his father, for his mother's sake.

Then he remembered that Uncle Frank and Auntie Kate regarded him as their son now. They wanted him to stay with them. He wanted to stay with them. He wanted to take over Low Farm, when Uncle Frank retired. He wanted to keep the shorthorn cattle, the Dales pony, Billy the half-wit, and other endangered species.

Where did that leave his father?

Had Henry not been in such a state, he might have made a better show of resisting Lorna Arrow. She was sitting on the dry-stone wall, swinging her long, thin legs, smiling her toothy smile.

She led him to one of the field barns, on Kit Orris's farm, at the back of the village. It was full of animal fodder. It smelt steamy and warm.

One of the best-known facts of human life was that girls were useless and soppy, yet Henry liked being with Lorna Arrow. He liked her husky voice, with the slight lisp. It made him tingle strangely. Why? He knew that grown-ups liked women. He knew that he was advanced at all his school subjects. Who could blame him, during the Lorna Arrow summer, if he deduced that the explanation was that he was advanced for his years?

The allies landed in northern France. The weather was wet, and Uncle Frank had great difficulty in gathering his hay. In the school sports Henry came second from last in the Sack Race, thus exceeding his achievements in the Hundred Yards, the Four-Forty, the Egg and Spoon Race, the High Jump, the Three-legged Race and the Potato Race. Yet Lorna Arrow did not desert him. He kept her apart from Simon. Some days were Simon days. Others were Lorna days. On Lorna days, they sometimes went to the field barn and he read her the comics. She didn't like reading. It made him feel good to read them, because he read well. Her favourites were Desperate Dan, Our Gang and Merry Marvo and his Magic Cigar. She laid her fair, toothy head against his chest, and he tingled as he read the exploits of Zogg, who turned Nick

Turner into the Headmaster of his Old School!, and of Wun Tun Joe, whose bones were so heavy that he weighed a ton. ' "Come here, Chink," snapped the bully,' he read. ' "No savvy," chirped Wun Ton Joe.'

'Let's be "Our Gang",' lisped Lorna.

'Not now,' sighed Henry.

'Do the Nigs,' commanded Lorna.

'I can't. I'm fair jiggered up,' protested Henry.

Lorna loved to enact the adventures of 'Our Gang'. She particularly liked Henry's accent when he portrayed Buckwheat and Billy, the darkies.

'Which does tha prefer – greengages or eggs?' queried Lorna.

'Both,' he responded.

'Tha can have a fried greengage for breakfast, then,' she exclaimed.

Once she brought him two Woodbines and insisted that he pretend to be Merry Marvo and his Magic Cigar, but he turned out to be Puking Pratt and his Soggy Ciggy.

When they ran out of comics, she made him read the All-Bran adverts. They were in comic strip form, featuring characters like Obstinate Oliver and Mary, Mary Not Contrary.

'Which would tha prefer? Seven hundred thousand tons of All-Bran, or a castle with six gold doors?' she said.

'Which would tha prefer? A smack in t' gob or a kick up t' arse-end?' said Henry.

She went home crying. It was all for the best. The boys were right. Girls were useless. So why did he apologise and take her out again?

'Which does tha prefer?' she said. 'Pencils or the Walls of Jericho?'

'Pencils,' he said at random. 'I don't rate t' Walls of Jericho, me.'

'Which would tha prefer?' she said. 'Come home to tea or a yacht?'

'A yacht,' he said.

Lorna's father came in late, and they started tea without him.

'Ee, I'm right twined,' he said grumpily, when he came in. 'I'm as twined as me arse.'

'Wash thy mouth out with soap and water,' said Lorna's mother.

'Which would tha prefer?' said Lorna. 'Two hundred bars of soap or a chest of sunken treasure?'

'Don't be silly, Lorna,' said Lorna's mother.

She *was* silly. Henry wished he wasn't there. But the next day, when he was with Simon, who was sensible, he longed to hear Lorna's husky, toothy lisp.

The summer slipped past. Paris was liberated. Henry wasn't. The weather was wet. Uncle Frank had the greatest difficulty in cutting his oats.

Fiona came over with her husband and his artificial leg. There was an element of the artificial about her legs, too. She had responded to the unavailability of silk stockings by using sun-tan lotion to give her legs the appearance of being stockinged, and had added the seams with eyebrow pencil. This was considered outrageously fast in Skipton banking circles, but then Fiona Brassingthwaite, née Turnbull, was known to be a law unto herself.

School resumed. Miss Candy rustled a lot. Her knickers were made of defective parachute silk. There was a war on. Miss Candy sometimes gave Henry glinting, conspiratorial looks. They embarrassed him less than he expected. The nit lady came. Lorna Arrow had nits. Henry vowed never again ever to have anything more to do with girls again ever.

The very next Sunday he ran across Belinda Boyce-Uppingham. She was riding, picking her way daintily through the little ash wood by the river. Henry was running home, to listen to a spelling bee between Post Office Workers and Red Cross Workers. He frightened her pony. The pony reared. Belinda Boyce-Uppingham, the great love of his life, because of whom all other loves were undergone, was deposited on the soggy, soggy ground.

He rushed forward to help her.

'Art tha all right?' he said.

She picked herself up and tested her limbs. Her face was scarlet with fury.

'No thanks to you, you. . .you bloody oik,' she said.

The wet weather continued. Uncle Frank's oats lay sodden in the fields, till well into November. The newspaper adverts began to look forward to a time of returning plenty. 'After victory, our familiar packages will re-appear in all parts of the country,' said Parkinsons' Old-Fashioned Humbugs. 'When they have finished their vital war service, Dagenite and Perdrix batteries will again be available to all,' promised Dagenite and Perdrix batteries. 'It's in the shops again! Reckitt's Blue!' thundered Reckitt's Blue.

If Reckitt's Blue was back, could peace be far behind?

But first there was the bombing of Dresden. Twenty-five thousand people were killed in one night, in a war that had already been virtually won.

Tuesday, May 9th and Wednesday, May 10th, 1945, were declared public holidays. Hitler was dead. Germany had surrendered. Union Jacks fluttered from big house and humble cottage alike. There was a victory peal on the bells of Rowth Bridge Church.

In Skipton there was dancing in the streets, to music relayed by loudspeakers. In Rowth Bridge Parish Hall, a dance was hastily laid on. It was widely agreed that a new piano was one of the first priorities of peace.

The children lit many bonfires. Henry ran around uselessly in great excitement.

Forty people, many of them from as far away as Troutwick, climbed Mickleborough and lit a victory beacon.

Uncle Frank danced with Auntie Kate. Jackie, the land-girl, danced with anybody and everybody. Even Jane Lugg, Pam Yardley and Lorna Arrow bore no grudges that night.

Pools of light. Tinkling of a bad piano. Chunter of assembled Luggs in the Three Horseshoes. Bonfires on all sides, and a ghostly beacon roaring in the wind among the Mickleborough clouds. It was not entirely unrestrained. There was still war in the Far East. People had seen the end of a war to end all wars before. People were tired. But it was victory, and Rowth Bridge did its best. The little village celebrated with pools of light and noise in the dark, silent dale.

Uncle Frank died peacefully in his sleep. It was a dreadful shock for Auntie Kate, of course, but everyone said what a wonderful way it was for Uncle Frank to go. At peace, in victory.

5 What About the Crispy Bacon We Used to Get Before the War?

Auntie Kate insisted on coming with him, although she had problems enough in keeping the farm going until the sale went through.

A Labour government had been elected. The Cold War had begun. Britain had given her blessing to the dropping of atomic bombs on Hiroshima and Nagasaki. Henry was going back to Thurmarsh.

'I want to stay here, Auntie Kate,' he'd said.

'It's not possible, Henry,' she'd told him. 'The farm's sold. I'm going to live wi' Fiona in Skipton. It's not possible.'

He'd done most of his crying at night.

Simon Eckington came on the bus with them. Mrs Eckington and Patrick were there to wave goodbye. So was Billy, the half-wit, who waved furiously, exaggeratedly. Henry said, 'I hope there's lots of eggs tomorrow, Billy,' and Billy said, 'Nay, t' hens know tha's going. T' hens like thee.'

As Henry clattered out of the village, three girls sat on the hump-backed bridge. They were Jane Lugg, Lorna Arrow and Pam Yardley, whose father had not yet been demobbed. Henry waved. They stuck their tongues out.

And so Henry Pratt, liked by hens, hated by girls, rode out of hill-womb and began the long journey back to world-cobble. His heart was heavy. They rattled through Five Houses. He was glad there was no sign of Sidney Mold.

Miss Candy was at Troutwick Station to see him off. She was fifty-eight now, and even the tuft on her middle chin had gone grey. Miss Forrest had decided to put up with her till she was sixty, for the sake of her feelings.

'What's Miss Candy doing here?' Simon said.

'I don't know,' said Henry. 'She's probably meeting a friend.'

'Miss Candy hasn't got friends,' said Simon.

The engine screeched to a halt. Henry didn't care how many wheels it had.

He hated farewells, and there seemed to be so many of them.

He leant out of the window, smiling inanely.

Henry and Simon, loquacious explorers, vivacious naturalists, enthusiastic pursuers of Huns, were unable to think of a single thing to say to each other.

Miss Candy came to the rescue.

'Clemmie and Winnie send their love,' she said.

'Clemmie and Winnie?' said Henry.

'My seals,' said Miss Candy. 'I train them for circuses, you know.'

They waved until they were so far away that he couldn't see Miss Candy's moustache.

On the train, he closed his eyes and willed it that when he opened them it would be a nightmare and he'd still be in Rowth Bridge. He opened them to see telegraph poles flashing by on a wet July day, traffic on a main road, and the last cows and sheep he would see for many a moon.

They changed trains at Leeds. As the train slipped out of City Station, Auntie Kate said, 'Tha's all he's got now. He's had five years of fighting. He'll miss our Ada so it hurts.'

'Does tha miss Uncle Frank so it hurts?' he said, as they passed a wet, forlorn Elland Road.

'Happen I do,' said Auntie Kate.

'That's Elland Road,' said Henry. 'Miss Candy took me there. She shouted at t' ref.'

'Miss Candy is a strange woman,' said Auntie Kate.

'Does tha think Uncle Frank's up in heaven?' said Henry.

'If any man deserves it, he does,' said Auntie Kate with a sigh.

'He might meet me mam.'

He didn't tell her his private theory. There was no God. There was a heaven and there was a hell, but they were on this earth. Heaven was Low Farm, Rowth Bridge, Upper Mitherdale. Hell was number 23 Paradise Lane, Thurmarsh.

His dad was at the station to meet them. They hadn't expected him to look so gaunt and ill, his demob suit hanging off him like wool on a dying sheep. They hadn't realised that his swift demob had been on medical grounds. They hadn't expected that he would only have one eye.

'Grand snoek, this.'

'I don't like snoek, Dad.'

'Well tha'll have to lump it. There's a war on.'

'There isn't, Dad. It's over.'

'Tha wouldn't think so, would tha? No food. No clothes. No nowt. I mean, did we win or am I deluded?'

'We won, Dad.'

'I'm just slipping out to t' Navigation for a bevvy,' said Ezra. 'Will tha be all right?'

'Course I will. I'm norra kid. I'm ten.'

'I'll not be long.'

Please be long, because you don't belong and I don't belong, so be long, thought Henry. He had a lot of thoughts nowadays that nobody knew about. It was one of the best things about being a human being.

When his dad was in, Henry often went out. He'd enjoyed wandering around in Upper Mitherdale, in fact it had been a way of life. It was different here. The River Rundle was a sewer, compared to the Mither. The Rundle and Gadd Navigation was only marginally better. The little cobbled streets were mean and nasty. He hated the shared lav in the yard. He hated wiping his backside on squared-off bits of *Reynolds News*. He only liked two things in this environment – the trains and the trams. It was nice to stand on the footbridge, immediately over the trains, so that the smoke roared up behind you and then suddenly it stopped, and a moment later it roared up in front of you.

The best thing about the trams was that they led into Thurmarsh Town Centre, and there was a public library there. Auntie Kate had told him about the libraries they had in the towns, full of proper books, not comics. Just before he left Rowth Bridge, he'd read a Sexton Blake book which was ninety pages long! Everyone had been amazed.

Ezra gave him fourpence a week pocket-money. He spent it all on tram fares, to get books. The library was the only thing in Thurmarsh that was better than the worst thing in Rowth Bridge, which was its girls. There were girls in Thurmarsh too, but you ignored them.

His reading was wide and various. He read *Biggles Flies North, Biggles Flies South, Biggles Flies East, Biggles Flies West, Biggles Flies In, Biggles Flies Out* and *Biggles Sweeps The Desert*. They were written by Captain W. E. Johns, whose main virtue was that he was the greatest writer who ever lived. He had created four magnificent characters, Biggles, Algy, Ginger and Bertie, who defeated cruel Germans, wily orientals, unshaven dagoes and pock-marked mulattos in burning deserts, icy mountains, crocodile-infested swamps and spider-infested jungles, and never a woman in sight. But he read other books as well. He read *Gimlet Flies North, Gimlet Flies South, Gimlet Flies East* and *Gimlet Flies West*. Gimlet books were also written by Captain W. E. Johns and were better than everything in the world except Biggles books. Once he brought home a book called *Hamlet – A Shortened Version*, thinking it was Gimlet. It was rubbish, probably because it wasn't written by Captain W. E. Johns.

That evening, he found it difficult to concentrate. In the morning, he was starting at Brunswick Road Elementary School. Eager anticipation was not coursing through his veins. Even the works of Captain W. E. Johns couldn't take him away from his worries. If only they had a wireless.

Ezra returned, a little unsteady on his feet.

'Sorry,' he said. 'I were detained.'

'Why haven't we gorra wireless?' said Henry.

'We had one before t' war,' said Ezra. 'It's disappeared into thin air.'

'Only I were thinking,' said Henry. 'I wouldn't be that worried if tha stayed a bit longer at t' Navigation, if we had a wireless.'

High walls noise jostle confusion shouting bleak corridor smell stale greens green paint where to go tidal wave big room hubbub who are you Henry Pratt Henry Pratt? Henry Pratt ah! new boy returning evacuee no! lived with relations same thing how old ten ah! must be Mr Gibbins' class over there come with me sit here hubbub yell silence shuffling feet cough cough silence sing hymn sit let us pray oh God we thank thee for another term like hell we do notices shortages breakages cough cough stand shuffle off corridor smell stale greens green paint classroom big high cold dark damp dank clatter boys sitting don't know where to go stand small shy forlorn who are you?

He walked forward slowly towards the teacher's desk. Mr Gibbins was six foot four and entirely bald. How old? Age didn't come into it. He was Mr Gibbins, a fixture, an ageless chrome-dome.

'Who are you?' he repeated.

'Henry,' said Henry, determined that there should be no Ezra nonsense here.

'Henry what?'

'Henry Pratt.'

There was some laughter.

'Henry Pratt what?'

'Just Henry Pratt.'

Thirty-three white boys and one black boy hung breathless on the exchange.

'Are you new to this school?'

'Aye.'

'At your last school, if your teacher had said to you, "What's your name?" what would you have said?'

'Ezra.'

It came out before he could stop it.

'What?????'

'Ezra.'

'I thought your name was Henry Pratt.'

'Aye, but there was another Henry there, and they couldn't have two Henrys, so they called me Ezra.'

'I see. Now, Pratt, when you addressed your teacher, did you use a little word as a mark of respect to the teacher?'

'Oh aye.'

'Well we believe in respect for authority here at Brunswick Road, Pratt, so I'd like you to use that same word to me. Do you understand?'

'Oh aye.'

'Oh aye *what?*'

Henry shrugged, then did what he was told.

'Oh aye, miss,' he said.

There was a roar of laughter. He *hated* it when people laughed at him.

That evening, when Henry got home, he found that Ezra had bought a wireless.

The nights drew in. The *Beano* exhorted, 'We still need salvage, ton by ton – even though the war is won,' but Henry didn't read the *Beano* any more.

The only thing there was plenty of was shortages. Even professional men went to work in odd trousers and jackets! Miners threatened to strike due to a shortage of cigarettes. Four tons of dried-fruit slab cake were sent from Capetown. A third of all street lights were switched off. Britain had pawned herself, and there would be hard bargaining before America allowed her to redeem the goods.

The premises of Binks and Madeley Ltd had been destroyed in the Sheffield blitz, and Ezra was forced to swallow his pride, and take work making pocket-knives. The job didn't last, and he was able to go to the Navigation at dinner time as well.

Uncle Teddy sent Ezra the occasional sum of conscience money, not knowing that Auntie Doris, not knowing that he was sending conscience money, was also sending conscience money. Cousin Hilda, not knowing that either Uncle Teddy or Auntie Doris were sending conscience money, was also sending conscience money, in lieu of taking a closer interest in what was going on. Her Mother, over at Leonard's, had gone a bit funny, and ignored them completely. Ezra's father was dying, and his mother had her hands full making sure that love and dignity were at the bedside. Ezra made sure that Henry had enough to eat and went to school looking no less presentable than the other children. Ezra told the customers at the Navigation that Cousin Hilda was looking after the boy. The neighbours at number 25 were old and deaf. At number 21 she was on the game. There was nobody to object. Nobody knew that Henry spent evening after evening on his own, except Henry and Ezra, and neither of them would tell.

One evening, returning from the pub a little earlier than usual, and finding his son still up, Ezra told him that he had applied for a job at the steelworks that day.

'They said, "Sorry. No vacancies." Them were their exact words. I said, "Listen. Think on this. I spent six years fighting against the perils of Hitler's Reich. I lost an eye. If I hadn't fought, it wouldn't be Crapp, Hawser and Kettlewell. It'd be Krupp, Kaiser and bloody Goebbels." He said, "That's as may be, but I can't sack lads as have worked for me throughout t' duration." He said, "Tha wouldn't be up to t' work. Tha's not suited. Tha's a cutler." I said, "Get me Crapp. Fetch me Hawser. I want to speak to Mr Kettlewell hisself." '

'Did he fetch them, dad?'

'Did he hell as like. He told me to piss off.'

One Saturday, Henry borrowed four books from the library and settled down for a momentous weekend's reading. The four books were, as it chanced, all by Captain W. E. Johns. They were called *Worrals Flies North, Worrals Flies South, Worrals Flies East* and *Worrals Flies West*. He had read the complete canon of Biggles and Gimlet. Now for Worrals. He didn't start the books on the tram. He wouldn't waste them. He would wait till after tea.

At last tea was finished, and Ezra popped down to the Navigation for 'a quick bevvy'.

He opened the front page of the first book. Now for a wallow.

The dreadful truth hit him almost immediately. Worrals was a girl. Captain W. E. Johns, the greatest writer in the history of the universe, wrote books about girls.

He turned to the wireless, that faithful friend who had never let him down.

There was a roar of traffic. An old cockney woman shouted, 'Violets. Lovely violets.' The traffic stopped, and the announcer said, 'Once again we stop the mighty roar of London's traffic, and from the great crowds we bring to the microphone some of the interesting people who are "In Town Tonight".'

He found none of them interesting. He bitterly resented their good humour, their idle metropolitan and transatlantic chatter.

Worrals was a girl, the weekend stretched before him like a desert, and still they prattled on.

He was alone. He had no friends. He was in a rat-infested back-to-back terrace which was steadily falling to pieces. It all swept over him. And the little voice which told him that he must fight piped up again. You always have to fight, it said. Stop for even five minutes and you'll go under.

By gow, he would fight.

He got out a notebook, and pencil, and settled at the table. He'd show the world. He'd show Captain W. E. Johns. There'd be no girls in his books.

'Chapter One,' he wrote.

Inspiration failed him at this point in his endeavours. He thought he knew why. He must plan his book.

He decided to start by writing down the titles of his books. Then he would decide which one to write first, and begin.

Half an hour later, when Cousin Hilda, alias the sniffer, found him, he had listed six titles in his notebook.

1. *Pratt Flies North.*
2. *Pratt Flies South.*
3. *Pratt Flies East.*
4. *Pratt Flies West.*
5. *Pratt Sweeps the Desert.*
6. *What Is Happiness?*

Cousin Hilda looked round the room and sniffed.

'Where's our Ezra?' she said. 'He's never gone down the pub and left you on your own!'

She poured a reservoir of disapproval into the word 'pub'.

'He's gone for a walk,' said Henry. 'He likes walking.'

'Does he often leave you alone?'

'Well, not for long.'

'Does he ever go to the pub and leave you alone?'

He sensed that a total denial might not carry conviction.

'He might go for a quick bevvy every now and then,' he said.

Cousin Hilda sniffed.

She sat at the table and leant forward to talk earnestly to Henry.

'Does he feed you all right?' she said.

'Oh aye,' said Henry. 'We had whale today. I like whale.'

'Is he. . .does he treat you all right?'

'Course he does. He's me dad.'

'Aye, I know, but. . .war's a terrible thing, Henry. It upsets people. It upsets their nerves. Sometimes, people go. . .well, a bit funny. It's not their fault, so if they did go a bit funny, there wouldn't be any cause not to tell anybody about it, would there?'

'No, Cousin Hilda.'

'Is he happy?'

Henry considered the question. It wasn't the sort of thing you normally wondered about, in connection with your father.

'I don't think he likes not having a job,' he said.

'Does his having one eye upset you?' said Cousin Hilda.

'No. They've made a right good job of t' false one,' said Henry.

He hoped she wouldn't stay too long. His dad was often unsteady when he got home.

'It's right nice of thee to call,' he said, 'but I've gorrus homework to do.'

'Is that your homework?' said Cousin Hilda, taking the notebook before he could stop her.

She read his list of titles.

'Homework?' she said.

'We've gorra write a book,' he said. 'I'm planning me titles.'

'Daydreams,' said Cousin Hilda. 'Nay, lad.'

'Daydreams?' he said.

'They're all about you,' she said.

'That isn't me,' he said. 'That's me dad.'

It was easy, telling lies, once you got into the swing of it.

Cousin Hilda handed him the notebook.

'You don't loop your pees right,' she said. It was her way of telling him that all the other letters were perfectly formed, but if she said it straight out, it might spoil him.

'I'm going to set to,' she said. 'The whole place is in a right pickle. I don't reckon it's seen a duster since VJ day.'

Cousin Hilda took a square of old pyjamas from under the sink, examined it, sniffed, and went to the door to give it a good shake. Then she went upstairs.

Henry had to pretend to be continuing with his homework.

'Ezra Pratt, known to all his friends as Prattles, stood on the

98

steps of the Royal Aero Club,' he began.

Every now and then he could hear her exclaiming with disgust, as she found more dirt.

Ten minutes later Ezra returned, slamming the door.

'Cousin Hilda's upstairs,' said Henry hastily.

'What's she doing here?' said Ezra.

'Dusting.'

Ezra grimaced.

'Is that you, Ezra?' shouted Cousin Hilda.

'Aye.'

'I told her tha's been for a walk,' said Henry quickly.

'What? Oh. Oh aye.'

Ezra looked at his son in astonishment.

Cousin Hilda came downstairs, carrying the pyjama duster as if it were a maggoty rat.

'I just went for a spot of air,' said Ezra.

'Oh aye?' said Cousin Hilda. 'Three times round t' bar of t' Navigation?'

'Just o'er t' river,' said Ezra. 'Just round t' roads.'

He sat in the rocking chair. It was his place as of right.

'That rag rug's coming unravelled,' said Cousin Hilda. 'It's a pig-sty. I could write my name in t' dust on your wardrobe.'

Henry grinned, but only internally. His sudden talent for dissembling surprised him. He found it exhilarating.

What he was grinning at was the thought of Cousin Hilda writing in dust. He imagined her writing, 'I'm filthy. Clean me,' in the dirt on Uncle Teddy's car.

'Well done, lad,' Ezra said, when Cousin Hilda had gone. 'Well done. She'd have torn t' bollocks off me if she'd known I'd gone to t' Navigation.'

Only a few months ago, at Rowth Bridge, Henry would have been astonished to have been praised by an adult for telling a lie. But Rowth Bridge seemed centuries ago.

'It's lucky tha came back early,' he said.

His dad snorted, rocked slowly in his chair, and began the longest speech he ever made in his life. Henry sat at the table, his notebook open, his pencil poised, as if he was taking the minutes of the meeting, although in fact he wrote nothing down.

'Aye, well,' said Ezra. 'It seems I'm not welcome at t' Navigation any more. I knew it spelt trouble when I saw t' new name over t' door. Cecil E. Jenkinson. I never trusted that E. It's t' end of an era, I thought. Still, fair dos, give him a chance, I thought. So I did. I gave him a chance. He says to me tonight, he says, "I'm not banning thee. Come here from time to time, fair enough. But tha's here all night every night." Well, I were flambergasted. I said, "So what? Tha's open, i'n't tha? I'm entitled." "Tha's not entitled wi'out I say so," he said. "I'm entitled to refuse to serve anybody." "So what's tha saying, then, Cecil?" I said. "I can but I can't, is that it?" "It's me other patrons," he said. "They don't see eye to eye wi' thee." "Aye," I said, "I knew it were me eye. I lost that eye so they could be free to come into t' pub," I said. "Aye," he said, "I agree, bur it's nowt to do wi' t' eye." He looked embarrassed. I'll gi'e 'im that. "Patrons don't like tha going on about t' war," he said. "T' war's over." "Aye," I said, "because I bloody fought it. That's why it's over. Don't give me other patrons," I said. "It's thee. Tha's never liked me." That struck home, cos he hasn't. And I'll tell thee why. Cos I don't like what he's done to t' pub, and he knows it. Well, I didn't fight Hitler for five years so that he could put bright-green upholstery in t' snug. "Tha's never liked me," I said. "I go away for five years and what happens? My place in t' dominoes team gets taken. It's a bloody disgrace." "They couldn't play a man short for five years," he said. "Fair enough, Cecil," I said. "Point taken, Cecil," I said. "Bur I'm back now. Darts, fair enough. I'm a shadow of me former self wi' one eye. But not dominoes. I played Sid Lowson last night," I said. "I won six games end-away." "Aye," he said, "but I can't split up a winning combination." Sid Lowson, to his eternal credit, offered to stand down. I refused. "Thanks, Sid," I said. "Much appreciated, but no. I don't want to be the cause célèbre of a domino crisis. I couldn't never represent this establishment again. There's a clash of personalities, and that's all there is to it." But I never thought I'd be banned from t' pub. Because that's whar I am. Wharever he says. Banned. Well, I can't go in there and say, "It's all right, Cecil. I'm only staying twenty minutes and I won't mention t' war once." Can I? Course I can't.'

They sat in silence for a moment, a pale, emaciated embittered wreck with a glass eye and a pale, podgy, ten-year-old boy with a notebook and a pencil.

'Sorry,' said Ezra. 'I didn't mean to burden thee wi' my problems.'

They spent Christmas Day at Cousin Hilda's. Auntie Doris said, 'Next year you must come to us. We insist.'

Cousin Hilda lived at number 66 Park View Road, Thurmarsh. It was a stone, semi-detached Victorian house on the town side of the Alderman Chandler Memorial Park. It had a bay window on the ground floor. Cousin Hilda owned the house. She had been a paid companion to a rich, autocratic, invalid lady. The family had disapproved of her dancing to this lady's sour tune. The family disapproved even more when the lady died at Deauville and left Cousin Hilda several thousand pounds, a vast sum in those days, and not to be sniffed at even by Cousin Hilda.

Into her modest, but pleasantly situated house, Cousin Hilda crammed four paying guests. They paid one pound ten shillings a week for a bed-sitting room, breakfast, tea, supper and laundry. On Sundays they had dinner instead of tea. Cousin Hilda referred to them as 'my businessmen'. They kept her occupied and solvent.

One of Cousin Hilda's 'businessmen' was present that Christmas Day. He was Len Arrowsmith, a French polisher, and he believed in reincarnation. He had no family living, in recognisable form, although every holiday he went to see a giraffe in Chester Zoo. Also present was Cousin Hilda's friend.

Cousin Hilda's living quarters were in the basement, which received only a poor ration of daylight. They ate their Christmas dinner around a large, square table in a corner of the room, with bench seats along two sides. This was where the 'businessmen' ate. A little blue-tiled stove, with a front of four panes of blue glass, shone merrily. It was set in a blue-tiled fireplace. There were two armchairs, which sagged badly, and a dresser, on which there were several plates. All the plates were blue. Blue was Cousin Hilda's favourite colour, being the colour of God, in her opinion.

At the back of this room there was a small, crowded scullery where Cousin Hilda slaved all day, cooking, ironing, washing clothes in a huge tub, with liberal usage of Reckitt's Blue, and rinsing them through a formidable mangle.

Henry missed Rowth Bridge again that day. Not that Cousin Hilda didn't do her best. They had roast chicken with all the trimmings, and Christmas pudding to follow. Henry got the threepenny bit. In Henry's cracker there was a joke, which ran 'What kind of ant waits on people? An attend-ant.' Len Arrowsmith said that that was a good one. His dad was on his best behaviour. They listened to a programme that linked up English-speaking people right round the world. Then came the King's speech. They stood up for the national anthem. Len Arrowsmith hummed it tunelessly.

Cousin Hilda's friend's left stocking developed a ladder which grew slowly longer as the day darkened.

They went for a short walk in the Alderman Chandler Memorial Park. The slit trenches remained. Three or four hardy children were playing on the swings and roundabouts, but the little cluster of animal and bird cages was empty. The glass in the old men's shelter had been shattered in the Blitz, and had still not been replaced. They went back to Cousin Hilda's and had tea and Christmas cake and then they played a card game in which you started with the sevens and had to go up to as far as the kings and down as far as the aces. Cousin Hilda's friend couldn't quite get the hang of it, but Len Arrowsmith revealed an unsuspected ruthless streak. His father was on his best behaviour. When Cousin Hilda's friend reached up for her handkerchief, which she kept in her knickers, Henry looked up her thigh to see how far the ladder had got.

'All over till next year,' said Cousin Hilda as they left.

Thank goodness, thought Henry.

1946 began quietly. More footwear was promised soon for civilians. In the January clearance sales, boys' school shirts were offered at 2/1d by the Thurmarsh and Rawlaston Cooperative Society. Gents' merino vests and trunks were 2/- and half a coupon. There were plans to stamp children's footwear to prevent parents pawning it, and complaints from housewives about the illogicality of aprons being on coupons when floor mops weren't.

Henry spent the time quietly with his friends. He had many friends. He particularly liked the boy detectives, Norman and Henry Bones, on 'Children's Hour', and there was an exciting serial called 'The Gay Dolphin Adventure' by Malcolm Saville. 'Nature Parliament' had begun, with Derek McCullough, Peter Scott and L. Hugh Newman. He loved this, and 'A Visit to Cowleaze Farm', although they both opened up a vein of painful nostalgia. But he would listen to anything. When they heard that Ezra's father had died, Henry was in the middle of a talk on squash rackets, with recorded illustrations, by F. N. S. Creek. In the evenings he liked boxing, comedy and adventure. He listened spell-bound to Arthur Dancha of Bethnal Green v Omar Kouidri of Paris. He laughed at 'Merry-Go-Round' from Waterlogged Spa, Sinking-in-the-Ooze, at 'Music Hall' with Nat Mills and Bobbie, who said, 'Well let's get on with it' and everybody laughed. They all had their catch phrases. Leon Cortez said, 'There was this 'ere geyser Caesar,' and everybody laughed. It seemed a shame to Henry to laugh at Shakespeare, just because he was so much worse a writer than Captain W. E. Johns.

He thrilled to Paul Temple and to 'Appointment with Fear'. These were his friends. He had no real-life friends.

Then, one dark, dismal, dank outside as well as in, electric-lit morning in early February, an incident occurred in Mr Gibbins' class which was to have a profound effect on Henry's social life.

Although Brunswick Road Elementary School had become Brunswick Road Primary School, it remained a stone, Victorian fortress, with high Dutch-style gables, a steep-pitched roof and green guttering. The walls and windows were high. There were three doors, for boys, girls and mixed infants. Beyond the infant level, boys and girls were still totally segregated.

Mr Gibbins' classroom had bare walls with peeling plaster. There wasn't a lot of fungus. The desks were fixed to the floor by iron legs, and the seats were benches fixed to the desks by iron arms. Sharp corners abounded. On each desk there was an ink-well.

Absentees were Chadwick (cold), Erpingham (I forget), Lewis (flu), Barton (death of grandmother – genuine) and Pilling (death of grandmother — false — got idea from Barton).

Among those present were Mr Gibbins, Henry, Tommy Marsden, Martin Hammond, Ian Lowson (son of the peripheral Sid) and Chalky White, the West Indian.

They took a test each week, and changed places according to their results, moving to the front if bad, and to the back if good. Henry had risen rapidly to the back of the class.

Mr Gibbins caned them on the hand if they didn't get seven out of ten for mental arithmetic, but the biggest bee in his bonnet was English grammar.

'Today,' he announced, 'we'll deal with subjects and objects. You might say that the subject of the lesson is subjects and objects, and the object is to cram as much knowledge into your thick skulls as possible.'

To be honest, the class did not look as if they would be very likely to say that.

'Joking apart,' said Mr Gibbins, to their surprise, 'give me a sentence, Marsden.'

'Six months,' said Tommy Marsden from the front row.

'Six months what, Marsden?'

'Six months for nicking lead off the church roof.'

'Come here, Marsden.'

'Yes, sir.'

Tommy Marsden went forward and held out his hand. Mr Gibbins smacked it three times with the cane.

'Let that be a warning to you all,' said Mr Gibbins. 'Give me a sentence, Cuffley.'

Norbert Cuffley, a goody but not a genius, adorned the second row from the back.

'The teacher asked me to give him a sentence, sir,' he said.

'Excellent, Cuffley, if not wildly imaginative.' Mr Gibbins scraped the sentence agonisingly onto the blackboard. 'Now, what is the subject of the sentence, Pratt?'

'You asking Cuffley to give you a sentence, sir.'

'No. I mean, yes, that is the subject in the sense of what it's about. I meant, "What is the subject in the grammatical sense?" What word in the sentence fulfils the role that we call the subject? Milner?'

'Me, sir?'

'Yes, you. That's why I said Milner, Milner.'

'No, sir. I meant "me". "The teacher asked me." That "me", sir.'

'Why do you say that, Milner?'

A loud fart rent the air. Everybody laughed, except Cuffley.

'Who did that?' said Mr Gibbins.

'Me, sir,' said Tommy Marsden. 'I'm sorry, sir. I've got wind.'

'I choose to believe you,' said Mr Gibbins. 'I cannot believe that any boy would deliberately waste time, in the most important year in his school life, by breaking wind deliberately.'

'Exactly, sir,' said Tommy Marsden.

'Why is this the most important year in your school life?' said Mr Gibbins. 'Because we now have, for the first time, true equality of opportunity in education. At the end of the year you will take the Eleven Plus examination to see which of you are clever enough to win this equality of opportunity. Some of you will go to the grammar school, and the chance of being somebody in life. Others won't. It's up to you.'

'If we all work hard, sir, will we all go to grammar school, sir?' asked Tommy Marsden.

'No, of course not. There isn't room. The best will go,' said Mr Gibbins.

'So whether we all work or all do nowt, t' same people will go, sir,' said Tommy Marsden.

'Don't be silly, Marsden,' said Mr Gibbins. A thin bead of sweat was glistening on his forehead. 'Right. Hilarious joke over. Back to education. Milner, why did you say that "me" was the subject of the sentence?'

'T' teacher's like t' king, sir. So t' pupils are his subjects.'

'Ah! Very ingenious, Milner. I'm glad to see you're thinking, at any rate. It makes a change. Keep at it. You may find you grow to like it. But you're wrong. Hammond?'

'Is the subject the noun, sir?'

'Very good, but which noun?'

'Teacher, sir.'

'Very good, Hammond. Why?'

'Because it comes first, sir.'

'Well, that's not really the. . .'

A loud fart rent the air. Everybody laughed, except Cuffley.

'Who did that?' said Mr Gibbins wearily.

'Me, sir,' said Booth.

'Come here, Booth.'

'I couldn't help it, sir.'

'Come here, Booth.'

'It's not fair, sir.'

Booth held out his hand. Mr Gibbins smacked it twice with the cane.

'Let that be a lesson to you all,' he said. 'The subject of a sentence, and we did deal with the subject of subjects last week, the subject of a sentence is the nominative, the element in the sentence about which something is predicated. The object is that which is governed by a transitive verb or preposition.' Mr Gibbins looked at their blank faces and wished he hadn't started on this. The sweat was beginning to run down into his eyes. 'In simple terms, the subject is the doer, the object is that which is done to.'

'What's a doer, sir?' said Cuffley.

'It's t' thing in t' hoil in t' wall to stop t' draught,' said Appleyard.

'Write out fifty times "I must not make silly remarks in class", Appleyard,' said Mr Gibbins.

'Can't I have t' cane, sir?'

Mr Gibbins took a deep breath.

'The subject of the sentence is therefore the teacher,' said Mr Gibbins.

A loud fart rent the air. Everybody laughed, except Cuffley.

'Would your tiny minds laugh however often that happened?' said Mr Gibbins. 'Would you still laugh if it happened a hundred times – don't try it!!!! Right. Who was it that time?'

'Me, sir,' said Martin Hammond.

'You're an intelligent boy, Hammond,' said Mr Gibbins. 'You could go far. Sometimes I wish you would. Why do you deliberately break wind and ally yourself with these miserable cretins?'

'The working class must stick together. That's what my dad says, any road,' said Martin Hammond.

Mr Gibbins stared at Martin Hammond wildly.

'I won't punish you this time, Hammond,' he said, 'because I believe you to be fundamentally sensible.'

'That's not fair,' muttered Tommy Marsden.

'I heard that,' said Mr Gibbins. 'Come here, Marsden.'

'It's not fair, sir,' said Tommy Marsden. 'He makes a loud noise and gets nowt. I whisper one word and get caned.'

'I didn't say you were going to be caned,' said Mr Gibbins, realising that Tommy Marsden had a point, and back-tracking hurriedly. 'Come here.'

Tommy Marsden walked forward and held out his hand.

'Point to the subject of the sentence on the board,' said Mr Gibbins, handing Tommy Marsden his pointer.

Tommy Marsden pointed to the word 'teacher'.

'Good,' said Mr Gibbins. 'It's the teacher, because it's the teacher who asked. So what's the object?'

'Him, sir,' said Chalky White.

'Me, sir,' said Henry Pratt.

'No, sir. Me! Me! said Norbert Cuffley.

'Me,' said Mr Gibbins. 'Precisely.'

'How can it be you, sir?' said Appleyard. 'You're the subject.'

'I didn't mean me as a person,' said Mr Gibbins. 'I meant "me" in the sentence.'

Something approximating to order was gradually restored. Mr Gibbins' class didn't want to overthrow the law and order of the classroom, because they wouldn't have known what to do after they'd done it. A total collapse of discipline would have frightened them. It was a war of attrition, fought on safe ground, renewable every day.

Henry liked it when order was restored. He wanted to learn. Judge then of his discomfiture when he began to feel a genuine need to break wind. He fought against it. He was frightened of the cane. He had no wish to do anything but sit quietly, learn things (if possible) and give the occasional right answer without being a disgraceful goody like Norbert Cuffley.

Desperately he pressed his buttocks against each other. In vain! There emerged a piercing whistle of gargantuan duration. It was so high-pitched that only dogs, bats, all twenty-nine boys and Mr

Gibbins could hear it.

Everybody laughed, even Cuffley.

Henry could feel his cheeks burning. Then he realised that everything would be all right so long as he pretended that he had done it deliberately.

He grinned.

Mr Gibbins brought the cane down four times on his outstretched hand, but he could hardly feel the pain through the glory.

Henry had been made an honorary member of the Paradise Lane Gang, on account of a single act, the slow emission of a phenomenal amount of wind in the form of a high-pitched scream unique in the anal annals of the West Riding. The gang had never heard of Le Pétomane, but, if they had, they would have believed that the distinguished Gallic farter had a worthy rival in South Yorkshire.

Henry relished the fame uneasily, for he knew he was living on borrowed time.

'Do it again!' was the constant command of his new chums.

'On my birthday,' he said; and they accepted that. An artist of such rare talent was entitled to choose the stage for his performance.

He had four whole weeks in the gang. There were six members. Tommy Marsden, Billy Erpingham, Chalky White, Martin Hammond, Ian Lowson and Henry. They got on trams without any money, knocked on people's doors and ran away, pretended to be blind and got helped across roads by kind old ladies, dialled 999 and ran away, painted spots on their faces and went on a trolley bus disguised as an epidemic of chicken pox, gave each other haircuts, bought a bathing cap and some glue, and constructed a wig which they put in Mr Gibbins' desk.

On Friday, March 8th, Henry listened to Jackie Paterson of Glasgow v Bunty Doran of Belfast.

On Wednesday, March 13th, he faced exposure.

The Paradise Lane Gang laid on a birthday party for him. He would give the cabaret. Dress was informal. The venue was the waste ground between the Rundle and Gadd Navigation and the

River Rundle. Tommy Marsden brought a quart of pale ale, stolen from his dad. Ian Lowson brought a packet of Park Drive, ditto. Chalky White brought chewing gum. Martin Hammond brought a packet of digestive biscuits and a jar of strawberry jam.

I forget what Billy Erpingham brought.

The sky was bleak, and the light was fading. The wind was cold. There were a few flakes of sleet.

There was no escape. It was his birthday. He had boasted that he liked beer and smoking.

He ate three digestive biscuits, spread with raspberry jam, washed down by swigs of the nauseous, flat, bitter beer. Gamely, he struggled through the third cigarette of his life. He ate three more digestive biscuits, spread with raspberry jam, washed down by swigs of the nauseous, flat, bitter beer. Gamely, he struggled through the fourth cigarette of his life.

He took another swig of the beer, hoping against hope that it would help to produce some wind. To no avail! And he was fair perished with cold. Exposure of two different kinds was at hand.

He rushed over to the canal and was prodigiously sick into its murky waters.

He set off home, his head thumping. There could be no question of any performance now. The day of reckoning was postponed, yet he didn't feel cheered by this. His life was passing him by. When he was twice his present age he would be twenty-two. When he was twice that he would be forty-four. When he was twice that he would be eighty-eight, and already an old man. When he was twice that he would be. . .his head thumped. . .a hundred and seventy-six, and people would come from far and wide to discover the secret of his long life. Unless he was dead. Dead! He shuddered.

He'd be late home for his tea, but it didn't matter.

He walked slowly along the footpath under the brick wall that separated the cul-de-sacs from the canal. He didn't turn right into Paradise Lane. He didn't want to go home yet.

It was almost dark now, and sleeting gently. The cold wind soothed his burning brow, and provided a suitable background for his mood.

He walked on past the ends of Back Paradise Lane, Paradise

Hill, Back Paradise Hill, Paradise Court, Back Paradise Court and Paradise Green. He walked down Back Paradise Green to the main road. In a sudden surge of anger against life he ran across the road in front of a tram. The driver yelled at him. He went on down the side of Crapp, Hawser and Kettlewell. On all sides there were great sheds, topped by rows of narrow chimneys. Nothing moved around these stranded liners, but from time to time huge flashes of molten flame lit up the sky, and occasionally, through a ventilation gap, he would see the glow from a furnace mouth. He went right round the huge works of Crapp, Hawser and Kettlewell, his head thumping as if in time with some vast industrial hammer. A tiny shunting engine took its freight slowly across the road in front of him, blocking his path.

On an impulse he plunged deeper into this nightmare industrial estate. He would walk west, over the Pennines, to Liverpool, and there he would stow away on a cargo ship and work his passage when he was discovered. He'd break ship on a tropical island where there was plenty of sunshine and fruit, and no school or girls, and he'd live happily ever after.

It would serve them right. Nobody cared about him. Except Simon Eckington and Auntie Kate and Miss Candy. Maybe he wouldn't go straight to the tropical island. He'd call in at Rowth Bridge first.

It was very cold, and his headache was no better. He decided to go home, and set off tomorrow after a good night's sleep. This would give him a chance to write a suicide note, and really worry them.

He struggled back to the main road, very tired now. The main road seemed endless. He hadn't realised how far he had come. His mouth tasted as if it had been coated with shrimp and dead grasshopper paste. He began to compose his suicide note.

His father, Uncle Teddy, Auntie Doris and Cousin Hilda were sitting by the not-so-efficiently leaded range. They tried to hide their relief and show only their anger.

On the table there were sandwiches, a cake with eleven candles, and – unheard of for many years – a wine-red Chivers jelly.

There were also three brown paper parcels.

He burst into tears.

Ezra's father had died. Twice they had made the trip to the home of Penistone's leading coal merchant to see him. Now they went to see Ezra's mother, who was quietly fading away from sorrow. These trips made Henry uneasy, even vaguely frightened. He didn't know how to cope, or what to say. There was nothing he could say. He didn't even like it when he was given a shilling before they left. It seemed like payment for services that he had failed to render.

Family deaths often come in clusters, and now Her Mother was dying as well. She had gone funny, and hadn't wanted to see them. Now, in the face of the grim reaper, she had relented.

Henry hated everything about the visit to the hospital. He hated the long walk from the gates, in the torrential rain, following the signs for Radcliffe Ward. The hospital appeared to have been designed by someone whose only previous experience had been the creation of mazes, but at last they found the ward. It was a kind of Nissen hut, with six beds on each side, and a Nurse Waddle, who did.

Her Mother was in the end bed on the left. They collected two chairs from a pile of chairs at the end of the room, and hung their sodden coats over the backs.

'How's tha doing, then, Ezra? And who's this?' said Her Mother.

'This is Henry.'

'Nay. Henry's nobbut a baby.'

'That was years ago, Norah. Before tha went to our Leonard's.'

'I've only been at our Leonard's for a fortnight,' said her mother. 'Just to help her wi' t' bairn.'

'Tha lives there, Norah,' said Ezra.

'With Leonard?'

'Aye.'

'How long have I been there?'

'Six years.'

'Oh heck. I forget. How's Henry, then?'

'All right, thank you, Grandma,' said Henry. He longed to add something amusing, or compassionate, or even just vaguely

III

interesting. Nothing came. It never did in the presence of the old and ill.

Nurse Waddle waddled down the ward towards them.

'I'm sorry,' said Ezra. 'We're making puddles on t' floor.'

It was true. Why else should Ezra have said it? Quite sizeable puddles were forming beneath their coats.

'Never mind,' said Nurse Waddle. 'Worse things'll happen before t' day's done.'

Henry remembered another puddle on another floor. The shame rose off him like the steam off his drying coat. He felt himself blushing. He caught Nurse Waddle's eye, and believed that she had seen into his soul, and he blushed all the more. Nurse Waddle waddled off to get a sponge and a bucket and then she waddled back and cleared up the puddles before they spread.

'Tha shouldn't have come on such a wet night,' said Her Mother. 'I'm not feeling neglected.'

'Aye, but Leonard said this were t' best night for him not to come,' said Ezra.

'Who's that?' said Her Mother.

'That's our Henry,' said Ezra.

'It can't be. Henry's nobbut a baby,' said Her Mother.

'Tha's lived with Leonard for six years,' said Ezra.

'Six years?'

'Aye.'

'Oh heck. I forget.'

The woman in the bed opposite, who was very elderly and emaciated, began to get out of bed very slowly, with great difficulty. She began to sing 'Throw out the life-line' in a mumble as she did so.

'Press the bell,' said Her Mother scornfully. 'Get back into bed,' she shouted.

Henry pressed the bell, glad to be of use, yet frightened of pressing the bell, in case it was the wrong thing to do. He caught sight of the old woman's naked, creased body, and shuddered at the shocking thinness of it.

Nurse Waddle waddled briskly up the ward like a clockwork toy. 'Where do we think we're going, Mrs Purkiss?' she said briskly, and started putting the very old woman back into bed.

Any hope of Henry thinking of anything interesting to say was dashed when Uncle Teddy and Auntie Doris arrived.

Auntie Doris smelt like a perfume factory, and put a bunch of bananas in Her Mother's bed-side bowl.

Bananas! Henry stared at them in wonder. They were an unheard-of luxury. It was rumoured that there had been a few in the corner shop, and Billy Erpingham had thought they were yellow polony, but these were the first Henry had seen.

That was something he could say. He waited for a gap in the conversation, into which he would slip the bon mot 'Billy Erpingham saw a banana and thought it were yellow polony'. But, as luck would have it, there was no gap.

'Is it all right to have four visitors?' said Uncle Teddy. 'Only it says two at a time.'

'It doesn't matter,' said Her Mother.

'We could go out and come back when you go, if you like,' said Auntie Doris.

'Or you could go out now and wait for us. We can't stay long. I've got some business to discuss,' said Uncle Teddy.

'It doesn't matter,' said Her Mother. 'She's not too bad, this one. Not like t' other one.'

'Pity we all came on the same day,' said Uncle Teddy.

'We could have given you a lift if we'd known,' said Auntie Doris. 'Then you needn't have got soaked.'

'I'm saying nowt,' said Her Mother.

'You're looking grand, Mother,' said Auntie Doris.

'I'm dying, but I'm not complaining. I don't feel hard done by,' said Her Mother.

Henry thought that perhaps it was just as well not to do the banana polony gag. It might suggest that he was hinting that his grandmother offer him a banana, and, much as he longed for one, he knew that under these circumstances he wouldn't enjoy it.

It was stifling. The bananas were looking more cheerful by the minute.

Biggles wouldn't be stuck for something to say. Or would he? Henry had never actually come across Biggles doing hospital visiting.

'You've got to help us, Bigglesworth,' pronounced the Air

Commodore. 'You've proved yourself singularly adept at solving this kind of devilish mystery.'

Biggles' eyes narrowed shrewdly. 'I'm awfully sorry, sir,' he countered evenly. 'It's jolly decent of you to say so, although I fear you exaggerate my powers. I'd dearly love to have a crack at the caper, but I've got to visit my Gran in hospital.'

Suddenly Henry thought of something to say. It wasn't witty. It wasn't even interesting. But it was, without doubt, a remark, and as such it mustn't go to waste. It was, in fact, 'We had to wait twenty minutes for a tram.'

Imagine his dismay when he heard his father say, at that very moment, 'We had to wait twenty minutes for a tram,' condemning him to another ten minutes' silence.

'Who's that?' said Her Mother.

'That's our Henry,' said Auntie Doris. 'Isn't it, Henry?'

'Aye,' riposted Henry amusingly.

'Nay,' said Her Mother. 'Henry's not much more than a baby.'

'You haven't seen him for six years,' said Uncle Teddy.

'Six years?' said Her Mother.

'Tha's lived wi' Leonard for six years,' said Ezra.

'Oh heck,' said Her Mother. 'I get confused. Why did I go to our Leonard's?'

'Because Ada took Henry to the country,' said Auntie Doris.

'I didn't want to go,' said Her Mother. 'I don't like t' countryside. It's nobbut fields. They went to Kate's, didn't they? No, I were better suited at our Leonard's. I were right set up wi' it there, specially after he sent Lord Hawke off to be broken up for t' war effort. I want thee all to know, before I go, that I didn't feel I were being flung out like a used duster.'

'We'd better be going,' said Uncle Teddy.

'Have we time to give them a lift home?' said Auntie Doris.

'Not really. It's pushing it a bit. We said we'd see Geoffrey,' said Uncle Teddy.

'In connection with business,' said Auntie Doris.

'It's all right,' said Ezra. 'We're on t' tram route.'

'Are you sure?' said Uncle Teddy.

'I'm keeping out of this,' said Her Mother.

'Right, if you're quite sure, we'll be off,' said Uncle Teddy.

Uncle Teddy and Auntie Doris kissed Her Mother.

The emaciated old woman began to get out of bed.

Henry rang the bell.

Another bell rang, for the ending of visiting time.

'Take those bananas,' said Her Mother. 'Our Leonard brought them. I don't like them.'

They kissed her goodbye. Nurse Waddle waddled in and said, 'And where do we think we're going, Mrs Purkiss?'

As they left the ward, they found themselves side by side with the man who had been visiting the woman in the next bed.

'At least your one talks,' he said. 'I can't get owt out of my one at all.'

It had stopped raining, but an ambulance roared through a large puddle and drenched them from head to foot. They had to wait twenty minutes for a tram. By the time it came, Uncle Teddy was already discussing his business, which consisted of paying the barman at the Robin Hood in Sheffield for two large whiskies and a large gin and It.

At last they got home, and Henry had his first banana. The old master of the Mars bar made it last seven minutes. Life's pleasures were not taken lightly in those days.

Visits to hospitals and to the home of Penistone's leading coal merchant could not delay the moment of truth for ever. Today was to be Henry's day of reckoning with the Paradise Lane Gang. He was to meet them at the bridge over the Rundle and Gadd Navigation, to demonstrate on that brick edifice that his prowess at emitting wind was no fluke.

Uncle Teddy had done his bit at last. He had given Ezra a job, at his import/export business in Sheffield. His father didn't get home till half-past six, so Henry often got his own tea. On this particular day he chose a tin of baked beans on toast, followed by a tin of baked beans not on toast.

He walked up Paradise Lane, along the footpath, through the gate onto the towpath, and along the towpath towards the bridge. It was a clear evening, and there wasn't a breath of wind. He regarded this as a bad omen.

The bridge over the canal was attractive, with the shallow

curve of the towpath at either side perfectly proportioned. Only five things marred its simple, functional beauty. Tommy Marsden, Martin Hammond, Chalky White, Billy Erpingham and Ian Lowson. They stood in line on the top of the bridge. Immobile. Stern. Ruthless. The Paradise Lane Gang.

Henry climbed slowly up the towpath to the top of the bridge. He took up his position, slightly bent over. He strained. Come on, beans. Do thy stuff, he implored. He strained again. A tiny, barely audible, semi-asthmatic wheeze dribbled from his backside.

They threw him into the Rundle and Gadd Navigation. It wasn't the last canal into which he would fall, but it was undoubtedly the most bruising to his ego.

6 Pratt Goes West

Another September. Another beginning. Henry got off the Thurmarsh tram at the stop before the terminus. The grammar school was in Link Lane, next to the fire station.

Boys were converging on the school from all sides, in black blazers and black-and-yellow-striped ties. The new boys stood out among the scruffy stream like barristers in a public bar.

The school building was long, brick, many-windowed, uninspired but also unforbidding. He was looking for Martin Hammond, but found only Norbert Cuffley. Although he didn't want to be seen as an ally of such an outrageous goody, they clung together in that vast strangeness.

He caught sight of Martin Hammond in the school hall. The boys sat in rows, with the younger boys at the front. The masters filed in, and sat facing the boys. The hubbub subsided, and the headmaster, Mr E. F. Crowther, entered.

They stood and sang a hymn. They sat and the headmaster intoned a prayer. Henry also noticed Milner and Trellis from Brunswick Road. He was surprised to find that he was feeling quite excited.

Mr E. F. Crowther addressed the school. Mr Quell stifled a yawn.

'Welcome back, old boys. Welcome to Thurmarsh Grammar, new boys,' began Mr E. F. Crowther. 'You see before you our staff, as fine as body of men as can be found. . .in this building.'

Mr Crosby had heard this joke twenty times before, but he still laughed exaggeratedly at it.

'Thurmarsh. It is not perhaps a name that resounds throughout the educational world. It is not an Eton or a Harrow. But is it any the worse for that?' Mr E. F. Crowther paused, as if defying some miserable urchin to say 'yes'. Nobody did. Nobody ever had. 'I am proud to be headmaster of Thurmarsh Grammar,' he continued at last. 'Perhaps I am biased, because I am Thurmarsh born and Thurmarsh bred.'

'And Thurmarsh bread is very nice when it's fresh,' whispered Henry to Norbert Cuffley. He hadn't expected to say it. It just came to him. He was a budding humorist, an emerging character, and he felt exhilarated. Besides, it terrified Norbert Cuffley.

The headmaster paused, and looked in his direction. Careful, Henry.

'In the great war that has strained the civilised world almost to breaking point,' resumed Mr E. F. Crowther, 'Old Thurmarshians have been up there beside Old Etonians and Old Harrovians. I am sure that in the battle to rebuild our nation and take up once again our rightful place in the forefront of history, there will once again be Thurmarshians in the van.'

'The bread van,' whispered Henry.

The headmaster turned towards him.

'Did somebody speak?' he asked.

Oh, miserable and aptly-named Pratt.

'Who spoke?' thundered the headmaster.

The room resounded to the loud silence of six hundred boys. You could have heard an earwig breathe.

'The whole school will stay in for one hour, unless somebody owns up,' said Mr E. F. Crowther.

'It were me, sir,' said Henry in a small voice.

'Stand up,' commanded Mr E. F. Crowther.

Henry stood up.

'Who are you?' said Mr E. F. Crowther.

'Pratt, sir.'

There was laughter.

'Silence,' said Mr E. F. Crowther. 'There is nothing funny about a boy's name. People who find names funny are puerile. You're new, aren't you, Pratt?'

'Yes, sir.'

'You have passed your eleven plus, and are therefore considered fit to come here rather than fester away in a secondary modern school,' said Mr E. F. Crowther. 'Allow us to share the epigrammatical delight of your secret discourse, Pratt, and help us to judge whether we find you fit.'

'Sir?'

'What did you say?'

His mind was a blank. He could think of nothing except the truth.

'The bread van, sir.'

'The bread van, Pratt?'

'Yes, sir. Tha said tha hoped there'd be Thurmarshians in the van. I said "the bread van".'

'Are you related to Oscar Wilde, by any chance, Pratt?'

'No, sir.'

'I thought not. You're an imbecile, Pratt. What are you?'

'An imbecile, sir.'

'You will come and see me in my study after school.'

'Yes, sir.'

The headmaster resumed his address. Everyone would be sorry to hear that Mr Budge had suffered a stroke. Extensive repairs had been carried out in the boiler room. They could face the winter with more confidence.

At Brunswick Road, all Henry's lessons had been taken by Mr Gibbins. At Thurmarsh Grammar his development was entrusted to several teachers, and much of the first day was spent in finding their classrooms and taking part in roll-calls.

His first lesson was given by Mr Quell, his form master, who would teach him English. Mr Quell was five foot five tall, large-framed and barrel-chested, and he had an absolutely square-topped head. He gave the impression of being quite a tough man, yet he looked at Henry with something approaching awe.

The boys in Henry's class were Astbury, Blake, Burgess, Crane, Cuffley, Dakins, Elmhurst, Hammond, Harrison, Huntley, Ibbotson, Jones, Larkins, Longfellow, Milner, Norris, Oberath, Openshaw, Pratt, Prziborski, Quayle, Smith, Stoner, Taylor, Tunnicliffe, Turner, Weston, Wilkinson, Wool and Yarnold.

After the day's chaotic activities were over, and a relatively ordered basis for the future had been established, Henry made his way uneasily towards the headmaster's study.

'Good luck, bread van,' said a senior boy, whom he met in the corridor.

He knocked.

'Come in,' said Mr E. F. Crowther.

He entered.

Mr E. F. Crowther sat behind a large desk on which there were several piles of papers arranged on spikes. His study was airy. The walls were liberally festooned with rosters and graphs. The room stated, 'Things get done here. We are plain, practical men, concerned with achievement, not pretension.'

'Good afternoon, Pratt,' said Mr E. F. Crowther.

'Good afternoon, sir,' said Henry.

'Thought up any more little gems, Pratt?'

'No, sir.'

'A pity. I've had a hard day. I was looking forward to being entertained.'

Mr E. F. Crowther picked up his cane, then let it fall onto the top of his desk.

'Can you furnish me with any arguments that might persuade me not to cane you, Pratt' he enquired.

'Yes, sir.'

The headmaster raised his eyebrows in eloquent surprise.

'Then do so.'

'I were excited, sir.'

'It's "I was excited," Pratt. You'll have to learn to speak grammatically here. After all, it is the grammar school.'

'I *was* excited, sir.'

'Why?'

'Coming to Thurmarsh Grammar, sir.'

Mr E. F. Crowther gave Henry a searching glance. He prided himself on his searching glances. Sometimes, he was so keen on making sure that his glance was searching that he forgot to look for the thing for which he was searching.

'I must warn you that I have the sole franchise for all sarcasm uttered between these four walls,' he said.

'Please, sir?'

'Are you seriously telling me that you said "the bread van" because you were excited about coming to Thurmarsh Grammar?'

'Yes, sir.'

Mr E. F. Crowther leant back in his chair. Behind him, a hazy autumn sun shone. There was a beam of dust in the air.

'Explain,' he said.

'Well, sir, I didn't like it that much at Brunswick Road because it were. . .it *was* mainly Reading, Writing and Arithmetic, with just a bit of Geography and that. I were. . .I *was* looking forward to learning all the different subjects, like, like History and French and that, and with seeing all the older boys and everything, I thought about everything I was going to learn and how after I left school I might get on in t' world and be summat, and I felt like my life was just starting at last, and I gor over-excited, sir. I'm only eleven.'

The headmaster stared at Henry with his mouth slightly open.

'Try to stay excited,' he said, 'but try not to get so carried away with your enthusiasm that you say "the bread van" while I'm talking. Run along now.'

'Yes, sir. Thank you, sir.'

Martin Hammond was waiting for him outside. He was astounded when he heard that Henry hadn't had the cane.

'I never wanted to throw thee out of t' gang,' said Martin Hammond. 'It were Tommy and Billy and Chalky and Ian. There was nowt I could do, not on me own.'

The Rawlaston tram was only half full. Most of the children had gone home, and the evening rush-hour had not yet started.

The tram dropped into the Rundle Valley, and swung round to the right, running alongside the canal for about a hundred yards. Then the cul-de-sacs began and they saw them waiting at the bus stop. Tommy Marsden. Ian Lowson. Billy Erpingham. Chalky White. Four boys who had not passed the eleven plus. On another day, the results might have been different, and the tramp ships of their lives might have been sent to different ports. But they hadn't, and now they stood facing each other, two grammar-school boys and four secondary-school boys.

'Art tha coming out tonight?' said Tommy Marsden. 'Well, we're all still members of t' gang, aren't we? Tha's not turned snotty-nosed just cos tha's gone to grammar school, has tha?'

'Course not,' said Martin Hammond.

'I was never made a proper member any road,' said Henry.

'We'll make thee a full member on Saturday,' said Tommy Marsden.

'I can't,' said Henry. 'I'm going t' match.'

'At six o clock,' said Tommy Marsden. 'After t' match. On t' waste ground. Be there.'

The match was against Accrington Stanley, in the Third Division North. This time Henry was excited by the crowd of flat-capped men and boys pouring up Blonk Lane. He felt six inches taller as he went through the juveniles' entrance and rejoined Ezra inside the ground.

The boys were handed to the front row over the heads of the good-natured crowd.

There was a cheer from the sizeable contingent of Stanleyites when the visitors emerged, but it was nothing compared to the roar that greeted the Reds. Eleven giants in their red shirts and long white shorts. Rawlings: Thong, Ibbotson: Salter, Cedarwood, Smailes: Ellison, Bunce, Gravel, Thompson and Hatch.

The Reds attacked from the start. The Peel Park men, who were wearing yellow due to a clash of colours, were pinned into their own half for long periods. There were cries of 'Windy' when they made back passes. BUNCE put the Reds into the lead in the twenty-third minute following a sinuous dribble by Hatch. In the eighty-third minute, the ubiquitous SMAILES popped up by the far post, to head a second for the home team. Unfortunately, by that time the visitors had scored three times in breakaways.

It took a long while to get back to Thurmarsh, and by the time they got there the 'Green 'Un' had already been published. They read about the match they'd just seen. 'The visitors were lucky to be on level terms at the interval,' opined the writer. 'When the Reds took the lead through the medium of young BUNCE, the cheers could have been heard as far away as Rotherham. The 13,671 crowd enjoyed the fast and furious exchanges. There was no question of cotton wool and swaddling clothes for these boys.' 13,671, thought Henry. That included me. Without me it would have been 13,670. I'm mentioned in the paper. It cheered him up a little, but not much. They had lost, unfairly. They had been robbed. Life wasn't worth living. And he dreaded his initiation into the Paradise Lane Gang.

He wandered over to the waste ground in his scuffed shoes with soles flapping loose, socks full of holes, torn trousers, torn shirt, and heavily-stained pullover.

There, on the waste ground, stood Tommy Marsden, Chalky White, Billy Erpingham and Ian Lowson. For an awful moment, he thought that Martin, his one ally, was going to let him down. But then Martin came, slowly, owlishly, reluctantly.

The sun was a pale orb, still just visible through the returning mist.

Tommy Marsden got out a penknife, such as Henry's father might have made, in his palmier days. He flicked one of its two blades open. There were crinkles in his black hair, and when he smiled he showed long, irregular teeth.

Henry stood with the river on his left and the canal on his right, facing the other five, who all looked very solemn.

'Members of t' Paradise Lane Gang,' said Tommy Marsden. 'Be silent for t' president, me. Does anybody know owt why Henry Pratt should not be elected a member of the Paradise Lane Gang?'

Nobody spoke.

A train steamed past, invisible in the thickening mist.

'Hold out thy left hand,' commanded Tommy Marsden.

Henry held out his left hand.

Tommy Marsden advanced, holding out the knife in front of him.

Henry closed his eyes. Don't shake, hand. Don't faint, body. It's up to thee. There's nowt I can do.

'Full name?' said Tommy Marsden.

'Henry Ezra Pratt.'

'Age?'

'Eleven.'

'Say after me. I, Henry Ezra Pratt. . .'

'I, Henry Ezra Pratt. . .'

'Of this parish. . .'

'Of this parish. . .'

'Do agree. . .'

'Do agree. . .'

'To obey all t' rules of t' Paradise Lane Gang.'

'To obey all t' rules of t' Paradise Lane Gang.'

'I now make t' cross of t' Paradise Lane Gang on thy left hand,' said Tommy Marsden.

Henry felt a searing pain in his left hand. It seemed to shoot right up his arm.

Then the pain came again.

He felt unsteady. He opened his eyes. Blood was trickling down his hand from the two incisions. He felt faint. He willed himself not to faint.

'I, Thomas John Marsden, welcome thee,' said Tommy Marsden, shaking Henry's right hand.

'Thanks,' said Henry, holding his left hand out stiffly, with the palm turned up, so that the blood wouldn't flow.

Ian Lowson came forward.

'I, Ian Sidney Lowson, welcome thee,' he said, shaking Henry's hand.

Martin Hammond came forward.

'I, Martin Ronald Hammond, welcome thee,' he said.

Henry shook his hand.

In the distance, trucks were being shunted. The noise was resonant in the fog.

Chalky White came forward.

'I, Benjamin Disraeli Gladstone White, welcome thee,' he said, grinning sheepishly.

Billy Erpingham came forward.

'I, Billy Erpingham, welcome thee,' he said.

Henry had achieved what he had wanted for so long. He was a member of the Paradise Lane Gang.

He no longer wanted it.

He woke up at three o'clock the next morning. His hand was throbbing.

His father was screaming. He rushed into his father's room.

'Wake up, dad,' he shouted.

His father sat up with a start. His ill-fitting dentures were in a glass at the side of the bed. With his empty mouth he looked hollow and ill and far older than his forty years. Both Henry's grandmothers had died during June. It had added to his father's gathering gloom.

'What is it?' said Ezra.

'Tha were screaming,' said Henry.

Sweat was pouring off Ezra's face.

124

'I had a nightmare,' he said. 'I were dreaming about t' war.'

'Were they trying to kill thee?' said Henry.

'Nay,' said Ezra. 'It were all the ones what I killed, coming back to haunt me.'

'How many Germans did tha kill, dad?'

'I don't know. Tha never knows, tha knows. Leastways, not in t' artillery. Tha fires in t' general direction of 'em, like, and that's about it.'

Henry had to strain to hear what his father was saying, without his teeth in.

'It were their faces. It were their faces, Henry.'

Henry felt a tingle of horror. He didn't want to know what their faces were like, and yet he did.

'I didn't recognise them at first,' said Ezra. 'Then it came to me who they were.'

'Who were they, dad?'

'Rawlings: Thong, Ibbotson: Salter, Cedarwood, Smailes: Ellison, Bunce, Gravel, Thompson and Hatch.'

One never-to-be-forgotten evening, at the beginning of October, 1946, two events occurred. One of them marked the end of an era. The other, although Henry didn't recognise this at the time, marked the start of what was quite soon to become the beginning of an era.

The evening began with the end of an era, and ended with the start of the beginning of an era.

Henry and Martin had been leading a double life. By day, studious young citizens, beginning to unravel the mysteries of Latin, French, Geometry, Physics, Chemistry, Geography and History. By night, members of the Paradise Lane Gang.

Their activities were relatively innocent.

They went to the pictures, to see Gary Cooper and Franchot Tone in *The Lives of a Bengal Lancer*, and by means of those who had already gone in coming out and handing tickets to the others in the lav, they managed to get the six of them in on three tickets. The cinema was still a novel, exciting experience to Henry, and he wished that he could enjoy the film and forget about manking about.

They sat in different parts of a tram and all pretended to be Polish refugees who didn't understand English, thus driving the conductor into a frenzy.

They went to see Thurmarsh United play Gateshead. The Reds won 4–1, over-running the Redheugh Park side with goals by GRAVEL (2), BUNCE and HATCH. After the match, they locked themselves into the gents and waited there for over an hour, and then they went out and played on the pitch. Henry went in goal. He was actually between the posts, in the Blonk Lane stadium, with shots being rained at him from all angles. He even saved two (both from Martin). Then men came running after them and they scattered to all parts of the ground, shinning up walls and managing to get everybody out of the ground safely, except Henry. A phrase that he had read came to him in the nick of time and he said, 'We just wanted to play on t' sacred turf,' and the man let him go with just a gentle clip round the ear-hole.

Then came that October evening. The end of an era. The final act in the saga of the Paradise Lane Gang.

They met on the waste ground as usual. Tommy Marsden led them over the river, over the railway and into the rows of semi-detached houses that wound up and over the hills, as far as the eye could see. He led them to a small row of shops – a grocer's, a greengrocer's, a butcher's, a newsagent's and a little sub-post office. Opposite them was a trolley-bus terminus, and here there was a tiny public garden. It was almost completely dark, the garden was deserted, and there was no trolley-bus due for thirty-five minutes. Street lighting was dim. Tommy Marsden got out a catapult, and asked Martin Hammond to break one of the shop windows. Martin refused, unless Tommy Marsden did so first. Tommy Marsden promptly catapulted a stone and shattered the butcher's window, sending glass splintering all over the empty slab. They ran away by different routes, silently, with orders to meet up again on the waste ground. They did meet up on the waste ground. Tommy Marsden told Martin Hammond that it was his turn next. Martin Hammond refused.

'We never broke windows before,' he said.

'We were nobbut kids,' said Tommy Marsden.

'Knocking on doors and running away, fair enough,' said

Martin Hammond.

'Kids' stuff,' said Tommy Marsden. 'Even breaking windows is kids' stuff really.'

'What isn't kids' stuff?' said Henry.

'Stealing,' said Tommy Marsden.

There was a brief silence.

'I'm not stealing,' said Martin Hammond, chucking a stone into the canal in a gentle parabola.

'Bloody nesh grammar-school cissy,' said Tommy Marsden.

'That's right,' said Billy Erpingham.

'Bloody stuck-up, snotty-nosed snob,' said Chalky White.

'That's right,' said Billy Erpingham.

'Henry,' said Tommy Marsden. 'Tha's t' newest member. Thursday, bring us stolen bread, jam and apples for us tea. And I need a watch.'

'I'm not stealing either,' said Henry.

Tommy Marsden grabbed his arm and twisted it.

'Tha promised to obey,' he said.

'Give over, Tommy,' said Ian Lowson. 'Let him be.'

'Tha promised to obey,' said Tommy Marsden.

'So did everybody else,' said Henry.

'No, they didn't,' said Tommy Marsden. 'We never had no initiation ceremonies before.'

'It's just a put-up job,' said Henry. 'It's not our fault we've gone to t' grammar school.'

'That's right,' said Billy Erpingham.

Henry kicked Tommy Marsden, and suddenly it was all flying fists and boots. Henry and Martin had no chance. They were outnumbered two to one, even though they suspected that neither Ian Lowson nor Chalky White felt particularly vicious towards them, and Billy Erpingham only did what he did because he always did what Tommy Marsden did.

Henry flailed and pummelled and scratched. He received one tremendous blow on the nose, which started to bleed. He only got in one decent blow himself. Unfortunately, it was on Martin Hammond. Boots crashed against his knees and back. An elbow thudded into his private parts with squelching venom. His ears rang. He could hardly breathe. Blood was pouring from his nose.

'Give up?' said Tommy Marsden.

'No,' he shrieked, desperate to give up, but unable to.

All six of them were writhing in the mud. He was pinned beneath the heap, trapped, dying, getting smaller and smaller and falling, falling, falling into the arms of death. He heard Tommy Marsden, a million miles away, say 'Give up?', almost beseeching them to surrender, but he couldn't have said 'yes' if he'd wanted to.

Then the heap just rolled slowly over and lay panting all around him, and he slowly came back to life and managed to roll over onto his back so that his nose wouldn't bleed so much.

Chalky White was being sick into the canal, having been inadvertently punched in the stomach by Tommy Marsden. Martin was gasping for breath. Billy Erpingham and Ian Lowson sat calmly, waiting for their leader to speak.

'That's that,' said Tommy Marsden.

They limped to their various homes in the cul-de-sac. The Paradise Lane Gang had met for the last time. An era had ended.

The start of the beginning of an era (although he didn't recognise it as such at the time) occurred when he got home.

A man sat slumped at a kitchen table in a decaying back-to-back terrace in south Yorkshire. He had a quarter-full bottle of whisky in his hands. His speech was slurred. A boy entered the room and collapsed into the other chair at the table. His lips were puffed up, there were cuts on his face and arms and legs. His clothes hung in tatters. Bruises were breaking out all over him. He held a grubby, scarlet-speckled handkerchief to his nose. His face was deathly pale. Every now and then he gave a rasping cough and winced.

'Bastard,' said the man. 'Bastard. Bastard sacked me. Bastard. Own wife's sister's husband. Absenteeism. "I've been badly," I said. "Badly?" he said. "Hangovers more like." "That's a bloody lie," I said. Told me I can't handle heavy loads. "Nor would tha," I said. "Nor would tha if tha'd been marching through bloody desert day after day, fighting t' might of Rommel's army, instead of getting thisen rich on bloody black-market Australian minced loaf." Bastard.'

The man seemed to grow dimly aware that all was not well with the boy.

'Hast tha been drinking?' he said. 'Bloody hell. Have a drop o' this.'

The man pushed the bottle across the table towards the boy. The boy took it, as in a dream, and put it to his lips.

The boy thought his life had ended. He choked and gasped and spluttered and pushed the bottle back to the man.

'Bastard,' said the man. 'Bastard sacked me. Bastard.'

'I want to discuss your essay with you, Pratt,' said Mr Quell, who was Irish, and a lapsed priest. 'Come and see me afterwards.'

After the lesson, Henry went up to Mr Quell's desk. Mr Quell raised his glasses so that they rested on the top of his massive forehead, and looked at Henry quizzically.

'It's Henry, isn't it?'

'Yes, sir.'

'Let's go and sit down and look through your essay a bit,' said Mr Quell.

Mr Quell sat in Mick Tunnicliffe's desk. Henry sat in Stefan Prziborski's desk, and was tempted to pretend he was Prziborski. He envied Prziborski deeply. At first everyone had laughed at Prziborski, like they laughed at Oberath, because they had foreign names. Unlike Oberath, whose German name and sullen disposition condemned him to endless torment, Prziborski soon won popularity by his skill on the football field. It wasn't fair. Henry loved football, and went to every home game at Blonk Lane, but he was hopeless at it. He concealed the fact that this grieved him deeply, by laughing at himself before everyone laughed at him. 'I reckon I know what it is I lack,' he said. 'Skill, control, strength, accuracy and speed,' or 'At least I'm not one-footed like some folk. I'm no-footed.' All this flashed through his mind as he sat in the desk of the great Prziborski.

'You're a bit of a comedian, aren't you?' said Mr Quell. 'I hear glowing reports of the Welsh grocer.'

Henry blushed. It was quite true. He had blossomed at Thurmarsh Grammar into a budding little comic. Partly it was the good start that he had got off to with the bread van incident. Partly it was because he was enjoying school life more than home life since his father had been sacked by Uncle Teddy. Pupils at Rowth Bridge Village School or Brunswick Road Primary School would have been astounded to see him standing at his desk, if a master was slightly late, and entertaining his class-mates with his dazzling impressions of a grocer from Abergavenny. 'Biscuits indeed to goodness I do have, isn't it? I do have cream crackers, custard creams, digestives, assorted, broken assorted and dog indeed to goodness yes. Dog, is it, Mrs Jones, the wet fish? I didn't know you had a dog, isn't it? Oh, you don't. It's for Mr Jones, the wet fish.' Suddenly, the grocer from Abergavenny didn't seem the most hilarious thing in the world, now that he knew that Mr Quell knew of it.

' "The best day of my holidays," ' said Mr Quell. 'So many boys chose Christmas. You strove for more originality than that.'

'I didn't have a very good Christmas, sir.'

They had gone to Cousin Hilda's again. 'You must come to us next year. I insist,' Auntie Doris had said. It had been exactly the same as the previous Christmas, with the single, dramatic exception that neither of Cousin Hilda's friend's stockings had laddered. Once again, his father had been on his best behaviour. Cousin Hilda had taken Henry into the scullery and asked searching questions about life at home. He had lied in his teeth to save his father. Why? Why why why?

'You didn't choose New Year's Day either,' said Mr Quell.

Children in the mining villages had been given parties to celebrate the nationalisation of the mines. But Henry didn't live in a mining village. 1946 had seen the nationalisation of the mines, the Bank of England, Cable and Wireless and civil aviation. It had seen the passing of the National Insurance Act, the National Injuries Act and National Health Act. It had been the most momentous year in British domestic history. That was what Reg Hammond said, any road.

'Your day begins quite badly. You haven't slept well. Your father has had nightmares. You're tired. You break a plate getting breakfast,' said Mr Quell. 'So how is this to be "the best day of the holidays"? I am intrigued. I read on out of curiosity, not duty. That is rare, Henry.'

'Thank you, sir.'

'You seem to spend a great deal of the day reading.'

'I like reading, sir.'

'You don't have a wireless?'

'No, sir.'

Two momentous events had occurred concerning the wireless. 'Dick Barton, Special Agent' had begun, and had proved to be the best ever wireless programme ever in the history of the universe, and his father had sold the wireless.

'You read for three hours, pausing only to say "Oh. Goodbye." That is to your father?'

'Yes, sir.'

'Where was he going?'

'Don't know, sir.'

'The pub?'

'Don't know, sir.'

'All right. So you get the dinner. Your father comes back?'

'Yes, sir.'

'More reading ensues. You're having a simply rivetting day. You get the tea. You wash up. What about your father?'

'His nerves are bad. It's best if I do it.'

'Then you read again.'

Sometimes Henry went to Martin Hammond's and listened to Dick Barton there, but he hadn't put that in the essay.

'Yes, sir.'

'You go to bed. You hear your father come in. We may safely deduce then that he had gone out again?'

'Yes, sir.'

'Where to?'

'Don't know, sir.'

'The pub?'

'Don't know, sir.'

'You lie in bed. Your father comes upstairs, and tells you that he's been fighting a villainous plot to overthrow the government and kill the king. And your adventure begins. You go out with your father and help him save the nation and bring the villainous thugs to heel.'

'Yes, sir.'

'And this dream that you have, this fantasy that you have, in

131

which your father is a hero, this is what makes this "the best day of the holidays"?'

'Yes, sir.'

'It's imaginative. It's different. It's good. Do you have any other relatives?'

Mr Quell took him to see Uncle Teddy and Auntie Doris. Henry couldn't remember the way, but Mr Quell looked up their address in the phone book.

Mr Quell showed Uncle Teddy and Auntie Doris the essay. Then he talked to Uncle Teddy, while Auntie Doris took Henry into the kitchen and made a pot of tea. Auntie Doris cried a bit. Henry wished she wouldn't, in case it made him cry, and quite soon she stopped.

Henry carried the tray in. Uncle Teddy opted for whisky, and attempted to prevail on Mr Quell to join him, but Mr Quell declined, expressing a preference for tea 'under the circumstances'.

'Is there anywhere else he can go?' said Mr Quell, looking round the well-appointed living room.

'We'll have him, won't we, Teddy?' said Auntie Doris. 'Of course we will.'

Uncle Teddy looked at Auntie Doris, then at Henry, then at Mr Quell, then at his whisky, then at Auntie Doris again. Henry found it impossible to tell what he was thinking.

'He obviously can't stay at home. That's the first thing,' said Uncle Teddy. 'And nobody could live with the sniffer.'

'You shouldn't call her the sniffer in front of the boy, and she hasn't got room anyway,' said Auntie Doris.

'Of course we'll have him,' said Uncle Teddy. 'There isn't anywhere else.'

'Don't make it sound like a last resort,' said Auntie Doris, who always made things worse by protesting about them. 'We'll have him because we want him.'

Henry wanted to cry. He didn't want to live with Uncle Teddy and Auntie Doris. Once again his destination was being discussed as if he were a parcel. It wasn't fair. Sometimes eleven seemed so grown-up, compared to all his past life. Then suddenly it was almost a babyish age, compared with all the growing up he still had

132

to do.

Uncle Teddy drove them to Paradise Lane. They made a detour to pick up Cousin Hilda.

'If we don't involve her, there'll be ructions,' said Uncle Teddy.

'I can understand that,' said Mr Quell. 'I was born into a family myself.'

They drove through the centre of Sheffield. The cinema queues were hunched into their coats against the rising January wind.

Uncle Teddy drove under the Wicker Arches, and up out of the Don Valley on the long Thurmarsh road. He was weaving inside and outside the trams in expert fashion.

In the back, Auntie Doris put an arm round Henry until she realised that he didn't want it. She withdrew the arm a bit at a time, as if hoping that Henry wouldn't notice that she was being forced to do it.

They dropped down into the smoking, glowing heavy industry of the Rundle Valley. A left turn would have taken them to Rawlaston and the Barnsley road. A right turn would have taken them to Paradise Lane. But Uncle Teddy drove straight on up the hill towards Thurmarsh.

'Are you a reading man, sir?' asked Mr Quell.

'I like a good book,' said Uncle Teddy.

'The boy has the spark,' said Mr Quell. 'He definitely has the spark. Yes, sir. Henry Pratt is a young man who can make you feel proud of him. Do you think it will snow?'

Uncle Teddy went into number 66 Park View Road and emerged a few minutes later with Cousin Hilda. Her face was grave.

'Well well well,' she said, and sniffed. On this occasion her disapproval was for herself. 'I've been remiss. But my businessmen take up so much of my time.'

Uncle Teddy drove even faster, now that Cousin Hilda was in the car, because he knew it frightened her. She had once accompanied them, on an outing, when Henry was two. She had kept up a stream of propaganda, aimed at Uncle Teddy, in the guise of a running commentary, aimed at Henry. 'Uncle Teddy'll slow down in a minute, because of the corner.' 'Watch Uncle Teddy put on the brakes, in case that car pulls out.' She could hardly do that now.

The car was spacious. There was no squeeze, even with three of them in the back.

'You have a pleasant prospect overlooking the park,' Mr Quell told Cousin Hilda, turning his huge, square-topped head.

They all fell silent as they approached Paradise Lane. Uncle Teddy drove very slowly over the cobbles.

The little terrace house was empty. The fire in the range was low. Its heat made little impression on the icy air. Mr Quell went down into the cellar and fetched more coal.

'Where'll he be, Henry?' said Uncle Teddy.

'Don't know,' said Henry.

'In the pub?'

'Don't know.'

'Which pub does he use?'

'He uses t' Navigation a bit, but he doesn't stay long. He goes up t' hill mainly. There's t' Pineapple and two or three others. Try t' Tennants houses first.'

Mr Quell and Uncle Teddy set off in search of Ezra.

Cousin Hilda made a pot of tea. 'It's mashing,' she announced, and sighed and sniffed at the same time. 'I've failed you, Henry,' she said. 'I were satisfied with the answers you gave, because I wanted to be satisfied. I pretended everything were all right. And I call myself a Christian.'

'We had no idea anything like this was going on,' said Auntie Doris. 'The state of the place. Poor boy.'

'He were all right till Uncle Teddy sacked him,' said Henry.

'Uncle Teddy offered him a job out of the goodness of his heart,' said Auntie Doris. 'He had no need to. He kept him on as long as he possibly could. But he runs a business, not a charity. Your father didn't help himself either, the things he said about your Uncle Teddy's war effort.'

Cousin Hilda sniffed.

'What's that supposed to mean?' said Auntie Doris.

'What?' said Cousin Hilda.

'That sniff,' said Auntie Doris. 'I distinctly heard you sniff.'

'I were breathing,' said Cousin Hilda, flushing blotchily. 'I'll try not to do it in future, if it upsets you.'

'You were insinuating that Teddy wasn't ready to do his bit,' said Auntie Doris. 'You were insinuating that his flat feet were a fraud.'

'There's lots I could say,' said Cousin Hilda. 'I could make some comment about guilty consciences. But I won't. I'll hold my tongue. I've been un-Christian enough already.'

Mr Quell and Uncle Teddy returned empty-handed.

'I need the smallest room in the house,' said Uncle Teddy. 'Where is it?'

"Ti'n't in t' house for a kick-off,' said Henry, fetching the torch. 'Tha goes up t' entry two doors away into t' yard. Ours is t' second one on t' left, beyond t' midden.'

Uncle Teddy shook his head, as if amazed that people could choose to live like that, as if he really believed that they did choose it. Then he put on the overcoat which he had just taken off, and set off into the street.

'It's starting to snow,' said Mr Quell. 'Do you think it's the harbinger of prolonged severe weather?'

Cousin Hilda smiled at Henry.

'I'll come and build a snowman with you, if it is,' she said.

Uncle Teddy came back in, very slowly. His face was white. He forgot to switch the torch off.

'What's the matter, Teddy?' said Auntie Doris. 'You look as if you've seen a ghost.'

'Switch the torch off,' said Cousin Hilda. 'There's no point in wasting batteries.'

'I've found him,' said Uncle Teddy. 'He's in the toilet. He's dead.'

The snow began in earnest that night, and Henry began his life at Cap Ferrat, the home of Uncle Teddy and Auntie Doris, in Wharfedale Road, in the salubrious western suburbs of Sheffield, among the foothills of the Pennines.

It was a substantial stone house, built in 1930. It had charmingly irregular gables, and to the right of the porch there was a tall, narrow window, in pale imitation of the high windows of a baronial hall.

In the morning, waking up in a sizeable bedroom, he couldn't think where he was. Then it all came back to him. His father was dead. Life stretched bleakly ahead of him. There was no point in getting up.

School! He got out of bed automatically. It was nice to feel a fitted carpet beneath your feet. If life was going to be bleak and awful, it might just as well be bleak and awful with fitted carpets.

He pulled back the curtains and gazed open-mouthed at a wonderland of white. The branches of huge trees sagged with the snow. It lay piled on the roofs of the substantial houses that rose and fell with the pleasant white hills. It was impossible to tell where lawns ended and flower beds began, and there would certainly be no school that day.

How could he be excited? His father had died. His poor, sick father had collapsed and expired in the outside lavatory they shared with number 25. And he had betrayed his father in his essay. One week more, and there would have been no need to betray him.

He didn't want to live with Uncle Teddy and Auntie Doris. His brain seized up totally in their presence. But there was no point in pretending that he disliked their bathroom. Soaking in the luxurious, fitted bath, with his face flannel lying beside the pumice stone on the rack that fitted onto the bath, it was impossible not to feel that this was the life. Not one inside lavatory, but two. He resented Uncle Teddy and Auntie Doris, of course. It was outrageous that some people should have two inside lavatories, one upstairs and one downstairs, while others had none. That was what Reg Hammond said, any road. But if you happened to live in a house with them, why not use them? Henry used them alternately, because they were there.

They gave him a wireless of his very own! It was one thing to resent Uncle Teddy and Auntie Doris and their eccentric life-style – they had dinner in the evening, and a meal called lunch at one o'clock. But, if you were there, you might as well enjoy the good food, the fitted carpets, the comfortable armchairs and settee, the view over the snowy garden through the French windows, the steaming baths, the luxurious lavatories, the bedroom which made such a deeply satisfying womb. A womb with patterned curtains, in russet and olive-green, a darker green carpet, a wardrobe, a chest of drawers, a reproduction of 'The Hay Wain'. A womb with a view.

One night Henry had a dream, in which a naked Lorna Arrow – he couldn't remember her body, when he woke up, but he remembered she was naked – said, 'Which do you prefer – your father or ninety-three thousand miles of fitted carpet?' And he didn't know the answer! He woke up all clammy and disorientatedly uneasy and not quite fitting the inside of his head. It was true, even when awake. He didn't know the answer. He had tried to be loyal to his father, and, until just before the end, he had been. But he'd never really liked him. He'd always been frightened of him. He'd spent several formative years apart from him. It was very difficult to feel any grief. Normal children grieved for their father. He didn't. Therefore he wasn't normal. Q.E.D.

At first he didn't go to school because of the snows. It was a long way to Thurmarsh Grammar, and the country was almost paralysed by the snow. Then came his mumps. By the time he was better, it was close to the end of term, the nation was facing a severe fuel crisis, the boilers at Thurmarsh Grammar had finally packed up completely, and there was no point in going back that term.

He read books about children who went sailing, children who went camping, children who went riding, and they were all good eggs. He read books about otters that talked, foxes that talked and birds that talked. They were all pretty good eggs too. Henry wished that he was a good egg, but if you weren't a good egg, the next best thing was to read about good eggs.

And his wireless poured forth its magic. 'Much-Binding-In-The-Marsh', in which people said 'Was there something?' and 'Not a word to Bessie' and 'When I was in Sidi Barrani', and everybody laughed. Henry wished he had a catch phrase. There was 'Ignorance Is Bliss' with Harold Berens and Gladys Hay. He could follow Dick Barton at last. There was Michael Miles in 'Radio Forfeits'. International boxing brought him Jackie Paterson v Cliff Anderson and Freddie Mills v Willi Quentemeyer. F. N. S. Creek gave hints about lacrosse. They might come in handy one day, or they might not, what did it matter? There was a new serial called 'Bunkle Butts In' on 'Children's

Hour'. Who needed real-life friends?

Henry did. Soon the summer term would begin, and he would see Martin Hammond again, and Stefan Prziborski. The thaws came, and with them the floods. The floods eased, and it was spring, and he couldn't wait to go back to school.

7 Oiky

'Oi. Oiky,' yelled Tubman-Edwards.

Henry turned and thumped Tubman-Edwards on the side of the head.

Tubman-Edwards knocked him flat.

'I thought you oiks could fight,' said Tubman-Edwards, walking away, but Henry was unconscious and didn't hear him.

When Henry came round, he couldn't remember where he was. It seemed to be becoming a frequent experience. What were these playing fields among the pine woods and rhododendrons? What was that large, brooding, ivy-covered mansion?

It came back to him with a thud only marginally less sickening than that dealt out by Tubman-Edwards. He was lying on the playing fields of Brasenose College, a preparatory school for boys, so named by its palindromic headmaster, Mr A. B. Noon B.A., in the hope that some of the educational glitter of the Oxford College of the same name would adhere to his crumbling pile among the rhododendrons (rhododendra? Mr Noon was nothing if not a pedant).

Mr A. B. Noon B.A. was approaching now, accompanied by his equally palindromic twin daughters, Hannah and Eve, who ran a riding school in Bagshot.

'What are you doing lying on the ground, laddie?' said Mr Noon, peering down at Henry.

'Nothing, sir,' said Henry.

'Splendid,' said Mr Noon. 'You evaded my little trap.'

Henry struggled to his feet. He felt dizzy and his legs were rubbery. He had no idea what little trap he had evaded. Luckily, Mr Noon explained to his daughters.

'I didn't ask him why he was on the ground,' said Mr Noon. 'I asked him what he was doing on the ground. He understood my question and replied, "Nothing". I have every reason to believe that he was speaking the truth.'

'Is he all right?' asked Eve anxiously.

'What?' said Mr Noon, a little irritated at this interruption of his linguistic flow. 'Are you all right, boy?'

'Yes, sir,' said Henry.

Mr A. B. Noon B.A. was – and maybe still is – a tall, shambling man with a long nose and a slight stoop.

'I shall now ask you the question which a less alert boy would already have answered,' he said. 'Why were you lying on the ground?'

'Tubman-Edwards knocked me out, sir.'

'Gentlemen don't tell tales,' said Mr Noon reprovingly.

'I'm not really telling tales, sir,' said Henry. 'He only knocked me out cos I hit him first.'

'You're Pratt, the new boy, aren't you?'

'Yes, sir.'

'Why did you hit Tubman-Edwards, Pratt?'

'I can't tell you, sir.'

Mr Noon raised his eyebrows.

'Oh?' he said. 'Why not?'

'Gentlemen don't tell tales, sir.'

It was just about the first good moment that Henry had experienced since coming to Brasenose.

Eve Noon, a tall, shambling girl with a long nose and a slight stoop, actually smiled.

'Touché,' said Mr Noon. 'Well done, boy. However, I, your headmaster, am now enquiring into an incident that happened at my school, so you will no longer be telling tales, you will be helping the authorities to arrive at the truth, and that is a very different matter. Why did you hit Tubman-Edwards?'

'He called me "Oiky", sir,' said Henry.

'Boys can be very cruel,' said Mr Noon.

The three Noons walked away, and a high-pitched roar came as a wicket fell in a junior cricket match. Hannah and Eve Noon, known to the boys as Before and After, turned and looked back at Henry. Hannah, a tall, shambling girl with a long nose and a slight stoop, looked at him as if she thought he was an oik, but Eve winked.

That night, in the dorm, when everyone else was asleep, Henry allowed himself to cry a little. He had felt like crying every day since Uncle Teddy dropped his bombshell.

It had been early evening in the living room of Cap Ferrat. The sun had set over the yard-arm, and Uncle Teddy had been enjoying his first whisky.

'You aren't going back to Thurmarsh Grammar,' he had said casually.

Henry had felt as if he was in a collapsing, plunging lift.

'It's too far away for you to go there every day,' Uncle Teddy had explained.

'Where am I going?' Henry had said.

'Brasenose College.'

'Where's that?'

'In Surrey.'

Henry had stared at Uncle Teddy in astonishment.

'It's a boarding school,' Uncle Teddy had explained. 'You come home during the holidays.'

Henry had protested that he didn't want to go to Brasenose College in Surrey. Uncle Teddy had explained that he was paying, out of his own pocket, to give Henry the privilege of private education. Some people had no choice. Others were lucky enough to have made enough money to be able to give the youngsters in their care opportunites that otherwise they would not have had. Maybe the system was wrong. Uncle Teddy didn't know. He was a businessman, not an educationalist or a politician. But, while the system existed, it would be very unfair of him not to give Henry all the opportunities he could, within that system.

'I'm your father now,' Uncle Teddy had said, as he poured his second whisky. 'You're my son. I'm sending you to boarding school. You're a lucky lad.'

Henry didn't feel like a lucky lad, lying in the dorm, listening to the ivy tapping gently against the windows, and the gurgling of a pipe somewhere in the water system, and the breathing of eleven sleeping boys.

Correction. Ten sleeping boys. Lush was awake.

'Oiky?' whispered that young worthy.

'What is it?'

'Are you asleep?'

141

'How can I be if I answered you?'

'Were you casing?'

Casing was Brasenose for crying.

'Course I wasn't.'

'You don't like being called Oiky, do you?'

'Would you?'

'I can't call you Pratt.'

'How about Henry?'

'O.K. I'm Gerald. I'll tell your fortune tomorrow if you like.'

'Thanks.'

'Night, Henry.'

'Night, Gerald.'

The craze in the school at the time was for fortune-telling. The method of telling fortunes was fairly primitive. You wrote out an enormous list of occupations, with numbers, and you asked the person to give you a number, and you looked the number up on your list, and told him what he was going to be when he grew up. The reader can no doubt imagine the many humorous incidents that resulted, especially when some of the occupations listed were of a somewhat ribald nature! Nevertheless, the craze only lasted for about ten days. After that, it was the most boring thing in the world, and all the lists were thrown away.

The conversation between Henry and Gerald took place during the height of this brief craze. He went to sleep feeling happier than at any time since he had discovered that he wasn't going back to Thurmarsh.

He had written to Mr Quell, telling him that he had been sent away to school. He had also written to Martin Hammond. He had imagined Mr Quell marching up to Uncle Teddy's house, and saying to Uncle Teddy and Auntie Doris, 'This nonsense must stop. The boy has the spark. I want to teach him. Brasenose College is useless. Thurmarsh Grammar is in the van. The boys have handed me a petition. "Get Bread Van back." They all signed it. Even Oberath. They chant it during morning assembly. "We want Bread Van. We want Bread Van." You've got to help us. Let him come back, and save our school.' He had received a reply from Mr Quell ten days later. He wished him luck and was sure that he would do well. Martin Hammond wrote to say that

Mick Tunnicliffe had broken a leg, Oberath was believed to be a spy, and people of working-class origins who gave their children private education were traitors. That was what his dad said, any road.

The next day was Sunday, and Henry wondered if Gerald Lush had forgotten all about the fortune-telling, not realising its symbolic importance to Henry as the first act of unsolicited kindness he had received at Brasenose.

They went to church in a crocodile. How Henry loathed that. He kept imagining that Martin Hammond and Stefan Prziborski, or even Tommy Marsden and Chalky White and Ian Lowson, would emerge from behind the rhododendrons, doubled up with mirth.

After church, many of the boys were fetched by their doting parents. Not Henry. Nor, on this occasion, Gerald Lush. Just as they were going in to dinner he said, 'Read your fortune afterwards.'

They had unidentifiable meat, with watery carrots and roast potatoes that managed to be extremely greasy and as hard as bullets at the same time. There was spotted dick and custard to follow. A purist would not have had difficulty in finding fault with the consistency of the custard.

The thing was developing a ridiculous importance. It was only a silly craze. It was impossible that the predictions could have any real validity.

After dinner, on the gravel area outside the boys' entrance to the house, Gerald Lush told Henry's fortune.

Also present were Bullock and Tubman-Edwards.

'Choose any number between one and eight hundred and sixty-two,' said Gerald Lush.

'Six hundred and thirty-six,' said Henry, for no particular reason.

Gerald Lush hunted down his huge list. Henry fought against his irrational conviction that this moment was of vital importance.

'Engine driver,' said Gerald Lush.

'Just about right for an oik,' said Bullock.

Gerald Lush walked away. He was prepared to tell Henry's

143

fortune and call him Henry in the middle of the night, but he wasn't prepared to stand up for him in public.

During the next few days, before the expiry of the craze, people rushed to tell Henry's future. It was impossible for him to refuse. His fortune always came out as something like 'sewage worker', 'burglar', 'lavatory attendant' or 'schoolmaster'. He suspected that the results were being falsified, especially as nobody would ever let him see the lists. He grabbed at Harcourt's list once, and it tore, and Harcourt beat him up. Perhaps the best result of all, to judge from the mirth which it provoked, was from Webber's list.

'Cricketer,' said Webber, and everybody fell about.

Under Mr Mallet's coaching, Henry discovered that he had certain valuable cricketing assets. He had a perfect forward defensive shot, a sound back defensive shot, a classical cover drive, an elegant force off the back foot on both sides of the wicket, a delicate late cut, a savage hook. There was only one snag. He never made contact with the ball. Never ever. In the golden summer of 1947, when Compton and Edrich set the land ablaze with the magnificence of their batting, and Henry alone at Brasenose College worshipped Len Hutton, who let him down by being out of form, every boy at Brasenose College who wasn't a total weed kept detailed records of his achievements upon the pitch. Henry kept his scores as diligently as anybody. They were 0, 0, 0, 0, 0 not out, 0, did not bat, retired hurt 0, 0, 4, 0, 0, 0 not out, 0 and 0. The 4 occurred when both he and the wicket-keeper missed the ball completely, but Penfold failed to signal four byes, and the runs were credited to him. Despite this appalling record, at the end of the term he completed his final averages, like everyone else. Innings 16, not outs 4, runs 4, highest score 4, average 0.3333333333333333333 recurring. It is hard to imagine a worse predicament for a youngster at an English preparatory school shortly after the war than to be appalling at sport. Add the fact that the youngster in question loved cricket and football passionately, and you will begin to imagine the depth of his unhappiness. Add to this stew of misery the fact that the school was in Surrey and Henry spoke with the flat-capped tones of south Yorkshire. Flavour this casserole of despair with the fact that his surname was Pratt and his legs were short and plump. Season this unappetising ragout of mental anguish with the reflection that he enjoyed reading books *and* was good at lessons, and you have a picture that would surely melt the stoniest heart.

In his first term at Brasenose College, Henry was several times near to breaking point, but he held on. He endured earth in his bed, a dead song thrush ditto, three apple-pie beds and being on the losing end of innumerable fights. With these physical humiliations, he could cope. He was developing a passive courage, a stoicism which allowed his tormentors to see no hint of his agony, and thus deprived them of the ultimate pleasure of the bully. What he found much more difficult to endure was his nickname. Oiky. Oiky Pratt. Because he believed it to be true.

He'd been told it at Rowth Bridge, by no less an authority than Belinda Boyce-Uppingham. He'd half believed it then. Now he knew it was true. He just didn't know how to cope when Tubman-Edward said, 'I say, Oiky, does your old man prefer claret or burgundy?' His oikishness was vividly brought home to him in connection with the name of Uncle Teddy and Auntie Doris's house. Cap Ferrat. The boys in his dorm accused him of not knowing what it meant. He reacted angrily, for he really did believe he knew what it meant.

'O.K., know-all, what does it mean?' said Bullock.

'It's a kind of hat they use in Yorkshire when they go rabbiting with ferrets,' he said.

How they all hooted.

He *felt* oiky. His body was inelegant. His movements were clumsy. He felt that he was never quite clean, however much he washed.

Once again, Henry was happiest when buried in his lessons. Throughout his school career so far, many of his fellow pupils had thought he was a swot. Some of his teachers had sensed the presence of that rare quality, a real enthusiasm for learning, and above all for learning to think. It grieves me to have to say that they were deluded. Henry still hadn't really grasped what education was all about. He liked lessons because they were safe.

There was no pecking order of bullying in the classroom. He liked lessons because he was good at them. He did them diligently so that he would continue to be good at them. It was as simple as that.

He was taught Latin by Mr Belling, dry as dust, a human Pompeii, who went round and round the class anti-clockwise firing staccato questions. Wrong answers were marked down, and ten wrong answers meant extra work at weekends. Henry rarely got extra work at weekends.

The French teacher, Mr Massey, had wanted to be a doctor, but he had failed his finals. A simple question about medicine would guarantee at least a ten-minute diversion, in English, often with diagrams on the blackboard. Hooper and Price-Ansty would faint, in that order, at the more grisly of Mr Massey's revelations. There was an awkward moment when Mr Noon came into the classroom to find a large diagram of the human kidneys on the blackboard. Mr Massey had hurriedly asked the French for kidneys. Nobody had known.

Mr Lee-Archer, the Maths master, hurled books at boys who got things wrong. Mr Lee-Archer had once represented Great Britain, at the discus, in a three-way international athletics match against Belgium and Finland. A Maths text-book hurled at one's head from ten yards with fearsome accuracy is almost as good an incentive to a lazy boy as fostering an interest in the subject, and a lot easier.

Mr Trench, the History master, was on the verge of a nervous breakdown. Mr Trench liked facts – names, dates, venues for the signing of treaties. He disliked ideas, theories, causes, effects, parallels, motives, anything that might necessitate delving into the reasons behind the facts. But he was now beginning to lose his grasp on facts as well, and was calling on the boys to reiterate constantly the diminishing fund of facts that he could still remember – the dates of the Battle of Hastings, the signing of Magna Carta, the Battle of Agincourt, Wat Tyler's rebellion, the length of the Thirty Years War, and a few others, round and round, with the boys embarrassed and helpless, not knowing what to do.

The Geography master, Mr Hill, had no disabilities except his age. He had been pressed back into service during the war, and had stayed on. He was a good teacher, but snoozed a lot. The boys read their Geography books while he snoozed, and when he was awake he tested them. It was a system that worked well for all concerned, and nobody rocked the boat.

The English teacher, Mr Mallender, believed that hand-writing was next to godliness. His pupils might not have much to say, but at least they would say it legibly. Twice a week, for the first fifteen minutes of the lesson, they would copy out a section of Keats' 'Endymion', to be handed in for Mr Mallender's inspection. If the hand-writing fell below a certain standard, you did the same section again the next time. When you got to the end of the poem, you were excused hand-writing and were allowed to read during the first fifteen minutes of the relevant lessons. But Keats' 'Endymion' is a long poem, and some untidy boys hadn't finished it when they left Brasenose. Henry, a late starter, had no chance of ever finishing it.

One day, around the middle of June, Mr A. B. Noon B.A. entered Mr Mallender's classroom unexpectedly. All the boys stood, except Henry.

It had been a tiring day. Mr Hill hadn't fallen asleep once. Mr Lee-Archer had struck Henry a glancing blow with *Geometry for Beginners*. Mr Belling had fired irregular verbs at fearsome speed. Mr Massey had described a delicate eye operation in terms so specific that Henry had almost joined Hooper and Price-Ansty in unconsciousness, and Mr Trench's store of facts had diminished so much that Webber had calculated that the date of the Battle of Hastings was now coming round every three minutes and sixteen seconds. Henry was eleven pages into Keats' 'Endymion', with a hundred and twenty-three to go. After a good start, his writing had deteriorated under the strain, and there had been moments when he wondered if he would remain on page ten for ever. He kept making mistakes in the couplet:

Oh thou, for whose soul-soothing quiet, turtles
Passion their voices cooingly 'mong myrtles.

A jolly good couplet if you like that kind of thing, of course, even if not one of Keats' absolute humdingers. Nobody can be on top form all the time. Anyway, it did begin to pall on Henry after he'd copied it out six times. The first mistake he made was due to a lapse of concentration. The preceding lines are – well, you don't need me to tell you, especially if you're an Old Brasenosian:

> By all the trembling mazes that she ran,
> Hear us, great Pan!

Boys will be boys, and Henry's mind strayed to another pan, made by Cobbold and Sons of Etruria. A chance association can have the power to unlock memories of the past. Proust touched on this, and now it was happening to Henry. He was not concentrating, therefore, and "mong myrtles' is a killer if you aren't alert. On this day, Henry had at last got onto page eleven. He was writing the lines:

> Their ripen'd fruitage; yellow-girted bees
> Their golden honeycombs; our village leas
> Their fairest blossom'd beans and poppied corn;
> The chuckling linnet its five young unborn,
> To sing for thee;. . .

Relieved to have got over the myrtle hurdle, Henry made the fatal mistake, as any copier will tell you, of concentrating on the meaning of the lines. The village came to life in his mind, and he was gripped by a severe melancholic nostalgia. Memories of Rowth Bridge flooded over him. He was miles away when Mr Noon entered the room and all the other boys leapt to their feet. He was up on the high fells with Simon Eckington when the clip on his ear-hole came.

'Stand up, boy,' said Mr Noon.

Henry stood up.

'Why didn't you stand up when I came in the room?'

'I was working so hard I didn't see you come in, sir,' said Henry, who no longer used 'thee' and 'tha', although there was nothing he could do about his accent.

'Nonsense, boy,' said the headmaster. 'You were dreaming. You were in a brown study, weren't you, Pratt?'

'Yes, sir.'

'You will come along to another brown study after school. My

148

study.'

When the lessons were over, Henry went along the stone corridor, past the door to the dining room, which smelt of the morning's cabbage, past the door to the kitchen, which smelt of the evening's rissoles, past the stairs down to the changing rooms, which smelt of dungeons, past Mr Belling's classroom, which smelt of dust, through the green baize fire-door into a wider corridor, past the common room, which smelt of pipe smoke, and so to the door of the headmaster's study.

He knocked.

'Come.'

He entered.

The headmaster sat behind an even larger desk than that of Mr E. F. Crowther. His study was oak-panelled, with a bay window, and one wall was lined with bookcases, filled with learned books which came with the house, and many of which were still uncut. This study announced, 'We are men of culture here. We will teach your boy civilised values. You are not throwing good money down the drain.'

'You're new to our customs, Pratt,' said Mr Noon, 'New perhaps to concepts of discipline and team spirit, of pulling together. Are you new to the concept of pulling together, Pratt?'

'No, sir.'

'When I enter a room, and you all stand up, it is not because I suffer from megalomania. It is because I am the symbol of authority. You boys are being groomed so that one day you will take up positions of authority yourselves. You must therefore learn to respect authority as a force beyond individuality. That is why I must thrash you, Pratt. Do you understand?'

'Yes, sir.'

Henry caught a brief glimpse of Mr Trench running stark-naked among the pines. His nervous breakdown had begun. Should he tell Mr Noon? Would he be believed, or would it be taken as a frenzied attempt to evade his punishment? He decided to remain silent.

'When a boy is beaten at Brasenose,' said Mr Noon, 'it is not a punishment. It is a part of his education, and therefore he should be grateful. That is why I insist on boys thanking me after I have

149

thrashed them. Do you understand that?'

'Yes, sir.'

'Bend over.'

Henry bent over.

'Put your hands behind your back and raise the flaps of your jacket well clear of your buttocks.'

Henry put his hands behind his back and raised the flaps of his jacket well clear of his buttocks.

Mr Noon made a practice swish with the cane.

Henry closed his eyes and gritted his teeth.

Thwack.

Not too bad.

Thwack.

Worse. Think of something nice.

Thwack.

Ouch! Think of the summer holidays.

Thwack.

Not quite such a bad one. I don't want to think of the summer holidays.

Thwack.

That did hurt. I'm dreading the summer holidays. I don't want to spend them with Uncle. . .

Thwack.

. . .Teddy and, oh God that was a bad one, Auntie Doris.

'Stand up. That's it.'

Henry stood up and turned to face Mr Noon. His backside was stinging and raw. The pain was spreading like a sunset.

'Thank you, sir,' he said.

One hot day in August, Henry woke early, in his spacious bedroom in the substantial detached house with the attractive irregular gables, in Haggersley Edge, a salubrious residential area situated between the mucky picture of Sheffield and the golden frame of the Peak District. He woke early, because he had plans. He was going back, to Paradise Lane, to see his old friend Martin Hammond. He had delayed too long. There was nothing to fear.

He pulled back the curtains, and gazed on another steamy summer morning. Already, the houses were shimmering in the haze. On the right, the high hills merged with the sky, green and blue mingling in the haze.

He washed himself thoroughly, twice. During the last few weeks of term he had ceased to be quite so spectacularly unpopular. You were never quite so unpopular once you'd had your first beating from Mr Noon. But he had still felt oiky, still had difficulty in persuading himself that he was clean.

He descended the wide, carpeted staircase of the vermin-free house.

They breakfasted on the patio. The Welgar shredded wheat, boiled egg, and toast and Oxford marmalade were a treat, even if he would have preferred Golden Shred.

Auntie Doris was wearing white shorts and a red shirt. Her legs were amazingly brown and smooth. Both she and Uncle Teddy had been very brown when he arrived back from school. (Not home from school. He couldn't quite think of it as home.) It wasn't surprising. They spent so much time on the patio during that wonderful summer. Auntie Doris's knees were varnished like stair-knobs. He caught himself wondering if she put furniture polish on them.

'You're the early bird,' she said.

'I'm going to Thurmarsh to see my old friends,' he said.

'Good idea,' she said.

She always said 'good idea'. She was glad to get him out from under her feet. He had the idea that if he said, 'I'm going to collect a pile of sheep shit and throw it at the Master Cutler,' she'd still have said 'Good idea'.

'I might be back late. I might go to the pictures,' he said.

'Good idea,' said Auntie Doris.

On Sunday, Uncle Teddy and Auntie Doris had taken him to a restaurant. They had met their friends, Geoffrey and Daphne Porringer. Geoffrey Porringer had blackheads on his nose. Daphne Porringer didn't. Geoffrey Porringer chose the wine. Daphne Porringer didn't. Geoffrey Porringer made Henry try it. 'The sooner you civilise the brats, the better,' he said. He described the wine as 'a thoughtful if slightly morose Burgundy'. Uncle Teddy laughed. Daphne Porringer didn't. Henry thought the wine was horrible, but then he was an oik.

Uncle Teddy came down to breakfast, and Henry's brain seized up.

'How's young Henry?' said Uncle Teddy, immaculate in his business suit.

'All right,' improvised Henry amusingly.

A wasp bore down upon the marmalade jar. Uncle Teddy crushed it with ease. Henry knew that if he'd tried it, it would have stung him. His body didn't feel like a part of himself. It was an enemy with which he constantly had to wrestle. He'd finished his breakfast, but he didn't dare get up until Uncle Teddy had gone, for fear of knocking the table over.

At last Uncle Teddy went, and Henry was free to go too. Auntie Doris gave him some sandwiches and a bit of extra pocket money. She was very good that way.

'Don't eat them too early,' she said.

'I won't,' he promised.

He said goodbye, hurried upstairs, and changed into scruffier clothes. He didn't want to look like a snazzy dresser in the environs of Paradise Lane. He crept out of the house in his filthy garb. Auntie Doris was on the telephone and didn't see him.

He walked down Wharfedale Road, past pleasant houses whose names suggested a conspiracy to pretend that the road was nothing to do with the city. Birchbrook. Beech Croft. Dane's Oak. Coppice View. Marshfields.

He caught a bus to the city centre, then walked through the oven of the city, from the bus station, through Fitzalan Square, and waited for the Thurmarsh tram down by the markets. The sunlight was filtering palely through the industrial smog.

He meant to change trams at Rawlaston Four Roads, but on impulse he decided to carry on into Thurmarsh and eat his sandwiches before seeing Martin. Otherwise he'd have to share them.

The tram terminus was in Mabberley Street, by the public library. He walked past the library, past the tripe butcher's, past the Thurmarsh branch of Arthur Davy and Sons, past Ted's Café, which gave out a hot whiff of potato and armpit pie, past the Maypole Dairy and the offices of the *Thurmarsh Chronicle and Argus*. The newspaper placards announced, 'Worse than darkest

1940 – Eden', and 'My night of shame – Thurmarsh Councillor'.

He sat on a wooden bench in the little gardens opposite the Town Hall. The clock on the Town Hall said 11.07. He might as well eat his sandwiches. Exhausted sooty sparrows and dishevelled starlings eyed him hopefully. The sun beat down on him. He opened the packet. She'd given him Gentleman's Relish again. What on earth had possessed him to pretend to like it when she had given it to him as a treat on the first day of the holidays? A fear of seeming unsophisticated, perhaps. An urge to shed his oikishness. Possibly, the reader will suspect, an hereditary streak of gastronomic masochism. His father, a dry meat man, had suffered his food to be drowned in gravy throughout his married life. For years all three of them had endured brawn together, each in the mistaken belief that the other two liked it. Now, a twelve-year-old boy with no relish for becoming a gentleman struggled through his Gentleman's Relish on a seat stained by starling droppings.

He finished his sandwiches at 11.16, flinging a token crumb towards the birds. Three sparrows fought for it. A starling pushed them out of the way and ate it. A small cloud, barely visible in the haze, briefly obscured the sun.

Would he talk to Martin about the strange teachers at Brasenose College, about Miss Prune, the matron, who had nailed her flag to the mast of clean underwear, about the boys all calling him Oiky? Would they discuss the amazing form of Compton and Edrich, and the fortunes of Yorkshire cricket?

He caught the Rawlaston tram. They clanked past the end of Link Lane. Four men were washing a fire engine, but there was no life around the grammar school. How small it looked. How tiny the houses were, as the tram moaned wearily up the hill. They breasted the rise, and looked down into the hazy valley of the Rundle. On the right, Brunswick Road Primary School, Devil's Island in a sea of brick. Their descent levelled out; the road swung right. On the left was the canal, smaller and weedier than in his memory. The canal swung away from the road, and the cul-de-sacs began. How minute they were. Everything was tiny except the vast, blank wall of Crapp, Hawser and Kettlewell. 'Paradise,' yelled the conductor. His legs wouldn't move. The tram stopped.

There was the corner shop. There was the chippy. How grimy it all was. He remained seated. A wave of relief swept over him as he realised that he wasn't going to get off, and then as soon as the tram was on its way once more, and the last of the cul-de-sacs was left behind, and the vast world of Crapp, Hawser and Kettlewell became past history also, the relief changed to regret. He should have got off. He hadn't. He wouldn't.

'I thought tha wanted Paradise,' said the conductor.

'I've changed me mind,' he said.

Steam escaped from the slender chimneys of the steelworks. Steam drifted out of gaps in the walls. Steam rose from innumerable shunting engines. A steam train roared along the line to Henry's left. The hills drifted steamily in the weak sun. Henry was adrift in a steamy world. These were the doldrums.

He got off the tram at Rawlaston, because it went no further. He was parched. He didn't know what language to use, even to himself. He was in a linguistic no man's land. 'Ee, I'm fair clammed,' had been left behind. 'Gosh, I'm absolutely Hairy Mac Thirsters,' had not yet arrived. He bought a bottle of Tizer, a newspaper, a packet of Nuttall's Mintoes, and a lucky bag.

He sat on a wall, behind which there would soon be a building site. He could smell a nearby chippy. He sipped his Tizer and examined the contents of his lucky bag. It contained sherbet, a little saying and a trick. The saying blew away in a sudden gust of hot wind, and the trick fell into the building site as he tried to rescue the saying.

He'd bought the paper to find out the cinema programmes. Fool that he was. It was a national paper. He skimmed through the headlines, for want of anything better to do. 'Attlee may sack five ministers.' 'Lords told "Rule or Quit Palestine".' 'Cannot call barrow boys crooks – Isaacs.' 'August heat above normal.' 'Julius napped at Haydock.' One of the adverts showed a man with a far-away look. The caption read, 'He's dreaming of the days when Vantella Shirts and Van Heusen Collars Are Easy to Get Again (with curve-woven semi-stiff collars and cuffs!)' Could anyone really dream of things like that? He crumpled the paper up and tossed it into the building site. A middle-aged woman said, 'Now then. Tha shouldn't throw litter, tha knows.' 'Why don't you drop dead, you fat cow?' he shouted. 'Young people today. I don't know,' said the woman, continuing on her way. He took a swig of lukewarm Tizer and dropped down off the wall. He deliberately barged into a woman shopper. 'Look where you're going,' she said. 'Oh go home and stew yourself in your knickers,' he riposted wittily. The mood passed. He finished his Tizer, caught a tram to Sheffield, and bought a copy of the *Star*.

Most of the films were 'A' or 'X'. He had used up all his bravado, and, in any case, there was no way he could pretend to be sixteen.

The only 'U' films were Elizabeth Taylor in *Courage of Lassie* at the Roscoe, Deanna Durbin in *I'll be Yours* at the Gaumont, Norman Evans, Nat Jackley and Dan Young in *Demobbed* at the Forum, Southey, *The Jolson Story* at the Lyric, Darnall, *Old Mother Riley Detective* at the Hillsboro' Kinema, Abbott and Costello in *The Time of Their Lives* at the Paragon, Firth Park, and *My Brother Talks to Horses* at the Rex, Intake. After ten minutes of agonised debate, he realised that he probably hadn't enough money to go to any cinema which involved an extra bus ride. He checked on the state of his finances.

All he could afford was the News Theatre in Fitzalan Square. He saw the news, a Laurel and Hardy comedy, two cartoons, one of which was a Donald Duck and the other of which wasn't, a semi-humorous feature on dogs, a film about ice sports, the news, a Laurel and Hardy comedy, two cartoons, one of which was a Donald Duck, and the other of which wasn't, a semi-humorous feature on dogs, a film about ice sports, the news, a Laurel and Hardy comedy, and two cartoons, one of which was a Donald Duck and the other of which wasn't. The best programme begins to lose its savour when you've seen it two and a half times, and he emerged blearily into the glaring, late-afternoon furnace that was Sheffield, city of steel.

It was still only twenty to five when he arrived back at Wharfedale Road. The tar in the road was tacky. His legs were stuck. The pavement was made of glue. He was walking, yet hardly moving, as in a dream. He would never reach Cap Ferrat.

He entered through the French windows, forgetting that he had secretly changed into scruffy clothes before leaving.

Geoffrey Porringer was sitting beside Auntie Doris on the

settee. They were drinking China tea.

'What sort of day have you had, young sir?' said Geoffrey Porringer.

'Very nice,' said Henry, but he didn't elaborate.

Quite soon Geoffrey Porringer stood up and said, 'Well. I'm sorry I missed Teddy,' and Auntie Doris said, 'What is it I'm to tell him?' and Geoffrey Porringer said, 'Tell him Bingley can't cope. We'll have to explore other avenues,' and then he nodded at Henry, said, 'Don't worry, Einstein, it may never happen,' and departed through the French windows.

Henry went upstairs and had a lukewarm bath and still didn't feel clean and lay on his bed, dressed only in his pants, as the evening slowly began to cool.

He dressed, and went down for dinner. He was a far cry from any boy who might have been in Rawlaston earlier that day saying, 'Why don't you drop dead, you fat cow?'

He was resolved to make more of a conversational show than he had managed heretofore.

An opening gambit lay ready to hand.

'Don't forget Geoffrey Porringer's message,' he reminded Auntie Doris.

'Geoffrey Porringer?' said Uncle Teddy. 'Has he been here?'

'He popped in this afternoon,' said Auntie Doris. 'With a message.'

'Why couldn't he ring me at the office?' said Uncle Teddy.

'I don't know,' said Auntie Doris. 'I'm not a mind reader.'

'Perhaps it was secret. It sounded pretty secret,' said Henry.

'What was this message?' said Uncle Teddy.

'I can't remember,' said Auntie Doris.

'He brings me a message so secret and important that he can't phone me at the office, and you forget it!' said Uncle Teddy.

'I remember it,' said Henry. 'He said, "Bingley can't cope. We'll have to explore other avenues." '

'I don't understand it,' said Uncle Teddy. 'What the hell does he mean? Bingley?'

'It's probably in code,' said Henry.

Uncle Teddy glared at Auntie Doris, then turned to Henry. 'That'll be it,' he said.

'Pretty useless code,' said Henry, 'if nobody knows what it means.'

Uncle Teddy and Auntie Doris said little after that, giving Henry a golden opportunity, over the bread and butter pudding, to raise a subject that had been worrying him.

'I think you've been done at Brasenose,' he said.

'Done?' said Uncle Teddy.

'Yes,' said Henry. 'You're paying lots of money, but the education's worse than at Thurmarsh, which is free.'

He hoped that Uncle Teddy would be so upset that he would remove him from Brasenose immediately. But it didn't work.

'It's what we call a preparatory school,' explained Uncle Teddy. 'You aren't there to be educated. You're there to be prepared.'

'What for?'

'Dalton.'

Henry looked at Uncle Teddy blankly.

'Dalton is one of the best public schools in the country,' said Auntie Doris.

'Where is it?' said Henry.

'In Somerset,' said Uncle Teddy. 'Rather a long way away. That's the only fly in the ointment.'

'I'm Labour,' Henry said.

There was a horrified silence in the dorm.

The financial crisis of 1947, even thought it was largely a result of the nation having bankrupted itself in order to win the war, was proof to all the boys of Brasenose College, except Henry, that Labour were unfit to run the country. 1947 saw the nationalisation of railways, canals, road haulage and electricity. It saw the school-leaving age raised to fifteen (not a good selling-point at Brasenose). It saw the final transfer of power in India to India. All this was regarded as unarguably awful by all the boys of Brasenose College, except Henry.

Why had he told them, thought Henry bitterly after lights-out in the bare-boarded, uncurtained, Spartan dorm, with its row of wash-basins down the middle? How could he establish any relationship with them? How could he ever talk to them about his past? What could he ever tell them about it? That he had lived in

157

a rat-infested, back-to-back terrace with a one-eyed, retired parrot-strangler?

Yes. Yes, yes, yes, yes, yes. The answer was so simple that he couldn't believe that he had been too stupid to see it before. There was no need of any grocer from Abergavenny here. He had himself. He would mock himself before they did.

He began to call himself 'Oiky'. 'Shut up, Oiky,' he'd say, or 'Come on, our Oik.' One day, at dinner, he convulsed the table by gazing at his plate and saying, 'It's months since I 'ad rat.' For years he had envied comedians their catch-phrases. Now, he had one of his own. It was a good 'un and all. 'It's months since I 'ad rat.'

That term, Henry discovered that he was as bad at rugby football as he was at cricket. He never once managed to repeat the successful tackle he had made on Pam Yardley. When he kicked the ridiculously shaped ball, he never knew where it would go. He even managed to achieve the near impossible by slicing it over his own goal-posts. Everyone collapsed with laughter, even Mr Lee-Archer, the referee, who wasn't sure whether you could score an own dropped goal at rugby. Henry stood there, looking sheepish. As the laughter died down, he knew that it was time for him to use his catchphrase.

'It's months since I 'ad rat,' he said.

It went down like a plate of cold sick. Why? Why?

Because it was inappropriate! Brilliant though his catch-phrase was, the opportunities for its use were too limited.

He needed something of more general application.

A catch-phrase must be ordinary. You couldn't imagine Oscar Wilde touring the halls and producing loud laughter every time he said, 'Fox hunting is the unspeakable in pursuit of the uneatable.' A witticism constantly repeated becomes a stale witticism. A catch phrase is, 'I won't take me coat off. I'm not stopping,' or 'It's agony, Ivy.'

Henry's came out by accident after he'd put his foot on the edge of his porridge plate while clambering to his place over the top of the bench. The plate tilted, and his portion of porridge flew through the air, like a slightly soggy discus, into his face. When the laughter died down, he said, 'E, by gum, I am daft.' It fitted him. It was comfortable. It was his. It was appropriate on all occasions. He was Henry 'Ee, by gum, I am daft' Pratt.

In the Christmas holidays, Uncle Teddy and Auntie Doris gave him a model railway, and he began to sample the delights of regular cinema-going. In the Easter term he discovered that he was as bad at hockey as at cricket and football. Mr Trench returned, having made an amazing recovery. He was helped by the fact that the boys never mocked him. In their eyes, a schoolmaster who ran naked through the woods had a certain heroic quality about him. Henry was past page fifty of Keats' 'Endymion' now, and if his French was a trifle sketchy, he could no doubt have had a shot at a simple appendectomy, had the need ever arisen.

One day, while Mr Hill dozed, Henry tried not to meander while reading why rivers did. So effective was he in this effort that once again he didn't know that Mr Noon was in the room until he received his old chum, the clip round the ear-hole.

'Why didn't you stand up when I came in the room?' said Mr Noon.

'I didn't hear you, sir,' said Henry. 'I was concentrating on my work.'

'Nonsense, boy, you were in a brown study,' said Mr Noon.

'No, sir. I wasn't,' said Henry.

'Come and see me in another brown study at the beginning of break,' said the headmaster.

'That's not fair, sir,' said Henry.

'Tut tut! Tut tut!' said Mr A. B. Noon B.A. palindromically. 'Not fair, eh? We'll see about that.'

In the break, Henry made the long trek to the headmaster's study, past the burgeoning sweat of rissoles, through the green baize door, past the acrid common-room fug.

'I really didn't know you were there, sir, because I was working so hard,' said Henry.

'I don't accuse you of lying,' said the headmaster. 'I merely say this. If you are lying, you deserve to be thrashed. If you aren't, then your thrashing will be unfair, and that will be an excellent preparation for life, because life is unfair, and it would be unfair of me to give you the impression that it isn't, so I shall thrash you anyway.'

Mr Noon gave him six of the best.

'Thank you, sir,' he said.

Back in the dorm that night, a bit of a hero because of his unjust thrashing, having shown his weals to the admiring throng, Henry was asked by Bullock, 'You've turned out not to be too bad a chap at all, Oiky. Are you honestly Labour?'

'Yes,' said Henry.

'Why?' said Bullock.

Now this was a shrewd question. Being Conservative or Labour didn't really have anything to do with politics. It was simply what one was. One was either Oxford or Cambridge, and similarly one was either Conservative or Labour, except that one was never Labour. Henry had accused them of being Conservative because they were sheep. Was he himself any better?

'Come on, Oiky. Why?' said Price-Ansty.

'I just don't think it's fair that some people should have so much more than others,' he said. He thought it sounded pretty lame, but it was the best he could do.

'They've earned it,' said Bullock.

'Not always,' said Henry. 'They get left it.'

'Their people earned it,' said Gerald Lush. 'You Labour chaps want to take everything away. That's what my father says anyway.'

'Don't you think there are working-class people capable of earning it?' said Henry.

'Of course I do,' said Price-Ansty. 'My father said that some of the working-class chaps in his regiment were jolly intelligent. He was quite surprised.'

'We're not getting at you, Oiky,' said Gerald Lush. 'You're pretty clever.'

'For an oik,' said Bullock, and everybody laughed.

Henry grinned too. Not as much inside as outside, perhaps, but if you grinned externally at a thing often enough, you did find that the internal pain began to ease.

By the end of his life at Brasenose, it was really quite tolerable. Nobody really seemed to hate him any more, except Tubman-Edwards, and he hated everybody.

Uncle Teddy and Auntie Doris were as brown as berries when he got home. He went to see Yorkshire play cricket twice and saw the first home games of Sheffield Wednesday and Sheffield

United. They took Cousin Hilda to Bakewell for tea, and Henry discovered that the greatest author in the world wasn't Captain W. E. Johns after all. It was a woman! Her name was Agatha Christie. He went to the pictures twice a week. You could forget all your worries there. You could even forget that before long you were going to Dalton College, and the whole painful business of beginning again was going to begin all over again.

8 It Rears Its Ugly Head

There were sixteen wash-basins round the walls and eight more in the middle of the room. On the floor there were slatted wooden boards. Beyond the wash-basins there were four large, heavily stained baths. The showers were downstairs, beyond the changing rooms. Such were the washing arrangements in Orange House, in Dalton College, in Somerset, and washing was still very important to Henry in the autumn of 1948. So diligently, with what thoroughness and vigour, did he ablute himself that he suddenly realised that he was all alone in a deserted wash-room.

A prefect poked his head round the door and said, 'Get to bed, you. It's past lights-out.'

He went out into the long, bare corridor. It was very dimly lit by a night-light at the far end.

He entered the dormitory. It was pitch dark. He knew that his bed was the third on the left. He felt his way round the walls. He edged past the first bed, walking very slowly, his left hand stretched out in front of him, his right hand clutching his towel and washing bag. His left hand connected with the second bed.

'Is that you, Badger?' whispered a voice from the second bed.

'No. I'm Pratt,' whispered Henry.

'Are you good-looking? If so, hop in,' whispered the voice from the second bed.

Henry moved on as fast as he dared in the impenetrable dark.

'Shut up, you blokes up that end,' shouted Hertford-Jones, the dorm prefect. 'Some of us want to get some crud.'

Henry edged his way round the third bed, and got in as quietly as he could.

'Get out,' yelled the bed's occupant, as Henry snuggled up against him.

'Shut up, Perkins,' shouted Hertford-Jones.

'No, honestly, Hertford-Jones,' said the one who must be Perkins. 'A raging homo's just got into bed with me.'

'Send him over here,' said another voice, and there was

laughter.

The dormitory was flooded with light. Henry was edging away from Perkins's bed, crimson with shame.

'I thought that was my bed,' he said, looking round desperately. Every bed appeared to be full, except the end one, and that must be Hertford-Jones's.

'I know moral standards are declining, but honestly,' said Perkins.

'Which dorm are you in?' said Hertford-Jones.

'South Africa,' said Henry.

'This is New Zealand,' said Hertford-Jones. 'You're in the wrong bloody dorm, you cretin.'

Henry edged his way out.

'See you later,' whispered the boy in the bed next to Perkins.

Henry closed the door of New Zealand carefully and groped his way down the corridor, away from the night-light, towards South Africa.

It was pitch black in South Africa. He felt his way carefully past the first two beds, still clutching his towel and washing bag. He was sweating freely. He might as well not have bothered to wash at all.

He found the third bed. This time he explored it with his hands before getting in.

It seemed empty.

He clambered into bed.

His feet touched something soft.

He screamed.

South Africa dorm was filled with blinding light, and alive with protestation.

'What the hell's going on?' said Nattrass, the dorm prefect.

'There's something in my bed,' said Henry, pulling back his bedclothes, to reveal a dead thrush.

Nattrass came over and examined it.

'It's a dead thrush,' he said. 'Who did this? Bloody little savages. I suppose nobody will have the guts to own up.'

Nobody spoke.

'What's your name?' Nattrass asked Henry.

'Pratt,' said Henry, knowing that laughter would follow as

163

surely as birth follows womb.

'Chuck it out of the window,' said Nattrass, and Henry picked up the horrible, lifeless bird, trying not to show his revulsion, trying not to catch its dead eye. The dead thrush at Brasenose College had been a song thrush (*Turdus philomelos*). This was the substantially larger mistle thrush (*Turdus viscivorus*). He hurled it far into the mellow Somerset night.

'Sleep on top of your sheets, Pratt,' said Nattrass. 'I'll get matron to change them tomorrow. Right, lights out. The fun's over, you bloody savages. Let's get some crud.'

The room was plunged into darkness, and Henry was glad of it, for he was on the verge of tears.

He lay on top of his sheets, reflecting on his somewhat unfortunate first day at Dalton College. Seeing that he was getting nervous about arriving at yet another new school, Auntie Doris had decided that he should be driven there. Uncle Teddy being too busy, she had driven him herself. On both his trunk and tuck box she had put sticky labels, which said 'H. E. Pratt. Orange House. Dalton College. Dalton. Somerset.' Henry had objected, on the grounds that the luggage was unlikely to go astray in transit while in the boot of their own car.

It had been a long drive to Somerset, and Auntie Doris had got lost twice. Eventually they had reached an attractive little stone-built town, and there, unmistakably, was the school. Auntie Doris had driven up to the gates. Henry hadn't been able to lift his trunk out of the boot. Auntie Doris had asked a passing seventeen-year-old to help them, and Henry had felt mortified about the labels, which would surely strike the seventeen-year-old as ridiculously fussy.

'Dalton College?' the seventeen-year-old had said.

'Yes,' Henry had said.

'This is King's School, Bruton,' the seventeen-year-old had said, not without a hint of amusement.

Henry had put his tuck box back in the boot, and they had driven on. Auntie Doris had said, 'You see. It was lucky I labelled them. I might have dropped you at the wrong school and driven off.' He had got into a lather because they were going to be late. And when they had at last found Dalton College, it had been to learn that Orange House was not actually on the premises. It was a large, rambling, three-storied, purpose-built, late-Victorian mansion on the edge of the town. By the time they had found it, it had been seventeen minutes past seven. Forty-seven minutes late! He had found the greatest difficulty in restraining himself from bursting into tears.

The porter, Gorringe, had tottered out, gasping for breath, his arms long, his legs bent, deformed by long years of carrying the trunks of the young gentry. Gorringe had grasped one end of the trunk and Henry the other. It had been extremely heavy, containing as it did the large number of clothes demanded by the school. Cousin Hilda had insisted that she sewed on the Cash's name-tapes, announcing that each item was the property of 287 H. Pratt. She had sniffed as she sewed one onto his jockstrap.

Henry had returned for his tuck box, which was also quite heavy, containing, among other delights, twelve jars of Gentleman's Relish, one for each week of term.

Aunti Doris had clasped him in a perfumed embrace, and smacked a great kiss onto his cheek, and *she* had cried. He had waved as she drove off half-blinded by tears, and he had felt empty of emotion. Then he had picked up his tuck box and struggled into the bowels of Orange House, a plump, nervous boy with a south Yorkshire accent, who smelt like a perfume factory and had a large smear of lipstick on his right cheek.

Henry had found his junior study, which he would share with seven other boys, each having a partition which he could decorate as he wished, within the confines of decorum. Senior boys had a study between two. Junior boys fagged for senior boys for two years. The roster informed Henry that he was to fag for Davey and Pilkington-Brick.

'You'd better go straight along,' the fair-haired boy in the next partition had advised him.

And so he had presented himself, nervously, at the second study from the end on the left upstairs.

Davey, tall, slim, dark, with a long, sad face, only sixteen but looking immensely grown up to Henry, had said, 'You've got lipstick on your cheek.'

Pilkington-Brick, even taller, and massive, with a large

moon-shaped, cheerful face, also only sixteen, also looking immensely grown up to Henry, had said, 'You smell like a Turkish brothel.'

Davey had said, 'Have we a sex maniac for our fag, Tosser?'

Pilkington-Brick had said, 'It could be an interesting couple of years, Lampo.'

Davey had said, 'Henry Pratt. What a deliciously uncompromising name. How proudly banal.'

Pilkington-Brick had said, 'Don't you worry about a thing, young Pratt. You've got a plum position here.'

Davey had said, 'It's true. Tosser is good-natured to the point of terminal boredom, and I'm just a clapped-out old roué.'

Lampo Davey had smiled. His mouth was slightly twisted when he smiled. Henry had left the room clumsily, in total bewilderment, utterly out of his depth.

He had welcomed bed-time, not knowing what horrors it would bring. Now he lay on top of his sheets, taking stock. Dead birds, to date, three. Parrot. Song thrush. Mistle thrush. What more did life hold in store for him? A rotting blackbird in his desk? A headless cormorant stuffed down his trousers?

There was a symphony of deep breathing, grunting and near-snoring. The odd whistle of breath. An occasional roar from a lorry on the main road. Should he run away and hitch-hike back to Cap Ferrat? How thrilled Uncle Teddy and Auntie Doris would be!

At last, shortly before the clock of St Peter's Church struck four, Henry fell into a light, uneasy crud.

The next day, as he walked up the main road, away from the little stone-built market town, towards the school, Henry found himself beside Paul Hargreaves, the fair-haired boy from the next partition in his junior study. Paul Hargreaves told him that his father was a brain surgeon. Henry told Paul Hargreaves that his father was a test pilot.

The school was set in a valley, surrounded by lush, wooded hills. It was a real jumble, with the original stone Queen Anne mansion flanked on one side by a high-roofed Victorian chapel which cried out for a spire and on the other by a two-storey block in the Bauhaus style, designed by an old Daltonian who died when the avant-garde squash court that he had designed collapsed on him in 1934. Many people thought it just retribution for a man who had done more than anybody else to ruin the look of the school.

In the chapel the boys sat in long rows, facing each other across the central aisle. In the middle of the first prayer, fruitily intoned by the chaplain, the Reverend L. A. Carstairs (known to the boys as Holy C), Henry had a nasty shock. He caught sight of Tubman-Edwards, who winked at him.

Henry was in Form 1A, the form for the brightest of the new boys. So was Paul Hargreaves. Tubman-Edwards wasn't.

And so there began again the process of finding classrooms and going through endless roll-calls, which made the first day a relatively undemanding exercise, a breather before the rigours to come. When lessons proper began, and his Maths teacher (Loopy L) picked up a text-book, Henry instinctively ducked. He found that he was backward at Maths, but a star performer at Latin, thanks to Mr Belling. And all the time he felt a sense of security that had come to him rarely in his school life. Friendship, which had so often proved so difficult, was suddenly easy here. Henry and Paul kept finding themselves next to each other. They were both sensitive and shy. Already, by Friday evening, Paul Hargreaves was his best friend ever.

That Friday evening, after tea (sausage and lumpy mash, served by the wheezing Gorringe), Henry and Paul were beginning the decoration of their partitions in the junior study. Paul was favouring a kind of collage of works of art which had a significance for him. There were postcards of works by people Henry had never heard of, like Salvador Dali and Braque. His own display promised to be slightly less sophisticated, consisting as it did entirely of cuttings from the *Picturegoer*. Uncle Teddy and Auntie Doris had arranged for him to receive the *Picturegoer* every week, and his growing interest in films blossomed into an obsession at a time when it was impossible for him to go out and see any.

Suddenly a cry rent the air. 'All new-bugs to the shower room.'

The sixteen new-bugs in Orange House assembled slightly uneasily in the bleak, stone-walled shower room, with its ten showers.

They were met by Hertford-Jones.

'O.K., you blokes,' said Hertford-Jones. 'Line up against the wall.'

They lined up against the wall, their uneasiness growing. Nothing pleasant in life is preceded by being lined up against a wall.

'O.K. Drop your shonkers,' said Hertford-Jones.

They stared at him blankly.

'Shonkers are trousers,' said Hertford-Jones impatiently, as if everybody knew that.

They dropped their shonkers.

'Ready, doctor,' sang out Hertford-Jones.

A cold autumn wind whistled through the shower room, lifting their shirts like cat-flaps.

A young doctor entered, in a white coat. He carried a small torch and a notebook. He examined their genitalia and surrounds with his torch and said either 'yes' or 'no' to Hertford-Jones, who put either a tick or a cross against their names. Henry and Paul both got ticks. Feltstein, who was Jewish, got a cross.

'Right,' said the doctor. 'The following thirteen boys – Keynes, Wellard, Curtis-Brown, Pratt, Hargreaves, Mallet, Needham, Renwick, Pellet, Forbes-Robinson, Bickerstaff, Tidewell and Willoughby – will be circumcised tomorrow. Be at the bottom of house drive at seven-thirty. Bring an overnight bag, just in case.'

'Please, sir,' said Paul Hargreaves, going red. 'My father's a doctor. I don't think he'd like me to be circumcised without his permission.'

'We have parental permission,' said the doctor. 'We wouldn't dream of doing it without.'

The doctor and Hertford-Jones departed, and the new-bugs debated. Could it be a hoax?

'It sounds like a hoax to me,' said Paul. 'I'm going to see Mr Satchel.'

Paul walked straight through the library and into the housemaster's part of the building.

Quite soon he returned, a little abashed.

'It's genuine,' he said.

That night, in South Africa, Nattrass tried to ease Henry's worries.

'I've had it,' he said. 'Nothing to it. Snip snip, thank you very much. They use a local anaesthetic and you don't have to look.'

After lights-out, Fletcher whispered to Henry from the next bed.

'Pratt?'

'Yes?'

'Good luck tomorrow. There's nothing to worry about. Doctor Wallis at Taunton General is the second best circumcision man in England. Only old Thursby at Barts is better. He hasn't had *any* cock-ups.'

'Has Doctor Wallis had cock-ups, then?'

'Only the one.'

'What happened?'

'Let's just say it was a bit of a balls-up, and leave it at that.'

'What happened?'

'I don't think you ought to know. It might spoil your crud.'

But Henry's crud was already spoilt. So was Keynes's, Wellard's, Curtis-Brown's, Hargreaves's, Mallet's, Needham's, Renwick's, Pellet's. Forbes-Robinson's, Bickerstaff's, Tidewell's and Willoughby's.

In the morning, the tremulous thirteen set off down the drive with three bags each, one in their hands, and one under each eye.

Shortly after eight o'clock, they trudged back, sheepish and red-faced, but also relieved, to cheers from the faces at the dormitory windows. It turned out that the doctor was Hertford-Jones's older brother.

That night, in South Africa, Nattrass explained that the ritual of the thirteen circumcisees of Orange House went back over a hundred years. It was mildly unpleasant when it happened to you, perhaps, but a real hoot in the years to come.

'But even Mr Satchel pretended it was true,' said Henry, puzzled.

'It's a tradition,' explained Nattrass, but he wasn't sure that Henry understood.

In the next weeks, a chain of events occurred concerning Henry's parentage.

When Paul had said that his father was a brain surgeon, Henry had only half believed it. He had said that his father was a test pilot on impulse, half thinking that he was involved in a joke routine. But Paul's father *was* a brain surgeon. Henry hoped that Paul had forgotten that his father was supposed to be a test pilot.

The first link in the chain was forged during a French lesson, given by Mr Wrigley (Sweaty W). His classroom was light and airy, in the Bauhaus block.

'No, Mallender,' said Sweaty W. 'It's a *pris*. The perfect of *prendre* takes *avoir*, as in "*Le mecanicien a pris le livre tout de suite*".' Sweaty W wrote the sentence on the blackboard. 'What does that mean, Pratt?' he said.

Henry's heart sank.

'The mechanic. . .' he began.

'Yes?'

'The mechanic has put the hare all over the furniture.'

'Are you trying to be funny, Pratt?'

'No, sir.'

'Hargreaves?'

'The mechanic. . .has taken. . .the book. . .at once,' said Paul, pretending that he found it difficult, so as not to humiliate his friend.

'The mechanic took the book at once,' said Sweaty W. 'What did you learn in French at your prep school, Pratt?'

'How to take out tonsils and gall-stones, sir.'

'What???'

'He means he went to Brasenose College, sir,' said Mallender.

Sweaty W stared at Mallender.

'What?' he said.

'The French master at Brasenose is a failed doctor, sir. He spends most of his time telling the boys how to do operations, in English,' said Mallender. 'My father teaches English there.'

Henry stared at Mallender in surprise, and wondered if he'd ever had to copy out the whole of Keats' 'Endymion'.

Sweaty W believed in improvisation, to give a certain vitality and edge to his French lessons. Should a window-cleaner ever fall off his ladder and drop head-first past the window onto the asphalt, no boy would have been allowed to go to his assistance until the class had produced the French for 'a window-cleaner has just fallen off his ladder and dropped head-first past the window onto the asphalt'.

'In French, Mallender,' said Sweaty W now. 'In French. My father is an English teacher.'

'*Mon père est un professeur de l'Anglais.*'

'Yes, though perhaps *professeur*'s putting it a big high for Brasenose College, and the French don't use *un* before an occupation. It's "*Mon père est professeur*".'

They went briefly round the class then, saying what their fathers did. '*Mon père est fermier.*' '*Mon père est aussi fermier.*' ('No, he isn't, Fuller.' 'I know, sir, but I don't know the French for estate agent.') '*Mon père est. . .il. . .*he's a lawyer, sir.' ('*Votre père est avocat*, Tremlett.') '*Mon père a laissé mon mère pour cinq ans.*' ('It's *ma mère*, and *depuis cinq ans*, and I'm sorry, Bairstow.') '*Mon père. . .*' Henry hesitated. Did Paul remember that he'd said that his father was a test pilot? Whether Paul remembered or not, should he now tell the truth? How could he, since he didn't know the French for a cutler, or a maker of penknives? Wasn't it an academic point, since he didn't know the French for test pilot either? Wouldn't it be simpler just to say that his father was dead?

'*Il essaye les avions,*' said Paul. 'He's a test pilot, sir.'

'*Votre père est pilote d'essai*, Pratt,' said Sweaty W.

Fair enough, thought Henry.

The second link occurred in Dalton Town. Boys were allowed into the town at certain times, and one of Henry's duties as a fag was to shop for Lampo Davey and Tosser Pilkington-Brick. On this occasion, as it chanced, he required writing paper, envelopes, instant coffee, condensed milk, drinking chocolate, a loaf and a tin of sardines.

Two unpleasant incidents occurred on this particular day. As he trudged down Eastgate in the rain, he was drenched from head to foot when a Carter Patterson removal van ploughed through a huge puddle outside Boots.

The second unfortunate incident happened in the market place, outside Butcher's the draper's. A charming square, in those days, Dalton market place. A jumble of Tudor and Georgian stone buildings with the Georgian Town Hall at the east end and the cathedral-like early-English parish church at the west end. Those are still there, but the north side is now totally disfigured by the hideous new shopping precinct, built in the late-sixties balance-sheet style. On that day, in early October, 1948, the north side of the market place was disfigured by an equally unpleasant sight, a human portent of the institutionalised vandalism to come. Tubman-Edwards.

'I thought you were going to Eton,' said Henry.

'It fell through,' said Tubman-Edwards, colouring. 'What's it worth to shut me up?'

'I don't understand,' said Henry.

'It doesn't understand,' said Tubman-Edwards. 'Well it soon will. It's changed a bit since I first knew it. It's still a pretty oiky individual, but it has toned down its accent quite a lot. Not totally successfully, of course, but still, it stands a reasonable chance of avoiding the nickname "Oiky". Specially now its father turns out to be a test pilot. Amazing. When Fuller told me there was a chap from Brasenose in his class, and it was you, and your father was a test pilot, I said nothing. Quick thinking, eh, Oiky? The possibilities struck me immediately. What's it worth for me not to reveal the truth, Oiky?'

Tubman-Edwards smirked. It was not a pretty sight. The church clock struck two, and reverberated into silence. Henry wished he was stronger than Tubman-Edwards.

'Seven hundred boys calling you "Oiky". Seven hundred boys knowing you're a shitty little liar. How much is it worth to shut me up, Oiky?'

'Twelve jars of Gentleman's Relish,' said Henry.

Perhaps, if it hadn't been for those twelve jars, he would have told Tubman-Edwards to shove off. The truth would have been out, and after some initial unpleasantness the matter might eventually have been forgotten. But it seemed like a master-stroke, a golden opportunity to get rid of Tubman-Edwards and his Gentleman's Relish at the same time.

'I don't like Gentleman's Relish,' said Tubman-Edwards.

'It's marvellous stuff,' said Henry. 'Every sandwich a treat.

Every mouthful a poem.'

'Why are you so eager to get rid of it, then?' said Tubman-Edwards.

'I'm not,' said Henry. 'But I've got to give you something, and it's all I've got.'

'I can swop them, I suppose,' said Tubman-Edwards. 'All right, you've got yourself a deal.'

Henry's reading had just passed through its detective-story period and was just coming onto its John Buchan, A. E. W. Mason and Scarlet Pimpernel stage. He should have been familiar with the old adage that 'the blackmailer always comes back for more'.

The following week, when he handed over his twelve jars of Gentleman's Relish outside Baker's the butcher's (they're all multiple stores now, but in those days an additional charm of Dalton market place was its cluster of shops whose proprietors bore the names of other kinds of shop), Tubman-Edwards said, 'That'll do for the first week.'

When they met the following week, outside Draper's the chemist's, Henry found himself committed to giving Tubman-Edwards all his pocket money for the rest of the term.

It was too late for Henry to tell the truth now. Tubman-Edwards was busily spreading false information about his father. Henry learnt that his father was testing amazing new prototypes. He was involved in a secret space project which might eventually make him the first man on the moon. He didn't need to boast. Tubman-Edwards did it for him. It was out of his control.

The following week, Tubman-Edwards took the money that he had been given by Lampo Davey and Tosser Pilkington-Brick for the purchase of instant coffee, condensed milk, drinking chocolate, mayonnaise, eggs and a tin of anchovies.

Henry walked back to Orange House in utter dejection, mocked by the soft sunshine of late October. The one ray of light in the whole gloomy business had been that Tubman-Edwards was in Plantaganet House. Orange House had remained a safe haven. How safe would it be, when he returned to Lampo Davey and Tosser Pilkington-Brick empty-handed?

He knocked timidly on their study door.

Davey was on his own, Pilkington-Brick having gone to train for the first fifteen.

Henry stood by the door, irresolute, silent.

'What is it, Pratt?' said Lampo Davey irritably.

'I dropped all your money down a drain,' said Henry, and to his horror his eyes filled with tears.

'Well for God's sake don't blatt,' said Lampo Davey.

Henry blew his nose and managed not to blatt.

'Sit down and have a coffee,' said Lampo Davey, his voice a mixture of kindness and disgust.

Henry sat down, and Lampo made two mugs of coffee, thickened and sweetened by the condensed milk. Henry felt ill-at-ease, a fag being made coffee by the boy for whom he fagged.

'Tosser'll be livid,' said Lampo. 'Serve him right. He eats the chocolate in powder form, with a teaspoon. He's disgusting.'

Mr Satchel (Dopy S) didn't allow senior boys to choose their study mates. He believed that you learnt more by being thrown together. Lampo Davey and Tosser Pilkington-Brick might have existed to justify his system. Total opposites, they had formed a bond of scorn and affection which was to survive a life-time.

'I am the most sensitive and artistic and subtle boy in Orange House, which isn't saying much,' said Lampo Davey. 'Tosser is a thick ape. Because he's good at games, House worships him. I have far too much natural good taste to be envious. You're not playing rugger today, are you? Good. Let's go for a walk before evening school.'

They turned right by the Methodist Chapel. 'They mistrust pleasure so deeply that even their buildings have to be hideous,' said Lampo Davey. They took the narrow lane that climbed up behind the town, winding through apple orchards, where sheep grazed between the trees. The countryside was a luscious green after the autumn rains. Now, the soft Indian summer had come and the trees were beginning to turn.

'Winter. I welcome it with open arms,' said Lampo Davey.

'Really?' said Henry.

'Oh yes,' said Lampo Davey, as if it was obvious. 'Autumn colours in England are beautiful, if a bit much. The first pale greens of spring have a certain brief charm. But winter! Ploughed

174

fields. Farm buildings. The magnificent outlines of trees. It's spare. It's strong. Summer in England is dreadful. The banality of all that bright green, which slowly fades into weariness. The grotesque excess of plant life. The English countryside in summer is a featureless confusion of weeds. Compare it with Tuscany, Pratt. Compare it with Umbria. The English summer, like so much of English life, is totally without taste. Give me Italy every time.'

'I prefer England,' said Henry. 'Italy's full of wops.'

'My father works in the Italian embassy in Rome. They're the most civilised people in Europe,' said Lampo Davey, with a touch of anger.

A grassy path ran along the edge of the woods, above the orchards. Lampo Davey flung himself onto the ground, beside the path. Henry sat down beside him, after testing the grass to see if it was dry. Lampo Davey laughed.

'Mr Sat On Wet Grass went rusty inside,' said Henry, and blushed.

'What?' said Lampo Davey.

'Miss Candy said things like that all the time,' said Henry. 'She was our teacher.'

'Priceless,' said Lampo Davey. 'Utterly priceless. Tell me more.'

'Mr Pick-Nose was carried off by the bogey man,' said Henry boldly.

'Priceless,' said Lampo Davey. 'When I first saw you, I thought, "Oh dear. Clueless clotto, I'm afraid." I didn't even think you were remotely pretty. A little fatty-legs, I thought. But I've decided that I rather like little fatty faggy-chops.'

Lampo Davey put his arm round Henry. Henry went red and wriggled free desperately.

'Don't be so shocked,' said Lampo Davey. 'We're in the nineteen forties, not the Middle Ages. Come on. Walkies. No further advances, I promise. I'm a connoisseur of sexual pleasure, not a child molester.'

They walked on into the woods, although Henry longed to go back, to the communal safety of Orange House. He felt shocked, surprised, even a little flattered, which shocked him also. He also felt a bit of a spoil-sport, which struck him as ridiculous.

An aeroplane zoomed loud and low over their heads, crossed the valley and disappeared low over the woods on the other side.

'Your father, perhaps,' said Lampo Davey.

'You what?' said Henry.

'Flying that plane.'

'Oh. Yes. Happen. I mean "maybe".'

'How could a father like yours have such a clueless clot as a son?' said Lampo Davey. 'You are a clueless clot, aren't you?'

Henry nodded. In the presence of this young man with the long, sad, slightly twisted face and the deep, sardonic eyes, he felt ignorant, innocent, ugly, unwordly, oiky and a liar. Yet Lampo fancied him.

'Oh, I'm all in favour of clueless clots,' said Lampo Davey, sensing that he'd hurt Henry more than he'd intended. 'Come on. Time to go home. Enough of Confuse-A-Fag.'

That evening, after school, when Henry was alone with Tosser Pilkington-Brick for the first time, Tosser grinned and said, 'Lampo's livid about your losing that money. He has the most affected eating habits. He would have hard-boiled two eggs, covered them in bottled mayonnaise and bits of anchovy, and pretended that he was sophisticated. He's pathetic. Don't worry, though. I'll defend you. He fancies you, you know.'

'Yes,' said Henry.

'You are actually rather more appealing than I thought at first,' said Tosser Pilkington-Brick. 'Any chance of a bit of "how's your father?"?'

'Sorry,' said Henry, feeling six inches taller because he wasn't blushing.

'No hard feelings,' said Tosser Pilkington-Brick. 'Getting any hard feelings yet? No? Late developer. Well, you will soon. If you do, promise me one thing. Don't get involved with Madame Lampo. She's devious. She's poison. She's a corrupter of youth. With me it would just be a bit of fun. Good, clean filth.'

The third link was added to the chain on the following Satuday. It was a raw, misty forerunner of winter. The venue was the Bald-Headed Angel, an ancient coaching house whose name constituted its only flirtation with originality. Henry was suffering from a minor ailment, made the mistake of ordering soup, and met an old flame in highly embarrassing circumstances. The minor ailment was a streaming code in the dose, the soup was oxtail, and the old flame was Belinda Boyce-Uppingham.

Henry had been invited to take luncheon with the parents of his best friend, Paul Hargreaves. Also present would be Paul's twin sister Diana, and Diana's school-friend, who was staying with the Hargreaves for half-term.

Paul and Henry were picked up at the school gates in the family Bentley after Saturday-morning school. Boys were streaming back to Orange House on foot and bike. All the pleasure of driving past them in a Bentley was destroyed by the presence in the car of Belinda Boyce-Uppingham. Even the fact that she had a brace on her teeth didn't cheer him up. The four young ones were squashed together in the back seat. Had Belinda recognised him? Had she ever known his name?

They drove through the market place, it charms ruined by its association with Tubman-Edwards. Dr Hargreaves steered the Bentley expertly under the narrow arch at the side of the Bald-Headed Angel, and parked in the long, narrow courtyard. They entered through a side door and made for the cocktail bar. The Hargreaves parents exuded elegance well-heeled enough to look as if it was attempting to hide how well-heeled it was. Dr James Hargreaves wore a sober, well-cut suit. Mrs Celia Hargreaves favoured the new Parisian 'tube look' in grey. When she took off her tight-fitting cloche hat, her hair was revealed in its daring, post-war shortness. Eating out was no longer a total mystery to Henry, thanks to Uncle Teddy and Auntie Doris, but he would have felt at his oikiest, in the world of brain surgeons and their elegant spouses, even if Belinda Boyce-Uppingham hadn't been there, and even if his nose hadn't begun to run, in the warmth of the cocktail bar.

The younger element had squashes, the grown-ups dry sherry. The head waiter gave them menus, and returned all too quickly to take their orders. Henry hadn't even begun to choose. How could he, when he was supposed to be the son of a famous test pilot, but was sitting next to a girl who might recognise him as the son of a private soldier who had made penknives in civvy street, and

177

whom he had knocked off her horse, to which she had responded by calling him an oik, providing a foretaste of the unpleasant soubriquet by which a whole school was later to identify him, and when he wanted to blow his nose but didn't dare in this elegant company, and when the whole menu was in French, one of his worst subjects?

The head waiter was standing over him.

'Are you all right, Henry? We're waiting for you to order,' said Paul.

'Oh. Right. I'll. . .I'll have the same as Paul.'

'That's silly,' said Diana.

'Not if it's what he wants,' said Dr James Hargreaves.

'It isn't,' said Diana. 'He's just saying it cos he can't decide.'

'Don't I know you?' said Belinda Boyce-Uppingham.

Henry's heart sank. On its way down it passed his blood, which was rushing up towards his cheeks. He went into violent internal convulsions, pumping, throbbing, sinking, burning. He sneezed five times.

'What on earth's wrong?' said Dr James Hargreaves.

'What did you say your other name was? said Belinda Boyce-Uppingham.

Henry opened his mouth, but no sound came.

'Pratt,' said Paul.

'I knew I knew you,' said Belinda Boyce-Uppingham. 'You were an evacuee at Rowth Bridge.'

'I wasn't an evacuee,' said Henry, finding his voice. 'I was staying with relations.'

'Of course he was,' said Paul, defending his friend. 'His father was fighting the war.'

Belinda Boyce-Uppingham frowned slightly. Perhaps she had just remembered calling him an oik, thought Henry.

Paul Hargreaves frowned too. His friend wasn't putting up a good show.

It was the memory of anger, not guilt, that had caused Belinda Boyce-Uppingham to frown. 'You knocked me off my horse,' she said.

'You called me an oik,' said Henry.

Belinda Boyce-Uppingham flushed.

'Surely not?' she said. 'I mean. . .'

'It's frightening when you're thrown off a horse,' said Mrs Celia Hargreaves. 'Do you ride, Henry?'

'No,' said Henry. How he wished he could have said 'yes', but he wasn't going to tell any more lies. If he did say 'yes', he'd probably discover that a string of thoroughbreds had been laid on for their post-prandial delectation.

'I think it was pretty rotten of you to remind Blin that she called you an oik,' said Diana. 'I think that *was* a bit oiky.'

'Diana!' said Dr Hargreaves.

'I don't agree,' said Paul. 'I mean you might forgive somebody for calling somebody an oik, if they were an oik, but not when they called you an oik and your father's a famous test pilot, even if they did knock you off your stupid horse.'

'Paleface was not stupid,' said Belinda Boyce-Uppingham, tossing her head, perhaps in sympathetic imitation of her erstwhile mount.

'I don't agree,' said Diana. 'It doesn't matter if you call somebody an oik if they obviously aren't, but if they are it's unforgiveable. Henry obviously isn't, so Blin's forgiven.'

'I think this is becoming a rather silly conversation,' said Mrs Hargreaves. 'I think we're all a little bit over-excited.'

'I'd like to meet your father, Henry. I hear he's fearsomely distinguished,' said Dr Hargreaves, not without a trace of smugness, as if he knew that Henry's father would have the utmost difficulty in being as distinguished as he was.

'What is all this about your father?' said Belinda Boyce-Uppingham.

'He's a famous test pilot,' said Paul. 'He tests all the new prototypes.'

'Well who was that funny little man with the bandage?' said Belinda Boyce-Uppingham.

'He was not a funny little man. He was my father. And he's dead,' said Henry.

'Your table's ready,' said the head waiter.

Henry found himself walking into the restaurant with the others, although he longed to run from the hotel. But he'd ordered, and social conventions are strong. Paul flashed him a look of fury, Belinda of scorn, Diana of encouragement. Dr and Mrs Hargreaves avoided his eye, which was easy, as he was avoiding everybody's eye.

He found that he had ordered oxtail soup. Its heat made his nose stream. Paul sat glaring at him as he continually blew his nose. The noise was like an air-raid warning in this temple of starched white linen and watery food.

The soup was watery, the conversation formal and evasive, till Paul said, 'For God's sake stop blowing your nose.'

'Paul!' said Mrs Hargreaves, reproving Paul for not giving Henry an example of what gracious manners were.

'Sorry,' said Henry. 'My cold's come out.'

'I wish you hadn't,' said Paul.

'Paul!' said Dr Hargreaves.

'Well, honestly, he's made me feel such an ass,' said Paul. 'He told me his father was a test pilot.'

'Yes, well,' said Dr Hargreaves, meaning, 'You feel an ass? What about him?'

The waiter advanced slowly, like one bad smell approaching another. They remained totally silent while he cleared the plates, as if it was of vital importance that he should know nothing about the matter.

Henry screwed himself up to provide some sort of explanation.

'Everyone at Brasenose called me Oiky,' he said. 'I hated being called Oiky. It wasn't my fault.'

It was Belinda Boyce-Uppingham's turn to go scarlet.

'Isn't embarrassment embarrassing,' said Diana. 'This is the most embarrassing meal I've ever been to.'

'Shut up, Diana,' said Paul.

'It really was mean of you actually, Blin, to call Henry an oik, because he really isn't,' said Diana.

The waiter ambled over with food that might have been hot when it left the kitchens. Henry found that he had ordered *le pâté de la maisonette* (cottage pie) *avec les choux du Bruxelles* (watery) *et les carottes* (tasteless).

'Waiter!' summoned Dr Hargreaves, as the waiter wandered off.

'Sir?' said the waiter.

'Tell the chef he does some amazing things with water,' said Dr

Hargreaves.

'James!' said Mrs Hargreaves.

The waiter sauntered off, mystified, across the half-empty room.

There was nothing Henry could have done to make matters worse, except to parody a clumsy young man in a restaurant by losing the top of the salt cellar and pouring all its contents onto his food. And that is exactly what he did.

'Never mind,' said Diana. 'It's horribly underseasoned actually.'

Henry scooped off what salt he could, and ate his meal bravely, although it did cause him to suffer a severe coughing fit just as his nasal flood had finally come to an end.

After the meal, as they were leaving the hotel, Diana pulled Henry back in.

'I don't think you're an oik,' she said, 'Knocking Blin off her horse like that, and pretending your father was a test pilot. I think it's a hoot.'

In the morning, there was a fire practice at Orange House. They descended down a canvas chute from their dormitory windows. South Africa dorm was on the second floor, and it was quite a long way down to the gravel. Runciman and Cranston held the chute rather high off the ground, and Henry took a nasty, scraping fall on the gravel.

'Terribly sorry,' said Runciman and Cranston in unison.

Henry caught sight of Paul, standing among a group of boys who had made their descent, grinning broadly.

'I paid them to do that,' said Paul. 'Serve you right for yesterday.'

They wandered along the path that led to the extensive vegetable garden.

'I'm sorry about yesterday,' said Henry.

'I won't tell anyone,' said Paul. 'Everyone will think your father's a test pilot except me.'

'But. . .'

'I'm your friend, aren't I?'

But for how long, thought Henry. Maybe Paul really was such a smashing bloke that his feelings wouldn't be undermined by the power he had over Henry, but what about Henry? Would his

181

feelings of friendship survive the guilt and gratitude that he would always feel in Paul's presence?

The answer was 'no'. The fourth and final link in the chain was therefore inevitable.

The opportunity arose the following day, when the English master, Mr Foden (Foggy F), set them an essay on the subject of 'A building that's important to me'. Seven long days later, the essays were handed back by Foggy F. He approached Henry, his slightly vacant face grave with disapproval.

'Not an inspired effort, I'm afraid,' he said. 'You look an imaginative enough boy, Mallender, but this is dead prose. Correct, organised, dead as a doornail.'

'But, sir. . .' Henry began.

'Don't argue, Mallender,' said Foggy F. 'You must be able to take criticism.'

'But, sir. . .'

'Silence. You haven't shown any finesse in your approach. Imagine me, the reader, approaching your work. You've held nothing back. Your first paragraph reveals all, making the rest of the essay almost redundant. You should tempt me. You should lead me up a figurative garden path.'

'But, sir. . .'

'There are no buts about it, Mallender. Now Pratt here. . .'

Foggy F turned towards Mallender.

'But, sir. . .' began Mallender.

'Don't argue,' said Foggy F. 'I'm about to praise you. You, Pratt, you may sit there looking about as imaginative as a pumice stone, but, inside that sponge-like edifice which passes for your brain, you are actually thinking.'

'Please, sir. . .' said Mallender.

'Silence, Pratt. You'll get nowhere if you're embarrassed by praise. You paint a picture of a world, a world of back-to-back terraces in industrial Yorkshire. The building you describe was jerry-built in the industrial revolution. It's infested with vermin. It's probably condemned by now. Do you live there? No. In your last paragraph you tell us why it's important. Not the first paragraph, Mallender. The last. That house is important to you because you do not live there, because it makes you appreciate the running water, the fitted carpets, the electric light of the house where you do live.'

'But, sir,' said Henry. 'I'm Pratt.'

'Mallender, for the last time. . .you're Pratt? Well, why didn't you tell me?'

'I tried, sir.'

'Well, anyway, Pratt, it's a fine piece of work. As for you, Mallender, sitting there accepting credit for work you didn't do, I hope you're ashamed. Now, I want everyone to read Pratt's essay. It's a thoroughly imaginative. . .'

'It isn't imagination, sir,' said Henry. 'I lived in that back-to-back terrace.'

'Are you sure?' said Foggy F. 'I understood your father was a brain surgeon.'

'No, sir. My father's a brain surgeon,' said Paul Hargreaves. 'His father's a test pilot.'

'Thank you, Fuller,' said Foggy F.

'My father isn't a test pilot,' said Henry. 'I made that up. My father made penknives, and he died sitting on the outside lats.'

The relief was intense. The truth was out at last. The future wouldn't be easy, but now his real life at Dalton College could begin.

The future wasn't easy. The news of his true origins swept Orange House. As an hors d'oeuvre, on Friday evening, he met an old chum, the noddle down the porcelain bowl. This bowl was made by Bollingtons of Tunstall, just up the road from Etruria. The incident linked the little village school at Rowth Bridge with the great public school of Dalton, and might have been said to be the only evidence Henry ever received of true equality of opportunity in education, had it not been for the fact that, due to the primitive toilet arrangements at Rowth Bridge school, even that had been an extra-mural activity.

The main course took place on Saturday evening. Cranston and Runciman grabbed him as he was collecting his clean pants, vest and socks from matron's cupboard under the stairs, with its overpowering smell of ironing. They led him out, through the

183

back door, into the dark November night. A thin drizzle was falling, and there was a light wind from the east.

Waiting outside were Shelton, Holmes, Philpot A. E., Philpot W. F. N. and Perkins. Philpot A. E. and Shelton carried coils of rope. Henry was led into a small corner of the gardens. The gardener had complained that the gardens were too much for him, and Dopy S had agreed to make his task easier by leaving a section as a nature reserve. It was known as 'The Dell'. They tied Henry to a tree in 'The Dell' with one of the ropes, the one carried by Philpot A. E. Then each boy gave him eight strokes with the other rope, doubled up. It hardly seems necessary to tell you that this was the rope carried by Shelton.

Eight strokes each from Cranston, Runciman, Shelton, Holmes, Philpot A. E., Philpot W. F. N. and Perkins. Fifty-six strokes with a doubled-up rope. They thudded into his backside until pain was an irrelevant word. He made no movement. He made no noise. He would die before he gave them the satisfaction.

They untied him, and led him back into the changing room.

'Did you have anything on, under there, for protection? said Perkins.

Henry shook his head, not trusting himself to speak.

They made him take down his shonkers, and examined his backside. They seemed awed by what they saw.

'Pull them up,' said Holmes flatly.

They seemed curiously subdued, almost crestfallen.

Henry decided that he must trust himself to speak. He must take a leaf out of the Brasenose book.

'Thank you,' he said.

And for dessert? There was no dessert. The bullying of Henry ended as abruptly as it had begun.

Not everybody was nasty to Henry.

Nattrass wasn't.

Nattrass summoned him to his study the next day.

'I believe something happened last night,' he said.

'No,' said Henry.

'Sit down,' said Nattrass.

'I'd rather stand,' said Henry.

184

Nattrass grinned.

'You had your buttocks beaten to pulp by a group of savages,' said Nattrass. 'This house is a cess-pit. It hasn't been cock house at anything since 1937. I want to clean it up. I want to turn it into a civilised, compassionate place. I want those bastards sacked.'

'I'm sorry,' said Henry. 'I want to forget it.'

'Shove off, then,' said Nattrass irritably, and added, in a kinder voice, 'If you're ever in any more trouble, come to me.'

Lampo Davey wasn't nasty.

On Sundays the senior boys often had fry-ups, cooked for them by their fags on the little gas stove in the alcove between the changing room and the showers. There were three favourite meals. Sausage and egg with fried bread and beans. Bacon and egg with fried bread and beans. Sausage, bacon and egg with fried bread and beans. Lampo opted for bacon and egg with fried bread but without the beans. The absence of baked beans was his way of asserting his sophistication.

To Henry's intense relief, he didn't break the egg. Tosser would eat anything, but it grieved Lampo deeply if the egg was broken.

Lampo signalled to him to sit down.

'I'd rather stand,' he said.

'Get me a coffee, then,' said Lampo.

The last November light was fading from the Sunday sky. Tosser was out. It was cosy in the study, with its smell of warm pipes and fried bread.

'Excellent,' said Lampo Davey, picking his way daintily through his fry-up. 'You're quite a good cook.'

'I'm not surprised you sound surprised,' said Henry. He was surprised himself.

'Priceless, this business of you being a slum kid,' said Lampo.

'It wasn't a slum,' said Henry. 'It was sub-standard housing, that's all.'

'Priceless, anyway,' said Lampo. 'Much better than that dreary old test pilot. He really was a bore. I bet he had a handlebar moustache. I'm so relieved to see him go.'

'I'm not too sorry myself,' said Henry.

'You worship Tosser, don't you?'

'He's pretty good at rugger.'

'You think the sun shines out of his arse. Well just as long as that's your only interest in that part of his anatomy. Now I've shocked you again. I understand why now. The working class has always hated homosexuality. All right, thanks for a nice meal. Dismiss, little Henry.'

Lampo Davey smiled his slightly distant, slightly crooked smile, and to his surprise Henry smiled back.

Paul Hargreaves wasn't nasty.

Paul hadn't abandoned him. He hadn't wavered when sentiment against Henry was running at its strongest. It seemed that although dreary to most people, Henry did have something, somewhere, that was not utterly and irremediably unattractive and boring.

On the Monday, two days after the beating, Henry took care during the Latin lesson of Mr Braithwaite (Busy B) not to make a mistake. Busy B ruled his class with a gymshoe of iron. The slightest mistake was rewarded with a sharp thwack across the backside. (It seemed to Henry that the most concrete thing which parents got for all the money they spent on private education was the knowledge that their loved ones would be beaten on the backside instead of the hand.) Henry sat, that morning, wary, alert, his backside throbbing, hoping that Busy B wouldn't touch on his Achilles heel, the gerund and gerundive. All seemed to be going well until Paul was asked to provide the supine of *rego*. It is, of course, *rectum*. Never did the old music-hall gag surface with such painful results. It sent Henry into a panic, from which there was no chance of recovery. Busy B asked him the second person singular of the past perfect of *audio*. You had been heard. *Auditus eras*. Normally a doddle, thank you very much, sir, tickety boo. Totally beyond Henry in his sudden panic.

Thwack. The impact of the gymshoe, which normally produced only a moderately unpleasant stinging, seemed to implode inside his rear-end. He had an image of Tubman-Edwards, huge, grotesque, filling the window with his smirking. Then the hallucination was gone, and he struggled back to his desk, resolved to end the threat of Tubman-Edwards.

After dinner the following day (egg and bacon pie with carrots and boiled potatoes, followed by sponge pudding with chocolate sauce), Henry took Paul with him into the market place.

There, outside Ironmonger's the newsagent's, they confronted Tubman-Edwards.

'This is my friend Paul Hargreaves,' said Henry. 'This is my blackmailer, Tubman-Edwards. Paul, tell Tubman-Edwards about my father.'

'The whole school knows that Henry's father made pocket-knives and died in the outside lats,' said Paul. 'So there's really no reason for Henry to worry about Shant knowing that he used to be called Oiky, and if you don't give everything back we'll tell the whole school what an inflated sack of blackmailing yak turd you are,' said Paul.

'I can't give it all back,' said Tubman-Edwards, who'd gone the colour of putty. 'I've sold the Gentleman's Relish.'

'The equivalent in cash value, in agreed weekly instalments, will do,' said Henry.

'Weekly?' said Tubman-Edwards weakly.

'Weekly,' said Henry. 'Otherwise I'll get my hatchet-men onto you.'

Henry had a rare stroke of luck at that moment. Tosser Pilkington-Brick walked past on his way back from the Coach and Horses. He was in a genial mood, and smiled as he said, 'Hello, Pratt.'

Tubman-Edwards gazed at Tosser's large frame, and his face changed from putty to flour.

'That won't he necessary,' he croaked.

Every Tuesday for the rest of that term and the next term, Henry met Tubman-Edwards in the market place and received his instalment.

Christmas was quiet, especially as the Porringers had gone to Canada. Cousin Hilda gave Henry a stamp album. Uncle Teddy and Auntie Doris gave him a Meccano set and equipment for his railway – two trucks, a guards van, four straight rails, two curves, a set of points, a turntable, a box of assorted conifers for scenery, a station platform and six mixed passengers. Henry wasn't interested in hobbies. He thought they must be a middle-class habit which he'd never acquired. Basic politeness demanded that he construct the odd Meccano monstrosity, stick the occasional desultory stamp in his album, arrange a conifer or two beside the track, even run a train once in a while when Uncle Teddy grew bored. He found Uncle Teddy's enthusiasm for the railway surprising and endearing, and felt dreadfully guilty about not being able to respond more wholeheartedly. What Henry loved were his books, his wireless – there was Jimmy Jewel and Ben Warris now, in 'Up the Pole', with Claude Dampier and Jon Pertwee, but Paul Temple and the Curzon Gang was spoilt because he'd missed the beginning and he'd have to go back to school before the last episode – and, above all, his new craze, the films. He went whenever he could, seeing, among others, *Scott of the Antarctic*, *The Winslow Boy*, *The Road to Rio*, *Green Grass of Wyoming*, *My Brother Jonathan* and *The Small Back Room*. Auntie Doris even came with him once or twice, although she liked to miss the second feature, especially when it was Ma and Pa Kettle.

Although he still dreaded his return to school, Henry found that he was looking forward to seeing Paul, and, more surprisingly, to fagging for Lampo Davey and Tosser Pilkington-Brick.

Lessons proceeded smoothly enough. The sports facilities provided wonderful opportunities for a boy who hitherto had only discovered that he was bad at cricket, soccer, hockey and rugger. By the end of his first year at Dalton College, Henry was bad at squash, fives, tennis and swimming as well. In the holidays, he no longer watched much sport. It wasn't much fun without friends. At school, he watched everything, especially if Tosser Pilkington-Brick was playing. Once again, Orange House failed to be cock house at anything. Plantaganet took rugger. (Blast. One up for Tubman-Edwards.) Tudor took hockey and cricket.

'All this sports watching will do you no good,' said Lampo Davey one Sunday evening in early March as he picked his way elegantly through Henry's egg, bacon and fried bread. 'You'll go blind. Has the slumbering giant still not stirred?'

'No.'

'Pour me a glass of claret.'

Lampo Davey and Tosser Pilkington-Brick kept wine under their floorboards. Henry poured Lampo Davey a glass of claret.

Lampo put his hand on Henry's knee.

'I wish you wouldn't do that,' said Henry.

Lampo removed his hand.

'I do wish you'd be my bit of rough trade, little slum boy,' he said. He saw the look in Henry's eye. 'Sorry. Little sub-standard housing boy. Maybe you will, when the slumbering giant stirs. You're probably just a late developer. At least you aren't interested in girls.'

'I used to be,' said Henry.

'When?'

'Till I was nine.'

'My God. You were nine before your latent sexuality period began. You *are* a late developer.'

Henry tried to let it all wash over him. He tried not to show how much the homosexuality still shocked him. He tried not to show how hurt he was at the suggestion that even his apparent precocity at Rowth Bridge had been nothing more than retarded infantilism. He still suffered some fairly fierce mockery of his humble origins, but he had learnt to cope now. Henry 'Ee by gum, I am daft' was back in play. He even tried it on Lampo Davey and Tosser Pilkington-Brick when he dropped a glass of claret. Tosser gave a snort of laughter and spooned some more powdered drinking chocolate into his capacious mouth. Claret and powdered chocolate were a favoured snack. Lampo showed no signs of amusement, but said, 'Priceless. Absolutely priceless.'

The high point of Henry's week was the arrival of the *Picturegoer*. He read it from cover to cover, from 'Should Betty Grable wear tights?' to 'Open pores – do they mar your beauty?'

One day, just before the end of the Easter term, he sat in his partition in the junior study, gazing at his montage of cuttings from the *Picturegoer*. The pictures were mostly of the stars at social functions. They had captions like 'At the Mocambo Club. William Powell selects a cigarette for socialite Mrs H. Bockwitz', 'Gene Kelly and Deborah Kerr found themselves having quite a serious conversation', 'Katharine Hepburn, seen with Lena Horne, caused top sensation. She wore slacks' (the accompanying picture showed only the top halves of the two ladies!) and Somebody must have called "yoo-hoo!" to judge from the faces of James

Stewart and veteran Frank Morgan'. They triggered off a fantasy world which might feature such captions as 'To judge from the friendly waves, it looks as though ex-oik Henry Pratt has won the hearts of the crowd at Elia Kazan's birthday party' and 'At the Mocambo Club, former slum kid Henry Pratt proffers a canapé to thrice-married Jasper K. Bungholtz. To judge from Bungholtz's expression, the tasty morsel is not unwelcome.' As Henry sat there, dreaming his fantasies of non-sexual social conquest, Paul butted in to announce that he had just had his second wank of the day, in the lats. Even Paul, elegant, shy, avant-garde, Braque-loving, discriminating, fractionally fastidious Paul was doing it. Henry sighed. His display suddenly looked very dull. He wanted to start wanting to offer people more than canapés.

The Easter holidays brought Chips Rafferty in *Eureka Stockade* and similar delights. The railway acquired another engine, two carriages, a tunnel and a footbridge. The slumbering giant remained a lifeless dwarf.

Henry remodelled the decoration of his partition. Out went the social events. In came the scantily clad females. The captions now were 'Possessor of these shapely underpinnings, of course, is Jean Kent, in her latest picture *Trottie True*', 'This is something like a pin-up. Gloria de Haven is wearing a striking swim-suit, although we doubt if she's ever actually dived off the deep end in it' and 'If you were running before the wind, wouldn't you like a sea nymph like Janice Carter, in contrasted slip and top, as part of the crew!' In Henry's fantasy, there were captions like 'Top glamour photographer Henry Pratt must have been up very early to catch this delightful pose by lovely Adele Jurgens. Poor fellow – or is he?' But the fantasy refused to come to life. The giant slumbered on.

One day, in the middle of June, 1949, two fourteen-year-old friends were watching Orange House play Plantaganet House at cricket on Middle Boggle. The sports fields were behind the school and slightly above it. They were on two levels, Middle Boggle and Lower Boggle. There had never been an Upper Boggle. This was just one more of life's many mysteries.

Orange House were 92 for 9. Tosser was 55 not out. From their position on the bank beside the Pavvy, they could see Lower Boggle studded with junior games, and the mish-mash of indifferent brick and stone buildings tumbling out of the back of the Queen Anne mansion like architectural faeces. Right at the back was the solid, pseudo-classical frontage of School Hall.

They could see Tubman-Edwards approaching. When he saw them, he turned away.

Tosser hit a massive six. They cheered lustily.

Lampo Davey walked past, ostentatiously reading a book on renaissance art and taking no notice of the game. Mr Satchel (Dopy S) glared at him. No wonder Orange never became cock house at anything if certain subversive elements preferred renaissance art.

Tosser preferred hitting sixes. Another massive pull brought up the hundred. Next ball he was out for 67. 104 all out. Not enough.

'I think I'll have a wank tonight,' said Paul, to cheer himself up.

'So will I,' said Henry.

'I didn't think you'd started,' said Paul.

'I started last night,' said Henry.

'Congratulingles.' Paul thumped his friend in delight.

'Thanks.'

'Fantastic, isn't it?'

'Fantastic.'

'The most fantangles thingles in the univingles.'

'Absolutelingles.'

Henry closed his eyes in dismay. Not at the awful new language which swept Shant mercifully briefly that term. At the stupidity of his lie. How many long weeks of pretence would follow? What a thing to feel the need to boast about. You pulled a bit of your body, it got longer, and some stuff came out. Amazingly clever!

'I don't believe it does make you go blind,' said Paul.

'Well if it did, everybody'd be blind,' said Henry.

'Exactly,' said Paul. 'I wonder if it ever makes people deaf.'

'Pardon?' said Henry.

'Oh, I forgot,' said Paul. 'I had a letter from mother today. She says it's perfectly all right.'

'Wanking?'

'Ass. You coming to stay for the first week of the hols.'

Henry's heart sank. He never wanted to see Dr and Mrs Hargreaves again.

'They won't eat you,' said Paul. 'They liked you. They understood.'

I know, thought Henry. That's what makes it so bad. They can see into my shallow, lying, dirty, oiky little soul.

'They've been burgled,' said Paul. 'All the burglar took was a wireless, a ball of string and two pounds of tomatoes.'

'Sounds like a nutcase,' said Henry. 'Perhaps he's going to bury the tomatoes in the ground, in rows marked by string, and play "Music While You Work" to them in the hope they'll seed themselves.'

'You will come, won't you?' said Paul as the Orange team made its way onto the field, followed by the Plantaganet openers.

'If my people will let me,' said Henry, who still found it odd to refer to his surrogate parents as his people.

That night Henry wrote to Uncle Teddy and Auntie Doris. He wrote dutifully, and found it hard to inject any real life into his efforts.

Dear Uncle Teddy and Auntie Doris [he wrote],

It's quite hot here. I am well. How are you? House lost to Plantaganet by three wickets today. We made 104. Tosser Pilkington-Brick, the one I fag for, made 67. They made 107 for 7. Tosser Pilkington-Brick took 4 for 36. Yesterday I played for Orange 4 v Hanover 4. Hanover 4 made 26. I didn't bowl. We made 17. I made 0. Shant (that's what we call school, it rhymes with pant) lost to Bruton by 8 runs on Saturday. They made 137. A bloke called Porringer made 43. I wonder if he's related to Geoffrey Porringer. Tosser Pilkington-Brick took 3 for 41. We made 129. Tosser Pilkington-Brick made 33. The blokes I fag for are really quite nice, compared to some of the blokes.

I did quite well at Latin and History this week. We're doing the Tudors. I told Toady D I thought some of the kings were no better than bullies. In chemistry my litmus paper went a different colour to everybody else's. Art is good. We just look at slides and Arty K talks about things and we don't have to write anything down.

We had a film show on Saturday in School Hall (that's Shant Shed in Shant Rant. [That means school language.]) It was *Monsieur Verdoux*, with Charlie Chaplin. It was very good, but rather boring.

Paul Hargreaves, who is still my best friend, wants me to go and stay with his people in Hampstead for the first week of the hols. They're frightfully posh and everything. His father's a brain surgeon. They live in Hampstead. Oh, I said that! Paul's got a twin sister, Diana. She's not bad for a girl. If I go I can have a brain operation. I need it. Joke. I hope. Seriously, I'm not bothered about going and if it's inconvenient I'd be just as happy to come straight home.

I finished the Gentleman's Relish yesterday. It was super.

With lots of love.

Henry.

Five days later he got a reply from Auntie Doris. Her replies came quicker than they used to, and were longer.

Dear Henry [he read],

Thank you for your nice, long letter. We're always really interested to read all your interesting news. Nothing much is happening here, business as usual. Your uncle is pretty fed up about the economy. He says the Labour government don't understand business. He calls them the groundnuts government. He says they penalise people like him who've got up off their backsides and done something with their lives. We were very interested in all your cricket scores. What a pity you aren't in very good form yourself this term. Uncle Teddy says everybody has these 'bad trots' from time to time. Yes, I believe I did hear that the Porringer brat is at Bruton. The Porringers have the same idea as your uncle, that a boy should go a long way away so as to learn to be self-reliant. We were very pleased that you did well in Latin etcetera. Where do you get the brains from? We were glad that the film you saw was very good, but sorry it was rather boring. We think it's a very good idea for you to go to stay with your friends. It's not that we don't want you for all the holidays, because we miss you very much, but it worries us that you don't have any friends your own age here. Stay longer than a week if you want to. Don't worry about us. Actually it fits in very well with our plans, as your uncle has some kind of conference thing to go to, and it means we won't have to rush back, which we would have been very happy to do, to be here when you got back. I enclose some more Gentleman's Relish, also eight Canadian stamps. Mum's the word.

With lots of love to our lovely boy, from Uncle Teddy and Auntie Doris XXXXXXXXXXXXXXXXXXXXXXXXX (Wipe off that lipstick!)

They took a taxi from Paddington to Hampstead. Mrs Hargreaves stood smiling at the door of the narrow, four-storey, Georgian town house. She looked elegant in a short yellow dress with straight lines, and high-heeled black leather court shoes.

Henry hadn't dared ask Paul if Diana would be there.

'No cold this time?' said Mrs Hargreaves.

'No,' said Henry. 'I don't usually get colds.'

'I know,' said Mrs Hargreaves. 'Only at the most embarrassing times.'

There was a faint hint of expensive perfume about her which Henry couldn't help comparing with Auntie Doris. She gave him an approving glance. He knew that he looked his best. He had grown quite a bit taller in the past nine months, and had lost some of his podgy look. But although there had been approval in her glance, he felt it to be the sort of approval a would-be owner might give a promising horse.

They had afternoon tea in the drawing room, on the first floor. The wallpaper, lamp-shades and curtains had a faintly Chinese air, and there was China tea. 'Isn't Diana here?' said Paul.

'She's upstairs, pretending not to care about Henry's arrival,' said Mrs Hargreaves.

'Ass,' said Paul. 'Girls can be asses. That appalling Brace-Uppingham girl isn't with her, is she?'

'Boyce-Uppingham, dear. She had a brace in her teeth, poor dear. I hope you like China tea, Henry.'

'Very much,' lied Henry. He'd had it at Auntie Doris's. It tasted like burnt rubber.

'Are you a post-lactarian?' said Mrs Hargreaves.

'No,' said Henry. 'I'm C of E.'

'Post-lactarian means you like the milk in last,' said Paul. 'It's considered correct.'

'I like the milk in first,' said Henry.

Mrs Hargreaves poured the milk in first. Henry sensed that she was trying to prevent her eyes from showing amusement. He sensed that he was Paul's funny little Northern friend, to whom they would all be very kind. He was also aware that he tended to imagine this even when it wasn't true, and that he sometimes played up to it, so he couldn't grumble.

Diana entered, dressed in skirt and scruffy old shirt, with flat shoes. Her cheeks were slightly pink.

'Oh hello, Henry. You here?' she said casually. 'Tea, please.'

Henry was aware that he was also slightly pink, and that yet again he couldn't think of a single thing to say. He was also deeply disappointed by Diana's appearance. She looked lumpy, like bad porridge. Her legs looked quite thick, her knees were uncompromisingly knobbly. In his memory she had been a cross between Mrs Hargreaves, Patricia Roc and Gloria de Haven, all much younger, of course. He had even felt vague stirrings of the slumbering giant as he thought about meeting her again.

'Henry's a pre-lactarian,' said Mrs Hargreaves.

'Sounds disgusting,' said Diana.

Her cheeks couldn't be pink because of him. Yet she had spoken nicely to him at the Bald-Headed Angel. He hoped she hadn't got a horrid schoolgirl crush on him, however flattering that would be. He didn't want this sack of potatoes round his neck.

With Diana such a wash-out, and the house so stiflingly elegant, and the tea tasting of burnt rubber, albeit better burnt rubber than Auntie Doris's, Henry didn't think he could stand a week of it.

'Your school's broken up too, has it?' he said.

'No. I'm still there,' said Diana. 'I have this amazing gift where I can send my body to lots of different places at once.'

Diana went off to her room, and Paul showed Henry the garden. It was quite small, terraced, walled, secret as only town gardens bother to be. Every square inch was used, and every plant was lovely. Probably the weeds all died of shame. Paul explained about the publisher on one side, the famous author on the other side and the potty professor at the bottom.

'I'll save the tour of the pictures for tomorrow,' said Paul.

'They're all originals, of course.'

Of course, thought Henry.

He was amazed to discover that Paul had an older brother, Jeremy, who was expected home from school within two or three days.

'You never even mentioned him,' said Henry.

'We don't get on awfully well,' said Paul. 'He's a little bit arty-crafty. My father sent him to one of these progressive schools, because it was such a Hampstead thing to do. He hated it at first. The headmaster asked him why. He said, "I like rules and regulations." The headmaster said, "Well, you can't have any here." He said, "Why not?" The headmaster said, "Because I say so." '

Henry laughed.

He washed and changed for dinner. By the time he came downstairs, Dr Hargreaves was back. Dr Hargreaves asked him if he liked sherry. He said he did. It tasted like razor blades.

Diana had changed into an elegant, short, black dress. She had moderately high-heeled shoes, which flattered the luscious fleshiness of her legs. No sack of potatoes ever looked like this. Only the cheery knobbliness of her knees revealed that she was still only fourteen. Henry caught his breath and hoped he wasn't gawping like a love-sick cod.

'Sherry?' said Dr Hargreaves.

'No fear. Your sherry tastes like razor blades. Lemonade, please,' she said.

With their dinner, in the olive-green dining room on the ground floor, they had claret. Henry said that he loved it, although he knew he hated it.

The stew was nice, though.

Back at Low Farm, casual conversation was discouraged at table, and Henry had always wanted to chatter. Here, table talk was de rigueur, and his brain seemed to have had gum poured into it.

'This stew's nice,' he said.

'It's boeuf bourguignon, ass,' said Paul.

They discussed art exhibitions and museums that they might visit. Paul said that Henry was good at Latin, and his French was coming along too.

'A great language,' said Dr Hargreaves. 'Are you familiar with Baudelaire at all, Henry?'

'I've never been to France,' said Henry.

Diana choked.

'Baudelaire isn't a place,' she said. 'It's a song.'

'It's no such thing,' said her mother. 'He was a great French poet.'

Henry couldn't be sure, in fact he would never know, but he suspected that Diana knew about Baudelaire and had diverted the correction onto herself to spare him. What a magnificent girl she was. How little taste he had. How could he ever have preferred the tight-knit, arrogant scrawniness of Belinda Brace-Toothingham? How could he have likened this magnificent creature to a sack of potatoes? How nice her breasts looked.

The slumbering giant stirred, yawned, stretched his legs. Not now! Not at the Hargreaves's dining table! Get down, ass!

He looked away from Diana hurriedly. He racked his brains for something even vaguely interesting to say. He recalled a story somebody had told him at school. Well, that would do.

'My people were burgled last week,' he said, 'Do you know what the thief took? A wireless, a ball of string and two pounds of tomatoes.'

Why was Paul glaring at him?

'That's incredible,' said Dr Hargreaves. 'We had a burglar too, and that's exactly what he took.'

Henry closed his eyes. The one good thing about it was that the awakened giant shrivelled up in embarrassment.

'It's obviously the same one,' said Diana.

'It could be two different ones,' said Paul.

'Oh yes. The country's awash with people stealing wirelesses, string and tomatoes,' said Diana.

'Where did this happen? said Mrs Hargreaves.

'Sheffield,' said Henry.

'We must let the police know,' said Dr Hargreaves. 'It could be a vital link.'

'No,' said Henry. 'My aunt's very nervous of the police.'

'We really ought to report it. It's our duty,' said Dr Hargreaves.

'I wouldn't like to do it without their knowing,' said Henry 'When I get back, I can tell them about your case and try and persuade them to report it.'

Dr Hargreaves agreed to that, but it had been a narrow escape. Henry suspected that they all knew that there had been no burglary, but he couldn't bring himself to admit it.

After dinner, he pleaded exhaustion.

'Ass,' said Paul, as they said goodnight. 'Cretinous ass.'

He washed himself from head to foot, in his determination not to sully the sheets.

It was a warm night. He got into bed without his pyjamas.

He stretched his legs. They ached with tension. He began to feel drowsy. He thought about Diana. She was a nice girl. He thought about her breasts. He pretended she was in bed with him, also naked. He pressed his body against hers and kissed her mouth. He put the sheet over his head and moved down to kiss her breasts.

'Diana, darling, I love you,' he whispered. 'Oh, Diana. Diana.'

The slumbering giant awoke, leapt up, and spat. It was brief, burning, terrifying, amazing, wonderful.

For ten seconds after it was over, he felt exhilarated. He wasn't a freak. He was a man.

Then he began to feel embarrassed about the Hargreaves's sheets.

9 The Day Pratt Broke Out

'I wouldn't go myself if I hadn't helped to organise it,' said Uncle Teddy. 'Rawlaston Working Men's Club isn't the Moulin Rouge, you know.'

It was pre-prandial drinks time in Cap Ferrat, on a wet evening in January, 1950.

'I've never been to a club,' said Henry.

'You're under age,' said Auntie Doris.

'I don't want to drink,' said Henry. 'I just want to see the cabaret. I've never seen a cabaret. They'll let me in if you're the organiser.'

'I don't like abusing positions of influence,' said Uncle Teddy.

'You never take me anywhere,' said Henry. 'I'm nearly fifteen. I can behave myself. Every summer holidays, when I come back, you're as bronzed as Greek gods. You think I don't realise that you've been on holiday, but I'm not as green as I'm cabbage-looking. That's why I never get any letters towards the end of the summer term.'

Uncle Teddy and Auntie Doris didn't look as bronzed as Greek gods at that moment. In fact they'd both gone deathly pale.

'You go to Cap Ferrat,' said Henry. 'It's your favourite place. You named your house after it. I used to think it was a hat for ferreting. I was naive. You've given me the chance to be sophisticated, and that means I can see through you.'

Auntie Doris burst into tears and left the room.

'Now look what you've done,' said Uncle Teddy.

'It's what you've done,' said Henry.

'You don't like us very much, do you?' said Uncle Teddy.

'I want to,' shouted Henry. 'I want to, but you won't let me into your lives.'

It was quite a large room, with thirty-two tables. Some of the tables were square, others oblong. They were arranged in straight lines. The men came in flat caps and many of them had square, rugged faces. They drank their pints from straight glasses. It was a world that had eschewed curves as the product of weakness. Henry loved it. It was also a dark room. The lights were low. The decor and furnishings were a tribute to the versatility of brown. All the men wore dark clothes. Many of the women looked as if they hoped they'd be mistaken for men. Here and there, there was a blaze of blonde hair, some real, more false. Occasionally, a woman in a colourful dress. One woman had a bright yellow drink. These were exceptions. Auntie Doris wore a low-cut, blue evening dress. Her figure was still excellent.

The room smelt of stale beer, fresh beer, cigarettes, cheap perfume, furniture polish, disinfectant and sweat. The atmosphere was smoky.

Also seated at their table was Jack Ibbotson, his wife Mabel and her friend Denise. It was because he employed Jack that Uncle Teddy had allowed himself, so untypically, to be roped in. He resented it.

'It's never been properly ventilated, hasn't this venue,' said Jack Ibbotson. 'Not within living memory, any road.'

There were three acts on the bill. The Amazing Illingworth (The Crown Prince of Prestidigitation), Talwyn Jones (The Celtic Droll) and Doreen Tibbs (The Tadcaster Thrush). The weak spots of the cabaret, if one wished to be hypercritical, were that the Crown Prince of Prestidigitation was so drunk that he was pushed to say magic, let alone prestidigitation, that the Celtic Droll had about as much comic personality as a tent pole and the Tadcaster Thrush had a shocking cold, with incipient laryngitis.

The concert secretary was none other than the peripheral Sid Lowson, who was to take no further part in this narrative after his performance as a domino substitute almost fifteen years ago.

'Good evening, ladies and gentlemen,' said Sid Lowson. 'All proceeds tonight go to that very fine footballer, Don Ibbotson, of Thurmarsh United, who's had to pack it in due to injury. He was a great servant of the club. If he'd had a bit of pace, who knows how far he'd have gone? Let's hear it for Don Ibbotson.'

Don Ibbotson stood up. The audience applauded. There were tears in Jack Ibbotson's eyes.

'Thank you,' said Sid Lowson. 'And now, without further ado, our special cabaret, who have all dispensed with their services tonight for nowt. Thank you, each. First, a legendary Tyke entertainer what I saw last week at Mexborough. I didn't rate him mysen, but then I don't like magic. Any road, let's hear it for the Amazing Illingworth.'

The Amazing Illingworth's act wasn't going terribly well even before the escape of the doves. They flew around the room, fluttering wildly, and it was only after a quarter of an hour, and the use of a ladder, that they were all recovered.

Sid Lowson returned to the stage and called for silence. Slowly, the hubbub died down.

'I have three messages,' said Sid Lowson. 'One. Will the bar please not serve the Amazing Illingworth? Thank you. Two. If anybody has a cleaning bill, we will honour them, though as this will come out of what we raise for Don, we hope there won't be. Three, and I should have said this at t' beginning, but in view of the Amazing Illingworth's condition I forgot. With great regret I have to announce the death of one of t' best-loved members of this club, Reg Oldfield. Reg passed away peacefully last night. He was a good 'un. We sent all our sympathies to Madge and the family, and we hope to have a bit of a do to raise summat for them later. T' funeral's on Tuesday. And now, comedy. Let's hear it for Talwyn Jones, the Celtic Droll.'

You're in trouble when you come on in a bright red suit, with a giant leek in your buttonhole, wearing a pith helmet and one roller skate, and nobody laughs.

'Good evening, ladies and gentlemen, and concert secretary,' said the Celtic Droll. 'My name is Taff the Laff. I just came over from by there to by 'ere. So where's the tapestry? By 'ere. Bayeux tapestry. Get it? Nor do I, much. So, you've never heard of the Bayeux tapestry. It's Plan B. Sex. You've heard of sex, have you? It's what the upper classes bring their coal home in.'

Uncle Teddy looked at Auntie Doris in something approaching panic, but excitement coursed through Henry's veins. Suddenly, without a shadow of a doubt, he knew what he was going to be when he grew up. A stand-up comedian.

'. . .Still, accidents will happen, won't they? Take my friend the undertaker. Jones the bones. No, I can't do that one.

Somebody just snuffed it. There were these two Welshmen, Paddy and Mick. Well, I can't do the Irish accent. Paddy says, "I'm walking to Pembroke Dock, isn't it, begorrah?" Mick says, "How long is it?" Paddy says, "I don't know, I haven't looked." Hasn't the rationing been terrible, though. Terrible, the rationing. Mind you, my wife's been rationing me for years. I'm talking about meat, madam. Rissoles to you too. . .'

Many people never find their vocation in life. Lucky is the lad who finds it at the tender age of fourteen. Henry was awash with an amazing exhilaration.

'You can take your gas-mask off, sir. The war's been over for. . .oh, sorry, you haven't got it on. Laugh? I thought you'd never start. Right. What else we got? Oh yes. Thurmarsh United. We slaughtered you last year nil all. I hear you've gone into the transfer market – bought a spectator from Liverpool. What about Stalin then, eh? He's a lad, isn't he?'

No matter that the comedian was bad. No matter that he was dying on his feet. Henry knew that *he* wouldn't die on his feet. It had all fallen into place. His search for a catch-phrase. The long hours listening to the wireless. His insistence on coming tonight. It had all clicked in his head.

'Music's great, though, isn't it? It's great, music. There's this Welsh tenor, see. . .on a string attached to a Welsh wallet. . .tenner, see?. . .What a state I'm in. Tennessee, state, get it? Nor do I, much. No, there's this Welsh tenor, see, from Welsh Wales, has to have this operation, on his throat, this tenor. Comes round, after the operation, doctor says, "How are you?" "Fine, doctor, but I couldn't half go a cup of tea." "All right, but you'll have to not take it through the mouth, you see, because of the operation, you'll have to take it through the. . ." The doctor paused, trying to be polite, like. "Rectum?" said the tenor. "Well, it didn't do them much good," said the doctor.'

No matter that the joke was in tatters. Henry felt like an old pro. He'd practically worked the rectum gag himself, with old Busy B.

'So they pours the old cup of tea in the old rectum, and the tenor screams. "What's wrong?" said the doctor. "Was it too hot?" "No," said the tenor. "You forgot to put any sugar in." Thank you

202

very much, and goodnight, ladies and gentlemen.'

There was sporadic applause, but Henry clapped wildly, less in tribute than in gratitude for having had his eyes opened.

Much of the night passed in a dream for Henry. He hardly heard the raffle draw, which was won by Cecil E. Jenkinson. He was barely conscious of the Tadcaster Thrush, her low-cut dress revealing the massive cleft between her huge breasts, her cold giving her the red nose the comic should have had. Her nasal voice gave her songs the sexual ambiguity of a Berlin cabaret in the thirties. After her first song, 'You're breaking my heart', somebody called out, 'You're not doing much for mine.' Henry was up on stage throughout the song, dreaming of a vast audience in stitches at his patter. He returned to earth to hear her graceful apology for her condition. 'Sorry about t' voice,' she said. 'I've got this dreadful cold. I'm right bunged up.' She launched herself into 'Now that I need you'. Henry reflected on the content of his act, trying out the odd phrase in his head to see how it fitted. It could be the big come-back for 'It's months since I 'ad rat.' During 'Far away places' he was in Hampstead, wondering what Dr and Mrs Hargreaves would make of this, how they would react to the drunk magician, the terrible comic and the singer who sounded like a man imitating Marlene Dietrich badly. She was embarked now upon 'I didn't dow the gud was doaded'. Henry thought briefly about Sid Lowson. Should he go up to him and say, 'I used to be a friend of your son before divisive social elements pulled us apart. Give him my best wishes, will you?' Next, Doreen Tibbs attempted 'Confidentially'. At one point the voice went completely, and somebody shouted, 'There's no need to be that confidential, luv,' and there was laughter, but she ploughed resolutely through it, and the voice returned. Henry's thoughts turned to Cecil E. Jenkinson, landlord of the Navigation, winner of the raffle. Should he go up to him and say, 'You virtually banned my dad from your pub. Well, he's dead now. I hope that makes you very happy.' There wasn't any point. All that part of his life was dead. It all seemed so very far away. It was amusing to touch it so secretly, so tangentially, tonight, by being in the same room as these people without their knowing. For her final number, the ailing Thrush (*Turdus Tadcasterus*) chose, 'I don't see be id your eyes ady bore'. Henry embarked upon a reprise of his opening number, the fantasy of standing on the stage, holding the multitude in his grip. Doreen Tibbs received the best ovation of her career. Her false notes, usually so clearly the result of lack of talent, were assumed tonight to be an unfortunate side-effect of her cold. It was an award for gallantry, and she accepted it with surprise and a sudden vulnerable charm. In Henry's mind the applause was for him. He had to restrain himself in order to remain in his seat. How embarrassed Uncle Teddy and Auntie Doris would be if he stood up and took a bow.

He sat suspended between his past and his future, in that dimly-lit, fetid, smoky, noisy, beery room.

'And now,' said a voice that filled the room, although Henry alone could hear it. 'Now, the moment you've been waiting for, our star turn tonight. He's droll. He's daft. He's Henry. Let's hear it for Henry "Ee By Gum I am Daft" Pratt.'

Dreams sometimes come true.

Life at Dalton College, in the spring term of 1950, still had its unpleasantnesses. Getting up at seven fifteen, in the freezing dorm, long before the dawn. The Spartan diet. The pale orange night-light in the stifling san when half the school went down with gastric flu, and the male nurse with the twisted lip came round with his night-time tray of Ovaltine, Horlicks or Milo, all of which made Henry feel sick. Hockey on Lower Boggle in a hailstorm, and a huge boy from Tudor House tripping him deliberately and sending him nose-first into the thick Somerset mud. The agony of those six-mile runs along the Somerton Road, gasping for breath, frozen, red, chapped legs smeared with mud, and the disgusting smell of Broadlees Farm's silage. The sound of crashing feet bounding off the walls of the gym as he struggled to climb a rope, hands cold, arms so feeble, up, up so slowly, and far below the supple vaulting of some natural athlete over the horse, across which he would shortly stumble in knee-wrenching, skin-scraping horror. Being beaten at table tennis 21–8, 21–7 by Brownlow, 21–6, 21–4 by Paul and 21–1, 21–2 by Prince Mangkukubono of Jogjakarta. There was the ever-present absence of Diana Hargreaves, in whose presence his courage had failed.

There was the pervasiveness of homosexuality, whose dark vapours invaded dorm and changing room. He interrupted glances, smelt entanglements, heard about orgies, and felt both disgusted and neglected.

But there were pleasant things, too. The friendship with Paul. The semi-sexual sparring with Lampo. The memorable day when Orange became cock house at hockey, beating Stuart 3–1, with two goals from Tosser Pilkington-Brick. How they cheered on Middle Boggle! With what fervour they sang 'Jerusalem the Golden' in house prayers that night, with the windows slightly open so that farmers, corn chandlers, labourers and auctioneers could pause on street corners in the little market town, if they so wished, and hear the proud, patriotic lines that sent the pimples goosing across the flesh of Dopy S and every boy except Lampo Davey, who closed his eyes and thought of Tuscany. Then there were the joys of self-abuse, and the redecoration of his partition, which consisted now entirely of pictures of Patricia Roc.

But lessons still took up the bulk of the day. It is time to consider Henry's progress at his lessons.

Art. This subject was not considered important at Dalton College. He sat quietly and caused no trouble.

Chemistry. 'Give me a test tube and I will show you a disaster,' might have been Henry's cry. Poor Stinky G. In Henry's hands even simple tests like the solubility of potassium permanganate or the preparation of oxygen from hydrogen peroxide H_2O_2 became dangerous adventures. As for the acids, whether sulphuric, hydrochloric or nitric, the less said the better. But Henry Pratt, budding comic, didn't seem to mind his disasters any more. He would grin vacantly. 'Ee, by gum, I am daft,' that grin would seem to say. Usually he came about twenty-first out of the class of twenty-five.

English. Doing less well this year, because Mr Lennox (Droopy L) didn't take to his style. Droopy L didn't take to any style. He didn't like style. He looked like a bloodhound which has lost its zest for life, but this morose exterior was merely a blind for his stony heart. Droopy L shredded your essays. His sole criterion of merit was that there should be no unnecessary words at all. ' "We set off *along the road*." You amaze me, Pratt. I thought you would have set off *on top of the hedge*.' Under Droopy L, he usually came about fourteenth.

French. Improving all the time, partly due to a secret ambition to become a bi-lingual comedian. Henri 'Ah par gomme je suis stupide' Pratt. Fifth to seventh.

Geography. Henry shared the enthusiams of his teacher, Mr Tenderfoot, who was hairy, grizzled, six foot three and known as High T. (This was a joke about food, not anticyclones, despite High T's preference for the latter over the former.) Henry and High T loved the bits of Geography without people in them. River erosion, corrasion and attrition. Lateral and medial moraines. Deltas, archipelagoes and gorges. Weather. Rainfall figures were High T's pornography, sunshine records his Bible. Once, in chapel, in the middle of a sermon given by the Bishop of Bath and Wells, High T strode boldly out, to watch a particularly severe thunderstorm. Unfortunately, Geography exams were mainly about the bits with people in them. Reasons for population densities, nature of farming, reasons for the location of industries. Fifth or sixth.

History. Henry sympathised with Mr Trench and his nervous breakdown. A very demanding subject, with its mixture of facts and interpretation. There was a lot to remember and a lot to understand. The understanding was not helped by doing History in blocks, so that you had no idea what happened before or after. It was a bit like studying a bottle of milk in order to understand the evolution of the cow. Not a lot like that, but a bit. Toady D claimed that Henry saw things too simply, because of his background. To Henry all history was the exploitation of the weak by the strong. This was simplistic. Usually about ninth.

Latin. His favourite subject, now that Droopy L had ruined English. Lampo Davey mocked him for this. 'But those Romans were so dreary, so greedy. All marching and plumbing and vomiting, and no imagination. Not like the modern Italians.' Could it be that Lampo was right about modern Italians, and the *Beano* wrong? 'The only Roman who comes over to me like a human being is Catullus,' said Lampo. 'I wouldn't have minded a stroll in the woods with him. No, forget the Romans. Go on to the Greeks.' Next year, Henry would. In the meantime, he usually came second in Latin.

Maths. He was doing worse as he came upon more advanced concepts. Calculus in particular was a closed book, and geometry and algebra sometimes hurt so much that he seemed able to feel the cracks in his brain across which the connections couldn't leap, and that gave him a pain in his toes, of all places, and made him worry about being dependent on such a complicated system of life-support as the human body. Had been as high as third, usually about fourteenth now.

Physics. It certainly wasn't as bad as Chemistry. Henry had difficulty in remembering the difference between Torricelli's experiment and Pascal's experiment, between Boyle's Law and Charles's Law. He tended to make silly jokes about this subject. 'I'm dense about density and relatively dense about relative density.' 'I'll tell you about good and bad conductors. What? Oh yes. There was this tram. . .' or 'The only magnetic pole I knew was Stefan Prziborski.' Partly this was due to a natural element of facetiousness in his personality, partly to his ambition to be a stand-up comic, but that alone would not explain why this eruption occurred so much more in Physics than in other subjects. The truth of the matter was that the nature of matter didn't matter to Henry. More, he felt that he couldn't function in the physical world *unless* he took it for granted. It was hard enough wielding a cricket bat without knowing about its molecular structure. He usually came about thirteenth in Physics.

Scripture. This subject was not considered important at Dalton College. He sat quietly and caused no trouble.

Henry's progress would have seemed very disappointing to Miss Candy, but it seemed good enough to him. He had no idea that anybody had ever had any special hopes for him.

In March, 1950, two events occurred, one of which showed Henry in a very negative light, the other in a much more positive light.

He was shown in a negative light during the general election. Shant held a mock election, with political meetings in Shant Shed. Henry went to the meeting of the Labour candidate, E. J. G. Holmes-Hankinson, of Stuart House. It was sparsely attended.

Only about fifty boys sat in the huge, tiered, semi-circular hall.

'In 1945,' said E. J. G. Holmes-Hankinson, 'this nation voted for a government of the people.'

'My father didn't,' shouted somebody.

'The people of Britain had fought together, as one nation, to win the war. Every man and woman, however humble, played their part.'

'My father didn't,' shouted another boy, and there was laughter.

'Now, they wanted a part to play in the peace that followed. Was that too much to ask?' said E. J. G. Holmes-Hankinson.

There were several cries of 'yes', and more laughter.

'The British people can no longer be cast off like old socks, when they've been used up,' said E. J. G. Holmes-Hankinson.

'Pity,' came a cry.

There were cries of 'S'sssh!' at this.

'They have rights,' said E. J. G. Holmes-Hankinson. 'They have proper unemployment pay and health insurance. They have the finest health service in the world, given by the Labour government. It will last for ever.'

Henry found it difficult to concentrate. E. J. G. Holmes-Hankinson's words about the achievements of nationalisation passed over him. He was imagining himself up on that stage, holding the school in thrall with his comical capers.

'Groundnuts,' shouted somebody.

'Do you think a government which has achieved so much, in such difficult times, should be pilloried for one mistake?' said E. J. G. Holmes-Hankinson.

There were cries of 'yes' and more cries of 'groundnuts'.

'Over a million homes have been built.'

'On our land.'

'Would you deny people the right to live? The Labour government has been forced to apply rationing and severe austerity longer than it would have wished to. Is that its fault? The nation was bankrupted by war. How could it recover over-night? Labour has sown the seeds for. . .'

'. . .more groundnuts.'

'. . .a gradual return to prosperity. The Labour government has

208

been criticised for allowing the breach with Russia to grow so wide. Did Labour invent the Cold War? It had been made inevitable before we came to power. The Labour government has behaved responsibly, moderately, some would say conservatively. It has expelled communists. It has begun the painful, but inevitable, process of decolonisation.'

There were roars of anger, and more cries of 'groundnuts'.

'Yes. Inevitable,' said E. J. G. Holmes-Hankinson. 'All you can find to say is "groundnuts". That proves how good the government's record is.'

A bag of flour exploded over E. J. G. Holmes-Hankinson.

'You fear the Labour government,' said E. J. G. Holmes-Hankinson, his hair streaked with flour, his shoulders white. 'Why? You're still here, aren't you?'

A few boys cheered and applauded E. J. G. Holmes-Hankinson. Others jeered. Henry remained silent. He simply didn't know enough to do otherwise.

At Westminster, Labour were returned to power, with a majority of six. At Dalton College, E. J. G. Holmes-Hankinson got eight votes. The Liberals got nine. The Conservatives got 657.

The event which saw Henry in a more positive light occurred two days before the end of term. He knocked on Lampo and Tosser's door, received no reply, and entered, to find Lampo rehearsing a mime.

'I didn't say "come in",' said Lampo.

'You didn't say "stay out",' said Henry.

'I couldn't say anything,' said Lampo. 'Mime is silent. In future, wait till you're told.'

'You like me to clean your study when you're out,' said Henry. 'If you're out, you can't say "come in" so if I have to wait for you to say "come in" I can never clean your study while you're out.'

'I'm sorry,' said Lampo. 'I was upset at being interrupted.'

'What were you doing?'

'I'm appearing in the end of summer term concert. I'm doing a satirical mime about Sir Stafford Cripps in Hell. I'm calling it "Austerity in the Underworld". It's a satire on the mean spirit of post-war Britain. It's going to be *a* sensation. A sensation. Tosser's appearing too.' Lampo Davey sighed. 'A ballet skit done by the rugger fifteen. I ask you, Henry. What is that but the hoary old anti-art gag in new clothes? I am trying to do something avant-garde. Tosser is about as avant-garde as a mangle.'

'My auntie had a mangle,' said Henry. 'I won't say she was ugly, but I talked to it for five minutes before I realised it wasn't her.'

Lampo Davey stared at him in astonishment.

'What?' he said.

'I'm practising for my act,' said Henry.

'What act?' said Lampo Davey.

'My act in the end of summer term concert,' said Henry.

Lampo Davey gawped at him. Henry would have gawped at himself, had it been physically possible.

He spent the Easter holidays researching for his act. Twice, he went to the first house at the Sheffield Empire. He went on the Tuesday. That way he could buy the *Star* and read the review of what he was going to see, and build up his anticipation.

To his astonishment, Uncle Teddy and Auntie Doris came with him. He would have preferred to be on his own, for professional reasons, but he couldn't say this. They had taken his January strictures to heart.

On April 4th, he saw the Five Smith Brothers, who sang with lots of energy. Second on the bill was Robb Wilton, a hero of his. He was upset because Robb Wilton wasn't top of the bill. Uncle Teddy explained that he was on the way down. Others on the bill were Kay 'On the Keys' Cavendish, Tony Fayne and David Evans, with amusing impressions of BBC performers, and Donald B. Stuart, more comic than conjuror.

On April 11th he saw the Mack Triplets, American close-harmony singers, sometimes saucy and always tuneful; Wee Georgie Wood, assisted by Dolly Harmer; Leslie Sarony; the Three Jokers, energetic knock-about comedians; Morecambe and Wise, amusing entertainers; Irene and Stanley Davis, clever dancers; Freda Wyn, who certainly knew the ropes; and Jackie, with extraordinary balancing feats.

Then there was Emile Littler's *Waltzes from America* for two weeks, so that was a dead loss, but he did persuade Uncle Teddy to go once to the Thurmarsh Empire, where the bill was headed by Confidentially, from Variety Bandbox, Reg Dixon. The Two Valettos provided an exotic touch with Eastern dancing, the Allen Brothers and June tumbled and glided in a sophisticated comedy routine, and the Two Harvards cut college capers with verve. Aimee Fontenay and her partner provided thrills on the trapeze. Margery Manners sang with an intimate microphone manner that was more than pleasing. Saucy Iris Sadler and ventriloquist Roger Carne provided plenty of laughs, and Victor Seaforth, the man with a hundred voices, gave an electrifying interpretation of Charles Laughton's *The Hunchback of Notre Dame*.

Henry loved it all. He had no idea that he was witnessing a dying art form, and that quite soon many of these theatres would be demolished for improvement schemes, and the rest would be given over to bingo.

He learnt a great deal. The successful comedians presented the audience with a false image of themselves. Not a true image of themselves, which might well be boring, or a false image without themselves, in which case there would be no contact. Contact was more important than the quality of the jokes.

But he still hadn't got his act. He needed something more, an external element.

It came in the shape of the headmaster, Mr Lichfield.

The shape of the headmaster, Mr Lichfield, was oblong, with a sphere on top. He had no waist, very square shoulders, and vitually no neck. He looked like a message hoisted for sailors, sphere above oblong, meaning 'easterly gales imminent' or some such thing.

After house prayers, in the panelled dining room of Orange House, with its list of house rugby captains since 1838 (1949 E. L. F. Pilkington-Brick, 1950 E. L. F. Pilkington-Brick, the first since 1857 to be house rugby captain for two years) Dopy S announced that the following day the headmaster would visit all the houses to talk to them individually on a matter of the greatest importance. They would assemble at 8.25. Dopy S was so concerned about this that he forgot his rubber cushion, which he was carrying on account of an excruciating attack of piles which all the boys except Lampo Davey found hilarious. 'The banal anal English,' said Lampo sadly.

The following day, House assembled round the bare wooden refectory tables. The headmaster entered with the housemaster. Mr Lichfield carried his mortarboard in his right hand. Mr Satchel carried his rubber cushion in his left hand.

House stood.

'Sit down, boys,' said Mr Satchel.

House sat down.

Mr Satchel arranged his cushion, and also sat down. The cushion sighed gently, perhaps for Mr Satchel's lost, unhaemorrhoidal youth.

Mr Lichfield remained standing, sphere over oblong. He looked very worried. He held his mortarboard in front of his private parts, as if he were naked.

He began to speak. He spoke slowly, slightly too loud, as if he had learnt the art of public speaking by numbers. He had a slight speech impediment, being unable to say a soft 's' without aspirating. He seemed to be drawn to his impediment like a moth to a flame.

'I want to shpeak to you today on a very sherioush shubject,' he said. 'Sheksh. In particular, the shin of homoshekshuality. Because it is a shin. Oh yesh.'

Henry stared fixedly at the table, through downcast eyes. This wasn't out of shame, for he agreed with the headmaster. It was out of the fear that, if he so much as caught the eye of another boy, he would begin to shake with helpless hysterical laughter. Was it his fancy that he could sense a barely suppressed communal quivering all round him?

The idea struck him like a swing door. Here was the very thing he had been seeking. And he wasn't even listening to it. He had missed a whole section of the headmaster's talk. He forced himself to concentrate on the peroration.

'At every boarding shchool there are isholated inshidents of thish short of shekshual mishbehaviour, which musht be dealt with on an individual bashish,' the headmaster was saying. 'But here, in thish corner of Shomershet, it has become an imposhible shituation. As I shee you shitting there, sho sholemn, sho shad, your expressions shuffused with shame, yesh, the shame shame that I myshelf onshe felt at my shchool, I confesh that my shpirits shag. I feel for you. The innoshent are at rishk from the guilty. However, I musht shay what has to be shaid. No shchool of which I am headmashter will be allowed to remain a shink of iniquity. Any boy found guilty of any kind of shekshual offenshe will be shacked.'

The headmaster's face had gone purple with embarrassment and honest feeling. The boys' faces had gone purple from their efforts not to laugh. Only the housemaster seemed unaffected. Mr Satchel's smooth face remained totally innocent throughout.

House stood, and they departed, the headmaster with his mortarboard, the housemaster with his rubber cushion, and Henry with his act.

It was the first day of the first test match at Old Trafford. Debuts: England – R. Berry, G. H. G. Doggart; West Indies – S. Ramadhin, A. L. Valentine; Dalton College auditions for end of summer term concert – H. Pratt.

The auditions were held in a small, bare room at the back of the stage in Shant Shed. It had mustard-washed brick walls. Kington, the producer, sat back-to-front on a kitchen chair, his chin resting on top of the back of the chair.

If Henry felt nervous, he didn't show it. Here at last was an area of life in which he was confident.

Kington watched his rough-hewn act, intently still, poker-faced, wanting to see how Henry reacted under pressure. Henry was concentrating so hard that he didn't even notice that Kington wasn't laughing.

'It needs a lot of work on it,' said Kington. 'A lot of work.'

'I know,' said Henry.

Kington nodded. He seemed pleased.

'You're very young to do a solo,' he said. 'You're still a fag. Don't you think it would be more sensible to wait till next year?'

'Yes,' said Henry, 'but who ever got anywhere by being sensible?'

Kington grinned for the first time.

'You can go on after the mime,' he said. 'They'll be so relieved that's over that you'll go down a bomb.'

The summer term passed pleasantly. His batting improved spectacularly. Scores of 0, 1, 1 not out, 0 not out, 2,0,0,3 not out, 1,0,0,0,0 not out, 0 and 2 gave him an average of 1, an all-time high. He just managed to pass his swimming proficiency test in the green, icy waters of the open-air pool. He began to feel that he belonged here. Next year, he wouldn't be a fag, and would be able to open one button on his jacket. The year after, he would have a senior study, he would be able to open two buttons on his jacket, he would be fagged for.

It was pleasant that summer, as Ramadhin and Valentine swept through the English batting, to lie on Middle Boggle, hearing the thwack of leather on willow, feeling your cock harden against the warm grass as you dreamt idly of Diana Hargreaves and Patricia Roc, while you chatted to Paul Hargreaves, or explained the rules, with deliberate incomprehensibility, to Prince Mangkukubono of Jogjakarta. Two-fifths of your mind on cricket, two-fifths on sex, the other fifth always thinking about your act.

The longest day came and went. So did Uncle Teddy and Auntie Doris. A visit! They took Paul Hargreaves out and went to Weston-super-Mare. The tide was out. Henry wished Auntie Doris's perfume didn't smell so strongly. Paul seemed to enjoy himself. 'Thank you very much,' he said at the end of the day, rather stiffly and formally. 'I've had a thoroughly enjoyable day.'

When they left, Auntie Doris hugged Henry, and Uncle Teddy clasped his hand firmly and pressed it.

'Well done, old chap,' he said.

Henry impressed Sweaty W with the revelation that he was reading Baudelaire. The trouble was that it was very difficult to enjoy something that was untranslatable. It was impossible to enjoy a line like 'les soirs illuminés par l'ardeur du charbon' because, although it sounded good, it was in a foreign language, and when you had translated it as 'the evenings lit up by the heat of coal' it was still impossible to enjoy it because, although it was in your language, it sounded awful. Henry was reading Baudelaire in

214

preparation for his second visit to the Hargreaves's home in Hampstead. This time he meant to impress. He intended to keep a clean sheet and not to blot his copy-book.

The day of the end of term concert approached.

He sat in his partition in the junior study, a small piece of land entirely surrounded by pictures of Patricia Roc. He had a severe attack of nerves. What a fool he had been to think he could make the whole school laugh.

He brought his stamp album up to date, for something to do. Auntie Doris had sent him five Canadian stamps. He could hardly control the hinges in his shaking fingers.

He counted the number of stamps in his album, to pass the time. There were 112. 57 of them were Canadian. 28 of them were identical.

Lampo Davey put his head round the door.

'Nothing to worry about,' he said. 'They'll be in such a good mood after my mime, they'll laugh at anything.'

He was sick. He walked to main school, head throbbing, saying to himself, 'It is funny. It is. No, it isn't. Yes, it *is*.' He was sick again, in the Shant Shed lats. Oh, presumptuous oik.

It *is* funny. Far funnier than the Celtic Droll. Nobody'll laugh at all. Everybody'll be in stitches.

He put on his dark suit, his comedy glasses and his mortarboard, ready for the dress rehearsal.

He felt better.

He went on for the dress rehearsal. He had refused to do his full act on this occasion, having read that this was what real comedians did. What did he mean, 'real comedians'? Wasn't he real?

'Ow do, I'm t' new headmaster waffle waffle waffle waffle waffle waffle waffle Moss Bros. Goodnight,' he said.

He felt much better.

He felt awful.

He was sick.

He gargled and cleaned his teeth.

The concert began. He became convinced that he would forget all his words.

215

Kington obviously thought he could do it. Or did he? Was it a deliberate plot to humiliate him in front of the whole school? That was it. He'd show them. No, that wasn't it. And he wouldn't show them. Yes, he would.

He heard the early acts as if from very far away. A parody of the school song. A sketch, with quite a few laughs. Another song. Warm applause. Then silence.

'Five minutes,' Kington told him. 'Davey's just doing his mime.'

Henry joined Kington at the side of the stage. The silence was total. His legs were leaden. He was shaking.

'He's dying on his arse,' whispered Kington. 'He's dying on his arse out there. You'll be terrific after this. A wow. A two hundred per cent copper-bottomed wow.'

There was a dribble of polite, bewildered applause for Lampo's mime. He came off fuming.

'Peasants,' he said.

Henry stood transfixed.

'Good luck,' whispered Kington. 'You'll slay them. If you're dying on your arse, get off quick.'

Kington pushed him. He walked forward as in a dream, feverish and disembodied.

They roared at the sight of him, fifteen-year-old Henry Pratt, dressed as the headmaster. After several minutes in which most of them hadn't even realised that they were watching the Chancellor of the Exchequer in the underworld, here was something they could understand.

All Henry's nerves left him. He felt the amazing, steadying presence of power. His neck disappeared. He became the headmaster, sphere over oblong. He waited for the laughter to die down, then waited a little longer, to show that he was in charge, to build up the tension, ready to defuse it with the next laugh. He knew about this. Amazingly, instinctively, he was a master of his craft.

"Ow do, I'm t' new headmaster, tha knows,' he said.

They laughed. It wasn't a joke, yet they laughed. He'd got them!

His voice was slightly silly, but not too silly.

'I want to talk to you tonight about summat very important

216

what I don't like and what there's too much of. Sex.'

They roared and applauded. He stood immobile, facing seven hundred laughing boys, and beyond them the masters, who might or might not be laughing.

'What is sex? It's what you snotty-nosed lot bring the coal home in.'

Yes, already he was not too proud to use old jokes.

'Another thing that there's too much of in this knacker's yard – sorry, school, that was my last job – another thing there's too much of is. . .er. . .homo. . .wait. I haven't finished. Don't laff just cause I say homo. Wait till I've finished. . . Sapiens. Far too many boys. Have to shack a few, I think. Now I'm a bit worried over t' acoustics of this converted abattoir, and whether I can be heard proper and all. If you can't hear me, shout out, and I won't hear you. I said I'm a bit worried over. . .never mind. Ee, by gum, I am daft.'

They'd been waiting for that, those who knew him, and they led the applause.

'Oh, I haven't told you my name yet, have I? I'm Oiky P, M.A. I were born in a slum, tha knows. I were. I come from a slum. One day, my dad said to me, "Henry." He were clever that way, cos that were me name. It still is. Ee, by gum, I am daft. "Henry," he said, "I've gorra pain in me eye." I didn't ask which one, cos he only had the one. He couldn't afford two. "Henry," he said. "Go into t' kitchen and gerrus t' eye-drops." I said, "I'm in t' kitchen." Well, we only had one room. We couldn't afford two. I won't say it was small, but the cockroaches and silverfish died of claustrophobia. He said, "Henry." Cos his memory was still good in them days. He said, "Henry, get t' eye-drops and gerrus dinner at t' same time. It's in t' oven. I opened t' oven door and there were this great big rat. I said, "Dad, there's a great big rat in t' oven." He said, "That's funny. I only ordered a little 'un." It's months since I 'ad rat.'

He paused, waiting for total silence, judging it was time to build the tension again. He adopted a pose of exaggerated innocence.

'Ee, I could do with a fag,' he said.

Homosexuality still shocked him, but he felt no guilt about pretending to be one, for the sake of his act. Anything went,

217

where laughs were concerned. He was a real pro, at fifteen.

'Right. My policies for this Borstal,' he continued. 'Education. We'll have some. Not a lot, but some. We'll get you off your buttocks. Not that I've got owt against buttocks. Never have had. Buttocks, I don't think you can beat them, me. "What about sport?" I hear a strangled cry. Tosser's got his jockstrap on too tight again. Yes, we'll have sport too. And I would like to thank Foggy F for putting up t' goal posts. It's actually cricket this term, but it was a nice thought. Ee, by gum, I am daft. I gorra go now, cos my suit's due back in Moss Bros. Goodnight.'

There was loud applause. Everyone agreed that he hadn't quite known how to end it, but that he'd been amazingly good for a fifteen-year-old.

As he came off, Kington grabbed him by the hand and said, 'Well done.'

He slumped, exhausted, into a chair in the crowded, communal dressing room, with its litter of make-up and costumes on all sides.

Lampo Davey came in, and stood by the door, gazing at him, smiling his twisted smile.

'Congratulations,' he said. 'You have discovered the grease-paint behind the agony. I'm going to kiss you.'

Lampo Davey kissed him full on the mouth.

'I'll probably never see you again after tonight,' he said. 'I'm leaving this Philistine island. I'm going somewhere where my kind of art will be appreciated. Crete.'

Henry couldn't sit for long. The adrenalin was still pumping. He wandered out into the warm, still night. A bat almost brushed his head as he wandered down the passage between the chapel and main school. He looked up at the mellow stone of the Queen Anne mansion, and no longer felt unworthy of it. He no longer felt like the Bauhaus block. He had toned in.

He returned in time to hear the roars that greeted the first fifteen's ballet skit.

'It confirms them in their belief that sport is superior to art. How the little cretins roar,' said Lampo Davey.

Henry went on stage to take his share of the final curtain. He had wondered if the applause would embarrass him. Now he wished that it would go on for ever.

There was a party, on stage. Henry enjoyed a glass of wine for the first time. He had reached maturity.

Lampo acted as his chaperone, choosing to bask in reflected glory rather than wallow in his own disgrace. Many people were leaving Shant the next day. Some of them would never know such glory again. The atmosphere was manic.

The headmaster came round briefly to congratulate them. Henry's heart beat a little faster as he approached.

'Congratulations,' said the headmaster warmly. 'It was a mosht amusing shkit.'

This made Henry feel guilty.

'Feeling guilty?' said Lampo Davey, when the headmaster had moved on.

'No,' said Henry.

'With what infinite subtlety the British ruling classes swallow up their opposition,' said Lamp Davey. 'That's the only thing I'm going to miss, in Crete.'

People paid Henry tributes, and they didn't embarrass him, for he regarded them as his due.

Only one thing marred his evening. He wanted to do the whole thing again the next day.

10 Oh God

In the morning, when he received the summons to go and see Mr Satchel, he assumed that his housemaster wished to add his congratulations to the many he had received.

He weaved his way cheerfully between trunks, parents and tuck boxes. The smell of warm gravel wafted in through open doors and windows. This evening he would see Diana.

He plunged into the stuffy gloom of Dopy S's private quarters, wondering idly what it must be like to have eighty schoolboys living in your home.

He entered Mr Satchel's study. At first he could see only Mr Satchel. Then he saw Auntie Doris. Her face was stricken.

'Congratulations on last night,' said Mr Satchel.

'Thank you very much indeed, sir,' he said graciously.

'I'll leave you two alone,' said Mr Satchel. He put his hand briefly on Henry's shoulder as he left.

'Come and sit down,' said Auntie Doris.

She looked gaunt. He could feel his heart thumping.

'You never really wanted to go away to school, did you?' she said.

'What's happened?' he said. 'What's happened, Auntie Doris?'

Her eyes were very moist. He wished she hadn't used so much perfume.

'Teddy's got problems,' she said. 'Business problems.'

A wave of relief swept over him.

'He's got problems with his English end,' she said. 'He's going to have to wind it up. Do you understand what I'm saying?'

'Well. . .yes. . .he's going to have to wind up his English end.'

'I'm saying that he's gone out East, to try to preserve his Oriental end. If he can preserve his Oriental end, all may not be lost.'

Oh God. Above the mantelpiece there were photographs of the cock house rugby team of 1937 and the cock house hockey team of 1950. He found himself full of sympathy for Mr Satchel, for the pain and humiliation which that long gap must have caused him. It was his mind's way of pretending that he hadn't got worries of his own.

'Do you understand what I'm saying?' said Auntie Doris.

Yes. I'm going to another school. Hong Kong High or Bangkok Grammar. The only English boy in a school of old school Thais. Oh God.

'I'm saying that he's going to have to live in Rangoon. I'm saying that I'm going to have to join him as soon as I've sold Cap Ferrat. Do you understand what I'm saying?'

'Well. . .yes.'

'I'm saying that we can't take you with us. I'm saying that there isn't room even if we could afford it. We're almost ruined. The receiver will take the money for Cap Ferrat. I don't mind for us. We've had a good innings. Uncle Teddy always says, "You can't lose money unless you've made it." But. . .do you understand what I'm saying?'

'Well. . .yes.'

'I'm saying that we can't afford to send you here any more. You're going back to Thurmarsh Grammar.'

Oh God.

'But, Auntie. . .'

'You liked it there. You didn't want to leave.'

'Yes, but. . . things are different now.'

'Everything's different now.'

'Yes, but. . .where will I live?'

'With Cousin Hilda, of course. We wouldn't send you out of the family.'

'You're back among your own folk,' said Cousin Hilda. 'I were never happy about your being at those schools. Getting ideas.'

She sniffed. Her tone suggested that she thought of ideas as if they were germs.

'Your tea's a bit dried up,' she said. 'I thought you'd be here before.'

It had been half-past seven before they had arrived at number 66 Park View Road. Auntie Doris had come in only briefly. The moment she had gone, Cousin Hilda had opened the windows wide.

He looked at his tea. It was roast lamb, with mint sauce, roast potatoes and runner beans. He felt too sick to eat, but he must.

Paul had been horrified when he'd heard the news. They had vowed to keep closely in touch.

He discovered that he was hungrier than he had thought. The blue-tiled stove was out. One of the blue glass panes was cracked. On top of the stove, for the summer, sat a blue vase filled with blue flowers.

This time last night he had been just about to go on. This time tonight he should have been with Diana. This year he would have had the courage to touch her, to tell her that he loved her, to steal secretly to her boudoir.

'Giving their house a French name. I don't know,' said Cousin Hilda. It was as near as she ever came to a direct condemnation of the behaviour of Uncle Teddy and Auntie Doris.

Henry thought of Tosser Pilkington-Brick, telling them about a taxidermist who had retired to Budleigh Salterton and called his bungalow 'Dunstuffing'. Lampo had thought that priceless.

A wave of nostalgia for Shant swept over him. He longed to be back in South Africa Dorm. Would he ever see the shower room again? He thought about condensed milk sandwiches, drinking chocolate eaten straight from the tin, the plopping of soft ball against squash court, the wheezing of Gorringe as he doled out the coley pie, the ever-present odour of male sweat. This time yesterday he had been standing on a stage, holding seven hundred boys in his grip.

'Mrs Wedderburn's very kindly lent you her camp bed, to tide us over,' said Cousin Hilda. 'I hope you're grateful to Mrs Wedderburn.'

He wouldn't care if Mrs Wedderburn's insides all fell out as she waited for the tram.

'Yes, I am,' he said. 'I'm very grateful to Mrs Wedderburn.'

He was sitting on one of the bench seats. Cousin Hilda sat opposite him, and watched him eat. He was trying to make his tea last a long time, because after he had finished it there would be several weeks with nothing to do.

There was rice pudding to follow.

'Your favourite,' said Cousin Hilda.

It was happening again! He didn't like rice pudding! First brawn, then Gentleman's Relish, now rice pudding.

'You'll have to sleep in my room. There's nowt else for it,' said Cousin Hilda. 'We'll see how we get on. If it's not satisfactory, I'll give Mr Carpenter notice. He's a journalist.'

Her tone of voice suggested that notice would be the least he deserved, if he was so stupid as to be a journalist.

'He still hasn't come in for his tea,' said Cousin Hilda.

He went into the little bedroom, at the front of the basement. There was only just room for the camp bed between Cousin Hilda's bed and the dressing-table. How could he live here? How would he ever invite Paul here? How could he share a bedroom with the sniffer? Where would she put her voluminous undies? How would he ever amuse himself? How would he ever abuse himself?

He decided to go for a walk in the park, but when he went back into the living room to tell Cousin Hilda, she produced a small parcel, wrapped in brown paper. It looked aggressively plain, that paper, as if to say, 'Those who use gift wrapping paper and such fripperies are on the slippery slope.'

'It's just a little thing,' said Cousin Hilda, shyly. 'I thought you might not have owt to read, and I know what a one you are for reading. I've never seen one like you for reading. I said to Mrs Wedderburn, "I don't know where he gets it from, but it's a pleasure to watch him with his little nose buried in all them words." '

I actually read with my eyes, Cousin Hilda, not my nose, he thought, and then he felt guilty about thinking it. He'd asked Auntie Doris why he couldn't still go to Paul's. She had said that Cousin Hilda would be very worried if he didn't go to her first and get settled in. He decided that he couldn't bear much more of this. He'd go the next day. With what? He had no money. You couldn't sting Cousin Hilda for train fares. Sting. Words like that belonged to Dalton.

'Well, aren't you going to open it?' said Cousin Hilda.

He realised that he'd just been standing there, holding his present, thinking. He didn't want to open it. It would be something wildly, embarrassingly unsuitable. *The Journals of St Paul. A Short History of Congregational Chapels in the West Riding, 1865–1898.*

'Oh. Yes,' he said.

He undid the parcel slowly, partly because he had never fully unravelled the mysteries of string, and Cousin Hilda was not the sort of person in whose presence you did anything so wanton as to cut string, and partly because he dreaded the effort of pretending that it was just what he had always wanted.

'You may have read it before,' she said. 'If you have, tell me. She said they could change it.'

He longed for her to shut up. His nerves screamed for her to keep quiet. He hated her nervous, pathetic, silly twittering. She was pathetic. He couldn't live with her.

There was only one last knot to go. As he fumbled with it, he had an image of Lampo Davey on a rocky shore, pretending to be Sir Stafford Cripps in the underworld to a group of unshaven men in navy-blue sweaters. Was that really the sort of thing Crete wanted? He'd like to be there with Lampo Davey. He'd even let Lampo kiss him. What was he thinking?

'Come on,' said Cousin Hilda.

Were there moments when he thought he might spend the rest of his life untying that parcel? Did he nourish a faint hope that Cousin Hilda would pass away peacefully of old age before he faced the embarrassment of hiding his contempt for her gift?

'I hope it's the right age for you,' she said, as he completed the unravelling of the string at last. 'It's difficult to tell. She said if it was wrong they'd be happy to change it if it wasn't soiled.'

Shut up!!!!!!!!

At last the paper was off. The book was revealed.

It was *Biggles Scours the Jungle.*

He looked across at Cousin Hilda. Her lips were working anxiously.

'It's marvellous,' he said. 'Thank you very much. It's the best thing you could possibly have given me.'

And it was, because his self-pity was swept away by a wave of compassion for Cousin Hilda.

'Open it,' she said.

He opened it. There was a card inside. It read 'Welcome home, Henry.'

'This is your home now,' she said.

Several years later, at half-past ten that evening, Cousin Hilda's 'businessmen' assembled in the basement room for their little supper.

Since we last saw him, Henry had unpacked his trunk and hidden his books in the loft. He didn't dare let Cousin Hilda see them. His literary tastes had changed, under the influence of Dalton in general and Paul and Lampo in particular. Paul had introduced him to Aldous Huxley, who had inherited the mantle of Captain W. E. Johns and Agatha Christie as the best writer in the history of the universe. It was also because of Paul that he had brought *Women in Love* and *The Rainbow* by D. H. Lawrence. Lampo thought Huxley dreary and Lawrence phoney, and had recommended the works of Henry Miller. Henry had borrowed the tropics of Cancer and Capricorn. In addition, he had brought *The Loom of Youth* by Alec Waugh, which was about homosexuality at a public school and therefore banned from Dalton, and therefore everybody read it.

For supper, there was as much brawn as you could eat, with a segment of tomato, a tease of cucumber and a pickled gherkin. There was also bread and marge, and tea.

'I seem to remember that you like brawn,' said Cousin Hilda.

'So do I,' said Henry.

'So do you what?' said Cousin Hilda.

'Seem to remember that I like brawn,' said Henry.

'If you don't, your aunt left a jar of Gentleman's Relish for you,' said Cousin Hilda.

'I love brawn,' said Henry. 'But I won't have much tonight, because I had my tea late.'

The first 'businessman' to arrive was Liam, a very shy bachelor Irish labourer in his late forties, with a slow mind and a slow smile. Liam was not the conventional image of an Irish labourer, being a virtual teetotaller and extremely quiet. He had a shiny red face, said, 'Pleased to meet you. Hasn't it been a grand day?' and then remained silent, though he smiled a lot.

Second to arrive was Tony Preece, an insurance salesman in his thirties, dark and quietly smooth, but with a bad complexion. He grinned broadly at Henry, and winked when introduced.

Next came Neville Chamberlain, who was the South Yorkshire Regional Sales Officer for a well-known paint firm.

'I nearly punched a man tonight,' he said.

'Neville Chamberlain!' said Cousin Hilda. 'Not in front of the boy.'

Henry groaned inwardly. Was he to be used as a spectre, hovering threateningly over the conversation?

'You don't know what it's like, having an awful name,' said Neville Chamberlain.

Oh yes I do, thought Henry.

'The number of people who hold up a contract or a bill and say, "I have here a piece of paper",' said Neville Chamberlain. 'And I don't think I ever said that anyway.' He went red, and corrected himself hastily. 'I don't think *he* ever said that anyway. You see. It's getting to me. I work hard. I go out for a quiet pint.'

'Neville!' said Cousin Hilda. 'Not in front of the boy.'

Oh God.

Tony Preece winked. Henry thought he probably quite liked Tony Preece, but he was allergic to being winked at.

'Up comes this idiot. "Hello, Neville, How was Munich?" Hi. . .bloody. . .larious.'

'Neville Chamberlain!' said Cousin Hilda. 'Wash your mouth out with soap and water.'

'How *was* Munich?' said Tony Preece, and he winked at Henry, his new ally.

Oh God.

Liam smiled.

'Which of you's the journalist?' said Henry.

'None of them. That's Mr Carpenter,' said Cousin Hilda.

'Has Len Arrowsmith left then?' said Henry.

'He's gone to meet the great French polisher in the sky,' said Tony Preece.

'Tony Preece!' said Cousin Hilda. 'You know I don't like that kind of talk.'

'I saw a little baby in the park this evening, by the bandstand,'

226

said Tony Preece. 'I thought, "I know you." Then I realised who it was. Len Arrowsmith.'

'Tony Preece!' said Cousin Hilda. 'I don't believe in reincarnation myself, but Len Arrowsmith held his belief sincerely, and you've no cause to mock it.'

Tony Preece winked at Henry, and the front door slammed.

'Mr Carpenter!' said Cousin Hilda grimly, and a tense silence fell on the gathering.

There were heavy, uneven thuds on the stairs, the door opened, and a dishevelled, middle-aged man lurched into the room.

'You weren't in to dinner,' said Cousin Hilda.

'I was out,' explained Mr Carpenter, swaying. 'Out. Not in.'

'Your tea is stone cold,' said Cousin Hilda. 'I could heat it up, but I won't. I could have kept it warm, but I didn't. I will not serve you your dinner drunk.'

'I didn't realise you were drunk,' said Mr Carpenter. 'So am I. Shall we go on somewhere? Make a night of it?'

Henry took over Mr Carpenter's room the following week. It was at the side, affording an excellent view of the side of number 67 Park View Road.

He found himself following a young boy with golden fair hair. It was raining. He overtook the boy just before the turning into Link Lane, and turned his head to look at the boy's face. He caught a glimpse of smooth skin, a delicate, sculpted nose and sensitive lips.

He plunged into the busy, steaming confusion of the school, looking round for Martin Hammond, or Stefan Prziborski. Even Norbert Cuffley would do.

He saw no one he knew.

He entered the assembly hall and sat about two-thirds back, as he judged a fifteen-year-old should.

The fair-haired boy's hair, many rows in front, shone out in the wet autumn gloom.

'Welcome back, old boys. Welcome to Thurmarsh Grammar, new boys,' began Mr E. F. Crowther.

All the other new boys were eleven, but Henry was fifteen.

'You see before you our staff,' said Mr E. F. Crowther, 'as fine a body of men as can be found. . .in this building.'

Mr Crosby had heard this joke twenty-four times before, but he still laughed exaggeratedly at it.

'Thurmarsh. It is not perhaps a name that resounds through the educational world.'

Mr Quell stifled a yawn.

'It is not an Eton or Harrow. It is not even a Dalton College.'

There was laughter. It was nasty of Mr E. F. Crowther, Henry thought, to add that. But perhaps it was expecting too much of human nature to imagine that any king could ever forgive a subject who said 'the bread van' in the middle of his address to the nation.

'But is it any the worse for that?'

Again, Mr E. F. Crowther paused, as if challenging any wretched boy, but in this case particularly Henry, to say 'yes'.

It wasn't his fault that he had left Thurmarsh. He hadn't wanted to, any more than he wanted to be back here now.

It would serve Mr E. F. Crowther right if he did say 'yes'.

He would say 'yes'.

Yes!

No!!!!

He began to sweat, but he didn't say 'yes'.

'I am proud to be headmaster of Thurmarsh Grammar,' the headmaster continued at last. 'Perhaps I am biased, because I am Thurmarsh born and Thurmarsh bred.'

Henry felt a ridiculous compulsion to interrupt again. Oh no. Oh no no no no no no no no no.

'We are still only beginning to rebuild the fabric of our civilisation after the recent war which stretched it to breaking point,' said Mr E. F. Crowther. 'In the war, Old Thurmarshians were up there in the front lines with Etonians, Harrovians and Daltonians. In the years to come, in the never-ending war against the enemies of liberalism and democracy, in the war against the self-destruction of the human race itself, I have no doubt there will also be Thurmarshians in the van.'

Was it just his fancy, or was the headmaster looking straight at him? Was half the school looking straight at him? Sweat poured off him. He tried to hold the words back. They were there, like a lump in his throat. He mustn't say them. Not again.

The tension eased. He wasn't going to. The temptation was over. The headmaster, perhaps relieved, perhaps disappointed, perhaps both, resumed his theme.

Henry found himself looking at the back view of the fair-haired boy. Just then, as if aware of Henry's gaze upon him, the boy turned round. He seemed to be looking straight at Henry. He really was remarkably beautiful.

He was getting an erection! Oh God. How often had he yearned after these elongations. Now they were cropping up at the most embarrassing moments. He had to get rid of it before they stood for the hymn. The whole row would notice it. It would be visible to the masters through a narrow gap in the standing ranks. Gradually the attention of the whole school would be drawn to it. Go away. Shove off. Concentrate on Mr E. F. Crowther. All be sorry to hear that poor old Mr Budge had passed away. Well, sorry to be callous, but never mind Mr Budge passing away. How about Mr Bulge passing away?

Concentrate. Extensive repairs to the boiler room, eh? Sounds good. Face the winter with more confidence. That's the ticket.

A boy? It wasn't possible. He'd spent two years at Dalton College being horrified by it. His working-class prudery, Lampo Davey had called it. Don't think about Lampo Davey! Concentrate. Improvements in the gymnasium! Two new ropes! Excellent news. The fair-haired boy'd look nice climbing a rope. Smooth legs, covered in downy fair. . .stop it! Count the windows. Sixteen, their top halves all open at an angle of twenty-five degrees, held in place by cords tied to cleats on the wall. Roof. Flat, dull, off-white. Lighting, strip. Like to see the fair-haired boy str. . . no! No!

Had Dalton College finally corrupted him? Had he fought it where it was rife only to succumb to it where it was taboo?

Oh God.

They sang a hymn. He managed to conceal it under his hymn book. Slowly, under the influence of the hymn, it went away.

A prayer followed. How drab and unimpressive it all was, after Dalton. Don't even think like that!

As they filed out of assembly, on a tide of talk, he came face to

229

face with Martin Hammond and Stefan Prziborski. How big they were. He hardly recognised them. Martin looked more like an owl than ever, a solid, robust owl. Stefan was medium-height, medium-build and had brown hair, and yet there was nothing average or dull about his appearance at all. There was a hint of foreign parts, of exotic sensitivity, in the rubbery mobility of his face.

'Hello,' said Martin.

'How do, then?' said Stefan, in his semi-pretend Yorkshire.

'Hello,' he croaked.

His voice sounded dreadfully middle-class and false, and he felt that the remark had not been a great success.

'How's things then, our Martin?' he said. 'How's t' football, our Stefan?'

It came out like his music-hall voice. It sounded false. It was false.

'Much the same,' said Martin.

Henry knew what Martin meant. He meant, 'Some of us have made the best out of our boring, unglamorous, routine lives while others have been gallivanting around chasing false gods, mocking their heritage, being corrupted by the sink of iniquity which is upper-middle-class life, learning to drink claret, put the milk in afterwards, cheer when the chaps scored a try, and betray their class, their family, their upbringing and their friends.'

If only Martin could have actually said it, instead of bottling it up.

Some of the boys mocked his altered accent. He soon acquired the soubriquet 'Snobby'. It was even more hurtful than 'Oiky'. It had not been his fault that he had been oiky, and at least he had had his anger and sense of injustice to sustain him. But he deserved to be known as 'Snobby'.

He had betrayed them all.

He avoided the company of Martin and Stefan, partly in order to spare himself the indignity of being snubbed by them, and partly also because he had something more important to do.

He had to establish a relationship with the fair-haired boy.

On the second day of term, he found himself walking out of the

230

school behind the fair-haired boy, who was alone. He followed him down Link Lane, past the fire station. The boy turned right, towards the town centre, where he took another right turn into Bargate. He popped into the sweet shop beside the Paw Paw Coffee Bar and Grill. He was buying sweets, which would ruin his teeth, silly boy. Henry stared at three-piece suits in the window of Dunn's till the boy emerged. He followed him as he turned left into Church Street, towards the Town Hall, which was streaked with pigeon droppings.

The boy turned right, along the Doncaster Road, past the end of Park View Road and into the Alderman Chandler Memorial Park. He walked diagonally across the park, skirting the bandstand and the pond, leaving the animal cages to his left, and plunged out into the maze of side roads in the north-eastern suburbs.

Henry followed him no further.

He simply hadn't dared to approach him. How could he, here, in Thurmarsh?

It was the most important year of his academic life. In June he would sit his 'O' levels. The change of school could not but handicap him. It was doubly important to work hard this year, yet the lessons passed him in a fog.

Latin was taken by Mr Blackthorn, who would come in disgruntled every Monday morning and say, 'Those damned Christians woke me with their bells again yesterday.' Mr Blackthorn worked off all his aggressions on the Christians. With his pupils he was patient and charitable. Yet Henry sat there in a fog.

The Maths master, Mr Littlewood, had a boyish, sandy-haired enthusiasm. If anybody could bring Henry and calculus together, it was he. Yet Henry sat there in a fog.

The Geography master, Mr Burrell, had only one eye. Was a return to Thurmarsh inevitably also a return to somebody with one eye? Was the number of people with one eye in the town a constant? Mr Burrell's glass eye, the left, was a fine piece of work, as these things go, and he laboured under the illusion that nobody realised that he only had one eye. He was therefore reluctant to turn his head more than would be natural in a man of two eyes.

Unfortunately, there were two rows of fixed bench seats parallel with three walls of Mr Burrell's class. The four boys at the end of these seats on Mr Burrell's left were therefore totally invisible to Mr Burrell at all times. He knew they were there, of course, and in order to ensure that they received their fair share of attention, he moved the class around from time to time. At this particular time the four invisible boys were Astbury, Longfellow, Prziborski and Wool. They sat with false red noses or women's hats on while the rest of the class behaved with total decorum. This added an exotic touch to a humdrum scene, yet Henry sat there in a fog.

The French master, Mr Telfer, had two eyes, but only one leg. He had lost the other one on active service in France, and this had confirmed him, if confirmation was needed, in his belief that the French were a chaotic, dirty and totally unreliable people who used sauces to cover up the fact that all their meat was horse and changed governments more often than their underclothes. Only a filthy nation would need so many bidets, he argued. Mr Telfer was sour and staccato. Teaching French was an act of masochism in the best puritan tradition. He taught it fiercely, coldly, by the book. No Arsène Lupin. No 'Auprès de ma Blonde'. Just irregular verbs and suffering. Just occasionally, if he was feeling generous or frivolous, or it was near the end of the term, they might be permitted to study the works of Racine. The boys were in awe of him, but Henry sat there in a fog, *auprès de* his blond in his guilt-ridden mind.

Mr McFarlane, the History master, had two eyes and two legs, but only one idea. It was Marxism. It was amazing how relevant the theories of a man born in Trier in 1818 were to every single thing that happened in British history between 1066 and 1485. All this should have been grist to Henry's dark, satanic mill, yet he sat there in a fog. Might catch a glimpse of the boy in the break. Oh, delicious prospect.

The final lesson of the day was English. The greatest of Mr Quell's many literary passions was Chaucer. One of the set books was *The Nun's Priest's Tale*. Mr Quell brought it vividly to life, yet Henry sat there in a fog, not even concentrating enough to be more than mildly disappointed that Mr Quell had said nothing especially welcoming to him on his return.

Good teachers, bad teachers. Happy teachers, sad teachers. Miss Candy's great hope, who never knew that he was Miss Candy's great hope, sat through all their lessons in a fog.

He hardly spoke to the other boys. His nerves were exhausted by all the new starts that he had made. He had nothing left to give to this school, and it was harder to readjust than to start from scratch.

Besides, he was busy. As soon as the lessons were over, he hurried out of school, tense, absorbed, tingling, determined that today he would talk to the fair-haired boy. Six times his courage had failed him. Today it mustn't.

It was a bright, rather hazy autumn afternoon. He walked past the old men's shelter, the glass restored now between the wrought iron. It was octagonal. An octagonal bench ran round the interior. There was no law to say that only old men might use this shelter, but only old men ever did. It was tradition.

He wandered over to the bird cages. There were five guinea fowl, a macaw, two rather scruffy peahens, three Lady Amhurst pheasants, seven assorted doves and twelve sparrows which had got in through the mesh. In the animal cages there were two marmots, two unidentified small deer and an extremely listless ocelot. All the while, only half of Henry's mind was occupied by this rich cornucopia of animal life. He was watching out for the fair-haired boy.

Here he came. If only he came over to the animals, Henry would be able to say, 'Oh, hello, haven't I seen you at Thurmarsh Grammar,' and the thing would be started.

Yesterday, Henry had stood by the pond, and the boy had come past the cages. Today he came nowhere near the cages, but lingered by the pond. Tomorrow. He'd definitely try tomorrow.

The following day saw the fog thicken. It cleared slowly outside, but not at all in Henry's head.

After school, he walked briskly to the park. This time he sat in the bandstand. It had a classical pillar at each corner and a green copper dome. The sun was a yellow plate riding through the mist, and a raw little breeze blew through the bandstand.

Here he came. Henry took deep breaths and his heart raced. This was it. Zero hour. He set off on an expertly timed walk which brought him across the boy's bows.

Right up till the moment when he said it, he wasn't sure whether he was going to say it or not. Out it came. 'Hello. Haven't I seen you at the grammar school?'

'Aye. That's right.'

The accent was broad Thurmarsh. That didn't make the thing any more probable.

They were heading towards the pond. In the middle there was a small reedy island, with a few stunted trees. A colourful board gave names and pictures of all the ducks which might be found on the pond.

'There's a fine collection of ducks,' said Henry.

'They haven't got half what they say on t' board.'

The boy seemed calm. Had he any idea what Henry was thinking? Did Henry's voice sound odd? Was the park keeper watching?

'You what?'

'They haven't got pochard. They haven't got shoveler.'

'They've got tufted duck.'

'Oh, aye, that's what they mostly are, tufted duck. But they're not very exciting, aren't tufted duck.'

'They've got teal.'

'They haven't got marbled teal. They haven't got falcated teal. It's only in t' last week they've had mandarin.'

Close to, the boy's features were not quite as fine as he had thought.

'They've got wigeon,' said the fair-haired boy.

'Have they got pintail?'

'Have they heck?'

'You like birds, do you?'

'Not really. I just look to see what it says on t' board, and what they haven't got. Then I complain to t' park keeper.'

The park keeper limped slowly towards them, examining a line of bleak, rectangular rose beds.

'Hey,' shouted the fair-haired boy. 'It says there's shoveler. There isn't.'

The park keeper approached them. He addressed himself to Henry.

'I keep telling him,' he said. 'There's been a war on. Ducks is in short supply, same as owt else.'

'Shouldn't be on t' board if tha hasn't gorrem;' said the fair-haired boy stubbornly.

'I'd better be getting home,' said Henry.

And that was that. He walked away, as flat as a pancake. That was what his great homosexual passion amounted to, one discussion about the lack of duck on the park pond.

He couldn't face smiling Liam, winking Tony and complaining Neville Chamberlain. He walked back into Thurmarsh, scuffing his shoes angrily against the pavements. The mist was closing in.

He'd been in love with a dream, a vision culled as much from literature as life. What a dreadful fool he would have made of himself, if anybody had noticed. Perhaps they had noticed.

He hadn't disliked the fair-haired boy. But he was just a little pre-pubertal grammar-school kid, aggressively determined not to be short-changed by life. He'd have run a mile if Henry'd tried anything. Or he'd have demanded money. Henry shuddered. He imagined himself flinging himself on the boy, the boy resisting and fighting, the awful humiliation of it. He began to shake, a shuddering mixture of the cold and self-revulsion.

'You're sick,' he told himself.

Oh God.

He caught the Rawlaston tram, barely conscious of what he was doing, certainly not responsible for his decisions.

The tram climbed past the end of Link Lane. New slums were being built on one of the bomb sites.

They breasted the rise like an immensely slow big dipper and groaned down into the Rundle Valley. There, on the right, looming like a battleship in the mist, was the fortress of Brunswick Road Primary School. Had he really been there; he, Henry Pratt, the same person as this?

In the Rundle Valley it wasn't mist. It was fog. The tram went into it so suddenly that Henry expected a collision. It was rank and sulphurous.

He could tell by the flattening out that they had reached the valley floor. They were swinging right. The canal would be on his left.

'Paradise,' said the conductor.

He got off. This was what he had come back to do. Visit his roots.

There wasn't a breath of wind. The factories were pumping filth into the autumn mists. It was almost as dark as night, but yellow instead of black.

He struggled along the pavement to the corner of Paradise Lane. The frail and the elderly walked with handkerchiefs over their mouths and noses, the home-made gas-masks of peace.

Footsteps rang hollow. Cars crawled. A man spat quite close to him. It was ridiculous. What was the point of revisiting old haunts when you couldn't see them?

It was perfect! The real trip was in his memory, anyway, and he certainly didn't want to be seen.

He felt his way up to the terraced houses. Visibility was about a foot and a half. He passed the entry to a yard. Number 15. 17. 19. 21, where she'd been on the game. 23. They'd got a new door with curved, patterned, frosted glass. It removed the only architectural merit the row could ever have been said to possess – simplicity.

'I don't like that door,' he said.

'Give over,' said Ezra. 'It's their one little chance of being individual. Would you deny them that?'

He jumped out of his skin. He looked round. If his father had been there, he wouldn't have been able to see him.

The sweat came out hot and cold all over him.

He was hearing voices now.

Oh God.

Yes?

What?

I am with you, my son.

He stumbled and fell, gashing his knee. No matter.

He had heard it.

Are you there?

Nothing.

If this was a blinding vision, it was strictly West Riding style. Two short sentences, in thick fog, on the Road to Nowhere instead of the Road to Damascus. He thought of Lampo Davey, who had said, 'Tosser has absolutely no religious feeling whatsoever. He thinks the Road to Damascus is a film with Bing Crosby, Bob Hope and Dorothy Lamour.' And Lampo Davey in Paradise Lane brought out the guilt – streaming, shuddering, dreadful guilt.

The fog began to swirl about him. It was turning into the faces of the ogglers and tackies, back at Shant. Ogglers was Shant rant for the waiters who served them at dinner. Tackies were maids. The boys never spoke to the ogglers and tackies as if they were human beings. It simply wasn't done. And now they were all about him, hideous, vaporous caricatures, reminding him, accusing him. And there was his father, a cadaver of fog, pointing an accusing foggy finger. You betrayed me, Paradise Lane, your own past, just to get laughs.

He stepped through the gate. It was a gate onto a canal towpath. It was a door into a world full of capital letters.

Guilt. Shame. The Scylla and Charybdis of Henry's voyage.

It was a perilous journey, along the towpath in the thick fog. There was a muffled explosion as a train detonated a fog signal.

He almost missed the bridge, where the towpath crossed the canal. He clambered carefully up, and down the other side onto the waste ground. He was shaking. It was the cold. Plus the Guilt. And the Shame.

He had heard Him. God had spoken to him. Of that he had no doubt.

He knelt on the waste ground and closed his eyes. He saw his dad, as he had been in the last days, shrunken, embittered, soon to die in an outside lav. He saw himself, standing in front of seven hundred boys, saying, ' "Henry," he said. "I've gorra pain in me eye." I didn't ask him which one, cos he only had the one. He couldn't afford two.'

A train whistled. A dog barked. Henry prayed in the fog.

'Oh, God,' he said. 'Forgive me.'

There was no reply. He didn't expect one. God had told him that He existed. Now, there would be silence until he had Atoned for his Sins.

He knew what he had to do. He understood the nature of symbolic gestures.

He got up, shaking, sweating, even crying, wretched, but happy. He edged his way forward towards the River Rundle, cautiously. It would ruin everything if he fell in.

He sensed the bank rather than saw it. Yes, there the land fell away. He knelt and reached out into the white nothingness with his hand.

No doubt the Ganges was polluted. A river was Sacred because Faith made it so. Otherwise, pilgrims would make only for trout streams, to the fury of angling clubs and water bailiffs.

Henry knew that the River Rundle was Sacred. Therefore, the River Rundle was Sacred. And it was truly an act of Faith, for in the thick fog he couldn't actually see that it was the river that he was stepping into. It might be the edge if the world.

It was the river. Once again, the foul waters of the Rundle closed over his head, but this time he meant them to. He was Purifying himself in its Holy Waters.

The police brought him home at twenty-five past ten, shaking uncontrollably, dripping wet, with a temperature of a hundred and five. Cousin Hilda had been at her wits' end, but his appearance was too terrible for her to be angry.

'Where have you been?' she said, sniffing only very mildly.

'Finding God,' he said.

He was in bed for two weeks. Two weeks in the bed with the sagging springs, which converted into a settee when required. Two weeks with the hiss of the gas fire, in front of which Cousin Hilda placed a saucer of water, in case it should get thirsty. Two weeks staring at the drab wallpaper, its pattern in dark blue and pink so small that from the bed there didn't seem to be a pattern. Two weeks staring at the massive, carved, slightly orange wardrobe. A signed photograph of Len Hutton stood on the mantelpiece. It was the nearest thing in the room to a personal touch, all the pictures of Patricia Roc having been thrown away, judged too racy for this establishment.

His fever died down, the magic of the fair-haired boy had gone, but the magic of God remained.

Many people never find their true vocation in life. Fortunate indeed is the young man who finds it at the tender age of fifteen.

But Henry has found his vocation before, a sceptic might point out. True, but that was only *a* vocation. This was *the* vocation.

He would devote himself to the service of God.

Cousin Hilda was delighted. She had been a little worried at first. His method of coming to God had been rather too unconventional for her nonconformist tastes. Once there, however, he seemed to be quietening down nicely.

At last he was well enough to go downstairs for his tea.

Liam possibly thought that he wasn't as much fun as he used to be.

Neville Chamberlain hardly noticed him. He was too busy wondering if he'd been over-impulsive in changing his bank that afternoon. Suffering from pains in the arm, worried that he might be on the verge of a heart attack, he had gone to see his bank manager, to make a will. The bank manager had said, 'I have here a piece of paper,' and Neville Chamberlain had almost had a heart attack then and there.

Only on Tony Preece did Henry's discovery of God make any impact. It was all because of a mouse.

When Tony Preece yawned and said, 'Sorry. Late night last night,' Henry had toyed with the idea of making some comment about Loose Living, but had decided against it. Now, however, he could not remain silent.

Cousin Hilda had discovered mouse droppings. She had seen tiny tooth marks. She had put down a trap by the door to the scullery.

'Got a mouse?' said Tony Preece.

'I'm afraid so,' said Cousin Hilda. 'It's probably come over from the park now the cold weather's come.'

'I hope the possibility has occurred to you that it might be Len Arrowsmith,' said Tony Preece.

'Don't be ridiculous,' sniffed Cousin Hilda.

'It's not at all ridiculous,' said Tony Preece. 'Where else would he come but here? He always liked it. And you know how he felt the cold.'

He winked at Henry.

'It's wrong to mock a sincerely held belief,' said Henry.

Tony Preece gawped at him, thunder-struck. He looked from

239

Henry to Cousin Hilda, then back to Henry again.

'My God, we've got two of them now,' he said, and he pushed his plate into the centre of the table and stormed out of the room, and Liam's smile froze on his bewildered face.

When Liam and Neville Chamberlain had gone, Cousin Hilda refused to let Henry go into the scullery, in case his fever returned. So while she washed up, he sat by the blue stove, gazing hypnotically at the glowing fire behind the cracked glass.

Cousin Hilda came and sat at the other side of the stove, with her knitting.

'Please don't say things like that to Tony Preece,' she said. 'You upset him.'

'You don't like him poking fun at reincarnation either,' said Henry.

'I know,' said Cousin Hilda, 'but he'll accept it from me. He won't from you, not at your age.'

'That's not fair,' said Henry.

'It's not just that,' said Cousin Hilda. 'I'm his landlady. I'm entitled. I don't want to lose him, Henry. This is a business, and he's a good customer, is Tony Preece.'

'Is he?'

'What do you mean?'

'I think he has Mucky Habits.'

'Mucky habits?'

'When he isn't in to supper,' said Henry. 'When he has late nights, like last night. I think he Indulges in Strong Drink and Consorts with Mucky Women.'

Cousin Hilda stared at him in astonishment.

'I know what he gets up to,' she said. 'He gives performances.'

'Performances, Cousin Hilda?'

'Tony Preece is summat of a Jekyll and Hyde,' said Cousin Hilda. 'By day, insurance salesman. By night, stand-up comedian.'

'Stand-up comedian?'

'It's his hobby. Very regrettable, of course, but. . .I wouldn't like to lose Tony Preece.'

Henry didn't feel that he was in a strong position to criticise people for being stand-up comedians. So he kept quiet in Tony

Preece's presence after that.

The following morning, in fact, although embarrassed, and unable to meet Tony Preece's eye, he forced himself to say, 'Sorry about last night.'

'That's all right,' said Tony Preece.

When Henry did meet Tony Preece's eye, Tony nodded in the direction of the scullery door, and winked.

The mouse trap had gone.

Mr Quell was worried about Henry. He didn't like the look of the boy. He had gone extremely pale and puffy. His face was waxy and lifeless. He was beginning to resemble a fish which has been on the slab too long. Either he was masturbating himself to death, or there were major problems.

Mr Quell believed that schoolmasters could often make matters worse by interfering too soon when they sensed the onset of a crisis. He had been careful to leave Henry to himself while he settled back into the life of the school. But you could also delay too long. He had delayed too long in the case of Oberath.

He invited Henry to tea on Friday. Henry was pleased. It would be a wonderful opportunity for talking to Mr Quell about Him.

They drove in Mr Quell's car. It was an ancient Hillman Minx with a rattling exhaust. Mr Quell drove at twenty-five miles an hour.

'It's a miserable month, November,' said Mr Quell.

'I quite like it,' said Henry.

Bad! No boy should wallow in mist and fog.

Their route took them through the town centre, and out onto the York Road.

'The United are picking up a bit,' said Mr Quell.

'Are they?' said Henry.

Small talk would prove to be a blind alley, thought Mr Quell.

Mr Quell pulled up at a newly installed set of traffic lights. A light rain was beginning to fall. The swish of the windscreen wipers was sad and comforting at the same time.

'There are certain practices which, if indulged in to excess, can prove very deleterious to health,' said Mr Quell.

'I've completely given up self-abuse,' said Henry, 'if that's what you mean.'

The Quells lived in a detached brick house, on Winstanley Road, near the edge of the town. There was a trolley-bus stop outside, and sometimes people waiting for a trolley-bus would drop sweet papers into their garden. This upset Mr Quell, but not his wife.

Mr Quell had to turn right to enter his drive. He was cautious, and waited a long while for a gap in the oncoming traffic. A queue built up behind him, and a driver hooted.

There was a monkey puzzle tree in Mr Quell's front garden.

They had tea in the front room, served by Mr Quell. There was a coal fire, with shelves in alcoves at either side of it. The tea was laid out on a trolley. Mr Quell divided up a nest of tables and placed a table beside each of their chairs.

Mrs Quell was small, almost doll-like, and very beautiful. She had small, regular features and dark hair. No lines of stress marred the oval perfection of her face.

Mr Quell served tea. His burly, barrel-chested frame and mass of greying hair seemed at odds with Dresden China ladies on shelves, and a Dresden China wife sitting very upright in the brown Parker Knoll chair. There were neat, thin, quartered slices of bread and butter and two bought cakes – a Battenburg cake and a chocolate cake. The Battenburg cake was stale and the chocolate cake had the consistency of damp sawdust. They drank cheap, unsubtle Indian tea out of tiny cups. Mr Quell could hardly get his gnarled finger inside the fragile handle of his cup.

Mrs Quell asked what colour Henry's eyes were.

'Brown,' he said, embarrassed.

'Brown!' said Mrs Quell, as if no other answer would have pleased her.

They asked gently searching questions about Henry's life at his various homes and schools. He replied precisely, without vitality. He only showed vitality when he explained that he had found God.

Mr Quell nodded when Henry told him this. He wasn't surprised. It had been one of his theories. He had seen quite a few religious people with this lifeless white puffiness, this soft, introverted righteousness.

242

Mrs Quell cut her Battenburg cake into four quarters, very carefully. She picked up one of the two yellow squares and took a delicate bite.

'Yellow,' she said, when she had eaten it.

'Correct,' said Mr Quell.

'I'll try for a pink one now,' she said, after she had finished the yellow square. She touched the second yellow square, then her hand moved on and she picked up a pink piece. She took a small bite and smiled. She ate fastidiously.

'Think how dull a Battenburg cake would be if I could see,' she said.

After tea, Mrs Quell left the room unaided. There was silence for a moment.

'Her face is beautiful because she cannot see how beautiful it is, and so does not worry about it becoming less beautiful,' said Mr Quell.

Henry couldn't manage any reply to this.

'Burrell is tormented by his refusal to admit that he has only one eye,' said Mr Quell. 'If only he could look at my wife and say, "Lucky old me. I have an eye that can see." If only the losing finalist at Wimbledon could say, "Magnificent. I'm the second-best player in the whole world. What an achievement." You find my comments specious. Didn't we make an abominable tea?'

'It was very nice,' said Henry politely.

'It was an abysmal repast,' said Mr Quell. 'All our food is brought in by Mrs Ellerby, who lives alone. It is quite the biggest thing in her life, buying our food for us. So, you've found God?'

'Yes, sir.'

'Less of the sir here, Henry. The name is Eamonn. This finding of God has made a great difference to you, has it, Henry?'

'Oh yes, sir. . .Eamonn. I want to devote my life to His Service.'

A trolley-bus hissed to a stop.

'I was going to be a monk, Henry.'

'Yes, s. . Eamonn.'

'I gave up to marry Beth. You would be wrong if you deduced that it was out of pity for her blindness. It was out of lust for her body and love for her soul.'

The trolley-bus resumed its journey.

'If the people on that trolley-bus could hear us, they'd be amazed,' said Mr Quell.

He went over to the hearth, lifted a small piece of coal with the tongs and placed it carefully on the fire.

'I remember thinking when I first knew you, "He's going to be quite the wag, that one," ' said Mr Quell, still with his back to Henry.

'I became very frivolous for a time,' said Henry. 'I even wanted to be a stand-up comedian once.'

Mr Quell came and sat opposite Henry and looked straight into his eyes.

'If you're going to do an act with God, don't forget he's the straight man,' he said.

'I don't quite understand,' said Henry.

'God has no need for bores,' said Mr Quell. 'Believe me, he has enough of those already. God wants you as you are. He wants you, not some lifeless image of how you think you ought to be.'

'That can't be so, s. . .Eamonn,' said Henry. 'If a murderer comes to God, God wants him to Repent of his Evil Ways.'

'We repent of the evil in us, but the good in us must not be subdued in accordance with some concept we have of what a religious person should be like. A man goes to a monastery. He says, "I want to lead a life of self-denial." The monk says, "Do you truly, deeply want to lead a life of self-denial?" The man says, "I long for it." The monk says, "Then the true self-denial is to deny yourself self-denial. Off you go now. Have a lobster thermidor, a bottle of chablis and a good woman." What does this illustrate?'

'I don't know.'

'Life is not simple, and we cannot come to religion in order to make it so. I believe that the search for simplicity has done great damage to religion. Good and evil are not on opposite sides of the road. Black and white. Them and us. Insiders and outsiders. Religion as a recipe for bigotry. One must always remember that there are many religious people who are more wicked than many people who are not religious.'

'It sounds as though you're trying to put me off religion, sir.'

'Eamonn. Of course not. I'm trying to persuade you to come to it in the right spirit.'

Mr Quell went over to the sofa and sat beside Henry.

'I am not a great thinker,' he said. 'I am just a man who has tried to live honestly and somtimes succeeded. I have learnt never to trust a man who says he has no doubts. Why are you suddenly seeking God in such an intense and overpowering manner, Henry?'

Mr Quell put his great hand on Henry's knee. He had goalkeeper's hands. Henry shrank away and Mr Quell hastily removed the hand and stood up.

'You think I'm a homosexual!' he said. 'Is that why you think I was so eager to get you to call me Eamonn?'

'No, s. . .Eamonn.'

Mr Quell selected another piece of coal and placed it carefully on the fire. He might have been an old charcoal-burner in the forests, so carefully did he tend his little blaze.

'You think *you're* a homosexual,' he said, wheeling round and smiling triumphantly at Henry.

Henry said nothing.

'That's it, isn't it?'

Henry nodded miserably.

'Tell me about it,' said Mr Quell, returning to his armchair, stretching his short, thick legs towards the fire, and not looking at Henry.

Henry told him about the fair-haired boy. His cheeks burned. It was the hardest thing he had ever had to tell anybody, but when he had finished he felt better.

Mr Quell asked him about life and homosexuality at Dalton College. Another trolley-bus came and went unnoticed as he talked.

'I'm certain you aren't a homosexual,' said Mr Quell when he had finished.

'Then why did I. . .?'

'All sexuality is ambiguous,' said Mr Quell. 'We love it and hate it. We hope for it and fear it. Male sexuality has to have feminine elements, in order to understand female sexuality, which has to have male elements, for the same reason. Virtue has elements of vice in it, and vice versa.' He lit a cigar. 'I suspect that it is because

245

many people know that they have some homosexual instincts that they are so extremely hostile to homosexuality,' he said. 'I'd like to ask you to try to use that knowledge to be more understanding and tolerant.'

'I will,' promised Henry. 'I really want to be tolerant. I can't stand people who aren't tolerant.'

Mr Quell put another piece of coal on the fire.

'What does God want of me?' said Henry.

'He wants you to try to be good, but also to try to be yourself,' said Mr Quell. 'He wants you to be tolerant to those of other faiths and to those of no faith. He wants you to get nine 'O' levels.'

Mr Quell looked at Henry.

Henry looked at Mr Quell.

Mr Quell laughed.

So did Henry.

He went to St James's Church twice every Sunday. He prayed for a peaceful ending to the Korean War. Perhaps he didn't pray hard enough. He prayed that the Labour Party would be more successful in its efforts to bring social justice to every corner of the land, and would manage to solve the growing balance of payments difficulties and reconcile its increasing split over rearmaments. Perhaps he didn't pray hard enough. When Hugh Gaitskell replaced Sir Stafford Cripps as Chancellor of the Exchequer, Henry wondered how this would affect Lampo Davey's career as a mime artist in Crete. Then he prayed for Hugh Gaitskell and Sir Stafford Cripps and Lampo Davey. When national service was increased from eighteen months to two years, he asked for the courage to declare himself a conscientious objector when the time came. He couldn't yet be sure if he had prayed hard enough. He prayed for forgiveness because during his two years in the enclosed world of Dalton College he had virtually forgotten that the outside world still existed.

On Friday evenings he went to St James's Church youth club, which had a thriving membership of a hundred and twenty-three. It was mainly table-tennis and darts. Kevin Thorburn beat him 5–0 at darts and 21–5, 21–2 at table-tennis. He made shy advances to Mabel Billington, one of the few people at the youth club who went to church. She beat him 4–1 at darts and 21–7, 21–8 at table-tennis. He prayed that the youth club would become more religious, and his prayers were answered. The youth club leader, Doug Watson, decided to introduce talks about aspects of religion, with guest speakers. In six weeks the attendance dropped to seventeen. Doug Watson abandoned the religious talks, and it became just darts and table-tennis again. Henry prayed for extra strength to help fight the Evils of Ignorance and the Forces of Darkness.

He tried to be Tolerant. He hoped that Tony Preece would joke about Len Arrowsmith's reincarnation again, so that he could demonstrate his Tolerance, but Tony Preece didn't. He prayed that Tony Preece would stop winking and that people would stop annoying Neville Chamberlain by saying, 'I have here a piece of paper.' When Aneurin Bevan resigned over the decision to introduce health charges to pay for rearmament, he prayed for Aneurin Bevan, for socialism and for the future of mankind. He asked God to give Uncle Teddy and Auntie Doris Strength to fight the Evils of Strong Drink. He even prayed for a cure for the blackheads on Geoffrey Porringer's nose.

He prayed for forgiveness for wasting God's time by praying too much.

He attended confirmation classes, given by the vicar of St James's Church. He had to fight against feelings of impatience. It was all so cool, so calm, so social. The vicar kept saying that reason wasn't enough, Christianity was far more than just a philosophy or an ethical system, it was Christ, it was Faith. Dryly, cooly, the vicar would say that this was no dry, cool business. It was the most exciting step in a person's life. Nobody looked excited, but then, to be fair, nor did he. Perhaps he should tell them that he had known all this, that God had spoken to him on the Road to Nowhere. He hadn't spoken much to him, but he had said, 'My son.' That made Henry Christ's brother in God. He didn't mention this, because it might seem like boasting, and boasting was a Sin. Maybe they were all concealing similar Revelations, but he doubted it, and then he felt Shame about his Doubt, and Prayed for Forgiveness.

One day, on a bus, he saw Chalky White, just as Chalky was

getting off. He said, 'Hello, Chalky.' Chalky looked round, and his face flashed into a grin, and he said, 'Henry!' and then he stepped off the bus. Henry's mind flashed back to the barn in Rowth Bridge, to reading about nigs and darkies to Lorna Arrow. He wondered how Chalky White liked reading about nigs and darkies.

The following day, during the Geography lesson, he had an idea. It was now his turn to be one of the four boys seated on Mr Burrell's extreme left. The other three were Dakins, Smedley and Martin Hammond. By this time Henry was being more or less ignored by the other boys. He was Snobby Pratt, who once said 'The bread van' in morning assembly and went away to a snotty-nosed public school down south, and came back ruined. Many boys would quite soon have admitted that it was not his fault, and tried to be moderately friendly, but he had given them no chance, and now, if you talked to him, he tried to convert you to Christianity. Between Martin and Henry, though, there existed the special tension of ruptured friendship, and on this particular morning Martin handed Henry a note which said, 'Bloody snobbish priggish goody-goody bastard.' Henry felt sad that Martin should do this, sad for their lost friendship, but mainly sad for Martin, who was Wandering in the Wilderness.

Why did Martin send Henry a note which said, 'Bloody snobbish priggish goody-goody bastard'? Because Martin was wearing huge false ears and a false moustache, Dakins had his jacket on back to front and Smedley had an unlit cigarette in his mouth and his feet on the desk, while Henry was taking no advantage of being in Mr Burrell's blind spot. This was due less to belated filial feeling for the one-eyed than to his Conviction that God did not want him to wear a fire bucket on his head as he studied Geography in the run-up to his 'O' levels.

And then Henry had his idea, which he would not have had if he had not seen Chalky White on the bus. In the next Geography lesson he would wear a black mask. He would sit there with a huge, black mask with smiling white teeth. The class would think he was taking advantage of Mr Burrell's blind spot, but God would know that he was in fact making a gesture of racial solidarity, an apology to black people everywhere for the insults meted out to them in the pages of popular literature.

He made the mask himself, with cardboard and some black paint given him by Neville Chamberlain out of rejected stock. It was crude, rough, badly finished, and the best thing he had made in his life.

He couldn't wait for the Geography lesson, but first there was Latin. Here too he faced a challenge to his religion. It came from that amiable enemy of organised religion, Mr Blackthorn. One of their set authors was Catullus, whose works had been so warmly praised by Lampo. Henry came to these personal, sexy, tortured, comic, blasphemous pieces at a time when there was no possibility of his finding them other than offensive. Catullus's passionate and unhappy love affair with Lesbia, a married woman, shocked him. If it could be forgiven in life, which was doubtful, it was inexcusable as a subject for poetry. All right, some subjects for poetry had been closed to the Romans. Tintern Abbey hadn't been built, let alone ruined. But didn't the Romans have daffodils, nightingales and ancient mariners?

The more scatological poems were ignored. They wouldn't figure in the exams. But Mr Blackthorn cast his net reasonably wide. Today, they were to translate the poem:

Verani, omnibus e meis amicis
antistans mihi milibus trecentis,
venistine domum ad tuos penates
fratresque unanimos anumque matrem?
venisti. O mihi nuntii beati!
visam te incolumem audiamque Hiberum
narrantem loca, facta, nationes,
ut mos est tuus, applicansque collum
iucundum os oculosque suavibor. . .

He began his translation. 'Veranius, standing out first to me from all my three hundred thousand friends, have you come home to your hearth and your brothers who are all of one mind and your old mother? You have come. Oh blessed tidings for me! I shall see you safe and sound and I shall hear you telling me of the places and deeds and people of Spain, as is your custom, and leaning on your pleasant neck I shall kiss your mouth and eyes. . .' Well! He couldn't go on. Poems about chaps leaning on each other's pleasant necks and kissing each other's mouths and eyes! He didn't want to be reminded of what he would have liked to do to the fair-haired boy, of Lampo, who had recommended Catullus, suaving him full on the os after the end of term concert. It outraged him that this sort of thing could happen during lessons. Was there to be no escape from the Sins of the World and from his own Sins?

At last Latin was over, and it was time for Geography. He entered, said 'Good morning' to Mr Burrell, and took up his seat. He put on the black mask. He had no idea what sort of reaction it received, because there was a design fault. He had forgotten to make holes for the eyes. No matter. All the better, in fact. It was now a symbol of solidarity with the blind as well as the black, with the handicapped as well as the victims of prejudice.

So this was what blindness was like. This was what beautiful Mrs Quell saw morning, noon and night, seven days a week, fifty-two weeks a year, ten years a decade.

Or was it? Henry could see darkness. Could Mrs Quell see darkness, if she was blind, or was there just nothingness, and what was that like?

They were dealing with the savannas. Norbert Cuffley, that inveterate goody-goody, had just become even more the apple of Mr Burrell's one eye by remembering that the word for trees that were biologically suited to withstand dry conditions was xerophytic (oh Norbert, much good may it do you in your career with the Gas Board).

The headmaster entered. Confusion! Luckily he had to stand with his back to the four boys in the blind spot, in order to turn towards Mr Burrell, and he had to go round almost to the front of Mr Burrell in order to be seen by Mr Burrell. There was hurried activity. Dakins took off his jacket and put it on the right way round. Smedley whipped his feet off the desk and pocketed the unlit cigarette. Martin removed his false ears, but forgot his moustache. Disturbed by the noise, Mr E. F. Crowther swung round. He didn't even notice Martin's false moustache. He was transfixed by the sight of Henry in his crude, home-made black

250

mask, with its uneven, grinning teeth. Martin remembered his moustache, coughed, covered his face with his hand and pulled the moustache off. Henry heard strange noises, but, oblivious behind his mask, he had no idea the headmaster was even in the room, let alone facing him grimly, until he heard, close by, the words, 'What do you think you are doing?'

Henry made no reply.

'I am speaking to you, boy,' said the headmaster.

Henry froze behind his mask.

'Me, sir?' he said.

'You, sir,' said the headmaster.

'Sorry, sir, what was the question?' said Henry.

'What do you think you are doing?' said Mr E. F. Crowther.

'Learning Geography, sir,' said Henry.

'Take that imbecilic thing off,' said Mr E. F Crowther.

Henry removed the mask.

The headmaster gazed at Henry's pale, religious face.

'It's Oscar Wilde,' he said. 'Any new goodies for me?'

'Excuse me, headmaster,' said Mr Burrell, who had been forced to turn his head to see what was happening, and could hardly admit that he hadn't known that Henry was wearing a mask.

'What is it, Mr Burrell?' said the headmaster impatiently.

'It was my idea that Pratt should wear the mask, headmaster,' said Mr Burrell.

'To what end, Mr Burrell?' said the headmaster.

'To an imaginative end, headmaster,' said Mr Burrell. 'We were considering the interior of Africa, headmaster, and I thought, headmaster, that Pratt might play the part of an African tribesman to. . .er. . .bring home to him, headmaster, what it's like to live in the interior of Africa, headmaster.'

'You don't need to address me as headmaster five times a sentence, Mr Burrell.'

'Sorry, headmaster.'

'Come on, then Pratt. I'll stay and watch this,' said Mr E. F. Crowther.

Henry put the mask back on and thanked God that Cousin Hilda had given him *Biggles Scours the Jungle*. Truly, everything, however apparently trivial, had its place in the Scheme of Things.

'My goodness, what a swamp,' said Henry. 'What a place full of jungle and rotting vegetation and big trees that blot out the sun, and poisonous snakes and deadly spiders, and muddy streams where logs are crocodiles. What a foul stench emanates from the stagnant waters. It's hard to believe that people actually live here, Algy.'

'Algy?' said the headmaster.

'Algae, green, slimy, cling to the rotting trunks of dead trees. I wish I could escape, but I do not have big metal bird like white man, sir.'

'Carry on, Mr Burrell,' said Mr E. F. Crowther. 'We'll have a chat about your educational theories later.'

'A pleasure, headmaster,' said Mr Burrell.

The headmaster left the room.

'You can take it off now. He's gone,' said Mr Burrell.

Henry took his mask off.

'I wonder what he came in for,' said Mr Burrell.

After that, Mr Burrell tacitly acknowledged that he had only one eye, and nobody needed to feel obliged to take advantage. They were free to concentrate on working for their 'O' levels.

Henry was convinced it was the work of God.

It was the proudest day of his life, and the happiest day of Cousin Hilda's life, when the Archbishop of York laid hands on him. He was at peace.

Why then did he find it difficult to concentrate on his 'O' levels? He could manage straightforward questions like, 'Give an account of the development of Parliament in the reigns of Henry III and Edward I' or 'Write an essay on the geographical aspects of the major contrasts in the world's grasslands and their more intensive future cultivation' or 'Simplify $(p+1)^3 - 3(p+1)^2 + 2$' or even 'Define the latent heat of vaporization of a liquid. Describe how you would determine the latent heat of vaporization of water.' He could translate into Latin, 'If we had started yesterday, we should not have been hindered so much by the contrary wind.' And 'Do you think Martial or Catullus is the more successful writer of light verse? Give reasons and examples,' was a gift. But it only needed the slightest connection with his own life to send him off at a tangent. When he tried to translate into French a passage beginning, 'When we lived in the country, we often went to the farm to buy cheese and eggs,' he found himself fighting against memories of collecting eggs with Billy, the half-wit. 'Write an answer to a person who asks, "Why waste your time reading poetry?" ' sent him straight into Mr Mallender's classroom at Brasenose, desperately copying out Keats' 'Endymion' and being called Oiky by everybody.

'Please, God, help me concentrate,' he begged.

A section of an ordnance survey map came with the Geography exam. It showed the Clyde estuary from Port Glasgow and Cardross to Clydebank, with Dunbarton and the Kilpatrick Hills, and 'Renfr' right on the edge. At the top of the map was the bottom of Loch Lomond. It would be nice to take Mabel Billington to Loch Lomond. There'd be steamers, and the skirl of the pipes. . .and get on with it! Your future depends on this.

When he addressed himself to the problem, 'A car of mass 2 tons, which is travelling due south at 45 mph, collides with a lorry of mass 8 tons, which is travelling in a direction 30° south of west at 20 mph. If the car and the lorry lock, find their speed and direction of motion immediately after the collision,' he found himself worrying about the drivers, especially the driver of the car, who had met this mad lorry driver, who wasn't following the road, but making sure that he travelled 30° south of west. A retired sea dog, with a compass in his cab, he followed his course across road, moor and peat bog, demolishing crofts and disturbing the grouse. Stop it, you fool. Answer the question.

What sober, mature, religious, well-adjusted, socially responsible, healthily ambitious student, when asked, 'What do you know of the following: a) Black Friars and Grey Friars; b) Anti-papal laws passed during the reign of Edward III; c) The reforms in the church advocated by Wyclif; d) The persecution of the Lollards?' had to fight hard to resist the temptation of replying, in his vital 'O' level examinations. 'Not a lot'?

11 Oh Mammon

One day in early September, 1951, Henry sat on top of a hill in the Peak District. He was alone with his maker and Mabel Billington. He was thinking more about Mabel Billington than about his maker. He was trying to think more about his maker than about Mabel Billington. The more that he tried to think more about his maker than about Mabel Billington, the more he found himself thinking more about Mabel Billington than about his maker.

In the eleven weeks since he had taken his 'O' levels, he had been to church thirty-three times, making eleven visits to holy communion, eleven to mattins and eleven to evensong. He had attended the church youth club eleven times. He had played twenty-seven games of table-tennis. He had lost twenty-six games of table-tennis. He had learnt that he had got nine 'O' levels. He had been to tea with the Quells three times, consuming four and three-quarter rounds of bread and butter, five slices of Battenburg cake, and one piece each of cream sponge cake, coffee cream cake and Madeira cake. He had written one letter to Paul Hargreaves. He had received two letters from Paul Hargreaves. He had had eight wet dreams.

A few details will help to flesh out these statistics.

'O' levels: his nine passes were in Latin, Maths, Advanced Maths, English Literature, English Language, Geography, History, French and Physics.

Table-tennis: his solitary victory had been over Derek Nodule, who was twelve, and had cried, saying, 'Even Henry beats me.'

Battenburg cake: twice it had been stale. Twice Mrs Quell had correctly guessed the colour of the squares. Once she had failed. Ironically, the time when she had failed had also been the time when the cake had not been stale, turning the eating of Battenburg cake that day into a pretty exceptional experience all round

His one letter to Paul Hargreaves: this had been more of an

epistle than a letter, being a detailed description of his discovery of God, of the difference it had made to his life, of the difference a similar discovery could make to the lives of Paul and Diana, and of how he could help Paul and Diana to make that discovery.

Paul Hargreaves's two letters to him: the first letter, which preceded Henry's letter, was an invitation to come to France with them for a fortnight, and to visit the Festival of Britain in Battersea Park. The second letter, which followed Henry's letter, was a withdrawal of that invitation, due to changed circumstances.

Wet dreams: These had occurred on June 22nd, July 11th, July 25th, August 8th, August 17th, August 25th, August 31st and September 4th. They caused Henry deep distress, especially as they were getting more frequent. A simple calculation (to one who has passed Advanced Maths, even if by only one mark, though he never knew that) using graphs, led him to the conclusion that at this rate he would be having a hundred and sixty-three wet dreams an hour by Christmas. If he lived that long. Wet dreams were unfair. They weren't his fault. He couldn't help them. But they made him feel profoundly ashamed, and all the more determined to atone. On six of the eight occasions he had remembered whom he had been dreaming about. They were, in chronological order, Diana Hargreaves, Patricia Roc, Mrs Hargreaves, Len Hutton, Mrs Hargreaves again and Mabel Billington. It was shortly after the dream about Mabel Billington that, on an impulse which he had almost immediately regretted, he had invited her out for a day in the Peaks.

She had turned up wearing hiking boots, orange socks, hiking shorts, a bright yellow oilskin jacket and a large rucksack, which contained a bottle of Tizer, two Double Gloucester doorstep sandwiches, two apples, a first aid kit and a Bible.

The bus from Sheffield had passed the end of Wharfedale Road. There were new people in Cap Ferrat now, and Henry felt ashamed of his nostalgia for its comforts.

They had walked for what seemed to Henry to be about twenty miles, but was actually nearer five and a half. Then they had collapsed onto the grass. Below them was a splendid view of valleys and hills. A river wound through a curving dale, a miniature green canyon. A tiny train came out of a tunnel and its smoke gave Henry a vague feeling of *déjà vu*, which he dismissed as an illusion, although it was thoroughly justified, for this was the very spot where he had sat with his father, when he was three, on the day when he had believed that his father was going to abandon him.

Earlier on this day he had felt like abandoning Mabel Billington. She had looked ridiculous in her gear, especially as her sturdy legs went a blotchy red when she walked. He had been unable to think of a single thing to say to her. When she had commented on the silence, he had come out with the old chestnut about true friends not needing to talk.

Now he was pleasantly warm, his weariness alleviated by the rest, his hunger assuaged by a Double Gloucester sandwich of massive proportions, his thirst half-slaked by warm Tizer. The slumbering giant in his trousers was stirring lazily with desire for Mabel Billington. Religion and sex were not mutually exclusive. Mr Quell had said so.

She looked at her best with her boots and yellow oilskins off. Even when she was lying on her back, her breasts bulged in her white shirt.

He rolled over and examined her. Her face was sturdy. It had character. It had grit. It was the face of a girl who was capable of taking God to Africa.

'Mabel?' he said, propping himself up on one elbow. 'Let's take God to Africa together.'

She smiled.

'All right,' she said. 'We'll travel up the rivers by boat.'

'We'll come to a village,' he said. 'The natives have blowpipes, but they're friendly.'

'They've never heard of Christianity,' she said.

'The women have bare breasts,' he said.

'We'll soon put a stop to that,' she said.

'They're sacrificing a goat,' he said. 'It's their fertility rites.'

'We'll save them from all their primitive rituals,' she said.

Henry's excitement was growing. He wanted Mabel Billington. Nothing else mattered, except that he should lose his virginity with Mabel Billington. He had no idea how she would react. She was religious. But then, so was he.

He decided to test the ground.

'Then, after a hard day's saving, we'll go back to our own hut,' he said. 'We'll go to bed early.'

'Definitely,' said Mabel Billington. 'I need my eight hours.'

'We'll go to bed at ten and get up at seven,' he said.

He watched a plane making a vapour trail as Mabel, who had not taken Advanced Maths, worked it out.

'That's nine hours,' she said.

'We need an hour before we go to sleep,' he said.

'What for?' she said.

'You know,' he said.

'Oh,' she said. 'Reading the Bible.'

'In that case, we'll have to go to bed at nine,' he said.

He leant over and began to kiss her knees. He moved his lips up, over her fleshy thighs.

She brought her rucksack down with a tremendous crash on his head.

'Why did you do that?' he said.

'What were tha doing?' she said.

'I fancy you.'

'I thought tha were religious.'

'I am religious. I'm also a man. God wants me as I am, not some wax image of how I think I ought to be. Religious people have sex, you know.'

'I never will,' she said. 'I'm saving my body for God. It's a sin, any road, if tha's not married.'

'God is forgiving. Redemption and Atonement are beautiful.'

'That's not supposed to be an excuse for sinning all over the place. I think all that stuff's awful, any road. I were nearly sick during sex education.'

'But God created all that. He wouldn't have created it if He meant you to be nearly sick during sex education.'

'He didn't mean it for having fun,' she said. 'It's for having babies. If He'd meant it for fun He'd have designed it all a lot better than what He did.'

'We'd better be going,' he said.

'I can't imagine anybody wanting to do things like that for fun,' said Mabel Billington.

When she stood up, in her hiking boots, orange socks and yellow oilskin jacket, with her knobbly knees and sturdy, blotchy legs, nor could he.

Mr Quell was in Ireland. Henry would find it difficult to speak of such things to the vicar of St James's, and he certainly couldn't mention them to Cousin Hilda. All he could do was pray.

That night, after a quiet supper with Cousin Hilda and Liam (Tony Preece performing at Togwell Miners' Social, Neville Chamberlain in Munich. 'Well, so many people have joked to me about it. I thought I'd see what it was like.'), he knelt down, in his ascetic bed-sitting room, with its view of the blank wall of number 67. He knelt in front of the settee, his head resting on its cushions, and prayed.

'Oh God,' he said. 'I wish I could convert myself into a good person as easily as I can convert this settee into a bed. I lusted after Mabel Billington today. I used you to try and persuade her to let me do things with her. I know that you have given me my sexuality in order that I may learn to control myself and put spiritual values above bodily ones. Help me to be strong, and concentrate on my studies, and be kind to Cousin Hilda, and redeem myself for the dreadful wrongs that I have committed. Help me to think about other people more than about myself, and to be thoughtful and kind and generous. Amen.'

He converted the settee into a bed. The room seemed suddenly to shrink. He thought of Lampo Davey, imagined Lampo looking down on him as he got ready for bed. How Lampo would laugh at him. And how proud he would be to be laughed at. How fervently, how utterly, he rejected the false idols of the sophisticated.

Before he went to sleep, he applied the principle of thinking more about other people than about himself. He wrote a letter to Uncle Teddy and Auntie Doris.

It was six days since he had received Auntie Doris's letter. He should have replied sooner.

Dear dear Henry [Auntie Doris had written],
It's far too long since we wrote. We are awful!!! Life in Rangoon

is colourful, but smelly. We love our little flat, overlooking the waterfront, but we are often homesick for our lovely Yorkshire. We miss the dusk. You don't get a proper dusk out east. As you can imagine, the price of whisky is another 'bone of contention'. We also miss the lawns. Uncle Teddy says you can't get a decent lawn south of Dover. It's something to do with the weather or the soil or something. As for the bars, well. . .your Uncle Teddy always said there wasn't a decent pub south of Newark. There is an English bar, complete with steak and kidney pud, but Uncle Teddy refuses to behave like a typical ex-pat! So he won't go out, and I like company. Next week I'm dragging him out to see the Rangoon Amateur Dramatic Association (Rada) doing *Major Barbara*. It's a British company, of course. Teddy hates it. He says the bar prices are ridiculous. I wish they'd do my lovely Noël Coward. I don't like Shaw. Still, you can't have everything, as they say! (Who's 'they', I wonder?) Oh yes. Guess who we ran into last week. Geoffrey Porringer, of all people. He's out here on business, sends his love. He always had a soft spot for you. Our business is so-so, no more. But I'm not writing to tell all this gossip. I'm writing to say we are sorry for not being good parents to you. Henry, my dear dear boy, we are a selfish old couple, but we *love* you. We hardly ever took you anywhere and never properly on holiday at all. If we were wicked, now we are paying with remorse. Truly. Anyway, you are better off with Cousin Hilda who is A SAINT. When I think what we sometimes said of her. So you be good to her and remember money and material things don't matter, it's love that makes the world go round, as they say.

Your mother was the good one, Henry. I'm the rotten one. But we love you.

Don't do anything we wouldn't do.

That leaves you quite a lot!!!!

Work hard.

With lots and lots of love,

Auntie Doris and Uncle Teddy.

XXXXXXXXXXXXXXXXXXXXXXXXXXXXXXXXX

P.S. I hope you don't think all those kisses are babyish. You must be so grown-up now.

Dear Auntie Doris and Uncle Teddy [wrote Henry],
Thank you for yours of July 19th. It took simply ages to get here. The stamp was nice, though I don't collect them now.

I really was very pleased to get a letter from you, but sorry to read how much you rebuke yourselves. There is really no need. You took me in, and I'm grateful.

Well, I got nine 'O' Levels, and now I'm going to take my 'A' levels. I think I'll do them in English, Latin and History. Some people can't understand why I do Latin, because it's a dead language. They don't realise that that's why I do it. I've only just realised myself. I think education is wasted on the young. The penny has only just dropped for me. The purpose of education is not to teach us facts but to help us to learn to use the faculties which God gave us. If I did French, it might help me get a job in France or something. Learning Latin is pure education, and that's why I like it. In fact I'd like to do Greek as well, but you can't at Thurmarsh Grammar.

No doubt you were amazed to see the word 'God' in that last paragraph. Yes, I have found God, and He has brought so much more into my life that I can recommend Him to you without reservations. I am going to devote my whole life to His service in some form or other. This is a wicked world, as I'm sure you've realised. God's love means that I look on you with gratitude for what you did do, rather than with blame for what you didn't do. I don't feel I need to forgive you, but if you feel it, then I do forgive you.

I cannot let this letter pass without touching on the subject of Strong Drink. You may feel that I am too young to have a right to say this, but because I love you both I must say it. Your letter is full of references to the subject. Reading between the lines, it seems to me that you are both 'knocking it back'. I beg you to give it up. Believe me, you will find yourselves happier without it. Why not make October a dry month? I shall pray to God to give you the strength to do it.

Does all this make me sound like a terrible goody-goody like Norbert Cuffley (a terrible goody-goody at our school!)? Well,

I'm not really. In fact I'm a Miserable Sinner. Today I wanted to Sin with Mabel Billington (from our youth club!). She wouldn't let me. I'm glad now. Sex is permitted with marriage, of course, but until then one must exercise control.

Cousin Hilda looks after me very well, and it's extremely pleasant here, all things considered. Her food is quite nice (though not as nice as yours) and so are her businessmen.

I was interested to hear about Geoffrey Porringer. Don't tell him this, but I prayed for a cure for the blackheads on his nose. Well, it must be awful to have blackheads like that.

On reflection, I think the three of us have a lot in common, to judge from your letter. I think we all feel that we have Sinned and are full of Remorse. Perhaps this is the Human Condition, and I hope that in the future we can all learn to help each other better than we did in the past.

It made me want to cry when you said you loved me, and I love you just as much. I certainly didn't think all the Xs were babyish. In fact, I think it's pretty babyish to find things babyish.

With lots of love. May God be with you,

Henry.

XXXXXXXXXXXXXXXXXXXXXXXXXXXXXXXX

P.S. That's exactly the same number as you gave me! Thirty-one! Now here's one extra each from my heart. XX.

When Henry woke up the next morning, he was once again applying some of the principles by which he now hoped to live his life. He was thinking of somebody else more than about himself, and he was being thoughtful and kind and generous to that person. Unfortunately, that person was Mrs Hargreaves, and the result was another wet dream.

He took regular cold baths. He went for long walks. He took up running. He mortified the flesh. He managed to think himself out of sexuality.

On one of his walks, he wandered in the vicinity of Drobwell Main Colliery. It might have been a model of an Alpine landscape created by a lunatic. The mountains were spoil heaps, some new and black, some old and grassy. The lakes were ground that had subsided and flooded. The water was heavily contaminated. Nature fought against almost impossible odds to re-establish itself. He came upon a deep pit, filled with rusty railings. They had been ripped out eleven years ago, for the war effort, and had ended up here.

There was a fence around the edge of the colliery. He saw a small group of miners, walking wearily. They didn't see him. One of them looked like Chalky White, but it was difficult to tell, as all their faces were black.

His life in the sixth form began. He apologised to Martin Hammond for his unfriendly behaviour during the previous school year. Martin beamed shyly.

'None of it's your fault,' said Martin. 'You're a bit of flotsam swirling on the flood-waters of a class-ridden society. That's what my dad reckons, any road.'

The following week, Martin invited Henry home for tea. The Hammonds didn't live in Paradise Lane any more. They had bought a semi in the streets over the river, quite close to the little row of shops were Tommy Marsden had fired his catapult at the butcher's window. The address was 17 Everest Crescent. An elderly Standard Eight stood in the open garage at the side of the pebble-dash semi. It was the day before the general election. They had fish-cakes. Reg Hammond ate quickly. He had two whole streets still to canvass, and then he had to ferry people to a meeting.

'There's nowt like a good fish-cake,' said Reg Hammond.

'And this is nowt like a good fish-cake,' said his son Martin. Everybody laughed. It was a family joke.

'They're grand, mother. Highly palatable,' said Reg Hammond, who was rising in the union.

'Very nice indeed,' said Henry.

With the fish-cakes, there were chips, Reg Hammond's favourite brand of baked beans, bread and butter and tea.

'You can keep your fancy foods,' said Reg Hammond. He made it sound as if he was talking about Henry's fancy foods.

'I don't like fish-cakes,' said Martin's young sister, who was eight.

'There's folk in India'd be glad of them,' said Mrs Hammond.

'Send them to India, then,' said Martin's young sister.

'Am I to give her summat else?' said Mrs Hammond.

'No. She mun learn,' said Reg Hammond, a fleshier owl than Martin, and with a touch of the hawk in there too. 'So, lad, tha's backed t' wrong horse,' he added, turning to Henry.

'Pardon?'

' "Pardon," he says. What's wrong wi' Yorkshire? What's wrong wi' "tha what?"?'

'Tha what, then?'

'Tha's backed t' wrong horse. God. Tha's gone up a blind alley there.'

'Reg!' said Mrs Hammond.

'What's the right horse, then?' said Henry.

Reg Hammond stared at him in amazement.

'Socialism,' he said. 'Socialism.'

'Are the two mutually exclusive, then?' said Henry.

'He's got you there!' said Mrs Hammond.

'Mother!' said Reg Hammond, as if to say, 'This is man's talk.'

Martin looked from his father to Henry, refereeing their talk. In the blue corner, God. In the red corner, socialism.

His sister began to cry.

'Ignore her,' said Reg Hammond. 'We've got to learn her. In t' war she'd have given thanks.'

'The war's been over six years, Reg,' said Mrs Hammond.

'Some wars are never over, mother,' said Reg Hammond. He turned to Henry, brushing off everything else as irrelevant. 'God promises a better world in the next world,' he said. 'Socialism promises it in this one.'

'Who's to say we can't have a better world in this world *and* the next one?' said Henry. 'There's no contest.'

'Careful, Henry. Don't deny him his fight,' said Martin.

'The church is all part of the ruling classes,' said Reg Hammond.

'Jesus Christ wasn't exactly a ruling class figure,' said Mrs Hammond.

Reg Hammond looked at her with a pained expression. She was ruining a straight fight by coming in on Henry's side.

'Martin's on my side, I know,' said Reg Hammond, openly making it a foursome.

'I'm afraid so,' said Martin.

'Why afraid?' said Reg Hammond.

'You never say anything I can disagree with,' said Martin. 'It's not healthy. It's stunting my development.'

Martin's sister cried on.

'The Tories are going to get in tomorrow,' said Reg Hammond. 'Does tha know summat? I don't trust them an inch. I wouldn't put it past them to have lost t' 1945 election deliberately because they knew whoever got in then stood no chance. 1950, let 'em back with a tiny majority. Get them to start tearing themselves apart, the ever-present curse of the left.'

'Just listen to his babblement,' said Mrs Hammond lovingly.

'Now the Tories'll nip in and reap t' benefit of all t' hard work we've done,' said Reg Hammond. 'They'll be in for years. Their hard times are over. Their brief decade of nightmare without servants. Now we've entered the decade of the consumer durable, but not too durable. Mechanical servants, made by the same class that used to be the servants. Everything appears to change. Nowt does.'

'The rubbish he comes out with,' said Mrs Hammond proudly.

'I hope it is rubbish,' said Reg Hammond. 'I just hope it is.'

He sighed deeply and sank into his chair.

'Are you really depressed, Mr Hammond?' said Henry.

'Aye, lad, I am,' said Reg Hammond. 'I hoped that 1945 meant that the middle class were losing their fear of Labour, and Labour would no longer be forced to be the sort of party they had any reason to fear. I hoped we could all go forward together. I really did.'

Martin's younger sister stopped crying, and ate a tiny corner of fish-cake. There was silence for about five seconds. Then it was shattered by a motor-bike spluttering into violent life in Matterhorn Drive.

'I said summat about it to that Crowther at t' grammar school,' said Reg Hammond. 'I don't think he knew what I were on about. Pillock.'

'Dad!' said Mrs Hammond. 'You shouldn't talk like that about their headmaster, not in front of them.'

'That's summat that *is* changing, mother,' said Reg Hammond, springing to his feet. 'From now on, authority is going to have to earn its respect. Pillocks of the world, watch out.'

'Criticise him, fair enough,' said Mrs Hammond. 'But there's no cause to call him a pillock. What will Henry and his God think?'

'God will forgive Mr Hammond,' said Henry. 'God will give him his tha what.'

'Tha what?' said Reg Hammond, turning at the door, half into his coat.

'Pardon,' said Henry. 'God will give you his pardon.'

Henry grinned.

Reg Hammond gave him an old-fashioned look, then laughed.

'By heck, Martin. Tha can't put much over on your Henry Pratt,' he said.

'He was brought up in a hard school,' said Martin.

'Several hard schools,' said Henry, but Reg Hammond had gone.

Reg Hammond was right about the election. Labour got the highest vote ever recorded by a political party in Britain, but lost by twenty-six seats.

Henry went to tea at the Hammonds every week after that. One day, as the last of the dusk was lingering, Martin accompanied him down the suburban roads, over the railway and the River Rundle, across the waste ground, over the canal, along the towpath, through the gate into the ginnel, along the ginnel as far as Paradise Lane, along Paradise Lane and across the main road to the tram stop outside Crapp, Hawser and Kettlewell's. They walked in silence, awed by their memories.

A youth was approaching, jaundiced by the street lights, a snappy dresser, a flashy young man. He carried a football under his arm.

'By heck,' he said. 'It can't be. It bloody is, though. Martin Hammond. Henry Pratt.'

'Tommy Marsden!' said Martin.

'Bloody stroll on,' said Tommy Marsden. 'Hey, are we to go for one in t' Navigation?'

'We're under age,' said Martin.

'To hell wi' that,' said Tommy Marsden. 'Barry Jenkinson's me mate. I often go up there, sup a bit of stuff.'

'Not me,' said Henry. 'Not a pub. Sorry.'

'He's religious,' said Martin.

'Oh heck. Bad luck,' said Tommy Marsden sympathetically. 'Why does tha think I've gorra football?'

'Why have you got a football?' said Martin.

'I've been took on by t' United.'

They looked at him in awe. They were boys. This was a man.

'Come on, Henry,' said Martin. 'Under the circumstances.'

'Well, all right,' said Henry. 'Under the circumstances. I won't drink, though.'

The smell of stale smoke, stale beer and furniture polish almost knocked Henry over.

He liked it. He fought against liking it, but he couldn't help it.

Cecil E. Jenkinson greeted them heartily.

'Evening, gents,' he said. 'All over eighteen, are we? Good. I have to ask. Heard about the flasher? Decided not to retire. Going to stick it out another year. He's upstairs, Tommy.'

'Line 'em up, Cecil,' said Tommy Marsden, going to the door marked 'private'.

'What's it to be, lads?' said Cecil E. Jenkinson, licensed to sell beers, wines and spirits. 'Pints all round?'

'Orange squash for me,' said Henry.

'Orange squash?' said Cecil E. Jenkinson.

'He's religious,' said Martin.

'He's norra Catholic, any road,' said Cecil E. Jenkinson, licensed to tell dirty jokes and use foul language. 'They're all piss-artists.'

'Have a beer,' said Tommy Marsden, returning. 'To celebrate. Under the circumstances.'

'Well, all right,' said Henry. 'Just a small one. Under the circumstances.'

Cecil E. Jenkinson poured three and a half pints of bitter. Barry Jenkinson joined them. Tommy Marsden paid. They raised their glasses.

'To Tommy,' said Henry. 'I really am thrilled, Tommy.'

Tommy Marsden pretended not to care, but you could see he was pleased.

'Henry Pratt,' said Cecil E. Jenkinson. 'Ezra's lad.'

'That's right,' said Henry.

'He was one of my best customers,' said Cecil E. Jenkinson.

Discretion proved the better part of Henry's valour. A tart comment would have provided a discordant note at what was, after all, a celebration.

The four under-age drinkers sat in the little snug. The stuffing was peeping out from inside the faded green upholstery. At regular intervals round the little room there were bells for service. On a shelf above the fireplace there were two sets of dominoes, two packs of cards and four pegboards. The window was of fine Victorian smoked glass. The fire was lit. If this was the Hell of Strong Drink, Henry found it surprisingly cosy.

He felt ashamed, but also exhilarated, as he sipped his beer. His conscience was eased by the fact that it tasted terrible.

'I may not play in t' first team for quite a while,' said Tommy Marsden. 'Mr Linacre says he's grooming me carefully for stardom. He says not to be disappointed if I don't make progress straight away. He says many a lad's been ruined by being brought on too fast, and I think he's right. He says I'm to remain level-headed whatever.'

'What position do you play?' said Martin.

'I'm an inside forward in the Raich Carter mould,' said Tommy Marsden.

Martin Hammond insisted on buying a round, and must have forgotten that Henry was only drinking halves. There was no point in saying anything. He needn't drink it all.

'Is this the same beer?' he asked.

'Yes. Why?'

'It tastes nicer.'

They chatted about old times, in the Paradise Lane Gang.

'We used to race dog turds in t' Rundle,' said Tommy Marsden to Barry Jenkinson.

Henry apologised silently to his maker for Tommy Marsden's language.

'I don't remember that,' said Martin.

'It's the only thing before the war I do remember,' said Tommy Marsden.

'What happened to Ian Lowson?' said Martin.

'He's in t' steelworks, like his dad. I don't see much of him.'

'What about Chalky White?' said Henry.

'He's gone down t' pits, where they're all black,' said Tommy Marsden.

'I thought I saw him,' said Henry.

'It's the pressure to conform,' said Martin Hammond.

'Don't say things like that,' said Tommy Marsden. 'Barry can't understand them. He's thick.'

'I am,' said Barry Jenkinson. 'I'm as thick as pig shit.'

Henry apologised silently to his maker for Barry Jenkinson's language.

'What happened to Billy Erpingham?' said Martin.

'God knows,' said Tommy Marsden, and Henry agreed silently that he did. 'I did hear summat, but I forget.'

A few other customers entered. Barry Jenkinson, not as mean as he was thick, rang a bell, and a waiter in a white coat came out with a tray, and Barry Jenkinson said, 'Same again, Gordon,' and Henry hadn't the energy to protest, and besides, the beer wasn't having any effect on him, so where was the harm?

'Is this the same beer?' he asked.

'Yes. Why?'

'It tastes nicer.'

Soon, Tommy Marsden said he must be off. 'Mr Linacre says self-indulgence has nipped many a promising career in t' bud, and he's right,' he added.

'I haven't bought a drink yet,' said Henry. 'Must buy a drink for Tommy.'

He borrowed three and eight off Tommy, and bought a round.

'I'm right glad you lot are pleased,' said Tommy. 'I thought tha might be too snotty-nosed.'

'Snotty-nosed? Are we buggery?' said Henry, and he forgot to apologise to God.

Their laughter grew boisterous. Cecil E. Jenkinson, licensed to be a crashing bore and have a son who was as thick as pig shit, approached them, and informed them that they had had enough.

268

'Banning me like you did me old dad, are you?' said Henry.

'Listen, young lad,' said Cecil E. Jenkinson, licensed to refuse to serve people for no reason whatever. 'Listen. I liked your dad. Don't get me wrong. One of t' finest human beings as ever supped a pint. There was only one thing wrong wi' him. He used to give the customers the screaming abdads.'

'You bloody bastard,' said Henry.

'Get your drunken friend out of here,' said Cecil E. Jenkinson. 'That's the last time I allow under-age drinking in here.'

He was right, too.

As Henry walked through the little gardens in front of the Town Hall, on his way home from the tram, the enormity of what he had done struck him and he burst into tears, and knelt to pray to God.

'And what do you think you're doing?' said the policeman.

Henry stood up, somewhat unsteadily.

'Praying,' he said.

'Oh aye? And I'm the Archbishop of Canterbury,' said the policeman.

'No, I *was* praying,' said Henry. 'I was praying for forgiveness.'

'Why? What have you done?'

'Tonight,' said Henry, desperately trying to focus. 'Tonight I have got drunk and used foul language.'

'How old are you?' said the policeman.

'Sixteen.'

'Where have you been drinking?'

This was his big chance to avenge his father for the wrongs that had been done to him by Cecil E. Jenkinson.

'The Navigation Inn,' he said.

It was several days before Cousin Hilda could forgive him for arriving home drunk.

Cecil E. Jenkinson never forgave him.

Henry wasn't sure whether God forgave him. He prayed for forgiveness, but received no reply.

He was beginning to have doubts about whether God existed.

He went through all the arguments over and over again. Cosmological. Teleological. Ontological. There must be a God because there is no other explanation of why the world began, or indeed of how it began. But what is the explanation of why there is a God and how there is a God and how God began? There are so many signs of order and purpose in Nature that it is inconceivable that there is not an over-all creative Mind controlling it. There are so many signs of disorder and chaos in Nature that it is inconceivable that there is an over-all creative Mind controlling it. There must be a God, otherwise how would we be able to have the idea of God? Well, there must be nuclear bombs because how else would we be able to have the idea of them? By inventing them. Have we not invented God? Does that make God any less God? Supposing every single person in the world believed in God? It would prove nothing. It's conceivable that everybody could suffer from the same delusion at the same time. Everything that is said is conceivable. Everything that is conceivable is said, many times. In the end either you plump for a God out of need or temperamental inclination, and that is grotesque, or God is Revealed to you.

In the end, every time, the question was, as he knew all along that it would be, did God speak to him in the fog in Paradise Lane? Of course it was possible that He did and of course it was possible that He didn't. He had been feverish. He could have had hallucinations. After all, he also heard his father. Of course it was possible that he had really heard God and imagined he'd heard his father. Or vice versa. Unlikely, but possible. He had also seen the fog swirl-pooling into the faces of the ogglers and tackies at Dalton, and that had definitely been an illusion (well, almost definitely), but then he had been impressed that God had not found it necessary to pull some physical trick. He had spoken, and that was enough.

Why had God said so little? Because He had said, 'I am with you, my son.' What else could He possibly add?

Why had God not spoken to him again? Because he did not exist, or because He did not make it so easy for you that you had no need of Faith? Christians were very clever at turning even the absence of proof and even the absence of the revelation of God into positive arguments for his existence. Was this speciousness, or the truth?

Three times he went to pubs and drank beer. He smoked five cigarettes. He resumed his self-abuse. Each time he did one of these things, he looked for a sign from God, perhaps even a thunderbolt. He wasn't sure whether he hoped for a sign, or feared it. Perhaps, if one came, he would know whether he was glad or sorry that it had come. But none came.

He told Mr Quell of these things, after Mrs Quell had left the room, on the occasion of his next visit for tea, a meal whose star attractions had been Battenburg cake and ginger cake.

'I don't think I'm cut out for the service of God,' he said. 'I've got all my work cut out trying to keep on believing in Him.'

'He gives us doubts,' said Mr Quell, 'so that we can test our Faith.'

'I doubt whether the doubts I'm getting are sent by Him,' said Henry.

'That doubt is part of the doubt that He has sent you,' said Mr Quell.

Henry's belief in God, which had come upon him so suddenly, dripped away like a leaking tap. He passed through a stage in which he believed that there was a God, but that he was incapable of believing in Him. He became convinced that the entire universe was part of God's grand design, except him. One day, during Religious Instruction, as it happened, he saw everything around him as divine, except himself. He sat in God's divine desk, dipping God's divine pen in His Holy Inkwell, and he was a stranger in the midst of all this revelation. A feeling of revulsion for himself shook him violently, and yet when he looked at his hands they weren't shaking.

Mr Seaton, the Scripture master, rebuked him for not concentrating. 'What's the point of my trying to drum some spiritual feeling into you if you're just going to sit there like a pudding?' he said.

The tap dripped on, and he came to see this stage as a form of temporary madness.

'You don't have to believe in everything in Christianity literally,' said Mr Quell. 'You don't have to take God absolutely literally.'

'You have to believe that He exists,' said Henry. 'You have to believe that He can be described.'

'I can't describe Him,' said Mr Quell. 'I can't say that He's an old man with a white beard. I certainly don't believe that He's an Englishman. Or even an Irishman, though that is slightly more likely.'

'You don't have to be able to describe Him,' said Henry. 'You can't, because you haven't seen Him. But you have to believe that He exists, somewhere, in some actual form, which we could describe if we ever saw it. Otherwise God is just a concept which we call a being, and that would be a con.'

A trolley-bus slid sibilantly to a halt outside. ('*Outside*! Amazing. I thought it would be *in the room*' – Droopy L.)

'I would disagree that God has to be physically describable,' said Mr Quell, 'but I would agree that we have to believe that His existence has a reality independent of ourselves. He clearly must be more than a symbol that we have created to satisfy our urge for Him. Wasn't that a particularly odious Battenburg cake that we tucked into this afternoon?'

'Appalling,' said Henry. 'If there was a God, He wouldn't allow us to eat such appalling cake.'

How long can a tap drip? Until the end of time, or a strike by water workers, whichever is the sooner, if it's attached to the mains. Until the container is empty, if it's attached to a container of finite capacity.

Henry's tap ceased to drip on the morning of March 13th, 1952. That it was his seventeenth birthday was of no account. It was the day they buried Chalky White.

Eight men were buried alive when there was a collapse at the face of the old seam at Drobwell Main Colliery. In three weeks' time that seam was to have been abandoned.

The rescuers fought their way through for twenty-seven hours. They could hear the weakening cries of the trapped men, but had to go slowly, excruciatingly, unbearably slowly, for fear of causing further collapse.

Four of the men were dead when the rescuers reached them. Chalky White died in hospital. Three men survived.

It was a joint funeral, and the little church was packed. All the miners had scrubbed their faces. Only the faces of Chalky White's relatives and friends remained black.

All the Paradise Lane Gang were there, except Billy Erpingham. Nobody could remember his address.

The vicar praised the courage of the rescue services, and of the great body of miners, who knew the risks of their jobs, and lived, and occasionally died, with those risks. There was quite a bit of coughing during the vicar's address, and Henry was transported back to the chapel at Dalton, Tubman-Edwards opposite him, Mr Tenderfoot striding out to witness the great storm. Then he returned to the present, bitterly ashamed of having been away.

The coughing at Dalton College had been the result of boredom. The coughing at Drobwell was the product of pneumoconiosis.

They filed out into the churchyard. A pale sun came out, just as the five coffins were lowered into the ground.

In the end it was nothing to do with arguments. It was simply that, as he stood there, beside Ian Lowson, who was a stranger, Henry knew that he believed that he knew that that was the end of Chalky White, that he was not going to a good place, or a bad place, but was going to rot in Drobwell churchyard.

Sales of Battenburg cake in south Yorkshire continued to boom.

'I still believe that it's better to be generous than mean, to be kind rather than cruel, to be tolerant rather than intolerant, to strive to bring order to society rather than chaos, to seek peace not war, and to try to have faith in man's capacity to overcome the evil in his own nature,' said Henry.

Mr Quell carefully selected a piece of coal, and placed it on the neat pyramid of his fire. The precision and delicacy of his movements never ceased to seem surprising in such a big-framed man.

'You're a humanist,' he said, 'and a refreshingly modest one.'

'Are you mocking me?' said Henry.

'Not at all,' said Mr Quell. 'Humanism is the religion of the coming times. It's a religion without services, without a Bible, and for that reason it might be assumed that it has no dogma. That would be incorrect.'

Henry hadn't heard the trolley-bus draw up, but now he heard the whoosh as it set off towards town. They were to be phased out soon, but they would live on in his memory, every time he thought about the great problems of existence. Sometimes it seemed to him that it was only in the trivia of life that individuality held any sway. The arguments about God had been made banal by repetition all over the world, but in Henry's case alone was God mingled inextricably with Battenburg cake and trolley-buses.

'Its dogma is that man can control the planet,' said Mr Quell. 'Its dogma is that by means of planning, and science, and technology, man will be able to restructure and improve Mother Nature. You believe that he will have a full-time job controlling his own nature, never mind Mother Nature. That is modest. I approve of that.'

The summer term dragged by, and they waited for something to happen. Being a humanist was something that went on all the time, and it didn't fill your Sunday like organised religion did. Henry no longer went to the church youth club. The trinity of God, table tennis and Mabel Billington had all lost their hold over him. There was no humanist youth club. The pleasures of reading, cinema-going and listening to the wireless were still all right, but they weren't the real thing. Self-abuse was all right, but it wasn't the real thing. Mock 'A' levels weren't till the winter and they weren't the real thing. If you did badly, it was ominous, and, if you did well, it was wasted. Henry's cricket continued to improve. His average this term was 1.75, which compared well with Martin's 4.55 but badly with Stefan's 84.41. But his development was too slow. Even if the graph of his improvement continued, he would be too old to play for Yorkshire by the time he was good enough. In fact, he would be 128 before he even got a trial. But even cricket wasn't the real thing.

The real thing was girls. Sex. Ceasing to be a virgin.

'I'm a humanist,' said Henry one endless Sunday in the Alderman Chandler Memorial Park, where clusters of teenagers were waiting to listen to the Top Twenty on their wirelesses.

'Has it got owt to do with girls?' said Stefan Prziborski, the best left-handed batsman ever to come out of Poland.

274

'It could have,' said Henry.

'How?' said Martin.

'Well, we could found a humanist society. Joint, with the girls' school.'

'Now you're talking,' said Martin Hammond.

There were still no marble or falcated teal on the pond. The ocelot had died. Henry saw the fair-haired boy occasionally, and nodded to him.

He went to see Mr E. F. Crowther in his study.

The study still said, 'Things get done here. We are plain, practical men, concerned with achievements, not pretensions,' but Henry was old enough now to realise that this was itself a pretension.

Mr E. F. Crowther refused to agree to the formation of a joint humanist society with the Thurmarsh Grammar School for Girls.

'Why not, sir?' said Henry.

'It might set a precedent,' said Mr E. F. Crowther.

'That way you'd never change anything, sir,' said Henry.

'I've made my decision,' said Mr E. F. Crowther.

Yes, and I know why, thought Henry. Because I once said 'The bread van' in morning assembly.

Pillock.

If they didn't meet in the park, they would meet in the Paw Paw Coffee Bar and Grill, in Bargate.

The Paw Paw Coffee Bar and Grill smelt of wet coats and steam when it rained and sweat and steam when it didn't. It never smelt of coffee, which wasn't surprising, since its coffee didn't taste of coffee. Its tea, on the other hand, tasted vaguely of coffee. There were glass-topped tables, and the tea and coffee came in glass cups, with glass saucers. Due to a design fault, the handles of the cups grew almost too hot to hold. It was self-service for coffee but waitress service for grills. They were never able to afford the delights of the grill. Few people ever did. Perhaps the sight of the very fat chef, standing in the kitchen, all stained white apron and tangled hairy armpits, put people off. If you asked the waitresses for sugar, they said, 'On the tables, luv,' without looking at you. When you got to the table, the sugar wasn't there, just the brown and tomato sauce bottles, with congealed sauce around their tops. The Paw Paw Coffee Bar and Grill was the only place in Thurmarsh where you could linger for hours over one cup of coffee, and chat up girls, and cheek the waitresses, and laugh sheepishly, and watch your youth waste away.

The Paw Paw Coffee Bar and Grill throbbed to the distant possibility of picking up a girl one day, and by the time you realised that you hadn't, it was too late.

When they made remarks to the waitresses, there would be blushing and giggling and the occasional shriek of good-natured outrage. Once, Stefan Prziborski pinched Rita's bum and she dropped a tray of dirty cups with an almighty clatter. But you couldn't be cross with Stefan. He was different. He had foreign blood.

Once Henry plucked up courage and asked the girl who worked at Macfisheries out. She told him to come back when he was three years older.

His virginity was written on his face. He was Henry 'Ee by gum, I've never had it' Pratt. Martin and Stefan had quite wide experience, in fact Henry was surprised that two such experienced Don Juans should still spend so much time hanging around the Paw Paw Coffee Bar and Grill.

The windows of the Paw Paw Coffee Bar and Grill were always steamed up.

That was how it was, so far as social excitement and gracious living were concerned, in the summer term of 1952.

Letters were exchanged. Auntie Doris wrote to him from Rangoon. She purported to be glad that he had found God. She made no reference to Strong Drink. They had been to see *Hay Fever*, performed by the Rangoon Amateur Dramatic Association. There was a dreadful shortage of English women in Rangoon, but Geoffrey Porringer had made a very brave stab at the role of Judith Bliss.

Henry sent a chatty letter back, explaining that he had lost God, and hoped they hadn't taken his strictures about strong drink to heart.

He wrote to Paul Hargreaves explaining that he was no longer religious, and wanted to found a joint humanist society with the girls' school, but couldn't, because the headmaster was a pillock.

He wrote to Simon Eckington, giving him all his news, including the finding and losing of God, and suggesting that he visit Rowth Bridge in the summer.

Simon Eckington replied briefly that he would be very welcome. He was working for the new people at Low Farm. They were all right. Billy, the half-wit, was dead.

Paul Hargreaves replied that all headmasters were pillocks, and invited Henry to come to Brittany with them for three weeks that summer. Diana sent her love.

This news gave Henry an erection at the breakfast table. As ill luck would have it, Cousin Hilda chose that moment to ask him to fetch more marge. She had been hard on him since he'd lost God. He was all right going to the scullery, but on his way back he felt that the obstinate bulge was obvious to all. It certainly was to Tony Preece, who winked and asked him who the letter was from. When he replied, 'My friend Paul,' Tony Preece raised his eyebrows. Cousin Hilda sniffed. Norman Pettifer, the manager of the cheese counter at Cullens, said, 'Oh well, time for all good men to come to the aid of the party,' and left. He said that every morning. He was only staying there till he found a house. He didn't fit in. Everybody missed Neville Chamberlain now that his firm had sent him to Kenya. Henry's erection died down slowly.

Henry wrote to Paul accepting the invitation. He wrote to Simon saying that he wouldn't be able to come.

He no longer needed to spend long, painful hours in the Paw Paw Coffee Bar and Grill. He loved Diana. She loved him. He wouldn't remain a virgin for long.

On the first Saturday of the summer holidays, in reverse chronological order, Henry met a girl on a bus, posed as a Frenchman, saw an idol, and had a very unexpected encounter. The names of the four people concerned were Maureen Abberley, Henri Bergerac, Len Hutton and Geoffrey Porringer.

The encounter with Geoffrey Porringer occurred at the top end of The Moor, in Sheffield. Henry was looking at the shops with Martin Hammond and Stefan Prziborski, prior to watching

Yorkshire play Middlesex at Bramall Lane. He carried a shoulder bag full of bloater paste sandwiches and apples. They had bought three bars of Fry's Chocolate Cream. They were wearing sandals and grey flannel trousers. And suddenly he was face to face with Geoffrey Porringer, in a lightweight fawn suit. He wasn't surprised, since he now believed prayer to be ineffective, to see that the poor man's nose was still festooned with blackheads.

'Hello!' he said.

Geoffrey Porringer looked at him blankly.

'Henry Pratt,' said Henry.

Recognition dawned slowly, and apparently not to Geoffrey Porringer's utter delight.

'Can I have a word with you?' said Henry.

'Of course,' said Geoffrey Porringer, a trifle uneasily.

'*Allez vous, mes braves,*' said Henry to Martin and Stefan. '*Je vous verrai à la petite rue de Bramall.*'

It was their latest little game, talking in French. It was all good practice for Henry.

'*Bon,*' said Martin.

'*J'espère que vous ne vous perdrerez pas, notre Henri,*' said Stefan.

'*Fermez l'orifice de votre gateau,*' said Henry. 'See you at the usual place.'

Geoffrey Porringer listened to all this with a mixture of incomprehension, irritation, impatience and distaste.

'Look, I am rather busy,' he said.

'Sorry,' said Henry.

Martin and Stefan set off for the ground.

'What is it?' said Geoffrey Porringer.

'Are you going back to Rangoon soon?' said Henry.

Geoffrey Porringer stared at him in amazement.

'Rangoon?' he said. 'Rangoon?' Then comprehension seemed to dawn. 'Ah! Rangoon!' he said. 'Rangoon! Yes. Probably. Well, almost certainly. Doris told you she'd seen me, did she?'

'Yes.'

'That was naughty. My presence there is supposed to be top secret.'

Geoffrey Porringer put his finger to the side of his blackheaded nose.

A lorry with a crane pulled up at a faulty street lamp.

'My business activities in Rangoon are just a cover,' said Geoffrey Porringer. 'Say no more, eh?'

Henry's mind went back to Cap Ferrat, and the secret message about Bingley. He couldn't recall it exactly now, but it had always puzzled him. Now it was all becoming clear. Geoffrey Porringer was a spy.

'Your secret's safe with me,' he said.

'Good man,' said Geoffrey Porringer.

'Will you do something for me?' said Henry.

'It depends what it is,' said Geoffrey Porringer cautiously.

'Will you take a present for Uncle Teddy and Auntie Doris?'

'If it's not bulky,' agreed Geoffrey Porringer, 'and if it doesn't take too long.'

They chose the present together. It was a set of six coasters with scenes of Yorkshire life – to wit, Robin Hood's Bay, Bolton Abbey, Richmond Market Place, the Shambles in York, Gordale Scar and the front at Scarborough.

'It'll bring a lump of nostalgia to their throats every time they have a drink,' opined the spy in the lightweight suit.

There was crowd of 17,000 at Bramall Lane, noisy, knowledgeable, hard to please. It was a strange ground, set between the cricket pavilion and the three-sided football ground. It made up in character what it lacked in charm.

Henry was in the mood to enjoy a game of cricket, but Martin and Stefan were feeling frivolous.

Middlesex batted and were in trouble from the start. On Henry's left there was a fat boy, who recorded every ball in his score-book. There always was.

Denis Compton was in a spell of terrible form, and the crowd gave him a tremendous, deeply moving ovation. Henry, who alone had been for Hutton in the summer of 1947, could afford to be generous now, and felt a lump in his throat as he clapped. He hoped Martin and Stefan wouldn't speak, and luckily they didn't.

Compton drove his first ball for four, but was lbw to Yardley without addition. Hutton took two fine catches off Eric Burgin, playing his first game in front of his home crowd. There were two attractive girls sitting behind them, and in the lunch interval

Stefan told them that Henry was a leading man in French cricket.

'Give over,' said the fairly pretty one.

'*Mais c'est vrai*,' said Henry. '*Je suis le président de l'association du cricket du Dijon. Je suis aussi enthousiaste comme la moutarde. J'aime très bien l'ouest equitation de Yorkshire.*'

'Give over,' said the very pretty one.

Yorkshire let Middlesex off the hook, dropping Leslie Compton three times in his innings of 91. Knightley-Smith made 57. Henry kept on having to pretend to be French.

'What position do you play?' said Martin, speaking slowly and loudly, as to a foreigner.

'*Troisième homme ou stupide mid-on*,' said Henry.

'Give over,' said both girls.

Henry felt that his day was being spoilt by all this pantomime. When Yorkshire batted, he was nervous until Hutton was off the mark. Hutton was dropped by Denis Compton (if only all the boys from Brasenose had been there) and was 21 not out at the close, with Lowson (no relation of the peripheral Sid) 15 not out. The fat boy sadly closed his score-book, and the three Thurmarsh boys wandered out of the ground with the two girls. Henry knew that Stefan would put his arm round the very pretty girl, Martin would put his arm round the fairly pretty girl, and Henry, who had done all the hard work of pretending to be French, as a result of which the girls thought him a total idiot, would put his arm round nobody. And so it was.

He told himself that he didn't care. Why should he? Next week he would be with Diana.

He cared. This was this week, not next week. He told them that he was going home, and their protests carried the authentic ring of true insincerity.

He sat in the off-side front seat upstairs on the Thurmarsh bus. On the near-side front seat sat a curvaceous brunette schoolgirl. Their driver did not seem terribly popular. Other drivers greeted him only curtly.

'Haven't I seen you in the Paw Paw Coffee Bar and Grill?' said Henry.

'I have been there,' admitted the curvaceous brunette.

He moved over to sit beside her. His heart was thumping.

'I'm Henry Pratt,' he said.

'I'm Maureen Abberley,' she said.

'I'm at Thurmarsh Grammar School for Boys,' he said.

'I'm at Thurmarsh Grammar School for Girls,' she said.

'We certainly go to the right schools,' he said.

'You what?' she said.

'If I went to the girls' school, it'd be ridiculous,' he said.

'I wouldn't mind going to the boys' school,' she said. 'I like boys, me.'

His willie perked up at this. Its owner decided that it was time to impress this curvaceous liker of boys with his worldliness.

'The driver isn't very popular,' he said.

'You what?' she said.

'The driver isn't very popular. The other drivers are waving, but only very curtly.'

'You what?' she said.

'I look at the other drivers,' he said. 'If our driver's popular, they all smile. They aren't smiling at our driver. They're giving the minimum acknowledgement they can without being downright rude.'

Your successful seducer is the man who recognises swiftly when he is on a loser. Henry changed the subject now.

'I'm a humanist,' he said.

'Oh aye?' said Maureen Abberley.

Curvaceous, sexy, but thick. Oh well, you couldn't have everything.

'Do you know what a humanist is?' he said.

'It's a person who doesn't believe in God, but believes in man's powers of reason to create an ordered and purposeful system of ethics,' said Maureen Abberley. 'That's the way I look at it, any road.'

Curvaceous, sexy and a genius.

He put his hand in hers. She didn't remove it. In fact, one nail gently stroked the back of his hand.

He put his left hand on her right thigh. It was solid and yielding at the same time. She didn't remove his hand. He couldn't believe it.

Suddenly masterful, pitying Stefan and Martin, he debated

281

whether to go first for the short-term or the long-term. It was a straightforward choice between, 'Would you like to be the girls' school representative on the Thurmarsh Grammar School Bisexual Humanist Society's Joint Steering Committee?' and 'Do you fancy a coffee at the Paw Paw Coffee Bar and Grill?'

Before he could decide which to choose, she suddenly stood up and said, 'I gerroff here.'

He was too surprised to say anything.

'Oh well,' he thought. 'It's probably all for the best anyway. I ought to be saving myself for Diana.'

The train arrived at St Pancras thirty-eight minutes late. Henry's heart raced as he walked towards the ticket barrier.

There was Paul, waving. No Diana.

'Super to see you,' said Paul.

He had forgotten how public school Paul was.

He tried to be casual, and it wasn't until they'd been in the taxi (taxi!) for several minutes that he said, so casually that its importance must have been crystal-clear, 'How's Diana?'

'Super,' said Paul, looking out of the window. 'Absolutely super. She's gone to spend three weeks with that Tooth-Braceingham horror in Rowth Bridge. She sends her love.'

The weather in Brittany was fine, the scenery pleasant if unspectacular, the villages drab, the small towns picturesque, and Henry tried hard to react in any way except dumb misery.

The first time they went swimming, he got an erection when he saw Mrs Hargreaves's long, elegant, ageless legs. He had to flop down into the sand, to hide it.

'Are you all right?' she said.

'Fine,' he said, craning his neck round so that he could see her while still hiding his erection.

She bent over him, concerned. Her breasts grew more pointed as she did so. He gritted his teeth and looked away, just managing to avoid an orgasm in the sand.

'Absolutely fine,' he said. 'I'll be along.'

She went away at last, and a few minutes later he deemed it safe to go into the water. He was sure they all thought he was mad.

He was very silly over the French food, refusing to eat anything except steak and chips. The Hargreaves ate oysters, langoustines, crabs, soles, crêpes de fruits de mer and gigot d'agneau avec haricots, and he ate steak and chips. He felt oiky again, and demonstrably a virgin. He felt that all these sophisticated French people could see that he was an oiky virgin, and he made it worse by behaving like one and by hating himself for it. He told himself that he was being loyal to his class, but it seemed a fairly pointless manifestation of loyalty even to him. It occurred to him that he was belittling himself in Mrs Hargreaves's eyes, in order to ensure that no sexual chemistry existed between them. Then he realised how ridiculous and shamingly ill-adjusted that thought was. Mrs Hargreaves noticed him as a sexual object even less than her daughter. Nobody noticed him as a sexual object. He longed to get out of this hole he had dug for himself over the food, and on the sixth day he simply ignored it and ordered langoustines, without comment, and after that he tried everything, and enjoyed most of it. He resented the fact that Dr Hargreaves was so rich, and he felt that he ought to refuse to eat all the food, in solidarity with his friends at home, but that would have made Dr Hargreaves even richer, so he ate extravagantly, and Dr Hargreaves was extremely generous about it, and this made him feel guilty.

Henry sat on a seat in the park, watching the ducks. Stefan was late. He wasn't surprised.

It was Sunday afternoon, when the dead hand of boredom clutches the throat. But Henry had vowed not to be bored at all during his last year at school. He was disgusted with his behaviour during the summer of ennui.

It was the last day of the holidays. There was an autumnal chill in the mornings, bringing him a desire for a new sense of purpose.

His purpose was to find an equilibrium between his mind and his genitalia, to rediscover the sense of purpose of his religious phase and ally it to a healthy sexual and emotional development. If he passed his 'A' levels as well, that would be a bonus, but exams could not be taken seriously, they were not a valid test of a man's worth.

If there was one point where Henry's mind and his genitalia

might meet, it was the Thurmarsh Grammar School Bisexual Humanist Society. Only two things had so far prevented the development of that society. It had no headquarters and no members.

He had already taken steps to remedy the second deficiency. He had acted with a decisiveness that had astonished him. He had looked in the telephone directory to find Abberleys living in the vicinity of the stop where Maureen had got off the bus. He'd been lucky. She was on the phone. She was in. He had taken her to the pictures in Sheffield, and kissed her in the back row, long wet kisses during a long wet film. She had promised to put a notice on the board at school, seeking a list of girls who might be interested in joining the humanist society. She had agreed to come out to Derbyshire with him the following Sunday, if it was fine.

Stefan wasn't coming, blast him. A wigeon quacked complacently, stupidly. He fought against his feelings of hostility towards it. Youth beheaded wigeon because friend didn't turn up. 'This callous crime,' says JP.

He shook his head, to get rid of the sudden headline, which had come from nowhere, and to get rid of even the possibility of doing such a thing.

'Sorry I'm late,' said Stefan. 'I bring good tidings. Who's a clever boy, then?'

'What have you done?'

'I've just seen Dickie Billet.'

'What about?'

'Guess.'

Dickie Billet was the captain of Thurmarsh Cricket Team. Stefan, perhaps the best cover point fielder ever to come out of the Baltic, had played four games for Thurmarsh that summer, and scored 72 not out in one of them.

'He's not getting you a trial for Yorkshire?'

'No chance.'

Dickie Billet had said, 'It's a pity you haven't got a residential qualification for Yorkshire. They'd never play a Pole. Born in Durham, they might stretch a point. Danzig, no chance.'

'What then?'

'Guess.'

'Oh come on.'

Stefan grinned.

'We can use the cricket pavilion for the meetings of the humanist society,' he said. 'Provided there's no alcohol or funny business.'

'There won't be,' said Henry. 'It's a serious project.'

'I suppose so,' said Stefan sadly.

They wandered up and down the park, rushed over to the swings and took turns on them manically, then flopped exhausted onto the tired, thin, browned, late-summer grass.

'Can you give me some advice about girls, Stefan?' said Henry. He needed Stefan's advice so badly that he felt it necessary to make an enormous admission. He swallowed. 'I'm still a virgin,' he said.

'You get too worked up,' said Stefan. 'You've got to play it cool. Make them chase you. That's the secret of my success.'

'Where do you get precautions from?' said Henry.

'There's a herbalist's in Merrick Street has them.'

'What do you say?'

'You just ask for a packet of three.'

'A packet of three what?'

'Just a packet of three. You know what they are, don't you?'

'Course I do.'

'Who are you taking out?'

'Nobody. It's just idle curiosity. Intellectual speculation. Thirst for knowledge. Like the humanist society.'

'Oh aye?'

'Oh aye. I'm serious about the humanist society, our Stefan. Any manking about, out.'

They wandered past the animal cages, three of which were empty. A family with two small children was examining them forlornly.

'There's nowt in this one either, dad,' said the small boy.

Henry felt that he must entertain Stefan, to show his gratitude for the advice and the arrangement over the pavilion, and also to win back a bit of respect.

'Excuse me,' he said to the forlorn family. 'There's four sloths in there.'

285

'Oh aye?' said the man. 'Where are they?'

'Asleep,' said Henry. 'They're very slothful, sloths.'

'Aye, well, I suppose they would be,' said the man.

'They sleep twenty-three and a half hours a day. They won't be up now while six in the morning.'

'Oh. Thank you very much,' said the woman.

The children stared at him.

'There's four chameleons in that one,' said Henry, pointing at the next cage.

'We couldn't see owt,' said the man.

'Well you wouldn't,' said Henry. 'They're masters of disguise, are chameleons. It took us fifty-five minutes to spot all four.'

'Oh. Thank you very much,' said the woman.

When Henry and Stefan looked back, the family were peering intently into the empty cage.

By the Friday evening, Henry's appeal on the school notice board for boys interested in joining the Thurmarsh Grammar School Bisexual Humanist Society had seventy-eight names. Some could be discounted, like Len Hutton, King Farouk, Freddie Mills, John Mills, John Stuart Mills, Ron Nietzsche, Busby Berkeley, Bobby Locke, Bertrand Russell, Jane Russell, Des Cartes, Sid Cartes, Plato, Pluto, Donald Duck, Karl Marx, Groucho Marx, Lorenzo Marx, Leibnitz and Landauer, Harry Stottle and all five Einsteins. When the silly ones had been eliminated, there were nine possible members.

Henry pocketed his list, and set off for Merrick Street, a little street of small shops that ran north from the back of the town hall. It was alive with shops for minority interests, but was already showing signs of social decay, and would soon be redeveloped.

The Merrick Herbalist's was situated between a religious bookshop and a model railway shop.

Henry looked in the window of the religious bookshop and felt ashamed of his lost innocence. Then he looked in the window of the model railway shop and felt even more ashamed of his lost innocence. Then he took a deep breath, walked up to the herbalist's, felt ashamed of the fact that he hadn't lost his innocence, and walked away up the street. At the end of the street he stopped, irresolute, walked half-way back to the herbalist's, then away again. Finally, when he was an object of interest to the whole street, he dived into the herbalist's, heart pounding. It was dark inside. He could hardly see the man.

'A packet of three, please,' he said in a squeaky voice.

To his dismay the man said, 'A packet of three what?' Then he added, 'Only joking,' and handed Henry his purchase. 'Good luck, lad,' he said.

On Sunday he took Maureen Abberley to a spot near the hill where he had lusted briefly after Mabel Billington. It was quite private there, but she said that she couldn't possibly make love to him in the open air. She caught colds easily, and besides, somebody would see. He supposed that he had been mad and naive to think that she would. He *was* mad and naive where sex was concerned.

An equilibrium between his mind and his genitalia.

It was definitely the mind's turn next.

As the first meeting of the Thurmarsh Grammar School Bisexual Humanist Society drew nearer, Henry began to panic. He was its founder. He ought to deliver an inaugural address on humanism. But what was it? The more he tried to study it, the less he knew what it was. Every time he tried to think hard about it, he ended up by having fantasies about going the whole way with Maureen Abberley. They went the whole way in the home dressing room, the visitors' dressing room, behind the scoreboard, even inside the heavy roller. He woke up one morning naked inside the heavy roller with Maureen Abberley, as it rolled the pitch for a test match between England and Australia. The two captains, Len Hutton and Lindsay Hassett, also naked, were tossing up. Len Hutton winked at him. Whatever the dream meant, it didn't help him to resolve the mysteries of humanism.

Cold baths. Early morning runs. Mind over matter. Perhaps as a result of the cold baths, or the early morning runs, he developed a streaming cold. All the girls would think him sickly.

The cricket ground was situated behind the football ground. Its southern boundary abutted onto the north terrace of the Blonk Lane stadium. The pavilion faced west, and from the road you had to trudge right across the sodden ground. The square was roped off to protect the wicket. The light was fading in the cloud-streaked west, but he could still just see that the scoreboard was set for the winter at 987 for 2 – last man 606. He let himself into the pavilion and flooded it with light. There was a wooden trestle table, at which the players sat for tea, as well as a few folding canvas chairs, which people took outside to watch the cricket on warm days. As Henry set up the chairs, he came upon a grimy, dust-covered jockstrap lying on the wooden floor. He hurled it into the dying nettles at the back of the pavilion. From this unpromising acorn, could any great tree of thought ever grow?

Famous philosopher mourned. Founder of 'Thurmarsh Movement' Lost at sea. 'This tragic day' – Bertrand Russell.

Nobody would come, except Martin and Stefan, who had promised. No girls would come. Perhaps that would be all for the best. His philosophical researches had revealed that there were no female philosphers, no Mrs Kants, no Daphne Spinozas or Gladys Wittgensteins.

Maureen Abberley arrived, with Betty Bridger, long-nosed and pale, Karen Porter, little, green-eyed and squashy, Beverley Minster, tall and buxom, and Denise Booth, sullen and pasty-faced. They brought three thermos flasks of coffee.

Good for them. Even if they didn't contribute much to the ebb and flow of the philosophical debate, they had proved their usefulness.

By half-past seven, five boys had arrived. Martin, Denis Hilton, small, serious and bespectacled, Bobby Cartwright, large, red-haired, freckled and gawky, Alan Turner, tall, languid, good-looking, with a sense of great intellectual power held in reserve, and Michael Normanton, who was a martyr to acne.

They sat, the eleven of them, a mixed cricket team, at the trestle table, boys on one side, girls on the other, Henry, their founder, at the end.

Henry's opening speech, which had caused him such worry, could have been criticised on the grounds that it did not grasp the nettle firmly in both hands. It might have been more impressive had it not been delivered in such a nasal, sniffy way. But the most churlish listener could not have accused him of tedious long-windedness.

'Welcome to the Thurmarsh Grammar School Bisexual Humanist Society,' he said. 'The first question we must discuss is "What is Humanism?"'

There was no applause. He hadn't expected any.

For an awful moment, he thought that nobody was going to speak.

'Humanism was founded in Italy by Petrarch and Boccaccio and people like that,' said Denise Booth.

Good for her, thought Henry. At least one of the girls had something to say for herself.

'They went back to classical literature, Plato and Aristotle and that, to find out how they could get better ideals and that so they could yank themselves out of the Middle Ages,' said Denise Booth.

'That's not how I understand humanism at all,' said Karen Porter.

Good for her. If two of the girls had thoughts on the subject, it looked as if they were in for a lively time.

It was when the third person to speak was also a girl that Henry began to get uneasy.

'Nor me,' said Beverley Minster. 'It means being kind, and nice to animals and things, and having charities, and visiting old people and things.'

When the fourth person to speak was also a girl, Henry began to get really worried.

'Why should you visit things?' said Betty Bridger.

'I don't mean visit things,' said Beverley Minster. 'I mean visit old people and people like that and things.'

'What do you mean "people like that"?' said Betty Bridger. 'What people like old people are there except other old people?'

'That's what I mean,' said Beverley Minster. 'We'll visit other old people as well.'

'My God. If we can't even define our terms,' said Betty Bridger.

'What do you understand by humanism, Beverley?' said Karen Porter.

'Being kind. Helping people. Bandaging sick animals and things,' said Beverley Minster. 'Running charities and things.'

'You're talking about being humane,' said Karen Porter. 'You're talking about humanitarianism.'

'That's what I thought it was,' said Beverley Minster.

'We're wasting time,' said Betty Bridger.

'Do you call bandaging sick animals and looking after old people and things a waste of time?' said Beverley Minster.

'We're here to discuss the philosophy of humanism,' said Betty Bridger.

'That's a great help to a sick animal,' said Beverley Minster.

'Look, if you want to bandage sick animals, you bandage sick animals,' said Betty Bridger. 'And visit things. There must be lots of lonely old umbrellas and hair-brushes would be glad of a visit. And we'll discuss philosophy.'

'I don't see how you can say that philosophy is more important than bandaging sick animals,' said Beverley Minster.

'I know how I say it,' said Betty Bridger. 'I presume you mean, "How can I justify saying it?" Well, that's a different question. Do we want to discuss that? On what grounds do we decide that one thing is more important than another?'

'Clearly there have always been philosophers and there have always been people who have visited old people and bandaged sick animals,' said Karen Porter. 'History records the achievements of philosophers far more than the achievements of bandagers of sick animals because history is written by intellectuals and not by sick animals, and philosophy is more important to intellectuals, while bandaging sick animals is more important to sick animals.'

'The two terms are not necessarily mutually exclusive,' said Betty Bridger. 'I mean, there may have been philosophers who visited old ladies.'

'And bandaged sick animals,' said Karen Porter.

'We've got to use language with precision, Beverley,' said Betty Bridger.

'I know what you mean,' said Beverley Minster. 'I should have said "bandage injured animals". You treat sick animals. You bandage injured animals.'

'Fine,' said Henry. 'I think we'd all agree this is a very helpful discussion. Atschoo. Sorry. But I founded this society with Maureen. . .' he smiled at Maureen, and she smiled back,

'. . .and it's a humanist society, not a society for doing humanitarian acts. I think you'd be happier, Beverley, if you left us and founded a society of your own for visiting old people and bandaging injured animals.'

'I think you're all horrid,' said Beverley Minster, and she left the pavilion in tears.

Henry longed for one of the boys to speak. He felt ashamed for them. And he longed for Maureen Abberley, whom he loved, to speak. He felt ashamed for her.

'Now there are quite a few people we haven't heard from,' he said. 'Somebody else, please.'

'Can I just say what I understand by humanism?' said Karen Porter. 'It's a dictionary definition. It's a philosophy that rejects supernaturalism, regards man as a natural object and asserts the essential dignity and worth of man and his capacity to achieve self-realisation through the use of reason and the scientific method.'

Alan Turner leant forward, and it was clear that he was preparing to speak. At last, a boy was going to contribute, and there was something impressive, calm, mature about Alan Turner. Everybody, even Betty Bridger, hung on his words.

'I agree with that,' he said.

'I don't,' said Denise Booth. 'Humanists didn't not believe in God. There were humanist popes.'

'How do you know?' said Betty Bridger.

'I've read it,' said Denise Booth.

'How do you know it's true? said Betty Bridger.

'How do you know anything's true?' said Denis Hilton, taking off his glasses and staring at them and leaping suddenly into brave, blushing, earnest life. 'How do you know anything? How do you know you exist? Maybe you're all a figment of my imagination.'

Rain began to drum on the roof. Karen Porter said that she knew that she often felt that she was a wraith-like figure, and that was probably the explanation. She was a figment of somebody else's imagination. Betty Bridger said that Karen Porter might well be right, but Denis Hilton was wrong, since, if anybody was a figment of anybody's imagination, they were all figments of hers. Henry said that if anybody was going to be a figment of anybody's imagination, as founder and secretary it was only right that they should be a figment of his imagination. He proposed that they should draft a set of club rules, which would include a clause to the effect that the society be deemed to exist, all members be deemed to exist, and a charge of threepence per head for coffee be deemed to exist. Betty Bridger suggested that at each meeting somebody should read a paper, as a basis for discussion. She suggested that, as she had suggested the idea, she should deliver the first paper, on the subject 'What is Humanism?' Just as they were about to start their coffee, Stefan arrived. Martin, Bobby Cartwright, Michael Normanton and Maureen Abberley didn't speak all evening. After the meeting, Henry suggested that Maureen Abberley and he stay behind to wash up and clear up and generally leave the pavilion as they would wish to find it. It was only fair that they should undertake this tiresome chore as they were the founders of the society in their respective schools.

When they had washed up and cleared up, Henry put his arms round Maureen's soft waist. But she shook herself free, and refused even to kiss him, for fear she would catch his cold.

Henry found it hard to avoid the conclusion that, taken all in all, the first meeting of the Thurmarsh Grammar School Bisexual Humanist Society had been a disappointment. No great new system of philosophy had emerged, and he remained a virgin.

Three days later, Cousin Hilda had a face like thunder. Norman Pettifer was not an unduly timid man. No man who holds down the position of manager of the cheese counter at Cullens can be unduly timid. Tony Preece was not a timid man. No man who braves the rigors both of trying to get laughs in working men's clubs and of selling insurance can be timid. Liam, though timid enough, was not a perceptive man. But at the sight of Cousin Hilda's face, all three men quailed. They dispatched their liver and bacon and tinned peaches at a speed that positively invited stomach ulcers, and fled.

'Well!' said Cousin Hilda, when only Henry was left. 'Well!'

'Well what?' said Henry.

Cousin Hilda's jaw was biting on the pain of it.

'I found a packet of. . .them things. . .in your pocket,' she said.

'I don't know how they got there,' said Henry. 'One of the boys must have put them there.'

'How do you know what I'm talking about, if you didn't know they were there?' said Cousin Hilda.

He noticed that there were now two cracked panes of blue glass in the front of the stove.

'I'm sorry,' he mumbled.

'Sorry!' she repeated bitterly. 'Sorry! I've done my best to be a mother to you. I've done my best to give you standards.'

He felt full of shame. Not shame at having had a packet of Durex. Shame at having been found with a packet of Durex. Shame at being Henry Pratt. Great philosopher! Distinguished humanist! He couldn't even avoid bringing misery on his poor surrogate parent.

Henry made no attempt to see Maureen Abberley before the next meeting of the humanist society. Let her do the pining and worrying.

He told Stefan that he was very upset with him. Stefan said that he couldn't stand societies and formal debates. They made him ill. He'd spent two hours plucking up his courage before he'd dared turn up.

He told Martin that he was very upset with him. He was his friend, and he hadn't said a word. Martin said he'd been shy. 'I thought you were going into politics,' said Henry. 'Where would the Labour Party be now, if Kier Hardie'd been shy?' 'That's different,' Martin said. 'That's my chosen field. All this humanism's just messing about.'

After school, on the day of the second meeting of the Thurmarsh Grammar School Bisexual Humanist Society, Henry went down to Merrick Street. He entered the shop hurriedly this time, head down, terrified he'd see somebody he knew.

'A refill, eh?' said the man. 'Well done, lad.'

As he set up the chairs and got the coffee mugs out of the cupboard, Henry tried to concentrate on humanism, not Maureen Abberley. Was it true what Martin said? Were they just messing about? How many people would turn up anway?

To his surprise, everybody came except two. He knew Betty Bridger would come, of course, and probably Karen Porter. He wasn't totally surprised that Denise Booth and Denis Hilton were there, and he'd expected Martin to come, out of loyalty if nothing else, but the presence of Bobby Cartwright and Michael Normanton, who hadn't contributed a word, and of Alan Turner, who had only said, 'I agree with that,' did surprise him.

The absentees were Stefan Prziborski, who was allergic to meetings and formal debates, and Maureen Abberley, who had a cold.

Betty Bridger read her paper. She said that she had changed its title from 'What is Humanism?' to 'What is "What is Humanism?"?'! They would have to examine the nature of statements, the nature of questions, the nature of definitions. But were they ready to do that? Shouldn't they first examine the nature of communication?

'I'd like to put this to you, in conclusion,' she said. 'Ought we not to consider the four questions "What is what?" "What is is?" "Is what?" and "Is is?" before we ask ourselves "What is " 'What is Humanism?"?'!

'That's ridiculous,' said Martin. 'There's a real world out there.'

'But is it real?' said Denis Hilton, kick-starting himself into stuttering excitement. 'I'm very interested in the question "what is is?" '

'Not "is is?"?' said Henry sarcastically.

'No. I believe we have to assume that is is, if we're to get anywhere,' said Denis Hilton. 'I was very interested in your father's comments on how we decide what a table is, Betty.'

Betty Bridger gave Denis Hilton an angry stare.

'Betty's father?' said Henry.

Some colour came to Betty Bridger's cheeks for the first time.

'My father's a philosopher,' she said.

'Aha! So he wrote your paper,' said Martin.

'He bloody well did not. He helped, that's all,' said Betty Bridger. 'He just suggested areas of enquiry.'

'Bloody stupid areas of enquiry,' said Martin

'Please, everybody,' said Henry.

'Not stupid at all,' said Denis Hilton. 'Unless you define your terms, you're talking in a vacuum.'

'Ah, but what is a vacuum?' said Martin.

'Your brain,' said Betty Bridger.

'Please!' said Henry. 'Please! This is not a philosophical society. It's a humanist society. If you want to form a philosophical society, do so.'

'I think I will,' said Betty Bridger, gathering up her papers.

'Good idea,' said Martin. 'Your father obviously can't help you quite so much on humanism.'

'I'm coming too,' said Denis Hilton. He turned towards Henry. 'I'm sorry,' he said, 'but that's my real interest. The wider field. I think the idea of confining it to humanism is a bit narrow for me.'

'Fair enough,' said Henry. 'Anybody else who finds the future of mankind too narrow and prefers the broader field of "What is is?" may as well go as well.'

Betty Bridger looked questioningly at Karen Porter.

'No, I'm staying,' said Karen Porter, grinning at Henry, who immediately felt glad that Maureen Abberley had a cold.

Betty Bridger and Denis Hilton departed. There were now two girls facing four boys, two of whom had not yet spoken.

'Right,' said Henry. 'So what is humanism?'

Alan Turner leant forward again, urgent, impressive, measured, as he had at the last meeting, when he had said, 'I agree with that.'

'I agree with what she said last time,' he said this time.

'Which "she"?' said Henry.

'The pretty one,' said Michael Normanton. His appearance improved briefly as the rest of his face and neck went as red as his acne.

'That's not a very nice thing to say of. . .of whichever girl you don't mean,' said Henry.

'He means me,' said Denise Booth. 'I mean I'm the one he doesn't mean. We all know that.'

'I looked up your medieval humanism stuff, Denise,' said Karen Porter. 'I must say I found it all very confusing.'

'I'm probaby on the wrong track altogether,' said Denise Booth. 'I'm probably stupid as well as ugly.'

She stormed out of the pavilion, slamming the door so hard that a photograph of the Thurmarsh Cricket Team of 1932 fell to the ground.

'Why have you come here, Michael?' said Henry. 'You haven't contributed anything.'

'I wanted to meet girls,' said Michael Normanton.

'What girl would look at you? You're covered in acne,' said Henry. 'You've got more spots than a set of dominoes. In fact we could have a good game of fives and threes on your neck.'

Michael Normanton flung himself at Henry. They rolled on the floor. Martin grabbed Michael Normanton's collar and attempted to pull him off. Alan Turner walked calmly over, yanked Michael Normanton from the pile of bodies and punched him on the nose. Bobby Cartwright made no move.

'Why did you hit me?' said Michael Normanton, sitting on the floor, holding a hankerchief to his nose.

'You attacked the chairman physically. That's anarchy,' said Martin.

'He made personal remarks about my face,' said Michael Normanton.

'You called Denise Booth ugly by implication,' said Karen Porter.

'To praise you,' shouted Michael Normanton. 'And, any road, his insults to me weren't by implication.'

'Now we're splitting hairs,' said Martin.

'Greasy unwashed hairs,' said Karen Porter.

'All right. I'm going, you sods,' said Michael Normanton.

Once more, the pavilion door slammed.

They poured out the coffee, and Henry asked Bobby Cartwright why he came.

'I like listening,' he said. 'I may not have owt to contribute, but I like listening.'

Nobody made any further references to humanism or to any further meetings. They cleared up, locked up, and went home. Henry insisted on accompanying Karen Porter to her door. She lived in Aylesbury Road, which was only two roads away from Park View Road.

'I suppose I can't come in or owt,' he said.

'Which?' she said.

296

'What?' he said.

'In or out?' she said.

'I meant in or owt like that,' he said.

'What is there like that?' she said.

'Oh, we're not onto all that again, are we?' he said. 'I meant, I don't want to say goodnight. Can I see you again, Karen?'

'There's no point,' she said, giving him a quick kiss on the cheek.

He grabbed her by her slender waist and bent to kiss her on the mouth. She averted her mouth.

'You find me repulsive,' he said.

She laughed.

'I'm sorry,' she said. 'I didn't mean to laugh. It was just the way you came out with it. No, I don't find you repulsive. I think you're probably quite attractive.'

'What do you mean "probably"?'

'I like you,' she said, 'but I've got a feller of me own. He's a friend of yours. Stefan Prziborski.'

Before he went home, he dropped the packet of three down a grating.

Twice he picked up the phone to ring Maureen Abberley. Twice he rang off before anyone answered. The third time he hung on, trying to sound cool as he asked for her.

'She's out,' said her father. 'Who am I to say rang?'

'It doesn't matter,' he said.

He regretted that afterwards. He rang again. Again her father answered. He tried not to sound like the person who had rung before. She was out again. How dare she be out all the time? 'Tell her Henry Pratt rang,' he said curtly, and rang off, before her father had any chance to sound amused.

He got a letter from her. 'I'm sorry we keep missing each other. Pick me up at four o'clock on Saturday.'

'That's right. Keep up the good work,' said the man in the herbalist's.

They went to the pictures. They kissed through most of the film. He took her home, and dropped his packet of three down a different grating.

He kept quarrelling with Stefan, because Stefan was going out with Karen Porter.

Christmas came and went. Maureen Abberley invited him to a party at the home of a friend whose parents were away. 'Nice to see you again,' said the man in the herbalist's. 'It makes you proud to be British.' He went home, intending to hide the contraceptives in his room while he had his tea. There was a telegram waiting for him. It said, 'No go stop sorry stop streaming cold stop Maureen.' He went out and dropped the contraceptives down a grating. After tea he wrote to Maureen. He told her how much he loved her and wanted her. Then he tore the letter into tiny pieces. Maureen wrote and said, 'I'm sorry about my boring old cold. I did miss you. Pick me up at four on Saturday, if my cold's better.' He couldn't because it was Tommy Marsden's debut for Thurmarsh United. He rang to explain, but she was out. At least her cold must be better. He left his message. She'd understand.

To most of the crowd who clogged up the streets surrounding the compact, unpretentious Blonk Lane stadium it was just another match, Thurmarsh v Darlington in the Third Division North. Henry wasn't sure how excited even Martin was.

Henry himself was wildly excited. Somebody he knew, who had been a fellow member of the Paradise Lane Gang, was playing league football. He regretted bitterly all the distractions which had prevented him supporting the Reds as he should have done. Boarding school, living in Sheffield, God, humanism, Maureen Abberley. A wasted youth.

The whole gang should have been there, but Chalky White was dead, Billy Erpingham had disappeared, Ian Lowson was sullen and unfriendly towards them.

The team was Isherwood; Plank, Reynolds; Ayers, Cedarwood, McNab; Bellow, Marsden, Gravel, Greenaway and Muir.

When the team came out, Tommy looked so young. The knot in Henry's stomach tightened.

The teams kicked around. The wind howled. Cedarwood, the veteran pivot, took his teeth out and put them in the goalmouth, wrapped in tissue paper.

During the first half, Tommy looked bewildered and out of his depth.

'Bring back Morley,' said the man on Henry's right. 'Tha's rubbish, Marsden.'

'Give him a chance,' said Henry. 'It's his first game.'

The man gave Henry a cold stare, then turned away.

Darlington were leading 1–0 at half time.

Teenage star transforms game in second half, thought Henry. From dog turds to Wembley for England's newest star. Knighthood for Marsden. The Tommy Marsden I knew, writes Henry Pratt.

In the sixty-ninth minute, MUIR equalised brilliantly after running onto a shrewd through-ball from Ayers.

In the seventy-third minute, Tommy had his first effort at goal. He packed a powerful shot, to judge from the way the ball thudded into the corner flag.

'Useless,' muttered the man on Henry's right. 'Tha's a great soft pudden, Marsden.'

In the seventy-ninth minute, the Darlington goalkeeper punched the ball out under pressure. It landed at Tommy's feet. Without time to be nervous, he lobbed it brilliantly into the goal. Suddenly confident, he soon split the defence to set up a third goal for GRAVEL.

'Where's tha been hiding him, Linacre, tha great twit?' shouted the man on Henry's right. 'That lad's a find,' he told anyone who cared to listen. 'He reminds me of Raich Carter. I can always spot 'em.'

Henry and Martin celebrated with two pints of Mansfield best bitter at the Forge Tavern. The headline in the *Green 'Un* read, 'Teenager Shines As Reds Shake Quakers'.

He sucked a mint before arriving back at number 66 Park View Road. The euphoria slipped gently away as he left the glory behind and drifted reluctantly back to his bed-sitter. He thought of the matches he had seen with his father, and then he thought of his mother. His eyes filled with tears, and the gale mourned for her bitterly in the telegraph wires.

Maureen wrote to say that he could get lost if she wasn't as important to him as a football match. He replied that he loved her madly, and was very sorry. He would never do it again. He replied that Tommy Marsden had been an old friend and if she resented his going to see his debut then she wasn't the sort of person he wanted to go out with. He tore both letters up. Maureen wrote to say that she was sorry. She realised that Tommy Marsden had been an old friend, and that he had to go to the match. He could pick her up at 3.30 on Saturday. This meant he'd have to miss Tommy's next home match.

They went to the pictures. Afterwards, he bought the *Green 'Un* and found that he had missed an impressive 2–0 home win over Bradford Park Avenue, with goals from MARSDEN and BELLOW. Maureen Abberley removed the paper and looked straight into his eyes.

'My parents are going to a party next Saturday,' she said. 'I'll be all alone in the house. You can come round if you like.'

'All right?' said the man in the herbalist's. 'That's the ticket. Have to discuss discount rates soon.'

Mr and Mrs Abberley had gone when Henry arrived, and the television was on.

Maureen was wearing rather a short dress, and her feet were bare. There was an electric fire and a cut-glass bowl of fruit on an occasional table. Maureen opened her mouth wide when he kissed her.

'I didn't know you had a television,' he said.

'We've just gorrit,' she said. 'Dad says there'll be a rush as the coronation gets near. Have you seen much television?'

'Hardly any,' he said.

'You can watch lots tonight,' she said.

'I don't want to watch television tonight,' he said.

'I promised my parents I'd be good,' she said. 'They trust me. I think trust between parents and children is too valuable to be trifled with, don't you?'

He had often longed to watch television. With what reluctance he spent his first evening in front of it. They watched 'Looking at Fish' with George Cansdale, an interlude on a Cotswold farm, and 'Café Continental' with l'Orchestre Pigalle, Père Auguste as Maître d'Hotel and Hélène Cordet as Mistress of Ceremonies. All the time they lay on the settee, semi-entwined, in the dark except

300

for the glow of the electric fire and the flickering white light from the television. He made a last big effort to prove so irresistible to her that she'd forget her parents. At first, as their kisses grew more passionate in time to the music of Shirley Abicair and her zither, he had a wild hope that all would be well.

Then came the close-down. Off went the set, Maureen Abberley smoothed her dress down, and said, 'You may as well go before they get back,' and a sad virgin bent to drop a packet of rubber goods down a grating, in a quiet suburban street which seemed to him to be alive with sexual satisfaction and excitement for everyone except himself.

The following Friday, Henry took Maureen to the pictures. He'd had to borrow the money, as he'd spent all his pocket money on unused rubber goods.

As they left the cinema, a boy stared at Maureen, and said, 'I thought you'd gorra cold.'

'It got better,' she said, blushing. She avoided Henry's eyes, then shot him a sudden, challenging look.

'Who did you go to that party with, when you told me you'd got a cold?' Henry said, as he walked her home.

He grabbed her arm and held it behind her back.

'You're hurting,' she said.

'Who?' he repeated, beginning to twist her arm.

'Norbert Cuffley,' she said.

'Norbert Cuffley? Norbert Cuffley?'

Girl found dead in duck pond.

Don't even think like that.

He turned and walked away, without a word. He didn't even look back, to enjoy the triumph of seeing her standing there at a loss.

Norbert Cuffley.

'Give up. You were never meant to be a lady-killer, our Henry,' he told himself.

Suddenly his 'A' levels were looming and he hadn't done enough work, and brave talk about exams not being valid tests of a man's worth were so much hot air.

Tommy Marsden played ten games and scored five goals. Henry watched him four times.

One Sunday, Tony Preece brought Stella, his new girlfriend, to dinner. She was a rather brassy blonde, with thin legs and lips. When she had left, Cousin Hilda said, 'Well!'

'She may have a heart of gold,' said Henry.

'Pigs may fly,' said Cousin Hilda.

Army medicals took place. Ears, feet and reflexes were explored, colour blindness and genitalia examined, anuses and rudimentary intelligence probed.

Henry and Martin were accepted as fit for national service. Stefan Prziborski failed. He had flat feet.

'Flat feet?' said Henry. 'He's the only one of us who can run.'

He listened to 'In All Directions', a radio comedy programme with Peter Ustinov and Peter Jones. In the first series they searched for Copthorne Avenue. In the second series they searched for more ambitious things, like Britain's heritage and true love. Henry laughed a lot, but he also felt pained. He had found his Copthorne Avenue. Would he ever find anything else?

Cousin Hilda got a television. She couldn't miss the coronation. Sometimes, Henry abandoned his studies for a while, to watch 'Animal, Vegetable and Mineral' or 'Kaleidoscope' or 'What's My Line?'.

Edmund Hillary and Sherpa Tensing climbed Everest. It was all a Tory plot. That was what Reg Hammond said, any road.

Tony Preece asked if he could bring Stella to see the coronation.

'I suppose so,' said Cousin Hilda.

They watched the coronation until their eyes hurt. The little basement room became London, City of Pageantry. 'All we need's a crate of light ale,' said Tony Preece. Stella grinned, and Cousin Hilda sniffed.

Mr McFarlane, History teacher and Marxist, suddenly copped out, and told the boys to be careful not to reveal Marxist bias in their exams.

Henry had dreaded his 'A' levels, but when they came he enjoyed them.

In the world of sporting action he could only watch the

triumphs of Tommy Marsden. Here, when told, ' "*King Lear* is not the tragedy of the downfall of a great hero: it is the story of a man who becomes great through tragic experience." Discuss,' or ' "All the intelligent characters in *Vanity Fair* are bad characters: only the stupid show kindness or honesty." Do you agree?' he came into his own.

In the world of sexual action, conventional morality did not even permit him to watch the triumphs of Stefan Prziborski. Far better to concentrate on 'Are there reasons for doubting Juvenal's sincerity?' and 'What tricks of style are characteristic of Tacitus?'

Even the world of intellectual speculation had proved a disappointment for Henry in real life. Here, in the quiet examination room, with the windows open on the buzzing of bees and the droning of traffic, he could enjoy wrestling with such matters as ' "Charles V was a Fleming rather than a Spaniard, and a Spaniard rather than a German. He was never an Italian." Discuss.'

Then it was over. He knew, with a deep inner conviction, that he had either passed or failed. He went for a final tea with the Quells. His school life drew to a close.

Britain was embarking on a new Elizabethan age, in which poverty and unemployment and snobbery would disappear for ever. As this great vessel steamed out of harbour, a little rowing boat bobbed uneasily in its wake. That boat was Henry, and as the great liner of optimism disappeared over the horizon, her wash eased, and he rocked almost imperceptibly on the slow swell of anti-climax.

12 Return to Upper Mitherdale

The sun glinted on the roof of a grey Standard Eight as it made its way between the dry-stone walls, up into the high hills.

In the car we.e four young men who had been rewarded by parents and guardians for passing their 'A' levels. Soon, three of them would be spending two years in Her Majesty's armed forces. The fourth, the golden boy, had turned out to have flat feet of clay.

Henry sighed.

'My God, why the sigh?' said Paul Hargreaves. Number 66 Park View Road and its businessmen, the Rundle Valley, Paradise Lane waiting for demolition, spittle on pavements, Fillingley Working Men's Club, it had been a world more foreign than Brittany to Paul. He had grated on Henry's nerves by looking brave the whole time. Now, for the first time, going into the country in Martin's father's car, to stay in a pub for a week, Paul looked relaxed. He wore the very scruffy old clothes of those who knew that they could afford to dress elegantly any time they chose.

'Because I'm happy,' replied Henry. 'I'm so happy I feel insecure.'

'Careful,' growled Stefan Prziborski. 'Don't mention the future.'

Stefan had been upset about his flat feet. He had been upset at getting the worst exam results of the trio. He had been upset that his inability to attend the meetings of the Humanist Society had revealed how fragile his edifice of insouciance was. He had been upset at his rejection by Karen Porter, who had suddenly left for London, because she found his pose of coolness so boring. It had caused a slump in his batting form, and he'd been dropped by Thurmarsh. The future was a hostile country.

'It's a good rule,' said Paul. 'No mention of the future, and no politics.'

'It's a stupid rule,' said Martin. 'All life is politics. That man with the bent back in that field is politics. Look at him, slaving away in his rags.'

'It's a scarecrow,' said Henry. 'Are you sure you're fit to drive?'

They were making good time. Martin drove as he lived, steadily, unspectacularly, but making better time than you expected. He was the man who surprised you by passing his driving test first time. He was the man you didn't notice until he crossed the finishing line in first place.

'I was thinking about last night as well, when I sighed,' said Henry.

Tony Preece had taken Henry and Paul to Fillingley Working Men's Club, beyond Doncaster.

Also present had been Stella, Tony's brassy blonde.

On the drive over, they had talked about comedy.

'Henry did a turn at the end-of-term concert at school. He was super,' Paul had said.

'Came on as the headmaster, did you?' Tony Preece had said.

'How on earth did you guess?'

'It's the obvious thing to do.'

'I suppose I was pretty cliché-ridden,' Henry had said.

'You were super,' Paul had said.

In the headlights the road had been like a long, narrow stage. A leaf that had died before its time had appeared stage left in front of them. A gust of warm summer wind had sent the leaf dancing across the road like a mouse on a hot-plate.

'I was at a working men's club when I decided I wanted to be a comic,' Henry had said. 'There was this Welsh comic there. He had a leek, and a pith-helmet, and one roller skate. I thought, "I could do better than that." '

'No good?' Tony Preece had said.

'Terrible.'

Tony Preece had driven into the rutted car park of a large, ugly brick building. It looked more like a giant public convenience than a palace of laughter, and Stella had expelled a deep, anxious breath at the sight of it.

'We're with t' turn,' Stella had told the doorman.

They had sat very near the stage. Paul had bought two pints of bitter and a sweet martini. Stella had called to him not to forget the cherry. He hadn't forgotten the cherry.

Henry and Stella had both gone very tense. It was worse than going on yourself.

Paul had appeared totally oblivious of the tension. He had gazed round the room with the detached eyes of a sociologist.

Before he announced Tony, the concert secretary had blown into the microphone.

'And now another comic that's making his first appearance at Fillingley,' he had said. 'Let's hope he's better than t' last one. Let's hear it for Talwyn Jones, the Celtic Droll.'

You're in trouble when you come on in a bright red suit, with a giant leek in your buttonhole, wearing a pith-helmet and one roller skate, and nobody laughs.

Stella had put a comforting hand on Henry's arm.

'Don't worry too much about it,' she'd said. 'He knows he's terrible.'

They stayed in the Crown Inn, Troutwick, since the Three Horseshoes in Rowth Bridge had no rooms.

The Crown was a low stone building in a tiny square just off the main square of the cluttered little town, where roads steered crazy courses between the damaged corners of old buildings.

Henry had not been content to let his youth end in anti-climax. He it was who had laid the plan. Now, when Simon Eckington arrived in the farm truck, the only four good friends he had ever had were assembled together for the first time, and the loose ends of a fragmented childhood were tied into a neater parcel than Henry had ever thought himself capable of making.

Simon was even bigger than he expected, tougher, slower, red-faced and weather-beaten.

'Sorry I'm late,' he said, as he placed Paul's soft hand cheerfully in his gnarled one. 'I had to cut up a pig.'

Simon was centuries old, a worker, uncomplicated, cheery, thirsty. Pints were drunk. Darts thudded into darts boards. No matter that Henry played badly. It was the others who were the performers. That night he was the impresario who had brought the bill together. A bill that, if successful, would run a week.

This was the life. A cheery bar. Hosts George and Edna were cheerfulness personified. Young men relaxing in the way they knew best. A stag evening, rich with the promise of many more to come. Henry had accepted that young ladies did not beat a path to the door of unathletic young men such as himself. Some, like Stefan Prziborski, are born to be ladies' men. But other young men collect engine numbers well into their thirties, sit at cricket grounds recording every ball in their score-books, or collect arcane objects and go away to meet other men who collect similar arcane objects. They are sensible enough to renounce sex before it renounces them. Henry had joined their ranks, and what a relief it was.

'Does tha remember a girl called Lorna Arrow?' said Simon. 'Tall, slim girl wi' a husky voice?'

'I used to read comics to her,' said Henry.

'She remembers thee all right,' said Simon.

'She had nits,' said Henry.

'She's grown into an attractive girl,' said Simon. 'She's a right belter now, is Lorna Arrow.'

'There was another one,' said Henry.

'Jane Lugg.'

'That's it. She was a tomboy.'

'She still is.'

'She had nits too. There was a third one. Evacuee.'

'Pam Yardley.'

'That's right. She was sex-mad. Kept grabbing me knackers. Couldn't stand you. She had nits too.'

'She comes back to stay wi' the Wallingtons every summer. We're engaged.'

The next day dawned warm and sunny. They drove back into Skipton, with the windows wide open to help ease their hangovers. Somebody had blacked-out the final letter of the Forthcoming Attractions outside the Odeon, changing 'Destination Gobi' into 'Destination Gob'. How childish, thought these four young men loftily.

They dropped Henry off outside the little bijou detached

residence where Auntie Kate lived with her daughter Fiona, with her husband, the assistant bank manager with the artificial leg, who was now the bank manager with the artificial leg, and with the baby they had finally had when all hope had been abandoned.

He knew that Auntie Kate would be old, and he had tried picturing her looking extremely old, so that he wouldn't be shocked when he saw how old she was. As a result, he was amazed how young she looked.

She embraced him till he could hardly breathe.

Fiona kissed him too and showed off her baby proudly. They'd waited so long. She was so excited. Henry felt awful about being a callous youth and not liking babies. The bank manager came home for dinner. The house was sparkling, the garden well-kept, the dinner palatable, the baby crawled in his play-pen, and Auntie Kate doted on him as much as Fiona did.

Fiona had forgotten reading him stories. She had forgotten that she had been a glamorous princess who had brought an aura of sexual mischief into a sick boy's bedroom. She had forgotten that she had been a naughty lady of exquisite beauty, who could have had anybody, and for two worrying years probably had.

Auntie Kate could not have forgotten that she had been a farmer's wife, taking jam to the sick, running W.I. stalls, making Low Farm a haven of good humour. But had she forgotten that she had been the sun rising in the morning? Had she forgotten that she had been the laughter that had rolled round the high fells and merged with the chuckling of the River Mither? Now she was an elderly lady, doting on her grandson.

Henry felt really mean about finding the past so much more exciting than the present.

That evening he found exciting, as Martin drove steadily up the winding, narrow road towards Rowth Bridge. Memories flooded back.

There were seven houses now, in the hamlet of Five Houses. A teenage boy leant against a wall on his bike, and turned to stare at them. Was this the boy, whose name he had forgotten, into whose clammy, frightened hand he had dug his nails?

Martin drove past the tiny school, where there were new

lavatories, past the Parish Hall, where there still wasn't a new piano, and over the hump-backed bridge. How tiny the houses were.

Martin drove through the village and up towards the head of the dale. To Henry's relief, the hills at least hadn't shrunk.

When they reached the track that led to Low Farm, they got out and stared at Henry's old home. It meant so little to the others, so much to Henry.

The cows were being led in by Simon, who waved at them. The cows were black-and-white Friesians. The shorthorns had gone. Billy, the half-wit, had gone. Uncle Frank and Auntie Kate had gone. Henry wanted to go.

Forewarned, the landlady of the Three Horseshoes gave them a ham and egg tea.

Simon arrived in the bar at ten to seven, with a demure, well-scrubbed, rather quiet, dark-haired, square-faced, nit-free girl, who would make him a grand wife, three healthy children and many excellent dinners. Could this really be Pam Yardley, that Hun of yesteryear?

'Lorna'll be here about eight,' said Simon with a grin.

Henry shook his head. If he struck a chord in her memory, it was far better that it remained there.

A burly young man entered with a noisy group, and said, 'Hello,' to Henry.

'Who's he?' whispered Henry.

'Jane Lugg,'. whispered Simon.

'That's a girl?' said Stefan.

They hissed at him to shut up. He smiled and downed a pint in one gulp.

Henry bought Jane Lugg a drink and they tried to find memories in common.

'I bet the wages here are well below what I'd call a dignified living,' said Martin.

Henry was totally unprepared for the tall, slender, toothy, husky, lisping sexuality of Lorna Arrow. She coloured as she talked to him, and her small but shapely breasts heaved.

'I were heart-broken when tha threw me over,' she said to Henry. 'I cried for months.'

'Give over,' he said. 'I wouldn't throw you over now, Lorna.'

'Why's that?' she said.

'You've become a great beauty,' he said.

'You haven't,' she said.

'I know,' he said.

'Tha's still my Henry,' she said. 'Does tha remember t' barn where tha used to read t' comics to me?'

'Course I do.'

'It's still there.'

Their legs rubbed together as they walked. The sun had long disappeared beneath the hills, and the evening light was blue. They walked round to the back of the village, and up to Kit Orris's field barn. Swallows and house-martins were gathering on the telegraph wires, and there were clouds of midges.

Inside, the barn was dark and sweet with rotting crops.

'We should have brought comics wi' us,' chuckled Lorna.

'I don't want to read tonight,' protested Henry.

'There's better things to do,' grinned Lorna.

'Oh, Lorna,' he gasped.

'Which would you prefer?' she queried. 'A fortnight's coach tour of Finland with the W.I., or me taking all my clothes off?'

She removed what few clothes she had on with all the grace with which a female gazelle would remove its clothes, if it wore any.

Henry undressed hurriedly, clumsily, and she laughed.

Her body was long, pale and exquisite in the dim light.

She put her bare feet on his, and pressed her naked body against his.

'You're hurting,' he cried urgently.

'Sorry,' she whispered softly.

'You're lovely,' he mouthed gently.

'Oh, Henry,' she lisped breathily.

'Oh, heck,' he ejaculated prematurely.

Breakfast at the Crown Inn, Troutwick, was an affair of mixed emotions, although George and Edna were hospitality personified.

Henry's emotions were of satisfaction, relief and pride. After their unfortunate start, events in the barn had proceeded much more successfully. He had lost his virginity at last. The first of two long journeys was over, and he could face the second, that of adult life itself, with more confidence than had at one time seemed possible.

Paul was disgruntled, because Stefan had been so wild, and Simon so quietly rural, and Martin so grumpily political, and Henry had deserted him.

Martin was disgruntled, because he had been driving his father's car, and he was a responsible young man, and so he had had to remain sober, and Stefan had been so wild, and Simon so quietly rural, and Paul so infuriatingly detached and complacent, and Henry had deserted him.

The waitress handed them their egg, bacon, sausage, fried bread and tomato.

'That'll put hairs on your chest,' she said.

Paul stared at her in astonishment.

'If you found out that waitress's hours and wages, you'd be shocked,' said Martin.

Paul groaned and imitated the winding up of a gramophone.

'It's all right for people like you,' said Martin angrily. 'Your father gets more in a week than these people earn in a year.'

'It's not my fault,' said Paul.

'Echoing the parrot cry of the German people,' said Martin.

'Please don't mention parrots,' said Henry.

'People like you make me sick,' said Martin, and he tipped his breakfast plate over Paul and strode from the room.

Paul sat immobile, deathly white, his dignity ruptured, as a fried egg slid slowly down his face.

The waitress returned.

'I'm afraid we've had a bit of an accident,' said Henry, and the waitress agreed.

George and Edna were tolerance personified.

Paul left, to clean himself up, and Martin returned, shame-faced.

'I'm sorry,' he said. 'He got on my nerves. You agree with me, don't you?'

'I believe brain surgeons should get less money than dustmen, because their job is more rewarding in itself,' said Henry.

'My God. You're more left-wing than I am,' said Martin.

'I don't believe you should make a fool of yourself and me by throwing breakfast over my friend,' said Henry.

He was furious with them both, for destroying his mood of complacent well-being.

'I'm sorry,' said Martin. 'I get none of the fun, that's all, because of the driving.'

'We'll stay in Troutwick tonight,' said Henry.

Paul returned, white-faced, clean-shirted.

'I'm very sorry, Paul,' said Martin.

'Oh, that's all right,' said Paul airily. 'These things happen.'

'If you're so unwise as to consort with the lower orders,' said Martin.

'I didn't say that,' said Paul. 'Do you want a breakfast over you?'

'Shut up,' screamed Henry. 'We've only got one week, and it's falling apart.'

'That's why it's falling apart,' said Paul.

Stefan appeared, comically hung-over, a parody of bloodshot vulnerability.

'What happened last night" he said.

'You bet ten bob that Jane Lugg was a boy,' said Martin.

Stefan groaned.

'She undressed on the bridge,' said Paul. 'You lost.'

'Narrowly,' said Martin. 'After a recount.'

'Give over,' said Henry. 'I like Jane Lugg.'

He could afford to be generous. Suddenly roles were reversed. He was a man, and they were behaving like children.

Stefan laughed.

'I really am terrible,' he said. 'I must get a grip on myself. No more drinking. What are we doing tonight?'

'Pub crawling in Troutwick,' said Henry.

'Fantastic,' said Stefan Prziborski.

They started their pub-crawl at the White Hart, the two-star hotel on the main square. The eponymous beast stood proudly upon a handsome Georgian porch.

They ended their pub-crawl at the White Hart.

312

Auntie Doris shook her head.

'I forwarded them to a friend in Rangoon,' she said. 'He sent them on.'

The penny dropped.

'I know who it was,' he said. 'Geoffrey Porringer.'

'Speaking about me?'

Henry looked up, to see Geoffrey Porringer standing over him, immaculate in evening dress.

'You remember Henry, Geoffrey,' said Auntie Doris.

'Oh yes,' said Geoffrey Porringer. 'I remember Henry.'

'Good do?' said Auntie Doris.

'No!' said Geoffrey Porringer. 'These dos are all the same. Be with you in two shakes.'

Henry's mind reeled as he looked at Auntie Doris. Suddenly it was all obvious to him. Coming upon Geoffrey Porringer at Cap Ferrat. All the Canadian stamps. She'd probably even spent the night with him in Bruton, when she'd taken him to Dalton and Geoffrey had taken his brat to Bruton. He felt ashamed of his naivety. How they must have laughed at him. He recalled buying coasters with him in Sheffield, and his cheeks burned. How they must have hooted.

'I'm sorry, darling,' said Auntie Doris. 'We didn't want you to know, my love.'

'I bought coasters for you.'

'They're very nice. Very suitable.'

His head was beginning to swim. Another thought hurled itself at him.

'What'll you do when he comes out of prison?' he said.

'I don't know,' said Auntie Doris. 'I just don't know, Henry.'

'You've got to go back to him,' he said. 'You've got to, Auntie Doris.'

'I never knew you liked him so much,' said Auntie Doris. 'He never knew you did.'

Did I? Or am I solely inspired by loathing for Geoffrey Porringer?

'A refill, young feller-me-lad?' said Geoffrey Porringer, returning in shirt-sleeves.

Henry shook his head. The clicking of dominoes continued.

The dour barman looked pointedly as his watch. Geoffrey Porringer brought drinks for himself and Auntie Doris.

'Come on,' said Geoffrey Porringer thickly, and Henry realised that he was drunk as well. 'Smile. It may never happen.'

'It has happened,' said Henry.

Oh no. He had written, in a letter, that he had prayed for a cure for Geoffrey Porringer's blackheads. Oh God. He hoped she hadn't shown the letter to. . .no he didn't. He hoped she had shown it.

He smiled.

'That's better,' said Geoffrey Porringer. 'No need to take it too hard. Life, eh? I mean, let's be brutally honest. What did Teddy ever do for you?'

'Geoffrey!' said Auntie Doris.

'He took me into his home and treated me as his son, to the best of his abilities,' said Henry.

'Only because he felt guilty because he thought he caused your father's death when he sacked him,' said Geoffrey Porringer.

'Geoffrey,' hissed Auntie Doris, who always made things worse by protesting about them. 'He doesn't know his father hanged himself.'

13 The End of the Beginning

It was Thursday, September 3rd 1953. The weather was cool and showery. Henry was on his way to join the Royal Corps of Signals at Catterick, sick at heart, sick at the grim prospect, sick at the interference with his freedom just when he was on the verge of manhood, sick at the waste of his childhood. It was the only youth he would ever have. It was gone.

The train clattered across the flat farming country of central Yorkshire. It was full of raw, clumsy, nervous young men. Henry read the newspaper frantically, in an attempt to take his mind off his worries. 'West to Russia: Talk it over.' 'Oil hopes are brighter.' 'Her baby born on platform four.' His had been a fragmented childhood, and he didn't know that an obsessive reading of newspapers in times of crisis, inherited from his father, was linking this, its last day, to the day when he was born. 'Dulles gives Mao two warnings.' 'Dustman dies in shrubbery.' 'Across Canada by tandem.'

The local train from Darlington crept closer and closer to the eastern edge of the Pennines, the backbone of England. 'Anti-burglar grille stolen.' 'More tinned milk is withdrawn.' He'd spent so much time being reluctant to escape from wombs. He hadn't realised that all the wombs and all the births had taken place within the protection of the great superwomb of youth. It was from this that he was now finally, at last, irrevocably to be born. 'Anna, the stay-put char, is back.' 'Feud splits a sleepy village.' 'Italy is a wonderful country, but it's no place to have an accident.' Italy. Lampo. Dalton. Paul. Diana. Lorna. Too many memories, too many partings, close your mind to all that. 'Mormon (he had 21 children) dies at 83.' 'When the army says "report", the pianist must change his tune.' Army. There's no escape even in the newspaper.

The line was among the hills now. Cows chewed peacefully,

infuriatingly unaware that this was a special day for anybody.

They were slowing down. There was a mass collection of scanty belongings, and then they were streaming onto the platform of Richmond station, a tidal wave of stick-out ears.

Step out of the womb, Henry. It may not be as bad as you think.

The wind was cold. He moved slowly, in short steps, with the sluggish human tide.

Be brave, Henry. Be positive. You have made so many disastrous starts, but you are older and wiser now.

Show them, Henry.

'You! What do you think you're doing?'

The words seemed far away, so that he only heard them a few seconds after they had been spoken.

'Oh sorry, were you speaking to me?' he said. 'I didn't hear you. I was thinking.'

He found that he was staring at a bull-like neck, in the middle of the station forecourt. He raised his eyes to the face, and suppressed a shudder.

'You were what????' bawled the massive sergeant. 'You were thinking? You're in the army now, laddie. What's your name?'

Here we go.

'Pratt.'

'Pratt. You know what you are, Pratt? You're a short fat blob of rancid turbot droppings. What are you?'

Henry stood as proud and erect as he could. He looked the sergeant straight in the face. He was unaware of the cold wind, the damp station forecourt, the waiting trucks.

'I'm a man, sergeant,' he said.